NEGOTIATING CAPTIVITY

HUMAN PETS OF TALIN

BOOK 3

Warning: Author is dyslexic as hell.

Beta reading team: Mary Alegre, Martha Collins, and Lauren Meghoo

Professional Editing: Amanda Brown Edits, LLC

Feel free to contact me with questions, requests, or comments: author@rk-munin.com

And, as with many writers, your reviews on Amazon, Goodreads, and/or Kindle help immeasurably, even if it's just clicking on the stars.

Thank you to all my readers!

CONTENT WARNING

FMC is blackmailed into the role of pet.

Kidnapping of FMC

FMC is trapped on a malfunctioning ship where several bad guys die

Fight scene where bad guys are injured or die

Sexual assault (not by the MMC)

CHAPTER 1

The Ollie regards Nalia with wide, fearful eyes. Or rather, he regards her with one wide, fearful eye because Ollies only have one eye. A nice big one right in the middle of their body-stalk, inches above their wide, lipless breathing and talking mouth. Their eating mouth, and other orifices, are hidden under the tentacles that ring the bottom half of their body-stalk.

Her Ollie's eye is so full of terror she knows he might shed a tentacle or two soon. Or maybe all ten. Most Ollies need to be under severe distress before they drop a tentacle but not Hax. He shed a tentacle once because he had a nightmare.

That they're currently being pursued by a military force who will execute both of them without a trial might cause Hax to leave a trail of tentacles until he doesn't even have enough to ambulate.

"Breathe, Hax!" Nalia shouts over the warning sirens issuing from several places on her control console. Manipulating the ship's manual controls is taking up most of her attention, so she can only spare a quick glance at him, but he doesn't seem to be following orders.

"If you drop even one tentacle on the deck, I'll shove it up your regurgitation hole!" she threatens. That seems to do the trick.

"That's disgusting," he declares in a wheezing voice, telling her he wasn't breathing before. "You say such shocking things, Nalia."

"I need you to function," Nalia says. "I don't know anything about this sector. Get on the navigation console and tell me what civilizations are nearby."

She hears Hax talking softly to the console followed by a pause; then he utters a few more words. When he looks up, his voice is a little calmer. "It looks like we are equal distances between two civilizations: the Marper homeworld and a Talin colony."

"Marper, not good," she mutters. Hax grunts in agreement. Marpers have no love for Ollies and would fry and eat Hax without doing him the courtesy of killing him first. "Certain death behind us. Certain death to our right. I guess we go to our left."

"What?" Hax asks as he waves a few anxious tentacles around in the air.

"It means we don't have a choice. Send me the coordinates for the Talin colony and let's hope they don't have any kind of reciprocity agreements with the Hamlershin." Coordinates appear on her display, and she changes the ship's trajectory. The only thing she knows about the Talin species is that they're setting up colonies in neighboring sectors. She and Hax were going to be dealing with them eventually. But it looks like it's going to be sooner rather than later.

The ship bucks, and she scrambles to steady the thruster feeds. Most of the automatic system controls failed long ago, so she and Hax had to learn to fly with manual inputs. It's exhausting, and when they need to move fast, it's hard to keep everything going smoothly.

"Create an open comm channel," she orders Hax.

"Done, wide-range broadcasting," he tells her.

"This is the ship Amity. We are being pursued and request sanctuary. Repeat, we are being pursued and request sanctuary. Two souls are on board. We have no weapons and no defenses. We are peaceful haulers and traders." She ends the communication and looks over at her friend.

Hax is leaning over his console, reading something off the display that makes his color turn a little deeper green. It can't be good news.

"Spit it out, Hax," she orders.

"The Talin are a slave-owning culture!" He says it so fast all the words end up squished together, so it takes her a few seconds to work out what he said. As much as she wants to have a nice little emotional meltdown, she needs to stay strong for Hax. If she shows any fear, he'll shed tentacles like a tree dropping overripe fruit.

"Well, we aren't slaves," she assures him. "We have all the paperwork to prove that we run a legitimate business. We're just dealing with a misunderstanding with the Hamlershin. I'm sure the Talins will be sympathetic once we explain everything."

That is assuming they aren't blown up the moment they hit Talin-controlled space. Some species can be damn territorial.

To her relief, the speech seems to work. Hax moves his tentacles around the console again, his color calming down a little.

"You're right, sorry. We aren't in hailing range of the Talin colony, but we're right near their major flight corridor. If we have any luck, a military or merchant vessel will pick up our distress call. They won't dare to fire on us if we're picked up by a Talin ship, even an unarmed one. No one messes with the Talins. It says here that they have a reputation for being brutal."

She casts him a quick look. She's not sure that reputation bodes well for either of them.

"Smuggling ship Amity, shut down your engines and surrender. We promise a quick and merciful death," the nasal voice of a Hamlershin comes over the comms.

Nalia snorts with derision. These Hamlershins are idiots when it comes to incentive. But then again, at least they're honest. She doesn't bother responding. She focuses on wrestling every last bit of power out of her engines.

"We shouldn't have done it," Hax mumbles as he flops back into his copilot chair.

"You know we had to," Nalia reminds him. "They were dying."

"But they're my people. I shouldn't have dragged you into it," Hax tells her with a small moan of distress. One of his tentacles is thinning out as he waves it, a sure sign he's about to shed it. "You're not Ollie. You shouldn't die because of us!"

"Hax, you're my people," Nalia tells him. "That means I care about who you care about. No matter what happens, I would do the same thing all over again."

"But you're not Ollie," Hax points out again, and Nalia just barely keeps from rolling her eyes.

"Doesn't matter. You're as close to family as I'll ever have. That means they are my family too. If we didn't risk Hamlershin space to get that colony those medical supplies, at least half of them would be dead within a year. They had young there," she reminds him. "Some of them from your same pod. We couldn't let them down."

"The negotiations were—"

Nalia cuts him off. "Were going nowhere. We both know we couldn't wait for the damn treaty negotiation to finish. They were talking those Ollie to death. We did what we had to do. So just shut it, Hax, or I'll put extra brine in your sleep tank."

Hax doesn't respond to her threat. He regards her silently for a moment, his tentacles all going still, an anomaly for the fretful Ollie.

"You might not be Ollie," Hax states grimly. "But you are family to me and my pod."

She feels touched by his words. Ollies are notoriously tightknit, and for Hax to call her family means a lot.

They started working together ages ago. When she hired on with Hax, she was shocked to find out that their first trip together would be his first trip ever.

It turns out that while he is skilled with navigation and calculation, he is inept at all other things. Seeing imminent failure, she took over the running of their small business. She picked their jobs. She haggled freight prices. She kept him calm on the rare occasion they flew illegal cargo. And somewhere along the way, she's grown to love the anxious, fidgety Ollie because no matter what, he's loyal.

Hax reaches out and wraps a tentacle around one of her wrists, literally grabbing her attention. She can feel his tension and fear in the shaking appendage. "No matter what happens, no regrets," he states quickly.

"No regrets," she agrees.

A new alarm sounds, making both of them look down at her side of the command console. A display pops up showing the Hamlershin ship is almost within firing distance. "Damn," she mutters. "I was hoping we'd get lucky again."

"Hailing freight ship Amity," an unfamiliar voice calls out over the comms. "This is the Talin merchant vessel Bountiful. Before we grant amnesty, tell us what species you are?"

"Good to hear from you, Bountiful," Nalia responds, her voice cracking a little from relief. "We have an Ollie on this vessel. Hax of the Teripina Pod." Ollies are well-liked by most species, so she hopes that's enough to earn them some assistance.

"You reported two souls on your ship. Are both of you Ollie?" Bountiful asks.

"One Ollie male, one human female," she explains and waits for the usual sets of questions: What's a human? Where do they come from? But I've never heard of your kind. And her most favorite question: Why are you so small?

For the most part, the fact that humans are so rare outside the few places they settled after old Earth was no longer inhabitable is helpful. If no one knows what a human is, she can tell them anything, like she is venomous or a male. Or her flesh is poisonous, so they shouldn't try to eat her.

When they find out about Earth, the questions can get annoying. They're always curious about the same thing: What kind of species destroys their own homeworld? Honestly, she doesn't have a good answer. What happened to the Earth was done long before even her grandmother was born. But that never satisfies the inquisitors.

Right now, they need rescue not questions. That's why the next words from the Bountiful throw her off. No questions, only statements. And oh how wonderful those statements are!

"Hamlershin ship in pursuit of Amity, desist pursuit and leave. Amity is now under Talin protection. We declare this ship ours, along with her crew and contents. Any form of aggression on either the hauler ship Amity or the Talin merchant ship Bountiful will be answered with deadly force."

Nalia watches with delight as the Hamlershin ship doesn't even bother responding. They just burn hard to turn around and hightail it away from Talin space.

"Hauler ship Amity, follow these coordinates. We will be taking you aboard the Bountiful," the Talin voice tells them over the comm, and Nalia's joy fades. She sets the course and sits back with a little frown.

Both of them are quiet as they wonder what will happen when they meet the Talins.

Hax breaks the silence first. "This reminds me of that human saying you like so much."

"The enemy of my enemy is my friend?"

Hax taps something on the console as he answers. "No, the one about jumping out of the cooking unit into the heating coils."

Nalia tries to give him a reassuring grin. "Let's hope it's inaccurate this time." She gets up from her seat and tugs at one of Hax's tentacles. "Let's doublecheck the cargo hold. It should be empty, but let's make sure we don't have anything in there that's illegal in Talin space.

The Ollie picks up an information square and follows her. At least it will keep them busy until they find out what their fate will be.

CHAPTER 2

"A human?" Navigator Yulian looks back at Derani, his back armor plates rattling faintly with wonder. "A female human is on that ship?"

"Apparently," Derani replies, a little in awe of his luck.

"And we're bringing her on board," Yulian states.

"Even if they run, that ship is small and old, we can easily force the issue," Negotiator Melanem points out. "They can't get away."

"They aren't running," Yulian assures them as he checks the readouts on his display. "They're burning slow, but they're heading toward us. If we keep the current burn rate, we'll meet them within the mark."

"Excellent," Derani says with a little rumble of satisfaction. "And the Hamlershin ship?"

Yulian sounds a derisive rattle. "Far away already. They burned hard right after your comm announcement."

Derani rattles his back plates in triumph. His ship might be a merchant ship with very limited weapons, but no one dares challenge any Talin ship, at least not for long. Firing on one would bring the might of the entire Talin military down on the arrogant aggressors. There's a saying among most species that deal with the Talins: *They might not start the war, but they will see it finished. And woe to those who test their resolve.*

"Did I hear we're bringing a human female on board?" Larimus asks over the inner-ship comms.

"There's one on the ship we're rescuing," Yulian answers with an excited rattle.

"A human female, just wandering around at the edge of Talin space? And we get her?" Larimus sounds an incredulous rattle with his back plates. "My father was right. Derani comes from a blessed clan. Have them dock in cargo hold two. It's empty and can fit their ship. I'll go prep the atmosphere generator. It's off line because I didn't expect to be using that bay on this trip."

"Acknowledged," Derani responds and taps the comm channel off.

"Do you think she's young or old?" Yulian interjects. "And she'll be soft to the touch, at least that's what I've read. I've never touched a human before. Do you think she'll let me hold her?" The navigator is the youngest member of his crew, and his lack of experience shows in those questions.

"Yulian," Melanem barks out, silencing Yulian's excited jabber. "Even if she wants to be touched by you, she belongs to the captain."

Yulian looks crestfallen and shoots Derani an aggravated look. "Yes, of course," he mumbles and turns his attention back to his display.

Derani catches the negotiator's eye and gives her a nod of thanks. Sometimes it's better to let his more experienced crew reprimand young Yulian, showing him by example how to behave toward a superior.

"But Yulian's questions do raise a point," Melanem says. "What will you do with her? She and her crewmate are in this area of space without permission codes. That means they're breaking Talin law by not having prior approval to be here. Talin space has to be their destination because we know they don't have permission to fly through Marper space."

"How do you know that?" Yulian asks.

Melanem answers easily, happy to educate their greenest crew member. "According to the current treaty laws, no one but Talins and Vicpors are allowed in."

Yulian sounds a rumble of understanding. "And the Hamlershin were chasing them for a reason. Any way you look at it, they broke someone's law."

Derani forces himself to give a casual rattle of his back plates. "Exactly. All things point to them being some level of criminal. Once they're on board, I'll interview them, assess their intentions and then make an appropriate offer."

The rumble that sounds from deep in Melanem's chest is one of amusement. "I'm sure you will."

Derani keeps his back plates from rattling with irritation, but only barely. He needs to leave the room before he lets any emotions show.

"Negotiator Melanem, you have control. I'm going down to bay two to help Larimus and great our guests." Both Melanem and Yulian rattle in acknowledgment of his order as he stands up and strides out of the control room.

He forces himself to take reasonable, measured steps out of the room and down the hall. There's no reason to rush. The Amity won't be safely secured for at least another mark. Telling himself he's just freshening up, not trying to impress anyone, he ducks into his quarters and changes his pants and belt. Talin rarely wear more than those two garments unless going into battle or they need to denote their profession like the healers with their knee-length green tunics. Most Talins find it uncomfortable to cover their armored back plates, and their thick skin certainly doesn't need to be protected from anything but the harshest conditions.

Derani takes a moment to examine his appearance. He's a good-sized male, with appropriately dense muscle mass and well-proportioned plating. He's been assured by several females that the plating on his brow ridge and along his head are particularly appealing because they are slightly darker than most other Talins, giving him a light brown coloring instead of the common light tan of his brethren.

He looks down and tenses his hands so his claws slide out. They're all a healthy black with sharp, pointed ends, good for either slashing or sinking into an enemy for grip in hand-to-hand combat.

He raises the quills on his forearm and checks their length. Only one is an odd length. But it's close to growing back to its full length after being broken off short while he helped Larimus secure cargo on the last trip. It's a minor defect and he can't imagine the human female will even notice it.

Overall, she should find him an appealing master. He's not a member of one of the elite clans, but his clan does very well and he can provide her with anything a human might need. He knows the negotiation will be difficult because she's probably a free-born human and might never have experienced captivity. But he's clever and patient. He can make her transition gentle.

Briefly, he considers bringing Melanem into the negotiation but then dismisses it. He wants to be the one she surrenders to, not Melanem, even if it's on his behalf. It's best to teach her that he has all the power at the start, so she doesn't think she can look to others for aid.

This won't be the first human he's met, unlike Yulian or Larimus. A few solars ago he visited Narlian, a friend raised in the same cresh. When he arrived, Narlian was sitting in the garden at his family compound with a little human female in his lap. He was feeding her from his hand and rumbling out encouraging sounds for her.

He sat across from his friend and watched the human snuggle up against Narlian's chest after she was finished eating. As they talked, she drifted off to sleep. Even in sleep, she kept one hand curled around his shoulders, and her face nuzzled against the small slip of unprotected skin that runs along the base of a Talin's neck.

It was the first and only time Derani experienced jealousy.

He's been hunting for a human of his own ever since. The only ones that have come up for sale on Talin so far were male and not affectionate. Those Talins who had affectionate humans never sold them. One of the reasons it's hard to find humans is that most clans jointly owned all their humans and put contracts in place to make it's impossible to sell or transmit ownership of them outside the clan.

Unable to find a human to buy on Talarian or any of the Talin colonies, Derani started searching elsewhere. Every time his travels take him near a slave market or auction house, he scours the place for human females or even a male young enough to be held and coddled.

He always came up empty handed. Until today, he thought his clan's reputation for luck might have deserted him.

He glances over at the meal he didn't eat that morning. It's not the first meal he's skipped. His people only require food once a rotation at most and can go several rotations without serious consequence. But he can't remember the last time he ate. It takes him a few submarks of calculating to realize he hasn't eaten in almost ten rotations, and that's troublesome. Loss of appetite is the first sign of the Fading.

No, he thinks as he shoves the plate of food into the waste receptacle, *the first sign is that nothing smells good anymore.*

The smells are there, but it's as if they don't trigger any feeling, not even one as basic as hunger. But despite that, most Talins don't realize what's happening to them until they lose their appetite. Fading happens to many of their species as they reach their prime reproductive years. No one knows why, or at least no one wants to admit to why it happens.

One of his aunts gave the best description of the Fading Derani ever heard. She told him it felt like her world turned to shades of gray. Nothing had color. Nothing had taste. Nothing touched her senses. Her mind was wrapped in a fog of bleakness. He didn't truly understand what she meant until his senses became muted. When eating became a chore instead of a pleasure, he didn't even have it in him to feel fear. He just felt resigned.

Derani checks his belt pouch one more time as he forces himself out of these dark thoughts. Then, with a determined stride, he leaves his quarters and makes his way to bay two. A human is arriving, and if everything goes well, food will taste again.

It's a well-known secret that owning a human can cure the Fading.

When he sees the Amity for the first time, his back plates rattle with displeasure. It's not the worst ship he's ever encountered, but it's close. He's surprised they didn't overheat an engine coil and explode the ship when they were running from the Hamlershin.

"I read a biography once that said *courage and determination can hold together even the most despairing situation*," Larimus mutters as he stands next to Derani, staring at the pile of garbage pretending to be a ship in front of them. "The human and the Ollie who run this hunk of salvage must brim with courage and determination because it's not possible that hull is structurally soundly enough to fly otherwise."

"When she called for help, her voice was fearful but full of strength and conviction," Derani comments as the hatch to the Amity hisses and jerkily slides open, starting and stopping along the track. He can barely keep from rattling with impatience as he's forced to wait to get his first glimpse of his soon-to-be pet human.

"Strength and conviction are two good qualities in a crewmate," Larimus comments. "But not in a pet."

Derani rattles his back plates in warning, and Larimus sounds an amused rumble from his chest. "But I'm sure you'll have her trained in no time."

"As to that, don't interact with the human," he orders Larimus, as he ignores the male's increased amusement at his irritation. "Not until she learns to trust me and turn to me with her needs."

"As you wish, Captain," Larimus agrees and takes a small step back to show deference. Although he's no longer rumbling, Derani gets the distinct impression the engineer is still laughing at him.

The hatch finally finishes opening, and a small, human female jumps down the short distance from the hatch to the deck. Then she turns around to help an Ollie twice her size out of the hatch.

The Ollie's eye is enormous, and its limbs are flailing about instead of helping him ambulate. One limb even knocks the diminutive human on the side of her head. She doesn't even blink, just grabs the limb and draws it down and away from her face. The Ollie pitches forward, and although she tries to slow his tilt, he falls right on top of her. With a muffled *umph*, the little female disappears under the wiggling mass of limbs.

Derani meant to wait with patient authority while the crew of the Amity approached him, but the moment the Ollie smacked his human with a tentacle, the confident, self-possessed captain he's trying to portray disappears.

With a loud, aggressive rattle of his back plates, he sprints forward and tosses the Ollie off the female, throwing him almost to where Larimus is standing. Remaining where he is, Larimus watches with rapt interest and no less amusement.

Leaning over, Derani snatches the female off the floor. Cradling her gently against his chest, he strides to the bay door, just barely resisting the urge the kick the Ollie as he walks past.

"Hey, put me down. I need to check on Hax. He's delicate. He might be hurt," the human objects. She's trying to wiggle out of his grip, but he ignores her struggles.

"Tell Melanem to join me in medical," Derani orders as he passes Larimus.

"I don't need medical, but Hax probably does," the human protests and fights his hold with more aggression. Her strength is negligible compared to his, and he easily disregard her thrashing, even when she smacks her palm against his chest plates in rhythm with her words. "Put. Me. Down."

"Quiet," he orders. She certainly is a free-born human. No slave or former slave would be so insistent or forceful. Her current actions imply that she's going to be a handful, but he doesn't mind. A difficult human female is better than no human female. "You will comply or I'll do a lot worse to the Ollie than just toss him across a bay floor."

That threat quiets her immediately. "Please don't hurt Hax," she requests in a subdued tone. Although he likes that she stopped fighting, he isn't pleased with the alarm in her voice.

"Behave and I'll have no reason to hurt the Ollie," he assures her.

"Right." She nods, and he notices how the light gleams off of her black mane. Unlike his friend's human, who had a light brown mane, this one's mane is so black it shines. She's wearing it secured at the back of her head in a knot, so he can't tell how long it is. He's looking forward to seeing it unbound and being able to feel the texture of the fine strands.

"I'm not hurt," she insists in a placating tone. "I've taken much worse falls. I'm probably not even bruised. Hax looks big, but he's kind of mushy. He doesn't have any boney or hard parts to impact with. And it's not the first time we've ended up in a heap together."

"My negotiator is a skilled medic. You will let her examine you. Then we will see about the Ollie," Derani tells her.

"Sure," she agrees as he walks her into Medical. Melanem is already there, digging out a scanner. When she turns and sees the human in Derani's arms, her chest rumbles out a comforting sound. It's loud enough to echo in the small room.

The human looks at Melanem with startled confusion. "Are you… purring?"

Melanem quiets her rumble. "What's a purr?"

"Uh, it's a sound, like what I heard when we came in just now," she explains, looking first at Melanem and then back at him.

"You mean the rumble?" he asks. When she continues to look puzzled, he rumbles a soothing sound out of his chest. She puts her hand flat on one of his chest plates.

"Wow, you guys purr," she murmurs.

"I've heard that humans like our soothing rumble," Melanem comments as she points to the exam table. "Please set her down right here, Captain. If your rumble calms her, you should continue."

Derani sets her down gently on the table. When she moves to withdraw her hand from his chest, he captures it with one of his own and presses down lightly, trapping her hand against him. "Do you like my rumble, little human? The purring, as you call it."

"I, uh," she stumbles with her words and the skin on her face darkens slightly. "Sure, I guess it's okay."

Melanem leans forward with enthusiasm to examine the human's face. "I've heard of that! The color change to her face means she's embarrassed or aroused."

"We blush for a lot of reasons," she counters and tries to tug her hand free again, but he doesn't let it go. She meets his eyes and her color deepens a little more. "Fine, the purring is nice," she mutters, sliding her gaze away from his and stops trying to pull her hand from him. Pleased at her subtle acknowledgment of his authority, he keeps up his rumbling.

"I'm going to scan you," Melanem tells her. "It will be quick and painless. If you can be still, that would help this go faster."

"Sure thing, we've got one on our ship too although nowhere near as nice," she mentions, eyeing the scanner with envy.

Melanem scans her quickly and looks at the small screen to read the results. She makes a slight displeased rattle, taps a few things, and then looks up.

"Nothing's broken, but the scanner is telling me she needs a more detailed scan at a medical center. She might have several minor issues that should be dealt with."

"I don't doubt it," Derani grunts. "She's probably malnourished and might even have parasites."

"*She* is sitting right here," the human grumbles, making Melanem rumble out a laugh. "*She* doesn't have parasites. And *she* has a name."

"Ah, yes, names. I'm Melanem, the ship's negotiator." Melanem smacks her palm to her chest plate to make a nice loud impact. The little human jerks at the sound, and Melanem makes an unhappy rattle. "Sorry, human. I didn't mean to startle you."

"Didn't it hurt when you hit yourself just now?"

"No, it's how we greet each other," Melanem explains.

"Oh, well in that case." She taps her own chest in a soft imitation of Melanem. "My name's Nalia," she tells them. "Nalia Gaborn"

Melanem makes a rumble usually used with infants and small children, which indicates she finds Nalia's action adorable. "Welcome to the Bountiful, Human Nalia."

"You're safe here," Derani adds, feeling it important she knows that. Humans are delicate, and she's probably spent most of her life skirting dangerous situations. "I'm Captain Derani of the Merchant Clan Anize."

"Me too," she says quickly. "I'm captain too."

Now it's his turn to rumble out a laugh. "Is the Ollie also a captain?"

She huffs out a breath and tries to cross her arms over her chest, but he still has one held captive. "I know the ship isn't much, but she gets the job done. And Hax and I work hard." She gives up crossing her arms and gives him a concerned look. "Could you please take me to Hax? I'm worried he's going to shed all his limbs out of fear if I don't get back to him soon. I don't want to have to drag him around until they grow back."

Derani shoots Melanem a look and sounds a questioning rattle, making Nalia jump in surprise.

The negotiator makes an affirmative rumble at his unvoiced question. "Ollies can detach a limb without damaging themselves. It's left over from when they were a primitive species. The limb could be left behind to distract a predator. In some Ollies, the instinct malfunctions and they shed their limbs even when no threat is present."

"I'm not so sure about the 'no threat' part. There seems to be a damn big threat present," Nalia grumbles, eyeing the two of them. Then she squares her shoulders and tries to look calm and commanding. "Look, he's an anxious shedder, so the sooner you get me back to him, the less goo and wriggling limbs you'll have to clean off your bay floor."

Derani rattles out a short, sharp warning. She only jumps a little at the sound.

"I'll let you check on him, but then you and I will talk alone. You need to make decisions that will impact both you and the Ollie."

"Yes, Captain," she mumbles, casting her eyes down. He puts his hand under her chin and lifts her head until her gaze meets his again. Her skin feels so soft under his hands, her bones fine and her appearance frail. He gives himself a moment to admire her eyes, a lovely combination of brown and green, with a ring of green around the outside. She's a beautiful human.

He leans a little closer and breathes in deeply through his nose, taking in her scent. She doesn't wear any altering substances, so all he smells are the products she uses to clean herself, a faint aroma of an engine, and her own delicate, unique human scent. It triggers some long-suppressed part of him and the gray fog that's been surrounding him for months begins to recede.

"Don't fret, little Nalia," he assures her as he rumbles out a purr. "I'll take care of you."

CHAPTER 3

An intense feeling of relief washes over Nalia the moment she sees Hax. Of course, that's quickly followed by dismay as she notices the three limbs littering the floor around him.

"Oh, Hax," she laments softly. She looks up at Captain Derani, who insisted on carrying her. She needs Derani's cooperation, so arguing with him isn't an option. But maybe gentle persuasion could work.

"Captain Derani, could you please put me down so I can check on my friend? I'm worried about him."

"Do not touch him or get too close," Derani commands and she just barely suppresses a snarky comment. What does he think Hax can do to her? On land Ollie are next to worthless in a fight. Unless there's a big body of sulfur water nearby, Hax isn't a threat to anyone.

"I won't," she promises. Derani reluctantly sets her on her feet and releases his grip. Once free from Derani's hold, she edges closer to her friend until the toe of her boot is touching one of his shed limbs.

"I need you to keep calm, Hax," she tells him. "I know you're scared, but it's going to be okay. I'm going to go talk with the captain about our release."

"He's going to hurt you! And he's going to hurt me! And—" Hax's words high pitched and fast. She knows better than to let him continue down this path.

"Cut it out," she interrupts him in a stern voice. He jams several of his tentacles in his mouth and starts sucking on them.

It's a self-soothing action most Ollie grow out of when they are still quite young, but Hax never did. She feels for him and wishes she could go up and hug him. When she grabs him tightly and holds him for a while, it helps him calm down.

She turns and gives the captain a pleading look. "Can I please touch him? He's upset, and a hug will calm him down so we can talk. You can see he's not a danger to me."

Captain Derani makes an unpleasant sound, very much like the sound of hardened projectiles being rapidly fired. She takes an involuntary step back, and the sounds stops. It's a fight, but she makes herself remain still while he steps forward.

"If you must touch the Ollie, I will allow it, but I insist on standing close." His tone is gruff and disapproving, but he only moves to shadow her as she makes her way around limbs on the floor. She wraps Hax in as best a bear hug as she can manage.

All his limbs go still, the three he was sucking on fall out of his big mouth, and his one eye closes. His breathing deepens a little and his color calms back down. She doesn't know what instinct the bear hug triggers, but it's sure effective.

She can feel Captain Derani looming behind her, so she puts her lips close to Hax's hearing bulb. "It's going to be okay, Hax," she whispers. "All you need to do for me is to keep calm. Remember the story exercise we practiced?"

"I remember," he whispers back.

"Good, do that. When I get back, you need to tell me all the stories you remember. Can you do that?"

"I can do that," he agrees. "I'll stay calm, and I won't shed anymore. I promise."

She tightens her hold on him for a moment. "I know you can do it. You're the best crewmate a girl could have."

"You're the best crewmate too," he responds. When she lets go and steps back, his color changes but only a little. It's a good sign. She just needs to get back before his anxiety becomes unmanageable again.

She turns to find Derani so close he's almost on top of her. With a little gasp, she tries to step away. In a move too fast for her to follow, he picks her up and cradles her to his chest again.

"I can walk," she reminds him.

"We are going to talk now," he tells her as he turns on his heels and strides out of the room, leaving Hax with the other Talin. "We will negotiate."

"Yes, sir," she replies with a strong sense of foreboding.

He takes them to a communal dining area and sets her down on a chair. Then he walks around the table and sits down across from her. She wiggles around in the large chair, finding that she can't touch the floor with her feet.

Trying to act more confident than she feels, she reaches out to rest her forearms on the table, but it's a little high and makes her feel awkward, so she pulls them back into her lap. She would think he's trying to make her feel small and uncomfortable on purpose to make the negotiation harder, but that's a pointless tactic. He doesn't need to do anything to remind her she's helpless. They both know she doesn't have many choices in this situation.

"There's no such thing as free humans in our society," he starts and she slumps a little. If that's his opening line, the rest of this conversation isn't going to go well for her.

"I'm free-born," she tells him. "I've never been a slave. No one in my family has ever been owned."

"That means nothing here," he explains. "We don't have any kind of treaty or alliance with humans, so according to Talin law I need to turn you over to the Hamlershin."

She feels herself go pale at those words but doesn't look away. He wouldn't go through all the effort of retrieving them if he was just going to turn around and give them to the Hamlershin.

"But that law only applies to persons, not property," he continues. "If I owned you, there would be no question that you would remain with me and not be turned over to the Hamlershin."

He's boxed her in nicely. But this negotiation isn't only about her. "What about Hax?"

"We have a trade agreement with the Ollies," he tells her. "If Hax isn't a declared outcast by his people, I have no reason to turn him over to anyone." He pulls a cube-shaped device off his belt and sets it on the table. She recognizes it as an Identification Cube. Several species use them as a combination of communication device, a way to access accounts, recorder, personal identification, and so many other things.

Right now he's using the cube to look something up. It projects a screen in the air between them. He taps at it a few times as a language she doesn't recognize scrolls across. He reads though it and finally looks back up at her.

"We only have a treaty of mutual trade consent with the Hamlershin. That means I can release Hax back to his people with no negative legal or political ramifications."

Relief fills Nalia. At least Hax is safe as long as she can keep him calm. He's going to have to pilot back on his own, but he should be able to do that as long as she sets the course for him. An Ollie colony is not too far away. If he makes it there, he can contact his family and they can fetch him. His attempt at independence will be over, but his family will be happy to have their anxiety-prone wayward podmate back home, safe and sound.

With Hax's safety assured, Nalia turns her attention to her questionable future. "So what you're saying is if I want to stay alive, I need to enter into captivity with you?"

"Correct," Captain Derani answers. "You'll be owned by me alone, not my family or clan."

"What duties would you expect of me?" she asks, hoping what he wants her to do is already within her skill set.

He's been gentle with her so far, but these Talins are a massive species. If he gets impatient with her, one angry swipe with his big hand would seriously injure, if not kill her outright. The best way to keep any captain happy is to know your job and do it effectively and quickly. She is young, strong, and smart. She can survive this until she figures out a way to escape.

"Duties?" Captain Derani echoes with a faint rattle. At that point she realizes that most of the sounds she hears him make are coming from the armor plates that cover his back. They must have a limited range of movement so they can be clattered together to create sounds.

So far, none of the Talins have changed facial expressions, so they must use their sounds to convey emotions. The purring from their chests and rattling from their back plates in the med bay are making more sense now.

This new sound strikes her as confusion or inquisitiveness. "Yes, sir, duties. As my owner, what will you require of me?"

"Your sole purpose is to please me," he explains.

She nods with understanding. On a lot of worlds, having a personal slave follow an owner around is a mark of status and wealth. The more exotic the slave, the better. At least her duties will be easy, just shadow the big captain and look exotic and subservient.

"I'm human," she starts. His rumbles interrupt her. It's not a purr like before, but his next words make her realize that this new sound denotes amusement, probably the Talin version of a laugh.

"I'm well aware of your species."

"Yes, well, I just want to make sure you know I might not be able to eat the same things you eat and a lot of stuff around here I won't be able to use because it'll be too big for me," she explains. She doesn't want to get in trouble because she can't carry, lift, or fetch something he orders her to get.

"I know all about humans," he assures her. "I know what to feed you. I know how to care for you. You're a common pet among my people. You'll be my first human, but I've read all the literature about humans and watched all the educational vids."

Pet. She tests the word out in her head and mentally shrugs. Pet or slave, it comes out to be the same basic thing—being owned.

"How long will this last?" She crosses her fingers under the table, hoping he's willing to negotiate a term of servitude.

"There will be no termination date," he declares. She deflates, her shoulders slumping. Her disappointment doesn't last long. His words aren't set in stone. They just mean she'll eventually need to run away.

I'm small, she thinks. *If all else fails, I'll just stow away in some Talin's luggage and get myself shipped off world.* She almost snorts at the image of her in a box, cutting little holes from the inside with a plasma saw so she can look out at legs as individuals walk by.

"Let me make sure I understand," she says. "Hax gets to go free with the ship. I stay with you as a pet, and you don't turn me over to the Hamlershin."

"You're correct on all counts."

"What if you get bored with me? Will you sell me to someone else?"

An angry rattle sounds. "Never. You are mine."

Huh, he's possessive. That's good in so far as he won't lend her out to others. But it might make him hypervigilant. She might have to wait a long time before he relaxes enough so she can slip away. That's fine. She's learned to deal with a lot of distasteful situations. He can't possibly be worse than the time she worked for a Veli. That guy had been petty, cheap, and mean. She finished out her contract with him but came close to death a few times. If she could survive that, she can survive this Talin.

His rumbling comes back as he speaks again. "I can promise you that your life with me will be a safe and comfortable one. You have no reason to fear."

He stands up and unhooks a bag from his belt she didn't notice before. He opens it and pulls out several items, lining them up on the table in front of her. One item looks like a simple, high-necked, unisex, wrap-around garment in a beautiful shade of turquoise, but she's not sure about the second item. Leaning over, she gives it a closer look.

It seems like some kind of jewelry, delicate links forming a circle with small links hanging down in regular intervals all the way around it. Small jewels have been set in each link, but she doesn't see a clasp to open and close it. It's too big to fit on a Talin's wrist and much too small to be a Talin necklace.

Then it hits her. "Is that a collar?"

"It's your collar if you agree to my terms," he tells her. "Engineer Larimus will bring the Ollie to you so you may discuss this situation with him before deciding. You must keep the table between you and the Ollie. I will be at the door watching, so don't disobey me. If you decide against my offer, just walk away from the table, leaving the clothing and collar behind. We will confine you both to a room until we've contacted the Hamlershin authorities to collect you."

"And if I agree to your terms?"

He purrs as he talks. "If you agree, simply change into the wrap and put on the collar yourself." He reaches down and picks up the collar. He thumbs a link that's slightly thicker than the others, and the collar opens. He sets it back down, careful to keep the open links separated.

"The collar will lock when you connect the ends. Only I can unlock it once it's on," he warns her.

"Sure, right," she says faintly, her eyes fixed on the collar.

"I'm sorry you must make such an important decision so quickly, little Nalia," he tells her as he continues to purr. "But I should warn you that if you want the Ollie safe, we need to launch his ship soon. Waiting much longer will mean Amity's trajectory will be compromised."

Stepping out the door, he calls to someone down the hall. Soon Hax appears in the doorway and makes his way to the table. His big squishy body collapses into one of the chairs, his eye never leaving her face. Derani steps into the doorway, watching them with an intense gaze. Nalia focuses on Hax, trying to ignore the big Talin staring at them.

"Engineer Larimus told me Captain Derani is going to keep you as a pet," Hax states, his voice upset and his color deepening.

"Don't do that," she says urgently. "If you get upset, I'm going to get upset, and then everything is going to go badly. Please, Hax. I need you to keep it together for me."

Hax lowers the tentacle he's about to stuff in his mouth. "I'll be strong," he promises.

"The short of it is this. If I agree to be his pet human, you get to go free, and neither of us will be turned over to the Hamlershin," she explains.

"I was afraid of this," he wails and flaps a few limbs around before he gets himself back under control.

"Look, I'm sure it won't be too bad," she soothes him. "I'm just going to be following the captain around. You know, like those exotic slaves the Vikary like to keep."

"The Vikary eat those slaves when they get too old," Hax whispers, and despite his best efforts shoves a limb into his mouth. Nalia gives in to the powerful emotions she's been experiencing and lets her head fall forward until it's resting on the table.

She hears a rattle and jerks up. Derani is halfway to them before she holds up a hand to stop him. "We're just talking. Everything is fine. Promise," she calls out.

"You collapsed," he says.

"No, no, I was just resting my head for a moment," she explains. "It's a human thing. Sometimes our thoughts are too heavy for our neck to support."

He stands stock still for a moment, and then a rumbling laugh sounds out of his chest. "You're a clever female."

He likes her humor. That's good to know. This might not be too bad after all. Maybe only beatings on the odd days of the month. Food almost every week. A square of floor to call her own. Ah, a girl can have such big dreams.

She's going to need to make sure her habit of joking doesn't get the better of her. Being amusing is one thing. Being mouthy is dangerous.

"I try," she agrees. "But Hax and I are still talking, Captain. You can go back to where you were standing. I'll keep my heavy head up from now on." Captain Derani rattles once in agreement and resumes his spot at the door. She turns her attention back to the anxious Ollie.

"I don't think they want to eat me," she tells him. "Besides, look at how big they are. I'm probably not even a full meal for one of those guys."

"You jest. You're about to lose your freedom because of me, yet you jest? You're a brave human, Nalia."

"I wouldn't change anything we've done," she tells Hax. "Except maybe I would have spent a few extra credits at the last station to eat a fantastic last meal. But other than that, I have no regrets."

"No regrets," Hax repeats. He lays a tentacle out on the table, stretching it toward her. She reaches out and rests her hand on it. Captain Derani makes a displeased rattle and they both withdraw.

"I have to put those on," she says, pointing to the collar and the wrap.

"Do you want me to leave first?" he asks.

"Yeah, I do. I don't want you to see me like that," she admits.

"Engineer Larimus said he will help me program Amity," Hax tells her. "I thought he was lying to keep me calm, but I see now it was the truth."

"Tell him to send you to the Garr Minor colony. It's the closest with diplomatic ties to the Ollies. When you get there, promise me that you'll contact your family."

"I will," Hax promises. "And I'll return with enough credits to buy your freedom."

Nalia casts a quick glance over to where Captain Derani is standing, arms crossed, eyes intensely focused on the two of them. "I doubt you're going to be able to, but I love that you want to try."

As the Ollie stands up, a few of his limbs are wiggling in her direction. She knows he wants to touch her, to say goodbye in the Ollie way by tangling several limbs together, but they can't with Captain Derani watching.

"I'll save you," he tells her before he moves away. She knows it's an empty promise. Hax can't even save himself from his anxiety, let alone figure out how to rescue her from captivity among the powerful Talins. But she gives him her best smile.

"I know you will," she lies. "Be well, Hax."

"Be well, Nalia," he replies and makes his way out of the room.

Captain Derani moves aside to let him pass and then turns his attention back to her. She picks up the wrap and turns her back on him. It's awkward, but she changes outfits without showing much flesh. She's reaching for the collar when Derani barks out an order.

"No boots," he commands. "You don't need shoes any longer."

Obediently, she tugs off her boots and adds them to the pile on the floor. The metal deck feels cold under her feet. She's worn shoes all her life. It's going to take a while before she's used to being barefoot. And she'll probably have some painful days ahead as her feet toughen up. But that doesn't worry her. No, the last item waiting on the table is filling her with unease.

Slowly, she picks up the damn collar. She takes a moment to observe the jewel-covered item. The glitter of the stones indicates they're real. She even recognizes a few of the stones. Rare and expensive, one stone from this collar is worth more than Amity.

Even if she could work her entire life and save everything she earned, she'd never be able to afford something this extravagant. And this Talin wants it around her neck.

Locked securely around her neck. Gilded cage indeed.

It feels light in her hands, but when she drapes it around her neck, the metal links feel heavy and cold. The click of the lock engaging is one of the loudest sounds she's ever heard.

"Good," Derani grunts the moment it's locked around her neck.

He strides forward and picks up her clothes and shoes, dumping them in a nearby trash receptacle. When he returns to her, he leans over and examines the collar. He slips a finger between the skin of her neck and the metal links, sliding it back and forth to test the fit.

"You will tell me if it becomes uncomfortable," he orders, and she nods. Suddenly, she feels strangely lightheaded and her heart is pounding.

Did she really just put a collar around her own neck?

"You will call me Master," he informs her, "or Master Derani. You must tell me when you become hungry or fatigued. You will stay where I put you or I'll start tethering you with the collar. Do you understand these orders?"

"Yes, Master," she says meekly. Now is the time to be meek and mild, to make Derani think she's helpless. It might take a while, but she'll get away. She'll find Hax. They'll work together again. Maybe even get a ship. It's only a matter of time, she tells herself as Derani picks her up and carries her out of the room.

She has to keep telling herself these things because it's the only way she'll keep from panicking.

CHAPTER
4

Derani carries his little human to his quarters, making the rumbling she refers to as a purr the entire journey. Soon the Ollie and that garbage heap of a ship will be gone, and Nalia won't have anything to focus on but him.

She's being docile and obedient now, but he's sure her clever mind is chewing on how to escape her new captivity. He's going to need to keep a close eye on his little pet, as she might prove herself too clever for her own good. The last thing he needs is for her to get loose and run amok on his ship or on a station.

His soothing rumble turns to one of merriment at the thought of having to chase Nalia around the ship. His change in rumbles makes her jerk and look up at him from the cradle of his arms.

"That's a laugh, correct?" she asks.

"Yes, that sound denotes humor or amusement," he explains.

"You seem to make a lot of distinct sounds. Maybe we could go over them so I know what they mean," she suggests as they walk into his quarters. The hatch slides soundlessly closed behind them, and she tenses a little, looking around the room with wary interest. He knows it's going to be a difficult transition for her—from free-born to pet. But he's determined to make the change as painless as possible.

"These are my private quarters," he tells her as he sets her down on his bed. Her feet don't touch the floor, and if she lay down crossways and stretched out, there would still be bed leftover. Humans are a rather small species.

Not just small but delicate and vulnerable as well. It's not surprising so few of them are left. According to the rumors, they're so abysmal at managing their resources that their home planet is nothing but a barren wasteland. Much better for her to be here with him.

"Stay," he commands, and her mouth twists up for a moment before smoothing out.

"Yes, Master."

He strides across the room and tugs out a bunk from the wall before digging out several pillows and blankets. He makes the bed with quick, efficient movements, wishing he had better bedding to offer her. It's well-known that humans like to nest in piles of plush pillows and velvety blankets.

She will have to make do with this bedding for now. They'll be stopping to drop off their cargo in less than a rotation. After that, they can stop by a station where he knows they can find human-specific items.

Straightening up from the bunk, he walks back over to her, pleased to see she stayed. Sitting down next to her, he lifts her onto his lap. Examining her mane, he finds that it's being held in a tight bundle with some kind of band.

Using two claws, he snaps the band in half and her hair unwinds itself, falling a little past her shoulders. The entire length is a perfectly uniform black and cut straight across the bottom. There isn't a hint of curl in the mass, unlike many other humans he's seen in vids.

When he nuzzles her mane with his nose, he finds it as soft as he expected it to be. The texture of her mane and breathing in her delicate scent reminds him that he needs to buy her gentle body cleansers. And he should acquire a few more wraps. The one she's wearing is the only one he has to give her.

"You'll sleep on that bunk," he tells her. "The cleansing and elimination units are through that door. You won't touch anything else in this room without permission. For now, you're able to open and close the cleaning and elimination room door, but if you cause damage, that privilege will be revoked. Do you understand?"

"Yes, Master."

"And you need to come to me with any issues you might have, especially if it concerns your health." She nods in the way humans do to confirm something. She's trying to keep her expression neutral, but he can tell she's anxious about the whole thing. It's fine. She'll relax once she realizes she's safe now. She has an owner to look after her. "Are you hungry?"

For the first time, she looks eager. "Very," she admits.

"Let's see what's available," he says as he stands up and carries her to the galley. It's empty, which isn't unusual for a crew of Talins who only need to eat once a rotation. If he hadn't been hiding the fact that he has no appetite, he would have been eating communal meals with his crew. Instead, he's been taking trays of food to his quarters. Then would stare at the food until it was cold and finally throw it away. He feared he would never feel hunger again.

But as he sets Nalia on the center table, the lingering smells of food filling the galley make him feel ravenous. Because no one is around to witness it, he gives in to temptation. Leaning over, he rubs his cheek along the top of Nalia's head, letting oil from his scent gland mark her mane before straightening up and letting go of her.

"What's that smell?" she asks.

"Smell?"

"Just now, like oranges and cloves," she explains. He doesn't know what either of those items are, so he gives a dismissive rattle of his back plates.

"It must be the smells left over from the last meal," he replies, lost in thought as he considers the food stores they have on board.

He taps a few commands into the food unit. "Have you ever eaten hargrim?" It's the only food he has in stock that's recommended for human consumption.

"It doesn't sound familiar," she admits. "I can eat Ollie fish cakes if that helps."

His back plates rattle with disgust. Ollie fish cakes are renowned for both their stink and disgusting mealy texture. His human will never be forced to eat one of them again.

"Right, that sounds like you don't approve," she comments with a light laugh. "They aren't that bad. I swear."

He selects several heaping plates of food from the food unit and returns to the table. He sets the food down and then pulls out a chair, sits, and pulls her into his lap. She makes a startled sound as she lands in his lap and one of her flailing arms barely misses a plate full of food.

"You need to warn me," she grumps as she situates herself. Once she seems settled, he pulls her back against his chest and encourages her to straddle his legs with her own so they can both face the table. She complies without comment, her eyes locked on the food.

"You'll become accustomed," he assures her. He could have warned her before moving her, but he enjoys all the sounds she makes. He picks up a bite of food and holds it up for her. "Try this."

"I can also feed myself," she points out, waving a tiny and adorable five-fingered hand. The smallest digit on the hand is minuscule. It's so short and skinny that she must be in constant danger of injuring it when doing physical tasks. Not that the rest of her fingers look particularly robust. How do humans accomplish anything with such small digits and puny musculature?

"Open," he orders, and she expels a quick burst of air and opens her mouth. He pops in the morsel and watches attentively as she eats. Humans make some sounds to convey emotions, but their range is limited, unlike the Talin with their back plates and chestbox. The literature he's read and the educational vids he's watched all stressed the high mobility of their facial muscles and the role of facial expressions and body movement in human communications.

Nalia tilts her head a little and chews slowly with her lips pursed. He's sure he knows what that facial expression means, but it's good to have verification. "Are you contemplating the taste of the food?"

She nods and swallows. "It's good," she declares, and he rumbles with pleasure at having accurately guessed her expression. "A little bland, but nothing some spices wouldn't fix."

He rattles his back plates in disagreement. "No spices. The list of foods that are healthy for you to eat doesn't include spices." She opens her mouth, probably to protest, but he uses the opportunity to feed her another bite.

"I'm going to be cautious," he explains. "When you visit the healer, I'll ask about any acceptable spices. Until then, this is your food. It's the only thing we have in the stock that is listed as safe for you to consume."

As she chews, he reaches over to his plate and picks up a piece of food for himself but then hesitates. He sits still, staring at the bit of molentikee pinched between his fingers. It's one of his favorites. Its briny smell wafts to his nose, teasing him, but he's afraid to try it. Afraid it'll be tasteless.

"Aren't you hungry?" Nalia asks. He looks down to see she's staring up at him with a concerned expression. "I thought that plate was yours, but you're not eating. You're just staring at it. Should I feed you? Is that one of my tasks?"

He rumbles out a laugh at her questions and pops the bite into his mouth. Flavor explodes over his tongue, making him rumble with a combination of relief and delight. It's been so long since he tasted what he ate that he chews slowly, savoring the experience.

Overwhelmed with relief and gratitude, he wraps both his arms around Nalia and grasps her to his chest, luxuriating in the feel of her silky skin and plush, warm body. No hard plates or quills scrape against him, just softness.

She makes a strange gasping sound, and he realizes she's banging on one of the armor plates on his upper arm. He pulls back a little to see why she's doing that, and she takes a gasping breath.

"Too tight," she wheezes. He rattles his back plates in embarrassment. At the same time, he starts up a soothing rumble as she pulls air into her lungs.

"I apologize, little Nalia," he says. "I'll be more careful." Cautiously, he pulls her into another embrace, stopping when she tenses. He holds her like that until she relaxes in his arms. He notes how tight he can hold without causing her duress and runs his cheek along the top of her head. This rubs the oil in his scent glands into her mane again. He can't help but enjoy the way his scent mixes with hers.

"There it is again," she murmurs. "Orange and cloves."

It must be his bonding oil she's interpreting as a familiar smell. "Does it bother you?"

"No, I like it. Mom used to make these scent boxes that smelled of orange and cloves. She had them all over the house. The smell reminds me of home and family. It's nice." He rumbles louder at her words, pleased beyond measure that she's already associating him with favorable memories.

"You can clutch to me if you wish. While we are alone or if you are under severe distress, you can request to cling or clutch to me so you can be soothed."

"Uh, clutch?"

"Yes, you humans require a lot of bodily contact to maintain your physical and mental well-being. I'm clutching you right now, but you can clutch back if you shift sideways and put your arms around my neck," he explains. He wishes she would do it naturally, so he didn't have to tell her. Perhaps it's a result of not being around other humans and having to push that part of herself aside. She must have grown so used to going without clutching or clinging that she's forgotten how vital it is for her health.

Because she wasn't born to the life of a pet, he'll need to be patient. He might even need to educate her on all the things humans are normally taught by their sires and dams.

"Oh, a hug," she says with a small nervous chuckle.

"Don't be anxious. I've told you that clutching and clinging to me is acceptable. You won't be punished."

She moves both legs to dangle on one side of his lap and then twists her upper body so she can drape her arms over his shoulders. Her movements are slow and hesitant, as if she's worried about his reaction.

"Like this?" she asks after her arms are over his shoulders. "Or this?" she wraps her arms around his neck and tries to touch her fingertips together.

"Either is fine, but be careful of my back plates," he warns her as she moves. "The edges are sharp. As long as you stay near my shoulders or neck, you're safe."

She arranges her arms so she's not touching his back plates and wiggles a little to settle herself. He reaches up and pushes her head down so it's resting on his shoulder.

"Put your face here," he tells her, tapping at his neck. She nestles closer. Her warm breath caresses the sensitive strip of exposed skin at the base of his neck.

Something in him loosens, settles, and calms. He never realized how hard it was to breathe until now as he expands his lungs with no effort.

For the last handful of solars, the back of his neck has always bothered him. In the spot where several of his plates overlap over a vulnerable bundle of nerves, the muscles constantly felt too tight. Turning his head always caused at least some discomfort. Sometimes it was agony and occasionally it was completely debilitating.

The healers couldn't do anything for him except tell him to stretch. Medications barely touched the pain. But with Nalia on his lap, that pain seems to have almost vanished completely.

"Blessing from the First Prime, you're eating!" Larimus declares as he strides in.

Nalia jerks in his lap and lets go of his neck so she can turn and see Larimus. He watches the tanned skin of her face color a little. As Melanem pointed out earlier, the color change can signify many things. In this instance, he assumes it means she's embarrassed. He's sure she'll become accustomed to her new role as a pet soon enough and no longer color when people see her on his lap. For now, he's more concerned over Larimus's words than Nalia's chagrin.

"Why would you say that?" he asks as his engineer takes a seat across from him.

"You stopped eating."

"I've been taking food to my quarters," Derani points out, skirting the truth.

"But you don't eat it. I'm sure you were just throwing it away."

"You can't know that," Derani challenges, alarmed by his engineer's astute observation.

"I can. Why else would you eat alone in your quarters? I've served you on this ship for six solars, and during all that time you've never eaten alone. There could only be one reason for the change. But it appears my fears are now unfounded." Larimus looks at Nalia and purrs. "Hello again, Nalia."

"Hi. How did—oh crap!" She snaps her mouth shut and looks at Derani with dismay. "Can I talk to others?"

Both he and Larimus rumble with amusement at the question and colorful language.

"You can speak to the crew without permission," he tells her. "Anyone else you need to look at me first for permission. Don't speak first. Always wait for the Talin to initiate conversation."

"Got it," she affirms, and he rattles his back plates with displeasure. "Shit, that sound means you're not happy with me," she mutters and then snaps her fingers as if remembering something. "I forgot the honorific. Got it, *Master*."

Larimus rumbles loudly with amusement. Derani ignores him and sounds a soothing rumble to reward her.

"Don't forget the title," he tells her. "I don't want you mistaken for anyone else's property."

"Don't worry," she mutters, running fingers over her collar. "I'm not going to forget that any time soon."

"Are you still feeling the Fading?" Larimus asks, drawing his attention from his impudent but amusing pet.

"I never said I suffered the Fading," Derani counters. The last thing he needs is for a rumor of Fading to get back to his clan. They might decide to strip him of his ship, his wealth, and all his possessions, including Nalia.

"I would never mention it to anyone," Larimus assures him as if reading his thoughts. "And before you ask, Yulian and Melanem are clueless. They think you're working on a proposal to extend the current trade agreement with the Ulk to include their colonies instead of only their homeworld."

Derani rattles in a slow, low tone of confusion. "Why would they think that? I've never even traded with the Ulk."

"Someone might have mentioned you were interested in founding a new trade route to bring honor to your family and prestige to your clan," Larimus says with a rumble of reassurance.

"You're a genuine friend," Derani tells him, echoing the rumble as realization dawns.

"The Ulk are such a difficult species to contact, and I'm sure any attempted trade agreement expansion would fall flat just from lack of response," Larimus expounds and Derani understands how brilliant the rumor is. If nothing happens, because he's not trying to create a new trade agreement, everyone will just assume the Ulk refused to even communicate. It's a rumor that not only satisfies his crew but his clan as well.

"Nalia, this is Engineer Larimus," Derani introduces them. "Our clans have been closely linked for generations. He's also my good friend."

"Nice to meet you," she says. "What's the Ulk trade agreement?"

"That's nothing you need to concern yourself with," Derani tells her quickly. He picks up a bite of food and holds it to her lips. She opens her mouth and accepts it, shooting him a mildly irritated glance. His little inquisitive human doesn't like it when her questions aren't answered, but along with everything else, she's going to have to learn to accept it.

"I programmed that excuse for a ship and launched the Ollie. He should make it to the nearest Ollie colony in two rotations," Larimus informs them.

"Did he shed any more limbs? Did you talk him through the engine reboot? He has a hard time with the storage bay hatches. Did you make sure the doors were all secured?" Nalia asks Larimus, her body tense with concern.

Larimus gives an amused rumble. "When I left him, he hadn't lost any more tentacles, and I checked and secured all hatches. I started the long burn engines for him remotely after he cleared our bay. Does that reassure you?"

She gives Larimus a little nod. "Thanks. He's not helpless. He's a whiz with navigation and good at figuring out advantageous trade routes. But he can't think at all when he's scared or anxious. He could easily forget to secure a hatch, launch, and get sucked out into space."

Derani feels a frisson of fear go through him. In no single situation could the Ollie have been able to protect Nalia if they ran into danger. Their ship is a disaster waiting to fall apart, and he suspects the reason the Hamlershin were chasing them was because they were smuggling. That's a dangerous endeavor for even the best-equipped ships. His little human might have died many times over, and it appears only luck kept her alive until she stumbled into his space. He hugs her to his chest, careful to keep the pressure at a level she can handle.

"That life is over," he declares as he nuzzles his face into her mane, enjoying the smell of her scent mixing with his own. "I will take good care of you," he promises. "You will come to like your new life."

CHAPTER 5

Nalia is exhausted by the time Derani declares it is time to start their rest period and takes them back to his cabin. After setting her down on her bunk, she watches with interest as he performs his pre-rest cycle routine. He rubs his face and head with a harsh pad and then goes into the cleansing room. When he comes out, he's wearing a baggy pair of pants and no belt. They must be his sleeping clothes.

Now that she only owns one article of clothing, it occurs to her it's going to be a pain to keep it clean. She'll need to take it into the cleansing unit with her, wash it, and then wait naked while it dries. Perhaps she can ask Derani to purchase her a second wrap so she can switch out every few days. She'll wait until the next time he feeds her. The simple act of putting food in her mouth seems to bring him a great deal of pleasure, and if he's in a good mood, he'll be more likely to grant her request.

She contemplates her new life as he pushes her to lie down on her bunk. She's been tasked with no labors so far and fed more in one sitting than she normally eats in an entire day. At the moment, her life feels luxurious.

But that could all change in the blink of an eye.

"I know humans can have trouble maintaining their core temperature, especially during sleep. I've set the room's ambient heat to a higher mark. It should accommodate your weaker body," he explains as he places a blanket over her. "If you need more covers for your nest, I've placed extra blankets you can use at the foot of your bunk."

"Thanks." She looking down at the blankets and then remembers and looks back up at him. He stands there staring at her as if waiting for something. Then she remembers.

"Thanks, Master," she corrects herself and he gives her a purr.

"Good, Nalia," he praises. "How long is your normal rest period?"

"The ship always pulled me out of my rest periods," she admits.

"I'll wake you when my sleep period is over and you will tell me if the amount of rest you received was sufficient," he instructs her. He leans over to nuzzle her hair, and the scent of oranges and cloves fills her nose again. She almost laughs at how long it took her to figure out the comforting smell was coming from him.

Straightening up, he takes the few steps to his barren bunk. Although her bunk is crowded with blankets and pillows, his only has one pillow and no blankets. Even though he claimed to have turned up temperature in the cabin, it still feels chilly. It's no surprise that the temperature doesn't bother him. Most species are more inured to hot and cold than humans. Even Hax, with all his anxiety and big spongy body, could handle almost any temperature short of boiling or freezing.

I'm nothing but a soft, squishy, thin-skinned alien, she thinks and cracks a smile. *No, not accurate enough. I'm a soft, squishy, thin-skinned alien **pet**!* Now she's forced to stifle the giggle. It might have an edge of hysteria to it, but it's still better than crying.

She's still grinning like a fool when he orders the lights off. She hears him move around in his bunk for a bit, and then he goes quiet. Everything goes quiet.

Sooooo quiet!

Amity was much smaller than the Bountiful and nowhere near as new. When she tried to sleep in the room she shared with Hax, she could hear the engines humming, causing her bunk to vibrate mildly. The biosystems room was right next to hers, so she heard the constant sound of air and water moving, systems turning off and on, and the clunk of old machinery.

Even before she and Hax bought the ship, she always lived in crowded quarters, sharing a room with at least three others and sometimes more. Many of the places she worked housed up to ten individuals in the same space. She learned to sleep no matter what was going on around her, including the occasional fights or hasty coupling in a bottom bunk.

Derani's quarters are completely quiet. No hums, no clunks, no vibrations, and no sounds from others as they move around. It's unnerving. How long is it going to take her to get used to a quiet rest period?

Even if she didn't find the silence disquieting, her mind won't let her sleep. Her body might be tired from the rigors of first running from the Hamlershin, then trying to soothe Hax, and finally accepting her new role as a slave, but her mind won't shut down.

Worry for Hax and questions about her future fill her mind, making her restless. If she was back on the Amity, she'd just get up and work until she felt tired enough to sleep. Something always needed to be repaired or maintained, but here she doesn't have that luxury, so she lies there, staring into the dark. There isn't even a port for her to watch the stars outside the ship.

If she had access to an information square, she could start learning about her new master and broaden her limited knowledge of Talin culture. She should probably wait until the next meal to ask for anything, but he doesn't need to purchase an information square. She can borrow one of the half-dozen sitting on the desk in the room. He doesn't even need to get up and out of his bunk. All he needs to do is give her access.

She listens intensely, trying to figure out if the Talin is awake or asleep. She pulls off her covers and slinks out of her bunk. If he's asleep, she doesn't want to wake him up. But if he's still awake, she can ask and won't need to spend half the night staring into the pitch black.

The room is so dark she can't see anything, but the layout is easy to remember. She creeps across the floor, her bare feet making almost no noise. When she feels the edge of his bunk with her hands, she faces toward his head.

"Master?" she whispers. She doesn't expect an immediate response, so she ends up making some undignified noises when Derani speaks and his voice is right next to her ear. She didn't even hear him move!

"Are you distraught, little human?" he asks. He doesn't wait for an answer. His huge hands grip her hips and her feet leave the floor. She's completely disoriented, and the next thing she knows, she is on his bunk. "I'm sure you're anxious about being in a new place. I'll comfort you until you feel better."

"No, I—" she starts, but he cuts her off.

"You're not in trouble," he assures her as he settles her down on the mattress next to him. "It's good that you seek me out for comfort. You humans are needy that way."

He puts a heavy arm around her middle and draws her back against his broad chest. She feels his face rubbing against the back of her head and the smell of oranges and cloves fills the air.

To her surprise, she's able to relax into his hold instead of feeling trapped by his much bigger body. Thoughts of asking to use an information square leave her head, and her eyes close on their own accord. The warmth of his body radiates through the thin material of her wrap, and his arm is a comforting weight draped over her.

"That's it," he encourages her. "I know free-born humans often sleep in pairs or groups for comfort and security, so you can ask to share my bunk any time you require. You're entirely safe now and I will give you all the affection you need."

She ignores his comment about humans sleeping in pairs or groups. It probably seems like they do that to outsiders who don't understand.

The truth of the matter is that most human colonies have few resources. Sharing a bed with a couple of siblings was the least uncomfortable thing she dealt with growing up.

"I'm not scared," she mutters.

The rumble he makes is a cross between a purr and amusement. She guesses it's his version of an indulgent coo.

"I'm not scared," she insists again. "But it's too quiet here. Too strange."

The moment the words are out of her mouth, she gasps and her eyes fly open. She tries to sit up, but his arm keeps her tucked against his body. "I'm sorry, Master. I didn't mean any offense by that. It wasn't an insult. I swear! I'm just used to a noisy old ship."

This time she knows the rumble he's making is one of laughter.

"Be at ease, little Nalia," he says as he replaces the laughing rumble with a purr. "I've read that humans are easily upset by a change in their environment. Don't worry. You'll become familiar with your new surroundings soon. Rest now and let your body recover. Cling to me if you become fearful in the night."

"Cling? Oh right, hugging."

"You shouldn't have a moment of worry while I'm holding you. But if you suffer from anxiety or fear in the night, cling to me. If that isn't enough, wake me, and I will soothe you."

"Uh, cling if I have a bad dream or something. Got it. Thanks—thank you, Master. I should be fine." Except for the time she would bear hug Hax to help him keep calm, she hasn't snuggled or hugged anyone since leaving her human colony and going to work on her first ship.

"Or wake me. I can purr for you and speak gentle words in a soft voice. As I'm doing now. I can tell you all the stories of my linage and clan."

"I should be fine." She thinks of something that forces her to stifle a giggle. She would hug Hax so his anxiety didn't get out of control. Now this Talin is hugging her for a similar reason, imagined though it might be. Her life has come full circle in some ways.

"I can feel you shaking a little. Should I turn on the lights? I forgot that your eyesight is so poor you probably can't see at all with only the infrared frequency being utilized. That explains why you walked over to me so slowly."

"No, it's fine," she assures him, feeling a little embarrassed that he could see her the entire time. She hopes she didn't look dumb with her arms stretched out, taking shuffling steps.

Then she thinks better of the request. What if she needs to use the bathroom?

"Maybe a little full-spectrum light? Just enough so I could make it across the room would be nice."

Derani orders the room light to adjust, and soon she can see. It's barely enough light, but she can make out the general outlines of everything. She feels a little stupid, but being able to see makes her feel better. The absolute dark was disconcerting and caused her more stress than she realized.

"I can feel you relaxing more. Excellent. You have been a brave little human, Nalia. But you don't need to worry or fear any longer. You're my pet. I'll take care of everything. Can you sleep now?"

"I think so."

"Good." With that, he goes still. Soon his breathing is deep and even, telling her he's probably asleep. Darn, this guy can fall asleep fast. She envies him. Sometimes it's hard for her to get her brain to shut down.

As she snuggles into his warmth, she contemplates all the strange ideas Derani has regarding humans. If her species are a common pet among the Talin, how can they believe such odd things? Where are they getting their information about humans? They make humans sound like the domesticated companion animals from old Earth.

Whatever source the Talins are using to learn about humans is skewed toward presenting them as weak, helpless, frail, and in constant need of reassurance and affection. The way he's constantly picking her up and holding her makes her want to argue that the one in desperate need of affection is the big Talin curled around her.

She wiggles around a little to get comfortable until she feels settled and then closes her eyes with a deep sigh. The embrace is pleasant. Her belly is full, she's warm, and the bed is reasonably soft. This isn't too bad.

When he starts softly purring in his sleep, Nalia lets it lull her into slumber.

Nalia wakes up alone. Yawning, she sits up to find that not only is the bunk next to her empty, but Derani isn't in the room at all. Standing up, she stretches and looks around. An information square is propped up on the desk, its screen flashing with the outline of a human. She picks it up, and when she taps it, a message written in the Common appears. Almost everyone learns Common along with their native language, so she reads the brief message easily.

You slept so deeply I determined you needed a longer rest period. I'll be planetside on Molina for most of the working cycle. We're unloading and negotiating for further trades. You'll find sustenance in the food storage locker. I've given you limited access to the UniBase from this information square.

You can't leave the room. If you require anything, tap the display next to the door. Engineer Larimus or Navigator Yulian will assist you.

Rest, eat, and behave.

Nalia sets down the information square and wanders over to the food locker. Inside is another plate full of the same food as yesterday. She's not hungry, so she closes the locker door and contemplates the room.

From her own experience of hauling for a Molina merchant, Derani isn't exaggerating about how long he'll be gone. The Molina like to take their time when interacting and often draw out even the simplest transaction with meals and entertainment.

She runs a hand through her hair or at least tries to. It's so tangled she winces as her fingers get caught in snarls. Time to take advantage of a fully functional cleansing unit.

Enjoying the luxurious cleansing unit, she washes her hair several times, finding it strangely oily. There're no combs or brushes, not a surprise considering the Talins don't have hair. She finger-combs her hair as best she can, thankful that she recently cut most of the length off. Any longer and it would be impossible to deal with. Once finished, she puts the same wrap back on and makes herself comfortable on her bunk with the information square.

To her disappointment, most of the content she has access to is in Talin, not Common, so she can't read it. The few things she can read are out of context and make very little sense.

Finding herself more frustrated than enlightened, she searches until she discovers she has access to a familiar strategy game. She finds several available platforms where she can play against others.

With nothing else to do, she spends the rest of her time pleasantly trouncing almost everyone she challenges.

She doesn't quit playing until her stomach grumbles. Distracted, she misses a key move and loses to her current opponent. The screen flashes with an offer for a rematch, but she declines and shuts down the information square.

Standing up, she stretches and works loose muscles stiff from sitting in one position for too long, and then makes her way to the food locker. Pulling out the plate of food, she sets it down at the desk and then looks around the room. He didn't leave her anything to drink. She could drink from the cleansing unit, but that will taste odd because that water is imbued with microbes that help wash off dirt and grime.

Would this be an acceptable reason to contact one of the crew members still on board the ship? Her interactions with Larimus were pleasant and she wouldn't mind seeing a friendly face. She can only hope she won't be left alone like this too often. She might go mad without company or anything to do for long stretches of time.

She touches the display next to the door and a face she doesn't recognize appears. "Pet Nalia, I'm Navigator Yulian. Are you well?"

"I'm fine," she assures him. "But I don't have any liquid to drink except cleansing unit water. Would it be possible to have a canister of drinking water?"

"I can help with that," Yulian tells her with more enthusiasm than she feels the situation warrants. Maybe he just wants to make a good impression on his captain by being nice to his newest acquisition. The display blanks out and Nalia shrugs. She's about to sit back down when the display chimes and the door slides open.

Because he's notably shorter than Larimus, Melanem, and Derani, she assumes this crew member is young. He also must have run from his post to get to the quarters so quickly. His eagerness to hand her the canister of water adds to the impression of youthfulness. The canister is large enough that she has to grasp it with both hands.

"Thank you, Navigator Yulian," she says, setting the canister on the desk.

"The captain said to provide you with anything you might need," he tells her. "You can't leave his quarters, but I can bring things to you." He's purring now, and she notes the difference in his purr compared to the other Talins on the Bountiful. His rumbling is slightly higher in pitch and a little faster. It reminds her of the way a human teenager's voice sounds different compared to an adult.

"I think I'm fine for now," she tells him. She tries to take a step away from him, but he steps forward, keeping her within arm's reach.

"But you're human," he protests, and she blinks in confusion.

"I am human," she agrees. "But Master Derani left me plenty of food. All I needed was some water."

"Yes, I read that humans require food and drink several times during a single rotation. Maybe even four or five meals!"

She grins at his incredulousness. "I'm good with this one meal."

Still, he doesn't leave, and she starts feeling a little nervous.

"But you're human, so you need to be held too," he explains. "Humans require it. You can become distressed if you aren't petted enough."

He reaches for her, and she steps back again. It's one thing to let Derani pick her up, carry her around, and cuddle her, but she didn't make a bargain with this young Talin.

"I don't need any affection right now," she tells him as he blocks her from moving around him. Now she's trapped between him and the desk.

"Captain Derani has been gone a long time, and he won't be back for many more marks," he warns her. "Only me and Engineer Larimus are here. He's busy with cargo, but I'm available to comfort you."

He reaches for her again and because there's no room to retreat, he easily captures her in his arms. He's not as big as Derani, but his strength is still impressive as he picks her up and cuddles her to his chest. He's not hurting her, so she doesn't struggle, not that it would do much good anyway.

"I need you to put me down," she insists as he nuzzles the top of her head with his cheek, exactly the way that Derani does. A smell similar to lavender fills her nose, but unlike Derani's scent of oranges and cloves, this one doesn't make her feel soothed. Instead, she feels slightly nauseated.

"Navigator Yulian, where are you? I need you in bay one," Larimus's voice barks out of the ship-wide comms, making Nalia jump and Yulian tense. His purring stops and his back plates rattle in a sound that Nalia recognizes as disappointment.

"I'm sorry, Pet Nalia," he says as he sets her down. "I must go. If you need me, just touch the door display again. I'll come right back."

"I don't need anything," she promises him quickly and doesn't relax until the door slides shut behind him.

Flopping down into the chair at the desk, she touches the top of her head. She feels an oily residue there. She brings her fingers to her nose and the smell of lavender becomes overwhelming.

"This needs to be gone," she mutters as she gets up and heads for the cleaning unit door. "And when Derani gets back, we're going to have a conversation about who gets to touch me."

CHAPTER 6

The tension behind his neck plates is bad enough to cause Derani's head to pound with pain. He stopped moving his neck more than necessary halfway through the negotiations to keep the nerves from becoming too irritated. It didn't work. Now as he stands stiffly in the transport shuttle, even the slight jostling as they dock sends agony piercing through his brain and down his spine.

"We did well this rotation," Melanem states with a rumble of satisfaction from her chest. "An entire solar's worth of contracts! That's the best we've ever done with them."

"Quiet," Derani commands in a low voice, hoping his head doesn't explode with that slight sound. His grip on the large box he's holding tightens, and he feels the semi-rigid material mangle under his broad, powerful hands. Forcing air into his lungs, he focuses on calming his muscles and keeping his head and neck still.

"You don't seem well, Captain," Melanem comments as she finishes docking the shuttle. "Maybe you should get a quick scan in medical so—"

"I'm fine," he tells her, trying for a more casual tone. "I'm just fatigued from dealing with the Molina all day. I don't like their tea, and they talk incessantly without actually conveying any information."

Melanem rumbles in agreement. "This is true. I'm ready for a good canister of soopi and maybe a game of gav with Larimus."

The shuttle dings to indicate the bay is sealed and pressurized. The hatch slides open and Derani strides out, eager to get back to his quarters and Nalia. Maybe he could get her to stroke between the plates on his neck with her soft little hands. Her fingers might just fit between the seams on the overlapping plates and be able to reach the muscles and nerves that are causing him so much pain.

"I'll be unavailable for the rest of the rotation," he informs Melanem as he leaves the shuttle. "We start our return journey at second mark next rotation. Inform the crew."

"Yes, Captain," Melanem answers to his back as he strides out of the bay.

The pain seems to calm a little as his cabin hatch slides open to reveal Nalia, nestled among the many pillows and blankets, dozing on her bunk. The information square he left her is resting on her chest and one leg is dangling off the side of the bunk. She must've been using the pad when she succumbed to sleep.

He sets the box of goods down on the desk and then turns his full attention to her. Carefully, he pulls the information square out from under one of her hands and sets it next to the box. Then he works his arms under her and lifts, cradling her against his chest. She makes a little snorting sound and mumbles something but then curls up against him, rubbing her cheek along one of his chest plates.

He carries her over to his desk chair and lowers himself into it. Then he props his legs up on his desk, carefully nudging the box aside to make room. Even with all the movement, Nalia remains asleep. When he shifts her slightly in his lap, she wiggles a little but doesn't fully wake. To his delight, she reaches up a hand and curls it around his neck, snuggling her body against his with another sleepy murmur.

He didn't say anything to Melanem, but he worried about Nalia the entire time they were planetside. It's the first set of marks she's spent alone on the ship, and although he knows it's unlikely anything would happen to her, he couldn't stop fearful images from filling his head.

Also, he doesn't know how needy Nalia might be. What if she suffered from lack of touch while he was away? It wouldn't kill her, but humans are so very delicate. It's well-documented by Talin healers that emotional damage can affect their bodies in adverse ways, even causing a shortening of their lifespan. The thought of Nalia's lifespan ending prematurely fills him with dread.

Rubbing his scent glands along the top of her head, he hears her take in a deep breath and sigh. The sound seems to loosen the muscles in his neck and the nerve pain calms a little. She must be growing familiar with his scent and starting to find it comforting.

He can tell she cleansed herself. Her smell is faint and all her own. None of his oils remain in her mane or on her scalp. He doesn't like that she isn't covered in his scent. But running his cheeks along her head and spreading his scenting oils into her dark mane is easily accomplished, and she seems to find it comforting if her deep sigh is any indication.

She must have bathed at least twice to clean his scent off her so thoroughly, perhaps even three or four times. Could this bathing be a sign of emotional agitation because she was left alone? Humans do like to bathe regularly, but excessive bathing can be hard on their delicate skin. More than one bathing a rotation is too much. He'll need to keep a close eye on her to see if she engages in any other potentially harmful activities.

Perhaps he shouldn't leave her alone for so long again. He can't risk her health, and it would be easy enough to take along a small kneeling pad so she can sit comfortably on the floor next to him as he goes over contracts with clients and negotiates deals.

He could also hand over more of the negotiation duties to Melanem. She has proven to be a clever negotiator since he hired her a solar ago. That would leave him more time to see to his pet and his duties on board the ship.

The hand Nalia curled around his neck twitches a few times. He purrs softly in an effort to ease her transition from slumber to wakefulness. Blinking open her eyes, she looks up at him and her lips curve into a smile.

"Oranges and cloves," she murmurs and then closes her eyes to yawn, showing off her adorable flat teeth.

"What are oranges and cloves?" he asks, remembering she said the same thing in the galley on the day she became his.

When she wiggles, he loosens his hold on her a little so she can sit up and stretch. She yawns again as she stretches her arms and legs before settling back down on his lap.

"An orange is a fruit from my homeworld. The colony my mom grew up in cultivated them. We had a little potted one that mom brought with her when she had to flee that colony. And cloves are a spice. Mom would make scent boxes by combining orange peels and cloves. It's a nice smell."

"Would you like me to find some of these oranges and cloves?" he asks. Although the human's original homeworld is a barren wasteland now, he could find the best approximation of an orange and a clove for her.

"Oh no, I don't need them," she assures him. "You make me think of them. You smell like oranges and cloves."

The oils from his scent glands must smell like that to her human nose. That the smell reminds her of her childhood domicile gives him pleasure. It shouldn't take much time at all for her to bond to his scent.

"Did your trip to the planet go well?" Her question makes him clatter his plates with annoyance.

"It was fruitful, but the Molina insist on spanning too many marks engaging in unnecessary pursuits while negotiating."

Nalia sounds one of her quiet human laughs. "They do like their food and tea," she agrees. "Even though Hax and I were just small-time haulers, we still spent a lot of time drinking tea with the contract agent."

He isn't surprised to find out she spent time on Molina. It's the biggest trade hub in this corner of the sector.

"Did you spend all the time I was gone resting?" he asks as he draws her hand back around his neck. She pets the back of his neck and he leans his head forward to create a bigger gap between his neck plates. She doesn't slip her fingers between them, but she runs her fingers along the edges.

"These aren't sharp at all," she murmurs thoughtfully.

"Only my backplates are sharp," he explains. "If you push your fingers between my neck plates, you can feel my skin and muscle under."

The moment those words are out of his mouth, he regrets it. He shouldn't encourage her to touch his vulnerable places. Not because he fears her, but because he wants her touch for entirely selfish reasons. He shouldn't be so weak.

But before he can tell her not to do it, she slides her fingers between the hard keratin plates. His soothing rumble hits a higher volume when her little fingers rub along his skin as she explores. His muscles loosen a bit more and the nerve pain recedes. She drops her head against his shoulder and puts her nose up to the strip of skin at the base of his neck. Her breath warms his skin, and the stress of the rotation fades away.

It takes a handful of submarks before he can think again because her touch is doing such wonderful things to his brain and body. Finally, he forces himself to talk and interact with her as if she isn't performing a miracle with her tiny fingers.

"Did you use the information square?" he asks.

"I did. Thank you for leaving it, Master. I can't read Talin, but I found a strategy game called gav and played that most of the day."

He left the information square full of his family's history but hadn't thought about the fact that she probably wouldn't be able to read Talin. His back plates buzz a little in embarrassment.

"I'll install a translation program on the information square," he tells her.

"That'll help. Playing gav was fun, but I can't spend all day every day doing only that. I'm not used to not having a job," she admits. "When I was growing up, you worked as soon as you could walk. Later, when I worked on ships, something always needed to be done. I've never slept so much in my life or been so lazy. It feels odd."

Her words worry him. Has his little human been rest deprived her entire life? There might already be irreparable damage to her dainty body. He needs to get her to the healers for a full check. That reminds him to ask about her use of the cleansing unit.

"Did you bathe today?" he asks, keeping his soothing rumble strong. He doesn't want to accidentally agitate her with his question. He doesn't expect her to huff out a laugh.

"I've never been so clean," she mutters. "I don't know where the oil comes from that gets in my hair after you guys hold me, but that stuff is hard to get off."

Sudden and intense anger makes his back plates rattle in a roar. Why would his little human deliberately try to strip herself of his scent?

His violent rattle makes her gasp and draw away from him. He straightens his head, snapping his neck plates closed. Then he looks down at her cringing form.

"You won't use the cleaning unit again without permission," he decrees.

"Sure, no problem," she responds quickly. "I didn't know I wasn't allowed to use it. I just felt really dirty and then after Yulian rubbed his smell on me, I wanted to get it off so—"

Rattling with fury, he stands up and sets her down on the floor next to the desk.

"Yulian touched you?" He knows he's speaking in a voice much too loud for the cabin, but he can't seem to help himself. The thought of Yulian not only holding his Nalia but putting his scent on her enrages him.

She flinches away from him, and he realizes he is terrorizing his human. Focusing on her comfort, he stops rattling and rumbles out a soothing sound. Her expression is still wary, but at least she straightens up and stops covering her face with her arms.

"I'd never hit you," he assures her. "Please explain to me what happened with Yulian."

Her little human face wrinkles in confusion. "I needed drinking water, and he brought me some. Then he said something about me being lonely. He kind of backed me up into a corner and picked me up. When he rubbed his face on my hair, it smelled like lavender and I got a little sick to my stomach. That's why I washed, but it took three times to get all the smell off."

That the scenting bonding oil of another Talin made her physically ill only lessens Derani's anger at Yulian slightly. It also helps that his little human tried to avoid the touch of another, but neither of those details are going to keep Yulian from feeling his wrath.

Nalia has gone silent, probably because the rattle of his back plates has become loud again. Without another word, he scoops her up and strides out of the cabin toward the galley.

He finds all three of his crew there, chatting and eating an elaborate communal meal to celebrate another successful trade. He carefully sets Nalia down on the floor next to Larimus, trusting his long-time crewmate and friend to look after her.

"Captain Derani?" He doesn't acknowledge Melanem's questioning voice. His entire focus is on Yulian.

Without saying a word, he grabs the young Talin by the neck and tosses him across the room with a roar. Yulian hits the wall hard enough to leave a dent in the metal plating and then crashes to the floor. Neither impact is enough to damage the young Talin.

"Captain!" Yulian exclaims as he scrambles to his feet. His back plates are rattling with agitation, and his chestbox rumbles with confusion. "What did I do?"

"You touched my human!" he roars at his young navigator. "You rubbed your bonding oil on her and made her sick. How dare you do such a thing!"

Yulian drops to his knees and lowers his head, making his neck plates gap as far as they'll go. He's rendering himself vulnerable to Derani.

"I just wanted to care for your human," he states, his chest rumbling with remorse. As he talks, he digs around in his belt pouch. "I didn't know my scent could make her sick. I didn't mean to scent mark her. It just happened. I couldn't help myself. When I held her, something came over me, and I had to run my glands over her mane."

Derani's anger calms as he realizes Yulian wasn't trying to steal his pet's affection. "Idiotic youth," he mumbles.

Yulian's hand emerges from his pouch clutching an Atonement Needle. With shaking fingers, he holds it out to Derani. "Please accept my most sincere apologies, my captain."

Derani stares at the needle. Everyone else in the room is silent as he contemplates how much punishment he should dole out to the youngest member of the crew.

Part of him wants to take the needle and stab it through Yulian's tongue and then make the navigator kneel there for a few rotations. Force him to bear the pain of both the uncomfortable position and holding his pierced tongue out of his mouth. Yulian is an honorable man so he will remain in that position until Derani formally forgives him by pulling out the needle and breaking it in half.

But in the end, Derani can't do it. Yulian acted out of ignorance and perhaps the same desperate need Derani himself was feeling. He can't blame the youth for this honest mistake.

"Your offer of atonement is noted but unnecessary," Derani intones. Yulian's shoulders slump from relief, and he drops the hand holding the needle to his side. "But you're still getting punished. You're going to clean the refreshing chamber from top to bottom by hand. No bots or portable cleaning units. Only your hands, a brush, and a container of cleanser."

Derani hears Larimus make a soft, sympathetic rumble. Cleaning the refreshing chamber is the worst task on the ship. The room stinks and is always covered in the thick black goo that the ship uses to lubricate everything. Normally bots clean it, or if the bots aren't working, one of the crew members can take a portable, high-powered cleansing unit in there and have the task done within two marks. Doing it by hand will take rotations. He might not even be done by the time they dock again.

"Thank you, Captain Derani," Yulian says, rumbling with relief. "I'll be quick and efficient in this task. I'm very sorry to have upset you or Pet Nalia."

The sincerity in Yulian's voice and his sad rumble make the last of Derani's anger vanish. He steps away from the navigator and quiets his rattling.

"Stand up," he orders. Yulian scrambles to his feet but keeps his head bowed.

"Humans can scent bond to us," he informs his young navigator. "Just like in the old days when we would scent-bond with each other. As with us, once they are bonded, the bonding oil of another makes them feel ill."

"That happened quickly," Larimus murmurs, and Derani looks back to find the engineer taking half a step away from Nalia and eyeing his pet with clinical interest. "I don't have any personal experience, but I've been told it can take many rotations for a human to scent bond to one of us. Sometimes it can even take an entire solar. You've owned her for less than two full rotations, and she's already displaying bonding behavior. That's interesting."

"Nalia is an obedient human," Derani throws out, as if her obedience means she pushed herself to scent-bond with him rapidly. It's a pleasant thought but ridiculous considering that scent-bonding isn't something that can be consciously controlled.

And judging by the confused looks she's casting around; she has no idea what they're talking about. Larimus sounds an amused rumble, denoting that he knows Derani is being illogical.

Derani moves back to Nalia and scoops her back up into his arms. Her eyes are wide, and she's tense, probably frightened by his display of violence, but she doesn't struggle against him.

"I'll be issuing guidelines and rules," he informs his crew as he holds Nalia firmly against him. "They will include how all of you can interact with my pet. Disregarding my decrees will result in immediate termination and a dishonorable report to your clan. Yulian, you can have your normal rest period, and then I expect you to begin in the refresher chamber."

A sound of acceptance rumbles out of Yulian at the same time surprised rumbles come out of both Larimus and Melanem.

Termination and a dishonorable report to a clan are usually punishments reserved for severely egregious behavior. If either felt brave enough, they might tell him later that he's overreacting, and he'd probably listen to them. Later. For now, he ignores them.

Turning on his heels, he carries his precious pet back to his quarters. He can always hire more crew. He'll never find another Nalia.

CHAPTER 7

When Derani sets her down on her bunk in his cabin, she stays still and quiet. After all the gentle touches from the night before, she didn't expect the violence her new owner displayed in the galley. Even though it wasn't focused on her, she still found it disturbing. Better to tread lightly than risk undesirable attention.

Instead of sitting at his desk, lying down on his bunk, or leaving the room altogether, he sinks to his knees in front of her. To her shock, he leans forward, craning his neck down until his forehead is resting on her lap. The overlapping armor plates on the back of his neck separate. The sound coming out of his chest isn't one she's heard before, but it sounds almost sad.

One thing is clear, he's upset and wants comfort.

Going on instinct, she slips her fingers between the plates and starts stroking the skin underneath. At first, it feels like the muscles under her fingertips are as rigid as the armor plates.

Then, as she moves her fingers back and forth, she feels the muscles relax fractionally. It encourages her to continue the stroking.

When the mournful rumbling stops and he purrs, the tension in her own shoulders abates.

"I'm sorry I failed you, little Nalia." His voice is muffled against her thigh, but she can still hear the words. "I told you I'd protect you. I told you that your life is safe now. Then one of my crew made you ill."

"I guess I don't need to ask you not to let anyone else touch me," she murmurs. Being a slave might be new to Nalia, but she's pretty sure most owners don't apologize to their property.

"Except for the healers, no one will touch you," he promises. His back plates rattle slowly, making a loud, rhythmic clacking.

"What does that sound mean?" she asks.

"I'm agitated," he explains.

"Right," she says. "I'm not hurt or anything. I felt a little sick to my stomach is all. You don't need to be upset on my behalf."

As she talks, his rattle slows and then stops. The purr becomes the dominant sound. More tension eases from the muscles in his neck. She watches as he takes a deep lung full of air, expanding the hard armor plating of his back and shoulders.

She finds herself matching her breaths with his. She's not sure how long they stay like that with her fingers buried under his neck plates, breathing in unison, his purr filling the room. A peaceful calm comes over her.

On impulse, she wiggles the fingers of her other hand under the neck plates. With two hands, she can better massage his tense muscles. His purr gets a little louder, and he brings his arms up to circle around her on the bed. That movement shifts his head a little closer to her stomach. His mouth is uncomfortably close to the apex of her legs, and if he was human, or one of the breeding compatible species, she might be worried.

Wait, that raises a question for her. Are Talins breeding compatible with humans? That might have been good information for her to have before she agreed to become a slave.

Not that the answer would have made a difference. No way was she going to leave Hax to the mercy of either the Talins or the Hamlershin. She needs to research Talins, if for no other reason than to know what to expect in the future.

Eventually her fingers fatigue and with regret, she withdraws her hands from Derani's neck. His purring quiets but doesn't stop. He sits up and moves his neck in a series of stretches, appearing far more relaxed now.

"You're a wonderful human, Nalia," he praises her. "I thank the ancestors that brought our paths together."

"Yeah, nice guys," she mutters under her breath.

His purring stops, and he sounds a questioning rumble. "Hmmm?"

"It's nothing," she states quickly and looks away. His rumbling stops altogether, and she gets the impression he's unhappy again. Not as badly as he was when they first got back to the room but definitely not as relaxed as moments ago.

"Are you hungry?" he asks. She's not sure, but his voice seems resigned somehow. As if he's calm but preparing to endure something. She's not sure how she knows, but he needs more from her. She's not one to let someone suffer, so she speaks, thinking no further than wanting to comfort.

"I'm upset. I need to be held," she states softly.

Her words galvanize him into action. He rises, dragging her to his chest. In one swift move, he turns and drops on her bunk, holding her tightly to his hard body. She's sprawled out on top of him and even though his grip is strong, she knows he'd let her move off of him if she wanted to.

She wiggles around a little to get comfortable. She curls into him and puts her mouth right next to the strip of skin not covered by hard plating at the base of his neck. She's not sure what to do with her hands, so she rubs one up and down on his chest. He probably can't even feel it much through all that hard keratin, but she enjoys the idea that she's petting him.

His purr starts up again, and he lifts his head to rub his cheek against her hair. The smell of oranges and cloves fills the room. When he drops his head back down, she stops petting him and runs her fingers through her hair to help distribute the oil from his scent glands.

She should be grossed out. She shouldn't want any fluid from his body on hers. But his bonding oil feels warm and satisfying as it covers her scalp. It also warms nicely as it covers the skin of her fingers. It reminds her of the expensive products her sister used to buy to keep her skin soft and shiny.

When it comes into contact with her skin, it absorbs quickly, leaving only scent behind. But the scent doesn't stay the same. It changes slightly as it interacts with her biochemistry. She's not sure how to describe it other than it becomes deeper, richer somehow. He inhales and makes a contented rumble.

"You're a perfect human," he breathes. "I'll make sure you want for nothing."

Derani wakes with a warm bundle in his arms. He breathes in a lung full of his bonding scent mixed with her unique human smell. It makes him purr without conscious thought.

After confronting Yulian in the galley during the previous rotation, he worried his little human might develop a fear of him. Although he almost never hears about a Talin who mistreated their pet, Nalia couldn't know that and might believe him capable of hurting her.

Once back in his cabin, he didn't know how to comfort her. Words seemed inadequate. Most of the literature he has read instructed owners to hold and soothe with a steady, continuous, soft rumble.

But that was for humans who were visibly distressed. Nalia hadn't been crying or shaking. She didn't flinch from him or try to get away. She was made of much sturdier stuff. All she did was watch him cautiously.

That wariness was his undoing. In the short time he'd known her, she'd displayed confidence, cleverness, and fortitude. To survive for any length of time on that old ship with only the Ollie as a crewmate, she must also be determined and resourceful. But now, because he lost his temper with the youngest and most inexperienced member of his crew, she watched him with cautious regard. Her expression was too close to one of fear for his comfort.

When he sank to his knees and put his head in her lap, separating his neck plates, his only goal was to make himself vulnerable to her and show her that she has nothing to fear from him.

It's something mates or close friends will do with each other as a show of trust.

Then he realized she couldn't have known the significance of the gesture. Feeling silly, he was about to sit back when she started voluntarily touching him. The moment her small fingers made contact, hope flared. Could his little human have already forgiven him?

Worried he might do something wrong and cause her to pull away from him, he remained perfectly still. Then her delicate fingers slid between his neck plates, and he understood that pure luck had led him to the most perfect human in the universe.

He could have spent an entire rotation kneeling before her, letting her wonderful human hands massage the tension and discomfort out of him. Nothing about his life before had filled him with so much tranquility.

During his supplication, her fingers also kneaded away the nerve pain that had been his constant companion for solars. Even now, marks later, his head and neck still don't hurt. All of that only cements the fact that Nalia is a gift beyond measure.

He draws her body tightly to his and watches with interest as she mumbles something in her sleep and wiggles around a little until they're facing each other. One of her tiny fists smacks harmlessly against his face and then draws down to nestle under her chin. The rest of her face nuzzles his chest. Her legs are drawn up against her body, and her knees jammed against his belly.

He doesn't mind. He can't imagine a scenario where she could hurt him with only her slim body, on purpose or by accident. Her small knees are nothing compared to his muscled torso. He likes it better when her back is to him, but he won't force her to turn over. She probably needs to move regularly in her sleep to keep circulation in her limbs.

Carefully he rearranges his arms so one of them acts as a pillow for her head. He drapes his other arm over her body, his elbow resting on her hip.

Humans are an odd species, he muses. He can understand why she needs to move so much in her sleep, but why does she make so many talking noises? Is it so the surrounding humans who are awake are assured that their fellow human is only resting and not deceased? It's curious, and he determines to do more research about it during his next work cycle.

With regret, he notices how many marks have passed on the small display over the bed. He'll need to rise soon to meet with his crew, but he can hold his little human for a little longer.

He'll need to be stealthy when he rises to keep from jostling his human. Nalia will require many more marks of sleep to be properly rested. As he holds his pet, he thinks of the tasks he needs to complete and how soon he'll be able to duck back to his cabin to check on Nalia.

The next time Nalia moves, her legs brush the flesh pouch that holds his mating shaft and seed sack. The touch is wholly unexpected and he can tell she didn't do it on purpose. She's still twisting and mumbling in her sleep. Her leg rubs him again and then presses with gentle pressure. To his surprise, he reacts to her unintended touch. His pouch gets tight, indicating increased blood flow to his mating member.

If he can't get control of his body's impulses, his shaft will emerge fully engorged and ready for copulating.

It doesn't help when she finds her next comfortable spot. She's turned over and snuggled up against him. Her soft, lush backside is nestled up against his pouch and he feels his inappropriate response worsen.

His mating member quickly fills with blood and the tip emerges. With horror, he realizes that even with his pants on, he could end up poking Nalia with a fully risen and ready mating shaft!

Trying to shift without waking her, he moves his lower body away, but little Nalia seems to follow him across the bunk. Now his shaft is fully engorging and pulling the taut skin of the pouch down, freeing his seed sack as well.

He's feeling trapped and on the verge of panicking. He can't let Nalia wake up to find him like this. Talins don't breed with pets. Talins rarely even breed with each other. Needing physical contact is a weakness no one wants to admit to. Newly married couples will mate to help cement their partnership, and young adult Talins will do it to alleviate overactive hormones. But he's a fully grown and highly trained adult.

This shouldn't be happening!

When he was younger, he and another willing crew member would occasionally share a bunk. Their interludes never took long. Breeding was always fast and efficient, a race to see who could climax first. He knew if the other crew member found her satisfaction first, she would leave even if he hadn't finished.

Words were exchanged between them beyond the most basic greeting. Their coupling was fast, and the moment she was finished, they parted ways. It was an opportunity many young males don't get to experience, but what he felt with that partner, and the few he's had since, are nothing compared to the strange need building in him now.

Ashamed at his lack of control, he extricates himself from the bunk. He's both relieved and strangely disappointed that Nalia doesn't stir at all.

He washes with icy-cold water in the cleansing unit, forcing his mating shaft to shrink back down. It's not pleasant, but by the time he exits the cleansing unit wearing a fresh pair of pants and buckling his belt around his hips, he feels in control of himself again.

Nalia slept through that short period of weakness so he can brush aside any shame at his lack of bodily control and focus on his daily tasks.

He spares a few submarks to lean over Nalia and check on her color and breathing. She doesn't even stir. It's yet another indicator that humans aren't equipped for survival. Sleeping that deeply would get some species killed earlier in their evolutions.

Picking up a convenient information square, he checks the roster as he leaves his cabin. It looks like Yulian is on shift and has started on the refresher chamber. He's not ready to talk to any of the other crew members yet, so he avoids the bridge and ducks into a rarely used cabin.

Checking the time on Talarian, the Talin homeworld, he finds that it's only the early evening there. He sends a contact request to his brother. The request is answered immediately and his brother's familiar face appears on the wall display.

Normally Talins only produced one male and one female child. But due to an unexpected natural disaster, too many male lives were lost. Families were requested to have two male children instead of only one in order to reset the balance between the genders.

Even with that request, many families didn't comply, fearful of reprisal even though the need was there. Three children for one family is considered extravagant. He and his brother belonged to one of the rare families who agreed to have three children.

It might have been legal and sanctioned by the government, but that didn't seem to make much of a difference to the way they were treated.

"Greetings, Derani," Lovialen says with a warm rumble of greeting.

"Greetings, Lovialen," Derani returns, enjoying the sight of his brother. Although everyone knew of the Apogee Assembly's request that the family produce an extra boy, he and his brother were routinely bullied growing up. Because of that, they enjoyed a close relationship, unlike most Talin siblings. It was always the two of them against everyone else—sometimes even their own parents.

"You seem well, so can I assume this is a social call rather than anything more serious?" Lovialen asks with a teasing rattle.

"I have news that will make your back plates fall off with jealousy," Derani tells him. Lovialen rumbles with curiosity.

"Do tell," he demands. "What could you possibly have that would make me jealous? We know my ship is nicer and I have the better property. And of course I'm Mother's favorite. What else is there?"

Derani rumbles out a laugh. "I'm Mother's favorite right now," Derani taunts him. "I brought her the naviora shells. Besides, your ship is only bigger; mine is nicer. My engines are newer, and I have Melanem. She decided to work with me instead of you."

"Only because she wants to form a marriage contract with Larimus," Lovialen counters. "But enough of this, what is your news? I'm impatient to hear what precious thing you've found now."

Derani debates torturing his brother a little longer but finds he can't keep the news to himself for even another submark. "I have a human!"

The rattle of astonishment from Lovialen is so loud it causes the display's audio system to crackle before it can readjust and compensate for the harsh noise. "You found a human! Male or female? How old? Are there more? Were you at an auction? Tell me!" Lovialen demands.

"No auction. I intercepted her ship," he explains. He tells Lovialen the story and his brother rattles loudly with keen disappointment.

"Will you let me meet her?" he begs. "I'll be very gentle. You know me. I have excellent control."

Fighting back a feeling of possessiveness, Derani sounds a reassuring rumble. "When we are both on the homeworld again, you can meet her. I don't know if she'll accept your touch, but you can ask."

Lovialen nods, sounding an eager, fast rattle. "I picked up some soft pillows on my last run. Is she tiny? One of the bigger pillows might make an excellent kneeling pad for her. What color is her mane? Her skin? Her eyes? Human coloring is so variant. Can you send me an image?"

"Calm yourself, brother," Derani rumbles out another laugh. He pulls his Ident off his belt and taps it until he finds the image he captured of her asleep before he left for Molina. "I just sent you an image."

He watches Lovialen fumble out of view of the display and then bring up his Ident. When the image Derani sent him appears, he starts up a soothing rumbling. "She looks so petite and delicate," he comments without taking his eyes off the picture the Ident is casting in the air in front of his face.

"She is small and fragile," Derani concedes. "And she's already scent bonded to me. My navigator rubbed his scent on her, and it made her ill."

Lovialen looks up and rattles aggressively. "Can I assume you reprimanded the navigator? Yulian, isn't it? Do I need to have a word with his family or clan?"

"It's been resolved," Derani assures him, glad his brother doesn't seem to be upset at the bonding news.

"I need to go," Lovialen says abruptly, looking at something out of view of the display. Glancing back, he pins Derani with his gaze. "If you ever find another human, she's mine." Then he pauses, realizing how that sounded like an order. Lovialen rumbles softly, and his tone takes on a pleading sound. "Tell me she'll be mine, brother. If you find another one, tell me I'll get her."

"Of course, brother," Derani agrees, wondering for the first time if Lovialen is suffering like he was before Nalia. "We'll find you a human of your own."

With a curt nod of his head, Lovialen shuts down the display and Derani regards the blank screen for a few moments.

Of the two of them, Lovialen was always the more jocular and charming. His easy humor made him the popular brother, not that Derani was ever envious. He couldn't be because Lovialen always dragged him everywhere, making sure Derani was including in his activities.

But could Lovialen's gaiety be hiding his suffering? Much like Derani hid his pain with work?

With that unpleasant thought, Derani leaves the small cabin and makes his way to the command deck, more than ready to start his day and fill his mind with tasks instead of worries.

CHAPTER 8

Nalia's been to large stations in the past that boasted sizable market areas, but she rarely bothered to visit any shops. Even if she could find products she wanted, it wasn't as if she and Hax ever had any extra money to spend. All their profits went into keeping their ship running and paying exorbitant docking fees. It was easier for her to avoid the market instead of running the risk of catching sight of something she wanted but couldn't afford.

Now that she's owned, she doesn't have a choice but to follow Derani into the market section of Kilkurn station. After she struggled to keep up with him at the dock, he slowed his stride. He tried to lift her and carry her, but she fussed enough to be allowed to walk.

Kilkurn is a major trade hub, so Nalia gets to see all the different species she knows about but many she's never seen firsthand. It's fun to hear all the different languages being spoken alongside the recognizable ones programmed into her intercranial translator. Thankfully, almost all the signs are in Common so she has no problem reading. This is her first time at this station, and she notices that every tenth person she sees is a Talin. They must be prevalent in this part of the sector.

"We need to go in here first," Derani explains as he leads them into a small, nondescript shop. The only person in there looks to be a Leemron, a species with cat-like features. The shop is thick with the smell of spices, and the Leemron greets Derani with friendly familiarity.

"Captain Derani, it's good to see you. I wasn't expecting you for another half a solar."

"Trade with the Molina finished sooner than expected—a rare occurrence with them," Derani explains. "And because I own a pet now, we left Molina as soon as we could to hurry here for supplies," Derani explains with obvious pride. He tugs at Nalia so she's standing in front of him.

The Leemron's gaze glides over her. He tries to keep his expression neutral, but she sees the distaste in his face. "She looks like a fine specimen," he congratulates Derani. Leemrons don't think much of most other species, and humans rank particularly low in their opinion.

"She is," Derani agrees, and she gets the distinct impression the rattle he makes is one of pride. "Nalia, this is Magluss. He owns this shop."

Refusing to act subservient with this Leemron, she meets his gaze boldly. "Greetings."

The Leemron's ears move back as if even hearing her voice bothers him. Then his ears fold flat against his head, and he lifts a lip to show sharp teeth.

Humans are one of the only species that show their teeth as an act of friendliness instead of a threat. Far from being a pleasant greeting, Magluss's actions are telling her that he doesn't like her and that she needs to keep her distance.

She's used to other species treating humans like second-class citizens, but this mild threat display is a surprise.

Derani finally notices that Magluss isn't impressed with having a human in his shop and the rattle of pride turns threatening. He pulls Nalia behind him, standing tall between her and Magluss. She watches the quills on his forearm rise and claws slide out of his finger. Damn, these guys have some fine natural weapons as well as the thick armor plating.

The Leemron's response is quick and placating. Magluss's ears shoot forward and his tail whips back and forth while he dips his head a little. "My apologies, Captain Derani."

Derani quiets his rattle but doesn't stop it. "What do you mean by showing my pet your teeth?" Derani demands. "We've been good trading partners for many solars, Magluss. But that could end right here and now."

The Leemron's pointed ears droop to the sides of his head in consternation. He looks back and forth between Nalia and Derani as if he's trying to figure out how to make amends. "I would keep the trade between us strong and enduring."

Ducking down, he goes through the items on a low shelf. When he emerges, he's holding a small bag of something. Curious, Nalia steps out from behind Derani and leans forward a little, but the opaque, silvery bag doesn't have any tags or labels on it.

"I don't normally trade in human items, but this was included in a shipment of orlan root, and I was thinking I might sell it to one of the human supply shops," he explains to them.

Now she's dying to find out what's in the bag, but his explanation makes her ask a different question. "Human supply shops?"

"We will go there after we've concluded our transaction here," Derani informs her. He hugs her close, pressing her back against this front. "Kilkurn isn't Talin owned, but we represent a large population here. That means that about a fourth of the market is geared specifically toward Talins and Talin interests."

"Like keeping humans as pets?" Nalia murmurs thoughtfully. It will be interesting to find out what items they'll have for humans. Hopefully, they will have some clothes. She could use at least one more wrap. The one she's wearing is feeling grungy, and she'd rather have something to wear while washing and drying it instead of going around naked or wrapped in a blanket.

Her thoughts are interrupted when the Leemron gives a low hiss of impatience and then shoves the silver bag at her. Reflexively, she grabs it. Curiosity makes her open it without hesitation, but Derani snatches it out of her hands.

"What is this?" he demands, shaking the bag at Magluss. "Humans have delicate constitutions. The wrong food can be toxic. Even touching some types of plants can kill them."

"I was told the crop is originally from her homeworld. A human colony produces it now that the human planet is uninhabitable," Magluss says quickly, taking half a step back and flopping his ears up and down a few times in supplication. "It's considered a delicacy among her kind."

With enough caution to make someone think there might be explosives in the bag, Derani opens it and peers inside. He takes a few sniffs and rattles out a disgusted sound. "She couldn't possibly digest this," he scoffs.

"Not raw, no," Magluss agrees. "They mix it in things."

Nalia is about to explode from curiosity. "What is it?" Then she remembers to add on, "Master."

Derani closes the bag, and that movement is enough for a hint of smell to hit Nalia's nose. It's a smell she didn't think she'd ever encounter so far from any human colonies. Derani is about to tuck the silver bag into the pouch on his belt, his eyes on the Leemron as he speaks, "Magluss, if—"

Because he's not paying any attention to Nalia, she's able to snatch the bag out of Derani's hand and open it.

"Chocolate!" she cries out. Wetting a finger, she dips it into the bag and then brings it to her mouth. The bitter richness of pure powdered cocoa hits her taste buds.

"Nalia!" Derani admonishes, his voice both surprised and upset. He tries to take the bag from her, but she turns away and tucks it against her chest. His rattle is dismayed and loud.

Looking at him over her shoulder, she pleads with Derani. "It's chocolate, and I haven't had it for a very long time. Years and years! Or I guess you would say solars and solars. Don't take this away, Der—Master. Please let me keep it."

The taste of the rare treat makes all kinds of familiar and happy memories flood her mind. The last time her family had cocoa, it was for her father's birthday. Within a year, both her parents would be dead from an industrial accident. This cocoa reminds her of the last time she was happy as a child. She wants it more than she can explain with words.

She doesn't realize that she's started crying until Derani begins to purr loudly and insistently. Throughout all of this, his crew has kept their distance, but now they step forward too. The Leemron steps back, his ears twitching back and forth in distress.

"What's wrong with her eyes?" Larimus asks, purring as loudly as Derani.

Melanem leans in close to get a better look at Nalia's face. "I've read about this. They shed water from ducts when there is detritus in their eyes. Or when they are in pain. There is nothing is her eyes, so she must be in pain."

"The powder must be poisoned!" Derani roars and his purring gives way to a rattle loud enough to make several canisters on a nearby shelf shake. Nalia watches in shock as his claws come out and his quills stand up on end, bristling down his forearm. He pulls his lips back in a growl and turns to face the Leemron.

"No, Captain Derani! I've done nothing harmful to the human!" Magluss protests quickly, backing up until he hits a nearby wall.

"Derani! Master!" Nalia calls out, grabbing hold of Derani's belt and digging in her heels. He stops advancing on the Leemron and looks down at her. Instantly, his claws retract and his quills lower. He scoops her up and holds her tightly against his chest.

"I'll save you," he promises as he purrs. He rubs his cheek on the top of her head and the scent of orange and cloves fills her nose. He's probably going to be pissed at her, but she needs to explain before anyone gets hurt or things go any further.

"Don't be mad," she starts and winces. That sounds like when she was a kid, but honestly, she feels like a child at the moment—a child who knows she's about to infuriate an authority figure.

"My emotional state is not because of you, Nalia. I'm furious with Magluss, who's trying to hurt you," Derani explains patiently. "But we can come back and deal with him later. Does it hurt if I hold you? We can get back to the ship faster if I carry you."

"We don't have any human-grade medications on board," Melanem points out quickly, her voice heavy with worry. "That was one of the reasons for making this stop, so we could stock up. We should take her to the medical facility here on the station."

"Absolutely not," Larimus objects. "They aren't trained for human anatomy. They could hurt her without even realizing it."

She doesn't want to, but Nalia is forced to raise her voice to be heard. "I'm not in pain."

Melanem rattles softly in disagreement. "But there is excess liquid pouring from your eyes. That indicates distress. Is the pain in your eyes? Did some of the powder attach to the surface and I can't see it?"

"No, there's nothing in my eye. I'm crying because I'm excited," Nalia says in a rush.

All three Talin go silent and stare at her. Their lack of facial expressions is freaking her out. She can't tell if they're shocked, angry, or amused.

They aren't even rattling or rumbling

Melanem is the first to talk. "Are you telling us that a strong emotional reaction is causing you to display a pain response?"

"I… uh, yes?" Nalia replies haltingly. Put like that, it makes her sound like an idiot. "Look, I'm sorry. I got super excited about the chocolate and then got scared that it would be taken away. I haven't had it in forever, and even when I was a kid it was a rare treat."

Derani still hasn't made a sound, so Nalia gets the feeling she's in big trouble. Oh crap, is there going to be punishment?

Thrusting the bag out, she tries to hand it to Melanem. "Here! I'm sorry I took it without permission. Please don't hurt me."

Now she really feels tears welling up in her eyes. Really? Tears again! Argh! She has to be the least stoic human ever.

Derani finally breaks the silence as Melanem takes the silver bag. He tightens his hold on her and starts purring.

"No, no more tears," Derani orders gently. "I'm not angry with you. This is my fault. I know humans are sensitive, emotionally demonstrative, and prone to outbursts. I should have been gentler when denying you something."

Nalia's jaw drops. "What? I'm not in trouble?"

"You are in trouble but not for the tears. You shouldn't have touched the contents of that bag until I tested it for you. What if it hadn't been human-grade? Or the substance inside wasn't what Magluss thought it was? You could have hurt yourself. The universe is not a benevolent place for your kind."

Derani's crew are making rumbling sounds of amusement.

Larimus stands up straight and stretches his neck to one side as if relieving some tension. "Now I understand why a lot of the literature cautions against giving humans direct access to their food or treats."

Melanem rumbles out a sound of agreement. "I concur. They have very little self-control and almost no sense of self-preservation. What species willingly puts untested powder in their mouth?"

"I could smell that it was chocolate," Nalia mutters. She's glad she's not in much trouble but isn't too thrilled by the conversation going on around her. "You can put me down. I'm not hurt or poisoned."

"Does being held like this cause you any discomfort?" Derani asks.

She knows if she says yes, he'll set her down. But she can't bring herself to lie. And truth be told, the way he's holding her is comforting. She doesn't want to be labeled as "overly emotional," but the barrage of memories that hit her after she tasted the chocolate has left her slightly shaken and a bit overwhelmed. Then Derani and his crew reacted so strongly to her tears that she was sure she was in trouble again.

Deciding to let Derani baby her, she snuggles down against his chest. "I guess this is fine." Derani's purr gets louder. She loves that purr.

Magluss steps around Larimus. "Captain Derani, is your pet well? Do you need me to summon emergency aid?"

Derani looks up at the Leemron. "Everything is fine. Let's conclude our business. I have other things I need to see to before leaving Kilkurn."

"Of course," Magluss says eagerly. "Would you like your usual order?"

Derani slides his eyes over to Melanem and gives her a sharp nod. She unclips her Ident and steps forward. Holding it up, she projects a list of items in the air. "In addition to what we normally order, we want these items as well."

The Leemron examines the list, his ears twisting back and forth as he reads. "Hmmm, I have most of this in stock. But this one," he puts a finger through the projection on the second to last item. "I don't have it. And as far as I know, no one else will either. That didn't make it off Earth when the humans abandoned their planet. It's effectively an extinct product."

That catches Nalia's attention. What are they trying to procure that would be from old Earth? She sits up and tries to see the list. It's an extensive list of human spices. She's not sure, but she thinks Magluss was pointing to turmeric, but Melanem has already tapped the Ident to dismiss it so she can't be sure. Either these Talins have decided to start trading in human spices, or Derani is getting them specifically for her.

A warm feeling fills her. They must be for her. The demand would be too low for it to be profitable. All this extra effort for her.

"Very well, get what you can," Derani instructs Magluss.

Straightening up, Magluss avoids eye contact with Nalia, going back to safely ignoring her. "I'll gather what I can, but I should warn you that I don't have any of those new items in bulk. The requests for it are few, and the quantities bought are small."

Derani stops purring to sound a mildly irritated rattle. "That's fine. Give me what you have."

"And these will almost double the price of your normal order," Magluss adds.

All three Talin are becoming annoyed with the Leemron now. Derani might be the only one rattling, but she can tell by the stiff way they're all holding themselves that Magluss has frustrated Larimus and Melanem also.

Melanem's fast rattle gets Magluss's attention. "You will charge us a reasonable increase or we'll start dealing with Damascul."

Her words have a powerful effect on the Leemron. His lips curl back and he snarls, "Damascul? Fine! You'll get your extra items at cost."

"Excellent," Melanem responds and brings up her Ident again. She projects a small display, taps it, and then shuts it back down again. "I've sent you the list."

"We're departing in three marks," Derani warns him.

"I'll have it to your ship in one mark," Magluss assures him. "Have a fruitful day."

"Thank you for your gift of time and skill," Derani responds, and Nalia gets the feeling that's a rote answer for Talins. Without another word, Derani turns on his heels and strides out of the shop, his crew right behind him.

CHAPTER 9

Even though Nalia is perfectly fine, Derani can't shake the unsettled feeling plaguing him.

When moisture started trickling from her eyes, he felt a kind of desperate helplessness overtake him. He hasn't felt that powerless since he started as an apprentice on his cousin's ship.

He still vividly remembers desperately wanting to make suggestions to his cousin but being unable to because of his low rank. He watched disaster unfold during a business meeting with a group of Matok merchants. The meeting went so badly that they were ejected from the planet, and their ship was chased out of Matok-controlled space.

Part of it was his cousin's inept management of his crew and arrogance that any species would do anything to trade with the Talins. The other part was the ship's negotiator's complete lack of knowledge about the Matok and his bungling negotiation tactics.

They all got out alive, but another merchant clan got the contract with the Matok instead of the Anize, and that was a blow his cousin never recovered from.

After that, he vowed to never feel that helpless again. He's worked hard to control his environment and reduce risk to below average levels. But Nalia is something wholly unpredictable. He would have never expected her to act so irresponsibly. No sane creature tastes an unknown powder!

However, he should have had an inkling of her complete disregard for her safety considering the wreck she and the Ollie called a ship. It's no wonder the human homeworld is nothing but a barren rock inhabited only by bacteria. If these humans can't be relied upon to see to their own well-being, it's reasonable to conclude that they wouldn't be able to successfully steward an entire planet.

Like the rest of Talin, Derani firmly believes that the best thing that ever happened to the humans are the Talin. As prized pets, humans can thrive despite their tendency toward harmful, nearsighted decisions. That conviction has been cemented in his mind by Nalia's recent actions with the silver bag full of powder.

Then she displayed a profound pain response because she was emotionally affected! What kind of species has a physical pain response to emotional distress? Poor little humans with their leaking eyes and tender emotions that match their soft, defenseless bodies.

His relief at realizing she wasn't poisoned and dying was profound. Already he can't imagine his life without the delicate little human at his side, and the thought that she might be hurt and even die was devastating.

No, from now on he will be much more careful and won't make the mistake of trusting her to act in her own best interest.

Nalia makes a sound of discomfort and moves in his arms. "You're holding me a little tight."

"Apologies," he grumbles and relaxes his arms fractionally. He rumbles out a soothing sound when she rests her head back on his chest.

"I've never been in Umally's shop before," Larimus comments as they walk.

"I've heard it's almost as good as the Yorium family's store at the Moravi Wares Plaza back home," Melanem comments.

"The Yorium family is the biggest supplier for human pet items, not just in the capital but on all of Talarian," Larimus points out. "If Umally's shop is even half as good, it should be very well-stocked."

"We're going to a store that only sells things for humans?" Nalia asks, bringing her head up to look back and forth between Larimus and Melanem.

"We are," Derani confirms. "I don't have all that you require and Umally's is the closest place that should stock necessary items."

"Poor Yulian," Larimus says with a small rumble of humor. "He was hoping to be done with the refresher chamber cleaning by now so he could see the station. He's never been here before. Looks like he's going to miss out on this trip."

"It's a minor disappointment," Melanem argues. "And we stop here a dozen times a solar. No doubt we'll be back soon enough. He'll be able to see it then."

"I think he wanted to buy Nalia something to make amends for unwittingly causing her discomfort." Larimus's voice is casual, but he gives Derani a meaningful look as he talks. Derani gets the message from his engineer. He needs to let Yulian apologize to Nalia so his guilt can be allayed.

"I'm not upset," Nalia comments. "He didn't realize what he was doing."

"You're a forgiving soul," Larimus tells her.

"Truly," Derani agrees. From what he's read, humans differ in their response to being damaged. Some will hold grudges and never trust again while others are quick to forgive. Nalia must fall into the latter category, but he's not sure if that's a good thing or not. On one hand, it helps him if he causes her distress. But it also means she'll be quick to trust others who have hurt her and might do it again.

The best recourse is to keep Nalia at his side as often as he can and, when he has to leave her, make sure only trusted Talins are looking after her.

Satisfied with that plan, he walks them into Umally's colorful and crowded shop. No sooner is he in the door than Nalia is wrigglingly vigorously and demanding to be put down. "I've never seen so much human-sized stuff all in one place. I need to look! Let me down!"

A Talin woman emerges from the back of the shop and lets out a rumble of amusement at the sight of Nalia flailing and whining in his arms. "You might as well let her roam. Humans are tactile creatures and she'll want to touch things."

"Are you sure?" Derani asks, eyeing the crowded shelves around him. If Nalia tried to climb one to reach an item, she might fall or pull something down on top of herself.

As if reading his mind, the woman sounds a reassuring rumble. "Everything here is within the reach of the average human, and nothing here will harm her. Anything that could be remotely dangerous is stored in the back behind a locked door."

"Soriana?" a voice calls out.

"I'm out front, Mika," Soriana responds and soon a human male appears from behind a rack of clothing. His eyes brighten when he spots Nalia, and he rushes over.

"Hello! I'm Mika," he states eagerly

Taking a small step back, Derani rattles out a warning. His loud rattle makes the male to a take stumbling step back and give him a confused look.

Derani read that sometimes human males will abuse those smaller than themselves, even to the point of forcing a partner to rut with them. Many research articles discuss how to properly and safely introduce humans to each other, and none of them say to let two humans meet for the first time in a crowded store.

"Mika is friendly and gentle," Soriana explains as she steps up behind the human and wraps her arms around him. He leans back against her, a smile replacing the confused expression from earlier. "He would never hurt anyone."

"Hiya, Mika, I'm Nalia," she calls out with a little wave. Then she points to him. "This is my Master, Captain Derani. And that's Engineer Larimus and Negotiator Melanem."

Derani can tell from the expression on Nalia's face that she's proud of herself for that introduction and both his crew are making amused rumbles.

Grinning broadly, Mika waves back. Then he looks at Derani. "If you set her down, I can show her things she might be interested in," he offers. When Derani still doesn't move, Mika's grin gets wider. "I have female siblings and a dam I'm very fond of. I know how to be polite and gentle around females. I'm a very good human. I promise."

Nalia snorts out a laugh when Mika proclaims this. "And so well-trained too."

Mika must have heard her because he laughs with her. "Are you a badly behaved human?"

"Usually," Nalia quips. This response not only makes Mika chuckle but makes the Talin holding him sound a rumble of amusement.

Even with this playful interaction between the two, Derani still hesitates. He looks over at his crew. Melanem gives the slightest of nods and Larimus rumbles out a sound of agreement.

"I don't see the harm. If a human owned by the Umally family can't be trusted with other humans, that would reflect poorly on both the family and the clan. They do specialize in importing and selling human items, after all," Larimus points out.

As always, his old friend's logic is sound. Reluctantly, he lowers Nalia to her feet. "Stay in sight," he orders her.

"Yes, Master," she responds quickly with one of her human grins. Why does he feel like she's laughing at him almost every time she uses his title?

Mika is examining her wrap with a critical eye. "Are all your wraps made of this same material?" he asks.

"Well, considering I only have this one, the answer would be yes," Nalia explains with a little laugh.

Instead of laughing with her, Mika casts Derani an accusing look. "She only has one wrap?"

Taken aback by Mika's boldness, Derani sounds a rattle of surprise. "That's why we are here, to buy more items for her."

Mika gives him an appraising look. "She'll need at least three more wraps, several omnies, slippers—well, you get the idea. You'll buy her everything she needs. Right?"

Derani is initially startled by this human's aggressive behavior. But far from feeling as if his authority is being challenged, he's amused.

He's not the only one. Mika's words make Soriana rumble out a laugh. "We need to work with what Captain Derani wishes to purchase, not what his human might want. You would have them buy half the store every time a new human visits."

Mika waves a hand in the air dismissively. "That's only because our store is so small. When we finally get to expand, I'll only encourage them to buy a quarter of our wares."

He then turns his attention to Nalia. "Come with me so you can try on a few of these wraps. They are much more comfortable and durable. Oh, and we need to pick out a few sleep wraps. What's your favorite color? Do you…" As he talks, he leads her off to a rack of wraps and other clothing items along the far wall of the shop.

Derani resists the urge to follow them. It's obvious Mika isn't going to do anything to Nalia. And he's already displaying his knowledge of the store's content and inquiring about Nalia's preferences. This human is an exceptionally good fit for Soriana to own.

"My clan owns twenty-two humans," Soriana explains as they all watch Mika shove items into Nalia's hands, insisting she touch and feel everything. "Most of the humans take turns living with the different families in our clan, except for Mika. He only wants to be with me here on Kilkurn, even though it means he rarely gets to see his sire, dam, or siblings."

"He seems like a very happy, well-adjusted human," Larimus comments. "But isn't it bad for humans to be by themselves too much? Don't they require contact with other humans?"

Soriana rattles out a negative sound. "Not necessarily. It depends on the human. He has a sister who will never want to leave her dam. Nel is a very gentle and easily scared human. She can even become distressed if she has to be seen by a healer. She would never survive here on Kilkurn with only me. But my Mika loves it here. Loves to meet all kinds of species and interact with the humans brought here by their owners. He's soothed a fair share of newly bought humans who have been terrified because they'd never been owned by Talins before and didn't know what to expect. He has a gift for kindness." She's sounding a rumble as she tells them about her human, showing a great deal of affection.

"You must see a lot of recently bought humans," Melanem murmurs thoughtfully. "Three major slave markets are within this sector."

"Four," Soriana corrects her. "At least a third of the humans brought to my shop have been bought at one of them. It's a sad sight to see. They're almost always severely malnourished and petrified of making their new owners angry. It can be hard for some of them to shake off their earlier slavery and relax with us." She pins Derani with her gaze. "Where did you get Nalia? She's obviously new to you if she only has one wrap, but she looks far too healthy to have come from one of the auction houses."

"We rescued her ship," he explains, wondering why Soriana seems so intense about Nalia's origins.

Soriana sounds a confused rumble. "Was she a slave on a ship you rescued?"

That makes him and his crew sound rumbles of amusement. "She was a co-owner of a ship along with an Ollie named Hax," Larimus explains. "Although calling it a ship is generous. The thing was a junker, ready to fall apart at any moment. It was her good fortune that she stumbled across our path."

"She's a wild-caught human? That's a rare find," Soriana comments. She sounds a mild rumble of concern. "Captain Derani, may I speak to you privately for a moment?"

Although he's curious about what Soriana wants to discuss with him, Derani is reluctant to move anywhere he won't be able to keep Nalia insight.

As if reading his mind, Melanem speaks up. "Larimus and I will keep a close watch on Nalia. And we'll help her and Mika find everything she might need."

"Although I don't think Mika needs much help," Larimus comments, and Derani follows his gaze to see a growing pile of items at Nalia's feet. "We might end up buying a good portion of the store if Soriana's human doesn't slow down."

"Try to keep the purchases from filling up the ship," Derani replies dryly, making both his crew sound amused rumbles. He could say something to Nalia about limiting her purchases, but he's wealthy and has plenty of room on the ship. It won't be a hardship to indulge his human, especially when the next stop they make will probably be unpleasant for her. It's well-known that no human enjoys going through processing with the healers to get registered.

When his eyes return to Soriana, she silently leads him through a door at the back of the shop. He finds himself in her living quarters. There is a table, chairs, and a few plush settees along with several kneeling pads scattered throughout the room. Soriana invites him to sit in one of the chairs as she takes another one.

Soriana beings questioning him right away. "Does your family or clan own any humans?"

"Several families in my clan own humans, but none are communally owned, so I've had no access to them. I'm sorry to say no one else in my family has acquired one yet."

"That would make Nalia your first human?" Soriana asks, her tone carefully neutral.

"Yes, she's my first. But I've made careful study of the literature and training vids," he assures her. Soriana must be worried that he lacks the skills and information to properly care for a human pet. It speaks well of her that she's protective of the pets that come into her shop and that she pulled him aside to quietly assess his knowledge base.

"Humans can be tricky creatures," she beings. "They—"

He's quick to cut her off, eager to display his worthiness to own a human. "I'm well-educated, even if I haven't had a pet before. Beyond taking all the standard human care classes, I've read everything the Committee for Pet Welfare has published and studied the list of vids they recommend. I also subscribe to the *Best Practices* journal issued by Pet Health from the Verda Healers Clan."

Soriana makes a rumble of approval. "All excellent resources, but you have a unique issue, Captain Derani. Wild-caught humans are rare. If a human is acquired outside of Talin-controlled space, it's usually from a slave auction. Slaves learn quickly to control their emotions and impulses. Slaves who are unmanageable don't live long."

Derani feels impatient. "She wasn't a slave, so I don't see how this pertains to my situation."

Soriana isn't bothered by his interruption. "That is actually part of my point. If she's never been a slave, she might be very demonstrative. Even more so than the humans we keep on Talin. Pets raised among us have never suffered the hardship that wild-caught humans often experience. Having to live in fear can create mental trauma in humans that is difficult to heal. And free-born humans are always unpredictable."

Derani can't help the rumble of amusement that comes out of him. "I had my first experience with her unpredictability before coming here." He tells the story of the chocolate and Nalia's tears.

Soriana is rumbling with laughter by the time he's done. "I'm afraid that's not out of the ordinary. But you handled it as well as you could. When you stepped through my door, I wouldn't have known any of that had happened, judging by Nalia's smile. I promise, you'll learn to read Nalia's emotions over time, and you will find it easier to judge when she's truly hurt or ill, or when her feelings are getting the better of her."

"I can only hope," Derani agrees and then pins her with a hard gaze. "Are you reassured now? Of my dedication as an owner?"

Soriana makes a rumble of satisfaction. "I'm convinced that you will be a conscientious owner, but that's not the only reason I called you back here."

"Oh? What else should I know."

"There are challenges to having a human who is isolated from other humans." The way Soriana says that makes Derani feel that she's choosing her words carefully. "As you may know from reading the literature, humans are rather lusty creatures and will often copulate every day. When they are in their prime breeding years, they may even perform the act several times a day."

That's not something Derani had thought about before now. "Yes, I'm aware of their rutting habits. I don't see how that is an issue here. There aren't any other humans on my ship, so I don't need to concern myself with impregnation or—"

"You misunderstand," Soriana states quickly, with a rattle of displeasure, cutting him off. "This isn't about reproduction. This is about pleasure. Humans who have all their basic needs met will want to rut. It's instinctual."

It finally hits Derani what Soriana is trying to tell him. "You're saying she'll want to seek a partner to rut with?"

"Or she will probably self-satisfy," she adds. "It's normal and healthy, but I don't want you to be shocked if you see it. Humans shed a lot of scent when they are self-satisfying, and it can be startling if you've never run across it before."

Derani isn't sure how to react to this information. On one hand, he feels like he should immediately start contacting other families in his clan and see about finding Nalia a male to pair off with. But he's also struck with the impulse to keep her away from those same males who can't possibly be trusted to treat his little Nalia with enough tenderness and care.

Perhaps he can give her medications to ease the symptoms of sexual neediness if she isn't able to self-satisfy. "Can I do anything about it?"

Soriana makes a happy rumble. "Absolutely! Let me get your Ident verification," she requests, holding out her Identification Cube. Pulling his off his belt, he keys it and then holds it next to hers. The Idents exchange information and then beep. Now the two of them can contact each other if they so desire.

"I'm going to send you some vids and literature that isn't widely distributed," she explains as she taps her Ident a few times. "The contents are considered slightly controversial. But I believe you want the best for your human, so you should have all the information available."

Derani hides his disappointment. He can't imagine there's much that he hasn't already read or at least seen referenced, but he gives Soriana a polite nod. "I'm always eager to gather new information."

They spend another twenty submarks discussing nutrition and what Talin foods are safe for Nalia to consume as well as how much exercise she might need. He's thankful for Soriana's wide range of knowledge regarding everything human and commits to memory a few Talin foods she recommends that appeal to human taste buds and are safe to consume. When they rise to leave, he's content that the meeting proved useful after all.

When they enter the shop area, they find no one new has entered. Nalia is standing next to an enormous pile of items with an apprehensive expression on her face. When she looks up at him, she tries to smile, but it only makes her appear more nervous.

Worried that Mika might be harassing or bullying her, Derani sounds a warning rattle and storms across the store.

CHAPTER 10

"Wait… what?" Mika says, his voice pitching high in disbelief. "You owned a ship? Like a complete ship?"

"Yes, a complete ship," Nalia repeats with a grin. "We weren't flying around inside half a ship."

They both chuckle at that image. Then Mika starts again. "I mean, were you in a ship that went into space?"

Nalia shoots him an annoyed look. "Where the hell else would a ship go?"

"No, I mean, it wasn't a planet jumper or high orbit shuttle, or something like that. I mean, was it a ship-ship?" Mika explains.

"Oh, yeah, it was a *ship-ship*," she says, mimicking him. That makes both of them laugh. "I owned it with an Ollie named Hax. We were small-time haulers. But, uh, we ran into some trouble and ended up getting rescued by Derani and his group."

Mika's expression goes from interested to concerned. "Sounds like something terrible could have happened to you."

"Every damn time we undocked," she confirms with a grin, automatically taking the thick maroon red wrap he's handing her. The moment she's touching it, she's struck by how soft it is. Bringing it up to her cheek, she rubs her face on the plush garment. "Oh, this is nice."

"That's an omnie," Mika explains, and his collar gleams a soft silver as he moves. Unlike her collar, his doesn't have any jewels or adornments. It's plain and serviceable. She wonders if that means anything or if it's a gender thing—girls in fancy collars and boys in plain ones.

"Omnie?" she asks, still petting the article of clothing in question.

"Think of it as a coat," he explains. "The lining is infused with nanos that will keep you toasty warm if the ambient temperature drops too low. It's also self-drying and self-cleaning because of the nanos." He takes it back from her and holds it up so she can slip it on. It almost reaches her ankles and secures at her waist with ties just like the wraps. One side ties at her left hip on the inside and the other side ties at her right hip on the outside. The moment it's on, she feels like snuggling down inside of it.

"It's so soft," she murmurs appreciatively.

"I have five of them," Mika admits. "I don't need them often, but I love them. This is a good color for you. It goes great with your dark skin. You know, Talins think humans with darker coloring are better?" He points to his long blond hair. "I'm not considered ugly, but they think those of us with lighter skin and mane color aren't as healthy as people with your coloring."

"There weren't many with your coloring at the colony where I grew up," she informs him. "But I can't imagine it makes much of a difference."

"Probably not, but I thought you might like to know," Mika tells her with a grin. "And they like our manes long. You're probably used to keeping it at this length, but Derani's going to want you to grow it out."

Absently, Nalia runs a hand through her tangled hair. "Speaking of long hair… er, mane, I mean. Do you have any brushes or combs?"

Mika lights up. "This way!"

Dragging her to another spot in the store, she finds herself confronted by all kinds of hair care products. She sees so many items that it takes her a moment to find the combs. Even then, she has dozens to choose from. Some even look hand carved.

Her hand itches to pick up one of the beautifully carved ones, but she knows better. They have to be expensive and the cheaper, industrially produced combs will do just as good a job on her hair. Picking out a sturdy-looking comb, she then moves to pick out a brush.

After she has picked out those items, Mika insists she choose several bottles of cleansers and personal care products. Then cleansing and drying cloths. Undergarments. Belts. Bedding. Plush kneeling pillows. Soon she has an uncomfortably large pile of items, but Mika still isn't done.

"You need slippers too," he tells her and urges her to sit down while he fetches half a dozen boxes. Larimus jumps in when it looks like the stack of boxes is about to tumble down. He helps Mika carry the boxes to where Nalia is sitting and then goes back to the front of the shop to continue his conversation with Melanem.

Kneeling next to her feet, he opens one of the boxes and pulls out a pair of deep blue, human-sized footwear.

"We don't call them shoes because that upsets the Talins. I don't completely understand why, but I think it has something to do with them equating shoes with slaves or wild humans. Because both slaves and wild humans are always working, they have to have shoes, unlike us pets. It's weird logic, so you have roll with it. But you need to remember to always refer to them as slippers."

She tries to take the pair from him, but he holds them away until she sticks out a foot. Grinning, he slides one on her right foot. It only takes a moment for her to realize why he's grinning in anticipation.

"They're like the omnie!" she exclaims as her cold feet turn delightfully warm. Because Derani took her shoes away, she's been plagued with cold feet whenever she has to walk on the metal planks that make up the floor of the ship. It hasn't been so bad that she's worried that her feet will be damaged, but it isn't comfortable either.

"They're made with the same tech as the omnie," Mika confirms. "The Talins don't need this stuff. They could sleep covered in snow and it wouldn't affect them. They get this stuff from the Marnox specifically to keep us comfortable."

"These feel amazing," she gushes.

Mika's grin gets wider. "The feel isn't even the best part! The soles of these slippers are made of some fancy tech they use for landing pads. If you end up on a slippery floor, they'll get grippy. If you have to walk on anything rough, they'll become more rigid. It's some sophisticated tech that will adapt, depending on what you might need." He puts one of his feet forward to show off a black slipper. "They've saved me from taking a spill on smooth floors on more than one occasion."

"This is so much better," she murmurs, curling her toes inside the slippers. "I didn't enjoy going around barefoot."

"Just be aware that if they put you in an enclosure on Talarian, or one of the Talin colonies, they'll probably take them away."

"Talarian is the Talin homeworld. Right?"

"Yup," Mika confirms as he pinches the toes of her slipper to test the fit. Then he picks up another box and starts opening it as he talks. "I grew up in Erigrid. That's a small town just outside the planet's capital, Moravi."

"How many times have you been sold?" She hopes that question will allow her to segue into finding out how humans are transported and maybe even get some insight into how often humans escape. What she isn't prepared for is for Mika to rear back with an affronted expression.

"I've never been sold," he spits out. "My clan would never sell any of us."

Holding up her hands, she backpedals. "Sorry! I'm new to the whole being a slave thing."

His expression softens, and his body relaxes. He drops the box he was holding and reaches out for her hand. She lets him take it, surprised when he sandwiches it between his own and leans forward with an earnest expression. "We aren't slaves," he explains gently. "We are pets. There's a big difference between the two."

She keeps her voice and expression neutral because she doesn't want to offend Mika again. "We're both wearing collars and can't leave of our own free will. That seems a lot like slavery."

That comment makes Mika chuckle. "You're not the first wild-caught human I've met, so I'm going to ask you a few questions that might help you understand. What was it like for the humans while you were growing up? I mean, once you understood how the world around you worked, not while you were a small kid and didn't know anything."

She has to think about it for a moment, not because she can't remember, but because she's always tried very hard not to think about the Wolder Colony.

"It wasn't good," she starts with reluctance. "The Malmarks let humans settle on one of their planets, but we had to pay a high tax and abide by strict laws about where we could go and what jobs we could have. The Malmarks are the closest civilization to old Earth, so they have the largest population of humans outside of Mars. Mom said her great-great-grandfather wanted to go to Mars, but only the most elite could live there. But honestly, he was lucky to be allowed to move to Malmark because not long after he got there, they closed their borders to any more humans. And by the time I was ready to leave Wolder, we got the news that the Mars Colony collapsed. We were some of the lucky ones."

"So you grew up around a lot of other humans?"

"Kind of. I was employed young, so I spent a lot of time among the Malmarks working for the city and planet maintenance crews. It was a lot cheaper to send a small, human kid into the tight places to perform maintenance on the enormous engines that powered everything instead of wasting money on expensive bots. It was good because I learned a lot about basic repairs and rebuilding, and I got to help my family."

Mika makes a soft, distressed sound. "That couldn't have been easy, working a job so young?"

She frowns at the memory. "Yeah, it was rough. No eight-year-old wants to work ten hours straight, but the money I brought in made the difference between us eating every day or every other day. Even after I got bigger, I worked for them until I left."

"I've heard similar stories. Humans on colonies forced to go to work at a young age. How old were you when you left?"

"Almost twenty standard Earth years. My parents died when I was only about five or six. Some kind of disease. Anyway, my older sister raised me. Then she died in a cave in the mine she was working in. After that, nothing was holding me there anymore."

Taking a deep breath, Mika gives her hand a sympathetic squeeze. "Right, now let me tell you about my life so we can compare. First, I've only ever seen one person die."

"Well, of course," Nalia says, feeling confused. "You live out here on Kilkurn. How would you see anyone in your family die from way out here?"

He shakes his head. "No, you don't understand. Ever! Even when I was growing up, I never saw a human die of anything but extreme old age. I'm one of eight siblings, and my dam was one of six. My father's dam had four children. All of them lived."

It takes Nalia a moment to digest this information. "You never lost anyone, not even in childbirth?"

If true, that would be incredible. Every year it seemed the Wolder Colony got smaller and smaller. One particularly terrible year it felt like she attended a funeral at least once a week. Only a quarter of those who died had been elderly. The rest had died of disease, childbirth, or industrial accidents.

"I'm not making that up," Mika insists. "My sire's dam was ancient when she died. The Talin family who took care of her mourned with the rest of us. They even gave her full Talin crossing-over honors as if she was a Talin instead of a human pet."

Nalia honestly can't believe what she's hearing, so she latches on to the one part of his description that doesn't make sense to her. "You mean the Talins who owned your grandmother gave her a funeral?"

"No, that family didn't own her. They had her for the last few years of her life. In the Omora clan, that's the clan Soriana and her family belong to, none of us are owned by any individual Talin or family. We are all communally owned by the clan. That means we take turns living with the various families that make up our clan. Sometimes we end up staying with a family permanently like my father's dam. She became very close to the female elder in that family and refused to be parted from her."

"And she wasn't forced to leave?"

"Absolutely not. If a human bonds to a Talin, it's considered harmful to make the human leave. The clan gave her permission to live there for the rest of her life."

Nalia makes a face. "You get to pick your owner?"

Mika shrugs, unconcerned. "In a way. In a few solars I'll be asked if I want to return to Erigrid or stay here on Kilkurn with Soriana." A look of happiness crosses Mika's face. "I'm going to stay. Soriana needs me, and I love her more than anyone else."

Nalia's at a loss for words. Mutely, she stares at Mika. He just described a life she never thought was possible for humans—a fantasy where her parents and sibling would have lived. Where there was no lack of food, shelter, or care. Where she wouldn't have worked long days at the tender age of eight and still couldn't afford more than the most basic medical care.

It's all too much, and she feels a strange combination of anger and sadness well up in her.

After a few beats of silence, Mika draws her in for a gentle hug.

"Everything's going to be fine now that you are owned by a Talin," he promises her. "They love us because they can't love each other. We're precious to them. And even though some nasty political maneuvering is going on right now, they're doing their best to keep us from getting hurt by it."

That last comment makes her think she should ask questions, but she can't get her brain to focus. Mika draws away and sees her confused and overwhelmed expression.

He huffs out a gentle laugh. "Right, you have no clue what I mean by any of that. And I probably just threw your world perspective on its side." He looks around and then sees a small data square. He grabs it and starts tapping at the screen. Then he hands it to her. She expects to see something on the screen, but it's blank. Before she can tap it, Mika speaks.

"I'm giving that to you. I downloaded some articles for you to read and it already has a Common translator program. I know the articles won't make any sense at first, but you'll begin to understand as you read through them. And don't be afraid to voice questions. Ask your owner about anything that makes you curious. It won't upset him. If he doesn't want to answer, he won't."

"Ask questions that aren't related to my job?"

Mika barks out a laugh. "What job?"

That makes Nalia feel uncomfortable. "Well, I haven't been assigned any duties yet. But I'm sure he'll get around to it."

Slowly Mika shakes his head, his grin never faltering. "No, he won't. You're doing your job right now."

"What, shopping?" she scoffs.

"Letting him hold you. Take care of you. Has he groomed you yet?"

"Groomed me?" she squeaks out. "Like brush my hair?"

"That and other things like bathing you and rubbing oil into your skin," Mika elaborates.

Nalia feels her skin flush with embarrassment. "I, uh… no."

"Brace yourself because he will," Mika warns her cheerfully. "Don't be afraid to tell him if he's being too rough. Talin skin is incredibly tough, so sometimes they can forget that our skin is easily damaged."

Nalia leans close and whispers, "Is he going to rape me."

It's a relief to her when Mika looks downright offended by her question. "Of course not! We are breeding compatible with Talins although you'd be hard-pressed to get one of them to admit it publicly. But they don't rape. It's not something they do to each other or any other species. They have some pretty powerful feelings and taboos about sex and sexuality."

"Yeah?"

"They see sex as something that distracts them from more important things. Powerful emotions in general aren't supposed to be displayed at all. Except for anger. But even then, it's supposed to be controlled and used productively."

Nalia holds up a hand to stop Mika's flow of words. "Wait, back up. If they're not supposed to be having sex often, how do they have kids? Artificial insemination?"

"Kinda. They use artificial wombs. A couple is expected to finance the birth and raising of two children, one male and one female." Mika's expression turns sad. "They don't raise their own kids either. Childbirth and child care are all institutionalized here. The moment they're pulled from the artificial womb, they're sent to a place called a cresh to be raised. Parents will visit them at the cresh, but they don't live together until the kids are almost adults and ready to learn about the family or clan businesses."

Nalia feels her eyes prick with tears. "They don't get to raise their own kids? That's horrible! What kind of law is that?"

"It's as much about social taboos as it is about laws," Mika explains. "Do me a favor, and read the articles. I left you a link tag so you can send me a comm request. You can ask Derani for comm access. Make sure he understands that you only want to talk and that you find me amusing. You could even say I remind you of a sibling or childhood friend from when you were growing up."

That specification confuses Nalia. "Uh, why the subterfuge?"

"If you're not careful, he might think you want to be paired off with a male." He gives her an exaggerated wink.

Chuckling, Nalia shakes her head. "You're a nice guy and all, but not ready for any weird co-habitation with another slave."

"Pet, Nalia," Mika reminds her gently.

"Right, sorry, pet. Still not up for it." Worried she might have offended him, she adds, "Not that you aren't handsome. But…"

He gives her a grin. "I'm not interested in you either."

That makes her giggle, and she realizes that over the course of a short time she's cried once, almost cried again, and has laughed more than she has in the last month. To say it feels like she's been through an emotional whirlwind might be putting it mildly.

"And so you know, if you tell them you're lonely and want a male, it probably wouldn't be me. They'd try to find a male owned by another family in your owner's clan or a family from a partner clan." At Nalia's frown, Mika continues. "But I get the feeling that Captain Derani isn't interested in sharing you yet, not even with another pet. I wouldn't be worried that he's going to pair you off against your will."

He leans in close, his expression conspiratorial. "Didn't you know loneliness can cause stress in humans? They're always worried about shortening our lifespans due to stress. Captain Derani's going to do the utmost to make sure you live a life as stress-free as possible. Try not to use it against him too often."

After the incident at the spice shop, the idea that she could manipulate Derani like that doesn't sound so far-fetched any longer. "Um, sure."

With a grin, Mika stands up. "Back to work!" he announces cheerfully as he gathers a few more boxes of slippers. "Four pairs of slippers should be good for now."

Thankfully, he didn't ask her to take the ones she's wearing off because her feet feel much too warm and comfy to comply. And the omnie is still wrapped around her. She can't imagine how expensive this wrap coat must be, so she braces to take it off and return it to Mika when Derani comes back.

Mika tugs her to her feet. "Come pick out some lotions and oils for your skin. They won't smell strongly to you because Talins have an excellent sense of smell and strong perfumes will bother them."

They stop in front of a display full of brightly colored bottles with elaborate stoppers. Mika explains which ones are lotions and which ones are body oils.

Nalia reaches for one of the bottles. If she's honest, she can't smell a difference in any of them, so she tells him to pick what she should have. She shouldn't be surprised when he pulls out six different bottles. Humming to himself, he carries them to the pile and then whisks her off to another corner of the store. For a relatively tiny shop, they've jam-packed a lot of items inside.

With growing dismay, Nalia realizes that the number of items Mika's accumulating is getting staggering. When he tries to drag her to a spot where decorative belts are hanging, she digs in her heels.

"We need to put some of this stuff back," she insists. Picking up several boxes of slippers and another omnie from the pile, she tries to hand them back to Mika.

"Nalia, you're going to need all these things," Mika insists.

Waving a hand over the pile, she grimaces. "This is more clothing than I've owned in my entire life!"

He casts her a pitying look. "Okay, that makes me sad. I've had humans bought at a slave auction who at least had a shoulder pack full of possessions. Are you telling me that a free human had less stuff than a few of the ex-slaves that have come through here?"

"All our money had to go into the ship," she responds grumpily. "And Derani made me throw out the clothes I was wearing. But look, the last thing I want to do is piss Derani off by making him look bad because he doesn't want to spend a ton of money on me. Let's put this stuff back."

Then she hugs herself, enjoying the feel of the soft plush omnie. Maybe if she reduces the pile to bare essentials, she can keep it. "Except this. I really want to keep this."

Mika steps away from the pile and links his hands behind his back. "You're going to end up taking it all, so I'd resign myself now if I were you."

She's already had one run-in with Derani today over the chocolate in the spice shop. The last thing she wants to do is cause another incident on Kilkurn station. She's feeling mildly panicky when Derani and Soriana come back in from the room they disappeared into. The moment she sees Derani, her mild worries turn into full-fledged alarm.

Then he comes storming up to her and all she can think is that her grace period is officially over.

CHAPTER 11

He can tell Nalia's upset about something. Ignoring his crew's rattles of alarm, he crosses the store in a few angry strides and sweeps her up in his arms. She squeaks out a sound of surprise and then curls herself in a tight ball. Turning, he walks to the front of the shop where his crew is standing at the ready. Melanem and Larimus can watch his back while he figures out what's going on.

"I'm sorry!"

Her words make him stop in his tracks. Why would she be sorry? Is this like the chocolate? Did she eat something she wasn't supposed to? Everything here should be safe for human consumption.

After what happened with the Leemron, Derani knows better than to assume anything. It takes effort, but he stops his rattling and concentrates on rumbling out sounds of reassurance.

Keeping her held tightly in his arms, he fights the urge to rub his cheek on the top of her head to soothe them both. It's not considered appropriate to scent mark a pet in public, even if most Talins make allowances if the human requires comfort. He still can't bring himself to do it, not in a place so openly and with his crew standing in view.

"Why are you sorry, Nalia?" he asks, working hard to keep his voice gentle.

She partially uncurls enough to look up at him. "I know Mika picked out a lot of things, but I don't need them. I don't. Please don't buy them because you feel pressured to. I don't want you to get upset later."

He turns to regard the other human, who's still standing next to a sizable pile of goods. Soriana's human looks concerned but not scared. He practically bolts to Soriana the moment she's through the living quarters' door and starts talking to her in a rapid whisper.

It's quickly becoming apparent that this is indeed the second misunderstanding caused by Nalia's quick emotions today.

Carefully setting her down, he then drops to his knees in front of her. He waits patiently for her to meet his gaze. "No one hurt you?"

She shakes her head, her expression puzzled. "No. Mika's nice, but he didn't understand that he was picking out too many things. I know it's offensive to be expected to buy items for a slave." She unties one side of the long-sleeved omnie she's wearing. The color of the omnie looks good on her, so he lays a hand on hers to stop her from taking it off.

"What if I *want* to buy these things for you?"

Her face registers shock, and she flounders for words. "You mean… but… really?"

Sympathy goes through him for his human. She's lived such a deprived life. Looking over at the pile of goods, he calculates the cost. He's unsure about a few of the items, but he knows enough to make an educated guess.

"I have routinely spent more on a good meal for my crew and me than what it will cost to buy double that pile," he explains. It's probably only a slight exaggeration.

Nalia shifts her gaze to the items in question and then back to him. "That can't possibly be true."

Melanem steps up behind him. She's sounding the loud, comforting rumble that only Talin females can achieve. "Since I've gotten to eat at several fine establishments, I can attest to the veracity of his statement. Every time we successfully negotiate a contract, he invites the crew out to dine at a Talin-controlled space station. I believe the schedule puts us at Hormin station next. Will you take us to Inol or Pakal for a meal?"

"Inol," he states without hesitation, keeping a careful eye on his human. "They have human food there so Nalia can join us."

An approving sound interrupts Melanem's soothing rumble. "Excellent point. And their Verian mash is better than Pakal anyway." Melanem leans a little closer to Nalia. "Are you less worried now? Even if you wanted to buy the entire store, Derani would just say no. He wouldn't get angry at you. You're safe here, little human. No one's going to hurt you."

"Well put," he compliments his negotiator with a rumble of approval and then goes back to sounding a soothing rumble for Nalia. All three of them are sounding soothing rumbles now, and between that and the assuring words, it looks like Nalia is relaxing. Her face isn't pinched in fear any longer and she's meeting his gaze instead of dropping her eyes to the floor.

"I really don't need any of that stuff," she mutters. "I didn't mean to make a fuss or anything, but I only need a change of clothes." Then she fingers the edge of her omnie. "And maybe this." Then she glances down at her feet and he notices she's wearing a pair of slippers. She slides one foot forward, biting her lip at the same time. "And these too, if that's okay."

Her multiple "ands" make him rumble out a laugh as he sweeps her up and carries her back over to the collection of items. His crew follows, probably curious to see all the things a human might need.

Mika and Soriana join them. "Have we calmed down now?" Soriana asks in a soft voice.

Derani nods. "I believe so. She became overwrought at the idea of owning these items."

"That's happened before," Soriana assures him.

"It has?" Nalia asks, drawing all their attention to her. She glances around at the curious looks, and her face flushes red. Understanding that this is a mild emotional reaction, Derani stifles his protectiveness. As a Talin, he needs to be in control of his emotions and instincts at all times. He's done a deplorable job of that today, but he vows to do better.

"May I approach your pet, Captain Derani?" Mika asks respectfully. "I'd like to give her a human clutch and see if she wants to cling to me for a moment."

"Mika is a gentle male and a clutch from another human might do her some good," Soriana comments to Derani.

His initial reaction to Mika's suggestion is jealousy, which is unacceptable, so despite his reluctance, he gives a rumble of assent. His rumble makes Nalia jump and look around at all of them with a bewildered expression.

"Clutch? Cling?" Nalia comments with a raised eyebrow at Mika as Derani sets her back down on the floor.

Mika gives her a big grin and holds out his arms wide. Derani watches comprehension dawn on her face and she steps forward to embrace. Mike isn't much bigger than Nalia, so they are both able to lay heads on shoulders as they wrap arms around each other.

"Oh, right, hugs," she murmurs out. "They're called hugs, damn it."

That makes Mika chuckle. "Get used to calling them clutching and clinging. And kisses are lip presses and—"

Nalia interrupts him with a laugh of her own. "Is falling over a vertical misalignment?"

That makes all the Talins rumble with laughter. "Aren't you an amusing pet?" Soriana observes.

"She's rather clever," Derani states proudly. "As I pointed out to you earlier, she survived on her own her entire life."

Soriana makes an appreciative rumble. "Most impressive."

"I'm right here," Nalia points out as she pulls away from Mika. Now that she's no longer clinging to Mika, Derani puts a hand on her shoulder. He tugs her against him, glad that she's finally seen fit to release the other human. Smiling, Mika steps sideways so he can press himself against Soriana's side.

"That's something else you're going to have to get used to," Mika informs her. "They talk over us all the time."

Nalia wrinkles her adorable human nose in distaste, but Soriana takes over the conversation before she can comment. "Enough of that, Mika. Someone will think you have no discipline at all," Soriana admonishes him.

Mika gives a little shrug and then goes on his toes so he can nuzzle his lips against the slip of bare skin where Talin natural amour plaiting leaves a gap at the base of Soriana's neck. She gives a quick contented rumble and then nudges his face away. Derani watches with curiosity as Mika doesn't pout or become upset. His expression is pleasant as he moves away from Soriana with confidence. This is a well-adjusted human. He glances down at Nalia. She'll be just as good someday. He's sure of it.

Soriana sounds a rattle of interest as she bends over the pile of goods. "Now, let's see what Mika and Nalia have picked out."

She carefully separates the items Mika carelessly jumbled together. Occasionally she'll make a rumble of approval, but mostly she just catalogs everything.

"If you wish to reduce the pile, you could do without the extra slippers or another omnie," Soriana explains as she straightens up. She slides a critical eye over Nalia and then makes a rattle of discontent. "But if I'm guessing correctly, your human might run a little cold. Having the extra self-warming slippers and omnie will help keep her much more comfortable."

That startles Derani. Has Nalia been suffering, and he didn't realize? "Are you cold?"

"Not right now," Nalia responds. He easily reads into her evasion.

"Why didn't you tell me?"

"It was just my feet," she states quickly, a worried look on her face. "You took my boots, so I didn't think I could have any shoes."

"You're not allowed to have shoes," he agrees. "But slippers are fine."

"Told you," Mika mutters under his breath, but all the Talins easily hear him. His soft taunt makes Nalia grin back at him before schooling her features into something more somber.

"One pair is fine," she assures him.

Derani knows better now than to listen to her, so he looks over at Soriana. "I don't think Nalia can be honest with me about her needs yet. Add anything she requires. I trust your judgment. Both your family and clan have a reputation for being honest traders and knowledgeable about human needs and care."

Soriana sounds a rumble of excitement. "Excellent. I'll have everything boxed and delivered to your ship within the mark."

"Very good," Derani says and taps his chest with his palm. The sound of his hand striking the natural armor on his chest makes Nalia wince. Then she winces again when Soriana does it back.

"And you're going to need to get used to that too," Mika murmurs to her.

"No problem," Nalia whispers back. "As long as I don't need to do it too."

Derani rumbles out a laugh along with everyone else. Nalia might have caused some emotional turmoil today, but she's also proving to be highly amusing. If those two things have to go hand in hand, he can't bring himself to care overly much.

CHAPTER 12

Tapping the corner of the information square Mika gave her to bring up the time-keeping display, Nalia sees that she's been reading for the last three marks. No wonder she's hungry and her eyes are feeling crusty.

It only takes her a moment to calculate what marks would be in Common. Talin timekeeping isn't complicated once you understand it. On the Talin homeworld sunrise starts the timekeeping with first mark, ending with thirteenth mark. Then the sun sets and that begins first strike and ends with thirteenth strike. Each mark and strike are comprised of a hundred submarks.

All the Talin-controlled stations keep the same time as their homeworld, Talarian. The colonies adjust how many submarks make up marks and strikes to adjust for longer or shorter rotation but continue to have thirteen marks and strikes on the clock.

The timekeeping along with using rotations instead of days and solars instead of years might take some getting used to, but those are minor issues. The bigger issue is the fact that, if she's accurately reading between the lines of the last five articles she's gone over, the Talin population has been steadily declining for generations.

The articles and interviews that Mika loaded onto the information square he gave her all point to several important facts:

1) A deadly disease referred to as Fading is ravaging the Talins, mostly as young adults.

2) Even though they are attempting to build more facilities to grow and raise children, it's not enough to make up for so many Talins dying young.

3) The instances of dying from Fading are seventy-five percent less likely for Talins who own or have access to humans. The correlation between healthy Talins and human ownership is undeniable, but it's also almost completely ignored.

That confused Nalia, so after reading most of what Mika gave her, she digs out the information square Derani allows her use. Although she has limited access to the Talin UniBase, it becomes obvious quickly that suffering from or dying of the Fading is considered deeply shameful.

That flummoxes Nalia. How can a disease be shameful? Especially one that isn't a direct result of some kind of activity. Talins don't get Fading from taking part in risky actions like flying in ships with poor radiation shielding. It hits them regardless of profession or gender. The only common denominator is that it generally strikes down Talins in their prime. But even then, many are still afflicted later in life.

Almost everyone who ends up with it hides it. Most who contract it are found dead without anyone even knowing they were suffering. That's a level of shame-based determination to hide that Nalia has never heard of. Most species are programmed to survive. But the Talins have developed a society where the fear of being disgraced is a bigger drive than survival.

Not that any Talin would receive much help if they sought aid from the medical community. The few articles on the actual disease all say the same thing. Death is inevitable and trying to extend life isn't recommended.

Tapping around, she finds the most common early symptom of Fading—lack of appetite.

The first time Derani fed her, he hesitated before eating, and Larimus mentioned Fading.

Shock makes her fingers fumble, and she ends up dropping the information square in her lap. Derani has the Fading!

She's not happy about that. Sure, he might have enslaved her, but he's made her life luxurious. She has a ton of clothes now, seven sets of slippers, and all kinds of products for her body and hair along with several plush omnies in beautiful jewel tones. The very worst thing she suffers from right now is boredom. That's not something she's ever encountered before.

Not only is she safe from abuse with Derani, but she doesn't even have any assigned tasks. When they got back on the ship from Kilkurn station, Derani promised that once they were underway and safely out of the Kilkurn space traffic, he would fetch her and let her spend time in the control room.

Even when she overreacted on Kilkurn, he was gentle and kind. The only retribution was that he took the chocolate away and told her that she had to wait to get it back until Larimus tested it.

That was it. That was the extent of her reprimand. And even after she upset everyone, he still purchased an insane amount of stuff for her.

How do free humans not know about the Talins? Not that many of them are left, but still, some kind of information should have been circulating among the human colonies. If this is how all Talins treat their human pets, some free humans may voluntarily accept captivity. Food, shelter, and safety are not small things. Freedom doesn't mean much if you're dead.

The door to the cabin opens, and Derani steps in. The sight of him makes a bolt of anxiety go through her. Instinct has her leaping off the bed and bounding over to him. He's not prepared for her actions and ends up dropping the information square he was holding. It hits the cold, metal floor with a hard thud as she wraps her arms around his middle and hugs him tightly.

"It's good to see you also," he murmurs and starts purring.

"Are you going to die?" The words are out before she even realizes she was going to say anything.

She immediately regrets her bluntness and tries to pull away from him. He doesn't let her. His muscled arms pull her into a tight embrace, and he rubs his cheek on the top of her head. The smell of oranges and cloves fills her nose as his purring fills her ears.

"I have no intention of dying and leaving you unprotected in the foreseeable future," Derani promises. "I cannot guarantee against random acts of the universe, but for now I'm hearty and healthy and enjoy the full confidence and backing of my family and clan."

Nalia lets herself be comforted. For the longest time, she was on her own. She worked on ships or stations where she was considered cheap labor. No one was there to watch her back, so she had to be extra diligent about her safety. Then she had Hax, and he needed a lot of looking after. She didn't have the luxury of being weak or needy. She never had the time to worry about nebulous concepts like happiness.

She would never trade her time with Hax for anything, but it's nice to have someone else to lean on for the first time in her adult life. She went to work on her first trawler at twenty and she hasn't been back to visit her home since. She has only run across other humans rarely. She seldom thinks about the people she left behind because none of them were particularly caring. She can't blame them. Everyone there was focused on survival. After her older sibling died, nothing was holding her to that colony.

But now she belongs to this Talin, and he seems interested only in keeping her safe and happy. The experience is novel and addicting.

That thought makes her hug him a little tighter, enjoying the feel of his muscles under his thick, tough skin.

"What has you so upset? Did you have a bad memory recall as you were sleeping?" he asks. "Is that why you're worried I might die and leave you?"

"No nightmares. I wasn't asleep," she says and pulls away from him. He lets her but makes sure she doesn't move further than an arm's length away. She's unable to stop herself as words start pouring out.

"But I was reading, and I learned about the Fading and then remembered Larimus mentioned it." She takes a deep breath and jumps in with both feet. She's the type of person who gives her loyalty to very few and the kind way this Talin has been treating her makes her want to extend that loyalty to him.

Having Nalia's loyalty means she's going to do everything in her power to keep you alive and healthy. Tilting her head so she can look up at him, she admits to some of what she was thinking about.

"I've been reading about the Fading and I got scared. That first meal we had together, you stared at your food and I thought maybe I was supposed to feed you. But you finally ate it and seemed, I don't know, relieved or something. And then I read that the first symptom of Fading is that you don't want to eat and so I thought maybe you had it, and I don't want you to die."

She talks so quickly that the words run together. She can tell it's taking Derani's translator implant extra seconds to catch up. But his purring never stops, only falters slightly when his translator finishes.

"I'm fine," he insists and rubs his cheek on her head again. "I'll be fine. Don't concern yourself with things like Fading or Ending."

"Ending?" Great, now she's got some other oddly named disease to be worried about.

"You don't need to know about either. Humans don't suffer from them," he assures her.

"I know that," she answers. "But if these diseases could kill you, I'm going to be worried. What are the symptoms of Ending? How should I monitor you? What can I do if you develop it? Is Ending like Fading, where you will be stubborn and not seek help? Maybe we should—"

"Nalia!" Derani's bark cuts off her questions. She startles a little at his sharp voice, but he never stops purring, and his next words are spoken calmly. "I need you to stop being alarmed. I'm not Fading and it's unlikely I'll succumb to Ending. I'd need to be scent-bonded first."

"Oh, good." She rubs her face on his tough skin while making a mental note to look up Ending and scent-bonding because it's obvious that he's not going to give her any further information. If Fading is shameful, then whatever Ending is might be viewed the same way, so he's probably not comfortable talking about it. That's fine. She's good at finding, consuming, and retaining data.

"I'm healthy," he adds. "I'm not going to suddenly die and leave you alone and defenseless. But if you have any apprehension about that, know that my brother would step up and care for you. He's a hard-working, dedicated Talin male and a good sibling. You won't ever be left to fend for yourself."

"I'm not worried about that," she says as she pulls out of his embrace. He lets her go. The purring stops, and a questioning rumble sounds.

"You're not worried about what, exactly?" he asks.

She hesitates for a moment, deciding whether she should be honest with him. There's no reason to prevaricate. He's literately negotiated her captivity, so he knows that she's used to being on her own. "If push comes to shove, I can take care of myself."

"Who would push and shove you?" Derani asks, rattling out a quick beat of anger. "Tell me who abused you and I'll find them and hurt them back."

That makes her smile. She's never had anyone willing to go out in the universe and beat someone up because she used an unfamiliar human idiom. It's sweet... in a bloodthirsty way. And it makes her want to do the same for this big, tough-skinned, emotionally needy alien. Maybe not brutalize other beings but definitely look after him.

"No one pushed me or anything. It's something my mom used to say all the time. It means is that if things become difficult, I'm good at surviving."

The purring starts up again. "You shouldn't be worried about merely surviving, little Nalia. My family does very well. We are the most successful traders in my clan. Even if the Bountiful fails, you never need to worry again. I can always find work on someone else's ship."

She grins up at him. "I appreciate that, big guy. But here's what I need you to understand. You're mine now. You need me as much as Hax did, so I'm adopting you. That means that I'm going to make sure you're safe and happy too."

Derani tilts his head a little as he regards her as though he can't make heads or tails of what she said. Then he rumbles out a laugh so loud it echoes in the room.

CHAPTER 13

"I can do this myself," Nalia insists for the third time as Derani guides her to sit in a chair.

"It's important for owners to groom their humans," Derani explains patiently. "All the literature agrees that grooming helps the human bond to their owners and aids owners in maintaining and monitoring their pet's health. I've let you bathe yourself so far, but I should see to your mane at least. It could become tangled and cause you discomfort."

"I know how to brush my hair… er, mane. It won't get tangled."

"I know it won't become snarled because I'm going to tend to it now. And I know you're diligent about caring for your mane, but it's short right now. Soon it will get much longer and then you'll need me to take care of it. It's good to become accustomed to my touch now while it's short and won't take long to brush. That way when it's longer and I need to devote more time, you don't become impatient or aggravated."

"I hold the right to take the comb and brush back if you pull out too much of my mane," she warns him.

"I've watched all the educational vids on mane care. I won't damage your mane or scalp," he assures her. "But I will need to insist on bathing you soon. Bathing is a good way to keep track of the health and well-being of humans. Some of you are stoic, and we might not find out anything is wrong until it's too late. Because many human illnesses will show on your skin, bathing is a good way to assess a human's general health. But we can put that off until tomorrow."

"You need to get me naked and wet to check on my health?" she mutters. "If you were a human male, I'd be calling foul."

Once again, Derani's translator helps him understand the words but not the meaning. She could be referring to poultry, something unpleasant, or dishonest activity. Because his desire to see to her health doesn't fall under any of those, he can only assume it's another wild-human saying.

Perhaps he should start a database of these phrases so when other wild-humans are acquired by other Talins, they don't have so many misunderstandings. But that's a task for later. Right now is about cleansing Nalia.

He's still bemused about her declaration of adoption but has decided to chalk it up to the strange way humans process their world. They are rather egocentric creatures.

He steps around her seated form and picks up the comb they bought on Kilkurn. Originally, he planned to take her up to the bridge after they left Kilkurn space. But now they're stuck in a long waiting queue at the exit corridor, so it will be many marks before they're in open space. She will probably be asleep by then, so he stole away from the bridge to spend some time with her before his crew will need him again.

"Now sit still while I groom your mane."

She grumbles something but doesn't move as he carefully works the comb through her dark mane. Although he has watched all the vids on grooming, this is the first time he's doing the actual act to a human. And not just any human but his human—one who's bonded to him to the point of claiming him. He would never admit it to anyone, but he's slightly nervous about causing Nalia any discomfort.

Starting only a finger's width from the bottom, he drags the comb through. It slides free with ease, and he rumbles out a sigh of relief. It's only the first pass and it will take many strokes with first the comb and then the brush to truly untangle her mane, but the feeling of accomplishment is monumental.

He never thought he'd have a human of his own to groom.

Keeping up a constant soothing rumbling, he diligently applies himself to the task at hand, keeping his movements slow, deliberate, and gentle. He hits a few snarls in her mane and one is bad enough that he puts down the comb and carefully separates the individual strands of her mane with his fingers. A few strands come loose and he's forced to remind himself that humans shed their manes. It's natural and not something to worry about unless it becomes excessive.

But what constitutes excessive?

Suddenly worried, he moves to the front of the chair and shows Nalia the strands of hair in his hand. "Are you sick and didn't tell me?" he demands.

She looks at the hair and then up to his face, her expression quizzical. "Uh, that's a pretty normal thing. I wouldn't worry about it."

"The educational vids said you would shed a little but not this much," he insists. Beyond concerned, he strides to the display near the door. Tapping it brings up Yulian. "Make our next destination Hormin station."

"Yes, Captain Derani," Yulian says quickly.

"And contact the healers there. Nalia needs to be seen as soon as we dock."

Yulian sounds a worried rumble. "I'll make sure she can be seen right after docking. Please look after her, Captain Derani."

Shutting off the display before Yulian can make any further comments, Derani strides back to Nalia, who's watching him with an amused tilt of her lips. "I'm not sick."

"You might not realize if you were," he explains. What will he do if Nalia is grievously ill? He can't lose her now. They need to hurry to Hormin station! It's the closest place that will have healers well-versed in human physiology.

Should he have Yulian jump the queue to leave Kilkurn? That might not only incur some hefty fines, but even worse, it could mean the station bans the Bountiful from future visits. This isn't the only station he utilizes, but it's a common stop, and it would hurt Bountiful's profit margin if he lost access to Kilkurn.

But what does that matter if Nalia needs help?

"I haven't been able to brush my hair for a few days," she explains, bringing him out of his thoughts. "I'm bound to have some extra loose hair. It's nothing to worry over."

Her words don't ease his concern. "The rapid shedding of a mane can be indicative of many maladies."

It occurs to him that he has yet to examine his human unclothed. She could have significant damage to her body that he missed and the scanner couldn't detect because they don't have the right programs for humans yet.

Desperately worried, he pulls her to her feet and reaches for the ties of her omnie. That's when he realizes that he's never seen her naked. He failed in the most important duties as an owner—to see to his pet's health and safety.

"What do you think you're doing?" she squeaks out as she bats at his hands. "Stop that."

"You need to disrobe," he orders. When she tries to pull away from him, he sounds a sharp, frustrated rattle. Far from being cowed, her expression turns stubborn. She determinedly tugs her omnie out of his grip. He could have held on, but he doesn't want her to struggle and cause injury on top of whatever illness is making her mane fall out.

"Derani… Master, I'm fine!" she insists and takes a step back. She comes to an abrupt halt when she runs into the bunk behind her. "Are we still within comm range of Kilkurn? Set up a comm link with Mika and his owner. Talk to them. They'll tell you I'm fine."

"Let me see you first," he insists. He couldn't explain it if anyone asked, but the need to see her bare flesh is paramount to him now. He needs to examine every inch of her and verify she doesn't have bruises, misshapen bones, suspicious swellings, or other indicators of ill health.

For a moment she stares at him silently, and he's worried she might be emotionally overwhelmed. Then she smiles. It's not one of her half-smiles that she used when she talked to Mika or the placating smile she uses with his crew. This smile makes the skin around her eyes crinkle and tells him it's a genuine display of positive emotion.

"You're worried about me."

A burst of irritation rattles out of him, filling the room briefly. "Of course I'm worried!"

Her expression softens. "I love that you're worried about me. It's nice to have someone care if I'm in pain or hurt or anything like that. But I'm fine, honest."

Every moment she delays is a moment he can't see where she might be damaged. "Clothing. Off. Now."

Her smile fades a little but doesn't disappear. To his relief, she unties her omnie. "I'll strip, but then you have to promise to contact Mika and Soriana."

"Yes, yes, fine," he agrees with an impatient rattle.

"And no funny stuff," she orders.

"I see no humor at the moment," he retorts. He doesn't understand why that statement makes her giggle, but the sound fills the room like music.

CHAPTER 14

The cabin isn't chilly, but gooseflesh still breaks out on Nalia's skin as she lets the omnie fall from her shoulders. Because the lining of the coat is so soft and plush, she often doesn't wear anything under it. Now the wonderful garment is pooled at her feet as she waits for Derani to do something.

Feeling shy, she keeps her face averted but looks up through her lashes at him. He's studying her intensely as he rumbles out a purr.

"I won't hurt you," he assures her.

"I know."

Her words embolden him to step forward and raise a big four-fingered hand. His fingers land on her neck and glide down to her shoulders. His hands are slightly rough and create a pleasant feeling as they run along her skin. After one pass from below her ears to her shoulders with only his fingertips, he places his entire palm on her and repeats the motion. This time he pauses every few inches to squeeze a little before moving his hands again to squeeze another spot. He doesn't stop at the slope of her shoulders and instead keeps going all the way down her arms, taking his time to check each finger on her hands.

She feels her nipples beading and tells herself it's because she's cold not because he's touching her.

Stepping behind her, he runs his hands down her back. Occasionally he'll knead the flesh under his fingers, but mostly he strokes and rubs as if checking for bumps or breaks. The muscles that run along her right shoulder blade were injured years ago during a maintenance accident. That spot always bothers her to some degree. To her surprise, when he gets to that bundle of tense muscles, he eases his fingers over it first and then starts massaging. She must have made a sound because he goes still.

"Did that hurt?"

If she could purr, she would. "No, that feels wonderful. Please don't stop."

"I didn't think you would enjoy the same type of touching I do," he murmurs thoughtfully.

That puzzles her. Looking over her shoulder, she asks, "Why wouldn't we?"

"You're so soft and vulnerable, I would think it would be easy to apply too much pressure to your delicate skin." He absently strikes a palm to the hard bit of armor over his left pectoral. "You couldn't press hard enough to hurt one of us. But the opposite is true between Talins and humans. Even a mild touch of my hand could leave you with skin discolorations."

She makes a scoffing sound. "I'm not that delicate. I like a good massage as much as anyone. And I don't remember massaging any part of your... wait. Are talking about when I rub between the plates on your neck?"

Derani's hands go still and his purring stops. Is her question impolite? Should she retract it? But why would it bother him? They're alone when she wiggles her fingers between those plates to reach his skin and she can feel the tension he carries in his neck. It's obvious her massaging helps because his whole body relaxes with only the firm touch of her fingertips. Maybe this is another Talin taboo?

Finally, he answers her, and as he begins, he moves his fingers at the same time. The purr is back also but muted. "Yes, you put your tiny fingers there, and it makes me feel much better. I won't make you do that again."

"What?" she steps away from his gentle touch so she can turn and face him. She feels at a disadvantage so she picks her omnie up to cover herself, wrapping it around her shoulders like a cloak instead of bothering to put her arms through the sleeves.

The moment she moves away from him, the purring stops and he drops his hands at his sides. "You no longer wish me to touch you?" he asks in a soft voice. "Have I disgusted you so much?"

"Whoa, we need to talk because I'm really confused," she admits. "Why would I be disgusted?"

"Humans are fragile and needy," he explains, and she barely keeps from rolling her eyes.

She nods. "Yeah, I know, we are all kinds of breakable compared to you guys. What does that have to do with anything?"

"Talins are one of the strongest species in the universe. We control more territory than anyone except the Hunga. This is possible because each Talin takes their responsibility to the species as sacrosanct. Each one of us must be strong and resilient."

Even though he stops explaining, Nalia nods. She's comprehending his logic. "You think that because you enjoyed me touching you, that makes you weak somehow?"

A sudden rattle bursts from him, startling her. She has to force herself not to take a step back. She's confident he'd never hurt her, but the sounds these Talins make can be disquieting sometimes.

He must have realized his rattle disturbed her because the rattling stops abruptly and the purring starts up again. "You don't need to fear me. I have excellent control."

"I'm not scared," she insists. "Why would enjoying my touch be a weakness?"

"I shouldn't need those things," he spits out, sliding his eyes away to stare at a nearby blank wall display. "I'm not wounded or damaged. I shouldn't need anyone to touch me, let alone a little human. I'm the caregiver, not you. I'm the one who needs to monitor your health. I'm the one who is in charge of your physical well-being. If I'm weak, I'm unworthy of possessing a human."

It takes Nalia a few moments to work out everything he said. He's packed a lot of self-recrimination in those words, and it's obvious he's internalized the Talin ideal that the desire for physical touch is a sign of weakness.

How sad.

"But I like it," she says softly. "I enjoy touching you and feeling your muscles under my fingers. I feel important because you trust me enough to let me touch such a vulnerable spot."

His eyes fly to hers, and his rumble falters for a moment before it starts up again, stronger and louder. "You want it?"

Nodding, she steps close and frees one arm from the confines of her draped omnie. She has to go on tiptoes, but she gets her palm on the back of his neck. He tilts his head forward, separating his neck plates and exposing himself to her. It's not comfortable, but she slides her fingers between the plates and starts stroking the flesh there without breaking eye contact.

"This pleases me," she whispers. "We humans might like to be touched and cuddled, but we want to touch back. The skin here is like that strip at the base of your neck that's exposed, soft and supple."

If there wasn't such a size disparity between them, she'd give the spot on his neck a little kiss. But unless he kneels, she can't reach it, so she keeps talking instead.

"You can't force me to trust you. You can't force me to want to touch you. My hand is here because I want to do this. Because I enjoy it. Because you feel good under my fingers. If anyone understands the importance of trust, it's us humans." She presses down harder and his rumbles change pitch. She's guessing that's what pleasure sounds like. "And this is a clear sign of trust. That means a lot."

He remains perfectly still until she's forced to withdraw her hand because her arm is getting fatigued. The moment she isn't touching his neck anymore, he lifts his head and pulls in a deep breath of air. Then he snatches up her and holds her tightly to his hard chest.

His rumble is so intense that it vibrates along her skin where she's resting against him. Her arms are trapped at her sides, but the hug isn't uncomfortable, so she goes limp and waits.

"You're precious to me, Nalia. I'll be diligent and make sure no harm ever comes to you. I'll provide you with the best life." His words sound like he's taking a sacred vow. Then he says something so softly she couldn't have heard it if he wasn't holding her so close. "You make everything bearable."

With that, he sets her down. His movements are slow and more reluctant. "For now, I need to finish checking your skin for any sign that you might be sick."

"Fine," she grumbles.

Understanding that he needs to do this because of his anxiety, Nalia pulls her omnie down around her waist and turns her back so he can resume where he left off. But he's not content with that. He tugs gently until she releases it, and then he drapes it over a nearby chair. Lifting her, he carries her to his bed.

"This will be more comfortable," he declares as he lays her out face down. She uses her arms to pillow her cheek and closes her eyes as he goes back to examining her.

His broad fingers are gentle but firm as he touches every part of her back. He pays special attention to the old injury, rubbing and massaging the skin and tight muscles. He moves on too soon, as far as Nalia's concerned. Maybe she'll ask him to rub that spot some more later, after he's finished making sure she's not dying.

She's surprised he didn't take her to medical to run a scanner over her. But then again, she heard him and Melanem grumbling about how inadequate the programing on the scanner is for humans.

She's amazed and touched that they've made plans to make the ship optimal for a human when they dock at the Talin station of Hormin. That includes getting all kinds of medications she might need in case of emergency, updated scanning protocols, and a bunch of other items.

She's also going to be examined and registered there. She's not looking forward to being registered as a slave or pet, but it can't be helped. She's not interested in fighting Derani about it. She's also comforted that very few species out there have required return-to-Talin policies for runaway pets. If things change and she decides to leave, it would be hard but not impossible. She would have to plan carefully and wait for the right opportunity, but the Bountiful visits so many places that slipping away is attainable. Once she's gone, she could make sure Derani doesn't find her.

If she wanted to.

Then his hands are on her ass and all thoughts of policies and protocols fly out the window. He's stroking her there and murmuring to himself. "So soft."

She would feel different from him. As far as she can tell, Talins don't look like they have much in the way of fat cells. They might not have any caloric storage system like that at all. Her round and soft shape appears to be an endless source of wonder for him.

She knows she shouldn't be getting turned on by this, but it's been a long time and his petting is affecting her. She wiggles a little, and he stops.

"Does that cause discomfort?"

"Not really?" It comes out more as a question than a statement. "I mean, it's not painful or anything. It's just, well, it's been a while… and… uh…" Right, no, she can't finish that statement with *it's been a while since I got laid and I'm horny as hell.* Nope, not going there.

"My poor touch-starved human. I'll make sure you never need to go without again," Derani promises and starts moving those big hands again.

They stroke lower, now caressing the curve where her ass meets her legs. His touch is firm enough that she can feel her cheeks being separated and feels her skin heat with embarrassment. Not that he cares if he sees the most intimate parts of her, but it's been a while since anyone looked at her down there.

Modesty has never been an issue for her. Shyness isn't something you can keep for long if you work on ships, especially if the crew's quarters are communal, which is most common. Before she got together with Hax, she shared a room with five other crewmates, all of them different species. She's seen a Gorgina shed all its skin, a Papol masturbate, and a Yamari regurgitate and re-consume his food. The last one took the longest to get used to, and she was thankful he didn't work on the ship for long.

But being naked and touched by Derani feels different from stripping down and bathing in a corner cleansing unit in shared accommodations. A few crewmates had touched her inappropriately in the past, but she was always quick to tell them off or even bash them with a convenient tool. Their touch felt wrong and forced. Derani's touch feels gentle and seductive.

He's not doing it on purpose, she grouses to herself. That little reminder doesn't help. She can feel her body getting warm from desire as his fingers move toward the most intimate parts of her.

Then she hears him take in a sharp inhale, and his purring stops. Without warning, she is unceremoniously flipped over. He puts his face down close to the apex of her legs and pulls in a deep breath through his nose.

"What does that smell mean?" he demands.

He can only be smelling one thing—her arousal. Well, damn, how to answer that?

"It's nothing," she hedges, but he isn't interested in letting her dismiss it.

"You're not scared. I know what your fear smells like." He brings his face to the skin of her belly and flicks his tongue across her abdomen. At first, she thinks he's flirting with her, but he sounds a contemplative rumble as he straightens up. She glances down at where he licked. Her brain feels witless because his tongue was rough and hot, making her wonder how it would feel if he licked her in other places.

"Your body temperature has elevated slightly. Your skin is slightly flushed. Are you having any other symptoms?" As he talks, he parts her legs and puts his nose so close the tip brushes the curls there.

She gasps and pushes at him. "Derani! No! Bad Talin!"

She might as well be pushing against the bulkhead for all the good it does her. He sniffs and then pulls his head back slightly as he rolls his eyes up to meet hers. "You're in rut!"

Trying one more time to push him away, she gives up and then ends up laughing because the whole situation is just too ridiculous.

"I've never heard that word before, but I think I can guess what it means. Could we not talk about this? Please!"

"You must be shy. The natural functions of your body shouldn't be emotionally discomforting," he insists. "I don't have access to male humans, and even if I did, I'm not comfortable letting them near you. Our males tend to be gentle, but because you're wild-caught there might be unexpected issues."

She lets her head flop back on the bunk. "I don't need a guy, just a little alone time. I promise."

Or you could keep touching me, she thinks and knows her face reddens even more with embarrassment. The articles Mika gave her point out that Talins rarely have sex with each other, let alone other species. She must be crazy to think she'd be a temptation to Derani.

He lets go of her legs and straightens up. "I'm going to do some research. I will find a solution for you, little Nalia. Now remain still so I can finish my inspection. Other than unexpectedly triggering your need to rut, is my touch bothering you at all?"

"No," she grumbles and shuts her eyes.

"Good," he declares with a purring rumble and starts his examination again—the tortuous examination. He runs his hands all over her body and if she even quivers slightly, he pulls back and demands she calm herself.

By the time he's satisfied nothing is obviously wrong with her, she's worked up to the point of distraction. She's had sex with a few humans and a couple of sexually compatible species, but none of them touched her with such slow, languid hands. She feels thoroughly seduced, and the worst part is that Derani didn't mean to do that and is actively horrified by the idea that she's turned on. This is inconvenient, considering he's the only male allowed anywhere near her.

Alone time. That's all she needs. A little alone time and her hand.

"You appear fine," he announces. "A thorough health check is part of the registration process, so if any malignancy is causing you to lose hair, it will be found and treated. Don't let yourself become fearful. We have some of the most advanced medicine among the known galaxies. There is little we can't cure."

"Nothing is wrong," she mumbles as she sits up.

Derani moves aside so she can slide off the bunk. "Come along. I'm probably needed on the bridge by now."

He hands her the omnie, and even though she's a little warm, she puts it on anyway. Eventually, she'll cool down and the garment will keep her toasty if the bridge turns out to be kept as cold as the rest of the ship.

"I could stay here," she offers.

"Are you fatigued?" he asks.

"No, not really." The moment the words are out of her mouth, she wants to kick herself. "I mean, I'm not super tired, but a nap might be nice."

Rumbling out a worried sound, Derani picks her up and cradles her against his chest. "I need to keep you close to monitor you. If you succumb to an illness here in the cabin, you might not be able to contact me for help. Until I'm sure you're well, you're not leaving my side."

Great. Looks like it going to be a long few rotations before she'll get to be satisfied.

CHAPTER 15

His human needs to rut. That thought keeps circling his brain. Now he understands why Soriana was so insistent that lone humans might need extra care. If she had outright mentioned this issue, he would have thought she was being overdramatic. But now he can see this is a common problem among owners of solitary humans.

Glancing over, he checks to make sure Nalia is still slumbering peacefully. He worked hard to wear her out. They walked the length and breadth of the ship several times, and even though he knew she was becoming weary, he didn't pick her up and carry her.

Then he handed her an information square and asked her to memorize the Talin governing structure. Then he quizzed her. That's when he discovered his pet has an impressive capacity for knowledge. She might even be as smart as an average Talin. After going over the reading he assigned only once, she could answer every question he asked. If not for the fact that he took the information square away, he might think she was cheating.

The physical and mental exercises worked. By the time the Bountiful was free of Kilkurn-controlled space and on the way to Hormin station, Nalia was showing signs of fatigue.

No sooner were they back in his cabin than she climbed into her smaller bunk and promptly fell asleep. He hopes she can make it through the night without needing to cling to him because he's not sure he can control his response again. It took a great deal of willpower to keep himself in check once he realized what her smell meant.

And that smell only got stronger as he continued to examine her. Humans are universal breeders, meaning they are both sexually compatible with a lot of species and can bear their young.

As universal breeders, it makes sense that a human would also be easily aroused by the touch of a nonhuman. But knowing that *any* touch would have probably caused this reaction in Nalia didn't help him with his own reaction to her scent.

He's also dealing with an extreme possessiveness that rears up in him every time he thinks of someone else touching her. He's never experienced an impulse so strong but refuses to examine it or worry.

That possessiveness makes one thing certain. No one is going to touch his human. Ever.

That means he needs to figure out how to help Nalia before the need to rut makes her miserable.

Tucking a transmitter into his earhole, he taps the information square he's holding until the two connect. Then he brings up the transmissions that Soriana sent him. Most of them are vids, so he taps the first one.

It's a lecture on human sexual anatomy by one of the premiere scholars on humans. He hasn't watched this vid before, but he has read all the articles this Talin produced. Most of it he already knows, but he discovers erogenous zones can vary depending on the human.

Once that vid is over, he moves to the next one. He expects another lecture, but this vid is completely different. It's not set in a classroom. It's being recorded in a human enclosure somewhere. There are two humans, one male and one female, sitting on a pallet and facing the vid capture. They're both naked and grinning.

"But why us?" the male asks someone outside the frame.

A brief amused rumble sounds. "Because both of you are so expressive. As I've explained, you don't have to do this." That must be their Talin owner.

The female gives one of those little movements of the shoulders that humans like to do to express a whole slew of emotions. Judging by her facial expression, this movement signifies that she doesn't mind being recorded.

"If this will make you happy, I'm fine with it," she answers, and the male nods.

"I don't think there are any better humans out there," the Talin off screen gushes. Both humans' faces light up with that comment. They obviously adore their master, and it's equally easy to see they're well-cared-for. Both look to be in their reproductive prime, healthy, and well-adjusted. What he can see of their enclosure makes the one back at his property on Talarian look paltry. Bushes are obscuring most of the view beyond the bars, but what little he can see looks extensive and elite. He wouldn't be surprised if these humans were owned by one of the wealthier families or clans.

"Begin whenever you are ready," the Talin instructs them.

"Do you want us to do anything specific?" the female asks.

"No. Do whatever comes naturally to you. This will be one in a series where I'm going to document the different ways humans copulate. Don't feel the need to act any differently. There is no deadline for the vids to be released."

The male turns to the female and gives her a big grin. "Hi there. You look pretty. Want to rut?"

She snorts out a laugh, and Derani gets the impression that was the reaction the male wanted. Leaning his head closer to her, his expression turns sincere when he whispers, "I love you."

Her expression is still amused as she echoes his statement. "I love you too, silly boy."

Then they press their lips together. Unlike the lip presses between humans and their owners he's witnessed before, this one is far more intense. Their mouths are open and they seem to be actively engaging their tongues.

Script scrolls across the bottom of the vid: *These two paired off several solars ago. The female is on suppressants for the time being, but note that humans don't necessarily equate rutting with breeding. Very often it's an act of affection or for base pleasure instead of a means by which to gain offspring.*

Derani isn't surprised to find out the female is on suppressants. It's common to limit births because too many can be dangerous for the female. The owner also might want to give the couple some extra time to bond before they reproduce. All the data agrees that strongly bonded humans produce and raise healthier pups.

A few other facts about the couple scroll across the bottom of the vid, but Derani ignores them. His entire focus is on the two humans. The male is murmuring soft words of love and affection to the female, and it's having the desired effect. She gazes back at the male between lip presses with absolute adoration.

Interestingly the male is not in a rush to sink the human version of a mating shaft into the female's reproductive orifice. It's clear that he's engorged with blood and ready, but he doesn't move to mount the female. Instead, he urges her to lie back and then spends a good amount of time kissing and sucking at her mammary glands. By the sounds the female is making, she's enjoying his attention.

When he kisses his way down her sternum and belly, she talks to the male but too softly for the vid capture to pick up anything except for an occasional word. From the few words he hears, Derani infers that she's begging the male to do something to her.

This time when scrip scrolls across the bottom, Derani reads it: *Although humans are inventive and varied in their pursuit of sexual gratification, direct oral stimulus to the genitalia is a common way to achieve sexual culmination. It can be done by either party, but I've noticed that with this couple, the male seems to prefer pleasing the female first and then himself. It's been noted by other researchers that this type of sexual generosity is common among happily bonded pairs.*

As Derani watches, the male licks and sucks at the female. She moves jerkily under him, mostly trying to press the apex of her legs harder against his face. Her tan skin is flushed, her body tense, and her breathing has become harsh, a sign that she's very near her sexual culmination. Then the male reaches up and covers one of her breasts with his hand, and it causes her to gasp and arch against him. She gives a soft cry and her body goes stiff, her eyes shut tightly, and her expression tenses. It's interesting to Derani that the human facial expression for pain is similar to the one for intense pleasure.

The male doesn't stop stimulating her until she gently nudges him. What surprises Derani is that she doesn't push him away now that she's satisfied. She tugs at him until his body is covering hers. She wraps her legs around his waist and lip presses him passionately, whispering words to him between lip presses. The male braces himself on a forearm so he can use his other hand to guide himself into the female. She tilts her hips to help him gain access and sighs happily as he slowly thrusts himself into her.

The Talin that produced this vid wasn't exaggerating when he used the term *sexual generosity*. He never thought human coupling would be like this. The technical articles he's read regarding human sexuality are nothing compared to watching the tender act between a bonded pair.

Although he knows that being so preoccupied with that kind of bodily pleasure is anathema to Talin teachings, he can't help the envy that invades him. What would it be like to share such intimacy and happiness?

For the first time in his life, he feels jealous of human pets.

With the same iron will he's cultivated his entire life, he squashes those feelings and forces himself to go back to watching the vid with clinical eyes.

The male is getting close to finding his own satisfaction. His hips are moving rapidly, almost violently, as he ruts into the female. The female doesn't seem to mind and looks like she might be close to reaching gratification a second time.

Only when the female goes stiff again and cries out does the male's rhythm stutter and a shout of pleasure escapes his lips. They have both found their releases, but the male doesn't roll off the female. He maneuvers them both so they're lying on their sides, the male still buried deeply inside the female. Breathing hard, they wrap their arms around each other. She closes her eyes and relaxes while he strokes her back with one hand.

More script brings Derani's attention to the bottom of the vid: *They remained like this for a full mark. The male's shaft will soften and leave the female, but they will continue to cling to each other. This is a common practice with this pair, independent of how they decide to please each other. An important aspect of human pair-bonding is touch—before and after copulation. Be wary if either is quick to leave the other after sexual interaction. An issue might be developing between them.*

After that, the vid ends and the menu takes over the information square's screen. Derani stares at the menu without really seeing it. Now he understands that his examination of Nalia caused her to become aroused. She's probably so touch starved that even the hands of her master are enough to provoke her sexuality.

He should probably find a male for her to visit, but he can't stomach the thought of anyone but him touching Nalia. Besides, no matter how carefully he vets the other human, he can't be sure Nalia will be safe.

No, there's no help for it. He's going to need to take care of her needs himself.

CHAPTER 16

In an attempt to be subtle, Derani slides his gaze down without moving his head. Nalia is engrossed in whatever she is reading on the information square on her lap. She's been like that for the last few marks. Even though he should be diligently going over the ship's finances, checking on Yulian's charts, or another of the many tasks he oversees as captain, his attention keeps being drawn to the human sitting quietly and contentedly on the kneeling pad next to his chair.

Or perhaps not so content. She keeps tapping her fingers on her leg and readjusting every few submarks. Everything leads him to believe she's mildly agitated, and he knows the cause. The delicious smell of her arousal has taunted him off and on for the last two rotations. He knows he needs to take care of her, but he keeps hesitating. The more he hesitates, the more he knows his pet suffers.

He needs to be bold and aid his sweet human.

His eyes glance at his engineer's empty seat. Larimus is enjoying an extended, off-duty period because he'll soon be forced to be ready for several entire rotations in a row. Docking at some stations is more problematic than at others, and Hormin station is one of the most complicated because of the high degree of traffic coming from almost a hundred different shipping corridors.

Melanem is at her control console, diligently sending inquires and requesting more details on contract requests that Derani flagged. Right now they are in a well-maintained travel corridor and there's little need for both him and Yulian to be in the control room at the same time. He finished answering the last of the long-distance messages in his queue and won't get replies for many more marks.

He could take his pet back to his quarters now if he wanted to. He could see about pleasuring her so she never desires a human male enough to ask for one. He doesn't want to deny her anything, but that's one thing he can't do. He can't share her attention. Not yet, at least. Maybe someday he will be able to, but right now the thought of her touching or being touched even by another human makes the muscles in his neck start to tighten.

No, he needs to be the one to pleasure her. He needs to be the one she seeks out if the urge to rut overcomes her.

He's sure he can be clinical about it. The incident where he became intolerably aroused was only because he wasn't prepared. With the correct mindset, he's sure he can remain unaffected and service his pet so she is healthy and happy.

His mind made up, he pushes his console away and stands. Looking up, Yulian sounds a questioning rattle. "Captain?"

"I'm going to finish my work in my quarters so Nalia can lie down," he explains as he reaches down and scoops her up.

"I'm not tired," she comments, even as she rests her head against his shoulder.

"Shhh, pet," he admonishes her gently. "You only need to lie down. You don't have to sleep if you don't feel like it."

Yulian sounds a cooing rumble at Nalia as he talks to Derani. "I'll contact you if anything changes, Captain Derani. Otherwise, I'll maintain comm silence."

Derani sounds a rumble of approval. "Very good."

It doesn't take him long to get back to the cabin. But once inside, a bout of nerves makes him feel like an uncoordinated youth. He almost dumps Nalia on her bunk and hurries into the cleansing unit with far more haste than needed. The moment the door shuts behind him, he leans back against it.

Control. He needs control. He looks down at his mating shaft. It's already starting to plump with blood at the mere thought of pleasuring Nalia.

"Stop it," he growls at himself. "You're not an untried youngster fresh from the cresh. You're a seasoned adult male, disciplined and in command of mind and body.

Claws slide out of his finger and he digs them into his palms, stopping short of drawing blood. The minor pain helps center him, giving him confidence in his control again.

"I can do this task," he tells himself. "I can see to my pet's needs without becoming engaged myself."

He repeats that phrase until he's mostly convinced it's true and then exits the cleansing chamber. Nalia is sitting on her bunk with a worried look on her face.

"Are you okay?"

He sounds a soothing rumble. "I'm fine. I need you to disrobe."

Eagerly, Nalia gets off the bunk and starts untying her wrap. "Are you going to rub my skin again?"

Part of what he'll be doing is rubbing a part of her, so he answers honestly. "Yes. Lie on your back on the bunk."

Naked, Nalia hops back onto her bunk and settles herself down. She smiles up at him as he approaches.

He pauses, his gaze sweeping over her soft body. A few scars mar her beautiful tan skin, most of them received when she was a child working on industrial machines. Far from detracting from her beauty, Derani feels they add to her loveliness. Those scars showcase her ability to survive situations that might have killed others—another example of how unique and wonderful his human is.

Bringing a knee up, he rests it on the bunk, but with her eyes boring into him, he can't go any further. "I need you to shut your eyes," he orders her. "If you find that difficult, I'm sure I can find something to cover them with."

She gives him a puzzled look. "I can shut my eyes. But I'd like to point out I'm the one naked here and you're still fully dressed. Well, fully dressed for a Talin anyway. Shouldn't I be the shy one in this situation?"

A rumble of humor sounds from Derani. "Close your eyes, Nalia."

"Fine." With a grin, she does as he asks, and he finds with her no longer watching him, he's able to focus better.

"Keep them closed or I'll stop," he warns her. Her soft laugh is the only answer.

Remembering the vid he watched, Derani looks down at her mammary glands. No, that's not right. Humans call them breasts. If he's going to help his pet find her pleasure, he needs to remember the human's words for things because when Nalia requests to be touched in specific places, she's unlikely to use the clinical terms.

Nalia laces her fingers together and moves them behind her head. That makes her breasts move a little and Derani can't hold back the need to touch them any longer. He covers one with his big hand, marveling at the contrast. Nalia gasps and tenses when he gently squeezes, but she doesn't open her eyes or move.

"It's about time," she mutters. He's not sure what she means, except perhaps she thinks he's still going to massage her. He needs to make sure she understands what's going to happen, so she doesn't fight her body's need for pleasure.

"I'm going to bring you to climax with my hands," he tells her. He's not sure what reaction she will have, but having her bend her legs at the knees and drop them open isn't what he expects.

"Yes!" she exclaims and cracks one eye open before shutting it again, the grin never leaving her face. "Tell me if you want any help."

Ah, so his pet understands. And is eager.

A laugh rumbles out of him, releasing the tension he was carrying in his neck.

He doesn't move to touch her between her legs yet. All the vids he watched and research he read pointed out that the human female orgasm can be slow to build, and he needs to pay attention to many areas of her body. He's also rewatched the series of vids of the two humans copulating so many times he has them memorized. Every move the male made. Every motion and every sound. He can only hope he'll be enough for Nalia.

Moving his thumb over her nipple, he pays close attention to her face. She doesn't respond to the soft touch, but when he rolls that soft bit of flesh between his fingers, she arches a little.

Shifting his body, he leans over and places his face over her other breast, eager to see if he can do as well or better by using his mouth. She gasps when he tugs at her, being careful to stay gentle and not pierce her delicate flesh with his sharp teeth.

Far from acting upset or fearful, his beautiful Nalia pushes her chest into his touch, silently demanding more. He continues to stimulate her and tries to ignore the effect it's having on his own body.

Soon the scent of her arousal is filling the room, and she's undulating under his touch.

"Please!" she begs, slitting her eyes open. She reaches her hands down and puts them between her legs as if to please herself.

He can't let her do that. Touching her there is his privilege!

Before he can consider what he's doing, he gently slaps her hands away. He grabs her hips and shifts her slightly on the bunk so her legs are on either side of him. Being so close to the sweet smell of her is intoxicating, and it takes several submarks before he realizes the loud, lustful rumbling is coming from him. It's so intense the bunk is vibrating.

"Yes," Nalia whispers, and tries to press her sex against his abdomen. With his grip on her hips, he keeps her still. She makes a frustrated whimper. Some rational part of his brain is yelling at him to use his fingers to distance himself both physically and mentally. But that part of his brain is overshadowed by the lust raging through him.

Hunkering down, he rubs his scent glands in the dark, curly hair surrounding her sex. Their scents mix and a bolt of satisfaction goes through him. She smells so perfect with the combination of her normal human smell, her arousal, and his bonding oil all merging.

Possessiveness roars through him. Her pleasure is his. Her body is his. He wants to hear her gasp and scream just like the woman in the vids. With gentle fingers, he parts the lips to her sex, revealing glistening flesh. He knows the labels for all the anatomical parts of her, but those names don't do justice to the delicate flower he's looking at.

"You're perfect," he breathes. She tries to say something, but her words end up a gasp as he flicks his tongue over her flesh. Her taste is indescribable. What little reason and logic he had in his mind flees as he buries his face into her soft, perfect sex. He licks, nips, and sucks until she's sobbing and struggling in his grip. She's not trying to get away. She's trying to push against him harder.

Wanting to feel her warmth, he lets go of one of her hips so he can gently work a finger into the opening of her wet, needy sex. She feels tight but gives easily to the pressure of his digit.

He's ready to pull away at the first sign that she doesn't like what he's doing. But judging by the sounds she's making, he's giving her a great deal of pleasure. He strokes her inner walls for a while as he works her little nub of nerves with his tongue. Then he slides a second finger into her, and finally pulls the nub into his mouth, sucking on it enthusiastically.

His mating shaft has long since become fully engorged and emerged from the flesh pouch holding it. His pants are made of strong, durable material, so they hold his mating shaft in check. It's painful but better than giving in and sinking into Nalia.

If he does that, he's seeking his own pleasure. What he's doing now is all about her, not him. This is about getting her through her need to rut. This is about maintaining her health and well-being. His arousal is nothing but an unfortunate side effect. As long as he doesn't give in to his base urges, as long as he maintains control, he's still acting appropriately.

At least that is what he keeps telling himself.

He's enjoying the taste and feel of her so much that he loses track of time. He doesn't know how long he's been sucking and touching her, but suddenly she screams and goes rigid under him. If he hadn't watched those vids, he'd think something was wrong with her.

He continues to stimulate her until her body relaxes back on the bunk. He only stops when she pushes him away, her body overstimulated and in need of a break.

Reluctantly, he sits up and inspects her flushed and sweaty face. She looks up at him through half-closed eyes, grinning and breathing hard. Her dark hair is splayed out over the light-colored pillow, her skin gleams from exertion, and her breasts move gently with her heavy breathing. With her legs spread around him, she looks wild, wanton, and gorgeous.

He wants to do it again. To touch her in such a way that she jerks and undulates under him. To make her frantic with need. To bring her to climax so she screams. Even with her taste still in his mouth, he wants more. So much more.

She sits up in a slow, languid motion. He follows her gaze down and finds his engorged mating shaft clearly outlined by his pants. She then looks up at his face with a welcoming smile on her lips. "Your turn?"

Those two words send a shock of fear through him because the only thing he wants to do is sink himself into her warmth. He's so tempted that his body shakes from the effort to deny himself.

His haste makes him clumsy as he gets out of the bunk.

"I'll be right back," he barks out as he hurries into the cleansing unit, hitting the display next to the door so hard he cracks it. Once he's shut into the unit, he calls up the coldest water the unit will supply and douses himself, pants and all.

It actually hurts when the cold water hits his mating shaft, but at least it causes it to shrink. Soon it's concealed again, and he takes a few deep breaths. He fights to find the iron control that's served him so well his entire life.

His pet might be happy and satisfied. He might have even reduced her stress enough to reverse whatever was causing her to lose her hair. But she'll probably never realize what it costs him to do this for her.

Ordering the water to shut off, he strips out of his wet pants and wraps a tight sankin wrap around his groin. Usually, the wraps are used to protect that area during training, but right now, he needs it to help him keep his instincts in check.

Pulling on a pair of sleep pants over the sankin, he takes a last deep breath and leaves the cleansing unit. He needs to see to his pet and remember his role.

This might be the hardest challenge he's faced yet.

CHAPTER 17

Larimus and Derani are discussing the upcoming docking at Hormin station and both seem excited. Well, as excited as Talins get.

She's already read all about Hormin station, including its traffic corridors, docking procedures, and laws regarding visiting Talins, non-Talin species, and pets. That means she only listens with half an ear as the two Talins debate about which corridor they should take to enter Hormin station space.

In her opinion, it shouldn't be a debate. For a ship the size of Bountiful, they should use Corridor A-33. According to the station's statistics, it's the best corridor for medium to large haulers and has the added benefit of being slightly faster because fewer ships use it. Sure, several of the other approach corridors are cheaper, but will add to their travel time by at least half of a rotation. The money-to-time ratio isn't advantageous enough to bother with.

Not that they've asked her. And she's not going to volunteer any advice. She doesn't think either of them will reprimand her, but they would likely dismiss her attempt to contribute to the discussion. She'll give it a little time and a few more stations or planet dockings before she'll make a suggestion or two. And she'll suggest something when she and Derani are alone. The last thing she wants to do is step on his toes as captain.

Her reluctance has little to do with her status as a pet and a lot to do with having dealt with arrogant and easily angered captains in the past. Derani isn't like them at all, but she still feels cautious.

She's sitting in her usual place on the kneeling pad next to Derani's captain's chair. Looking down, she tries to concentrate on the bylaw she's reading, which regards the transport of food to and from various Talin stations and colonies. She's read the same page three times and hasn't been able to retain any of it, which is an anomaly for her. Normally she only needs to read something once and then can remember it perfectly. But her distracted brain won't let her concentrate well enough to commit the words to memory.

No, distracted isn't the right term. Exhausted? Satiated? Flooded with orgasm hormones? Those fit better.

When Derani finally decided to be intimate with her, she never expected that he would be such an intense and skillful lover. He touched her as if he had experience, and when she tried to ask questions, he sounded an embarrassed rumble and made some comment about vids. Does that mean Talins have porn?

Not that it matters. Wherever he learned, she doesn't care.

But then, after that first orgasm, he acted oddly. He ducked into the cleansing unit so fast that she worried she might have offended him somehow. But when he came back out, he sounded a determined rattle and proceeded to give her another orgasm.

And then another one.

He wanted to try for a fourth one, but she begged him to stop, claiming exhaustion. She was asleep before he even shifted them to his bunk to cuddle.

When she woke up, she tried to return the favor. During her first round of pleasure, she had felt the guy's cock, rock hard and enticing in his pants. Then he'd ducked into the cleansing unit and changed. To her disappointment, he covered himself in some kind of binding material. She could still make out his outline but only vaguely. She tried to get him to take it off, but he adamantly refused. Then he gave her another orgasm before they got up to start the rotation.

It's been three rotations now, and each time it's the same. She gets to feel incredible pleasure while he keeps himself restrained. She knows he's affected. She'll catch him sometimes, rubbing against her and sounding needy rumbles. But then he'll go still and refocus on her.

Why won't he let her touch him? The most he'll allow is kissing. Why is she the only one getting off? It doesn't seem fair at all. And she wants to see that cock, damn it. She wants to know what it would taste like. What it would feel like sinking into her. Her mouth waters at the thought of it.

That he's denying her that part of himself makes her feel mildly crabby! It's almost enough to undo all the lovely orgasms he's been giving her.

"Very well, Corridor A-33," Derani comments, bringing her attention back to the conversation going on over her head. Ha! She knew Corridor A-33 was the best one to pick.

She's shifting a little on the kneeling pad. Noticing her movements, Larimus addresses her. "Do you need to get up and walk, Nalia?"

"Yeah, a walk sounds nice," she agrees. She's been sitting in the same spot for the past few marks and feels a little stiff.

Derani sounds an unhappy rattle. "I can't leave my console for another mark. I'm waiting for an important comm link from my clan. Would you be comfortable if Larimus walked you?"

"You're safe with me," Larimus assures her as he slides a quick look over to Yulian. "I'd never touch you uninvited unless there was an emergency."

"It's fine," she agrees.

Before she can stand up, Derani picks her up and cuddles her for a moment. He never rubs his scent glands on her when anyone else is around, but she can feel him fighting the urge. "If you become anxious, have Larimus contact me through the ship's comms. I'll come get you."

She pulls back and grins up at him. "I won't get anxious. It's a walk around the ship. Not an expedition onto a derelict station or uncharted planet. But if Larimus and I come across any space pirates, we'll leave one alive so you can have some fun too."

He rumbles out an amused sound. "Enough of your imagination." He gives her a last squeeze and sets her on her feet. "If

I didn't have to go over the ship's finances with the head of my clan, I promise I'd take you. But I've missed several meetings with her already and she's interested in finding out how the Bountiful has been performing. I had to talk her into investing clan money into this ship. She and several others in the clan were hesitant."

Larimus rattles out a slightly annoyed sound. "Hesitant is an understatement. You had to fight to get approval, and then you had to keep fighting the first three solars, even after we started making an excellent profit."

Derani sounds a rumble that strikes Nalia as resigned. "That's to be expected. I was so young."

"Your youth shouldn't have been a factor," Larimus argues. "You proved yourself repeatedly on ships owned by other families in the clan. They took advantage of you."

"You've stated that before, Larimus," Derani murmurs, distracted by something on his console. "But I have my ship now so it doesn't matter."

"It still matters because they would like an excuse to take the Bountiful away," Larimus mutters.

Sounding a dismissive rattle, Derani points to the open hatch. "Enough. Take Nalia for a walk and cool your own emotions."

Without further comment, Larimus walks out the room with Nalia falling into step next to him. She waits until they are several corridors away and won't be overheard before she speaks.

"If the Bountiful is making a profit, why would they want to take it away from Derani?" she asks.

Larimus sounds an irritated rattle but then stops himself. "I'm not sure I should discuss this with you."

"I don't see why not. It's important that I understand what's going on with Derani and his clan. I might be able to help." She winces the moment those words are out of her mouth. That statement might not go over well with Larimus.

To her relief, Larimus rumbles out a sound of amusement. "Of course you can help," he assures her. "You're such an excellent human, little Nalia. You started helping Derani the moment you agreed to stay."

Keeping her tone light, she keeps pushing for more information. "Why is Derani's clan so interested in him not having the Bountiful?"

"Are you worried about losing your home?" Larimus asks. "You shouldn't be. Even if they take the Bountiful away, Derani is so valued that they will let him take you on any ship he serves on. But it's unlikely he'll lose this ship. They can't argue with the profits he's been making."

"I guess I don't understand why they would give him trouble if he's doing so well," Nalia murmurs, baiting Larimus to tell her more. The Talin obliges with a frustrated rattle.

"The problem is that several of the more powerful families in the clan want him working under their captains on their ships. So they are putting pressure on the clan leadership to find some way to force him back into a subservient position. Every ship he worked on did well. The families want him back so they can make that profit again."

"That's selfish of them."

"It is," Larimus agrees. "Derani is the most skilled captain I've ever served under. He can do every job on this ship as well or sometimes better than the crew assigned to the task. That's not common, especially not with a ship as advanced and complex as the Bountiful. I don't know a single captain who can equal his knowledge of other cultures, trade routes, laws, and customs."

Nalia grins up at Larimus. "My Talin is better than other Talins," she sing-songs.

Larimus rumbles out a laugh. "He certainly is. But until he is finished paying his clan back for this ship, he has to give in to every little thing they demand."

"How long until the amount is paid off?"

Larimus rumbles out a thoughtful sound. "Probably another ten solars. Maybe sooner if our luck holds. But no less than eight."

"I bet I can get it down to seven solars," she brags. Larimus reacts as she expects him to, with laughter and indulgent questions. But by the time they've made half a circuit around the ship, he's asking her serious questions that she answers easily.

"But what about the anti-processed food laws?" he queries as their talk has turned to importing food items to Molina, a notoriously difficult task.

"If you read the free-trade agreement Molina has with the Hukan, there is no limit on food items. They can be raw, semi-processed, or fully processed. So to avoid the extra fees on semi-processed or fully processed food, we went to a Hukan Colony first."

"But you didn't buy the items on Hukan," Larimus argues.

"Doesn't matter. The fine print of the agreement says any food coming from a Hukan-controlled area into Molina space is fee-exempt. It's a giant loophole that the Molina try hard to keep hidden. In fact, you can't find a copy of the agreement anywhere on the Molina UniBase. You have to go to the Hukan UniBase to find it."

"And you did." Admiration is clear in Larimus's voice.

"I wasn't looking for it," she admits. "I was trying to figure out what we could import from Hukan to Molina. It's a safe trade route, and we were desperate for jobs that would pay enough to keep the ship going. Then I found that treaty. We loaded Amity up with boxes of meal packets and flew to one of the smaller Molina stations."

"Why a station and not a prime planet?"

"More need. I figured that would mean we would be less likely to get in trouble."

Larimus sounds an impatient rattle. "And what happened?"

"That first time, I thought Hax and I would end up in the station brig. But after I showed the Molina authorities the Hukans' copy of the agreement, they let us go and even said they wouldn't give us a hard time if we kept the knowledge to ourselves."

Larimus's rattle is aggravated. "That could have gone so badly for you. The Molina think nothing of throwing individuals from non-powerful species into their slave prisons."

"It was a risk," she agrees. "But it paid off. I think it helped that there was only me and Hax. I mean, how much could the two of us realistically haul? And the occasional shipment of cheaper processed food was needed at a few of the smaller Molina stations and colonies. Once I pointed out that it was a win-win for everyone, they let us go."

"I believe you're far shrewder than we originally assessed," Larimus murmurs. "I'm surprised you ended up in the dire situation we found you in."

"You and me both," Nalia admits. "If we hadn't needed to help a colony of Ollies trapped and dying in a demilitarized zone by treaty negotiations, we would still be doing the food import thing on Molina."

Larimus rumbles out a thoughtful sound. "I'm going to ask you questions when we are all in the control room. Answer honestly.

Give references. Derani might not listen to you all the time, but it would be a waste not to use your gift for laws and treaties."

Nalia does a little skip from happiness. "I agree!"

CHAPTER 18

Hormin station is Talin owned and operated, so when Nalia follows Derani through the docking area into the principal thoroughfare, she isn't surprised to see Talins everywhere. The powerful species crowds the area, filling the air with rattles and rumbles. It's a fascinating scene.

Now she's glad to be on her own two feet so she can swivel and take everything in. It was a battle to be allowed to walk instead of being carried. The winning argument was that walking would let her work off some of her nervousness about the upcoming visit to the healers.

By the way Derani makes it sound, no human likes to visit the healers. She can't imagine it's that bad, but she'll take advantage of his concern for her mental health if it means she can walk around for a bit.

As soon as the Talins on the station notice her, they gather around them. Derani and the crew try to move between her and the interested Talins, but with so many of them, they end up surrounded.

Derani's reaching back to grab her when she's suddenly pulled out from the protective circle.

"What an adorable human!" a female coos out, grabbing Nalia up in her arms before she can even turn her head to see who's talking. "But she's so skinny!"

"I'm not—"

"Her mane is short. Do you think she is ill?" another says as he rubs a hunk of her hair between two fingers.

"I cut it because—"

"You're right. She's much too small," another says as he leans in close and sniffs. "I don't smell any disease, but a few don't produce a smell."

"Maybe she's abused," the female holding her comments and tightens her hold on Nalia slightly.

That's when Nalia gives up trying to talk to these Talins and looks for Derani. He's busy pushing and shoving as more and more Talins gather around her. He's trying to talk over everyone, but the crowd is buzzing with agitated rattles. Except for the Talins closest to her, who are rumbling out purrs.

"Are you being denied food, little human?" the male who commented about illness asks. "We have laws about the treatment of pets. Do you need us to advocate for you? My clan collectively owns over twenty humans. We would take custody of you."

The female holding her sounds a challenging rattle. "No! I saw her first. If anyone is going to take temporary custody of her, it will be me. My husband's family owns several humans, and we have access to all the best care. She'll come with me."

Damn, these Talins are fighting over who gets to steal her? Mika wasn't kidding when he told her that Talins adore humans. This moment, more than anything else, makes her feel like a prized pet, but not in a good way.

"Release my human!" Derani roars as he rattles loudly enough to make the chattering come to a halt. He's stopped playing nice and asking others to move aside. Now he's shoving.

She waves a hand at him so he can see her in the crush of bodies. "Derani!"

The Talin holding her takes several quick steps back and rattles out a warning. "Her mane is short, and she's too small. We can see she's being abused!" That accusation is shouted at Derani and causes enraged rattles to sound all around her. The crowd turns on Derani and his crew.

"No!" she screams. "He's not abusing me! He's—"

Her voice is easily drowned out by the rattles and roars going on. She's seen enough brawls on stations to know that's exactly where this is heading.

The mob moves to stand between her and Derani. "Back away," one of them spits out. "I won't hesitate to disable you if you try to take the human. We're going to get the authorities here. You'll be judged and charged!"

"Nalia is my human!" Derani roars. "Release her!"

"She's thin and sickly. You don't deserve to have her!" the female holding her yells out.

"No! Stop! Give me back to Derani!" Nalia demands, but she might as well have not bothered. The only one who hears her is the female holding her.

"Easy, little human. You're safe. I'll make sure you are cared for."

"I'm being cared for!" Nalia insists. "Captain Derani takes good care of me."

"That can't possibly be true," the female replies. "Look at the state of you. And your eyes are filling with water! Are you feeling pain right now? Tell me where it hurts. I can help you."

"I'm not hurt. Give me back to Derani." None of this makes any sense to Nalia. She's eating better and feels healthier than she ever has in her life. Not to mention she owns nicer clothes and has more possessions than when she was a free human. How can this Talin think she's being neglected or abused?

Then it hits her. Mika was handsome but a little round. Could they equate slim humans with illness or deprivation? So far Mika is the only Talin-owned human she's seen, but it would make sense that a slightly pudgy human would equate to health in their minds. Among the human colonies, having a little extra weight is considered a sign of wealth because you had the money to spend on extra calories.

"I was free," she tries to explain.

The Talin sounds a confused rumble. "Free?"

It takes Nalia a moment to remember what the Talin term is. "Wild-caught. I'm wild-caught. I haven't been with Derani long."

The rumble of confusion turns to a purr. "Oh, you poor thing, no wonder you're in such poor condition. Don't worry. You'll be well-cared-for from now on."

Nalia wiggles in the Talin's hold. "Right, so that means you can put me down. You can give me back to Derani."

Not only does the Talin not release her, but she takes several big steps back until Nalia can barely see Derani or any of the crew. "Oh no, little one. Setting you down would be a bad idea."

And that's when the fighting starts. She flinches badly as roaring echoes off the high ceiling and the sounds of battle fill the air. Horrified, Nalia watches at least twenty Talins converge on Derani, Larimus, and Melanem. All three meet their attacks with quills bristling.

"*No!*" her scream is completely overwhelmed by the sounds of battle.

Talins in full fight mode are a sight to behold. They have impressive claws that slide out from their fingers and are sharp enough to put grooves in the natural armor of their opponent. Derani grabs his first challenger by the throat and tosses him into several others. But two more quickly come at him. He fights hard, brushing off blows to his body and head as if they're light touches.

The Talins can't seem to pierce each other without repeated blows to the same spot, so it looks like a lot of Talin fighting techniques include keeping blows from repeatedly landing in the same area. But even with all of Derani's quick movements and effective blocking, his chest is soon crisscrossed with deep grooves from other Talins slashing him. At least no one has drawn blood. Yet.

Derani's crew aren't deficient in the fighting department either. For a bunch of long-haul traders who focus on contracts and travel, they are holding their own in hand-to-hand combat with these station Talins.

Melanem takes down one of the foes to the floor. Once he's on the ground, she executes several rapid strikes to the same spot on his neck and he goes limp. Larimus does something similar to an opponent who's being pushed at him by the crowd. But no sooner are two adversaries knocked out than more are there. And Talins are pouring into the common area and joining the fight. It won't be long until the place will be wall-to-wall Talins.

If any non-Talins were here, they've quickly evacuated the area.

Nalia looks up at the female holding her. "We need to stop this!"

"We need to get you a safe distance away," the female counters as she turns and starts running.

The station passes by her in a blur as the Talin holding her runs away from the common area and down a narrower corridor. Before she knows it, they're in a private room and the door is sliding shut and locking.

Even though there is no threat of danger, the Talin doesn't put her down. Sitting in the only chair in the room, she settles Nalia on her lap and starts purring loudly. "You're safe now, little human. I won't let anyone hurt you. You can clutch me if you need to."

Nalia tries to keep her voice calm and reasonable, even though she's far from either emotion at the moment. "I'd like to be returned to my Talin, Captain Derani. His ship is the Bountiful. You could take me there, and we could wait for him to return."

A rattle of displeasure comes out of the Talin. "No, that won't do. You can't go back to him. You're mine now."

Nalia gives logic another shot. "I think that's stealing."

"You're not registered," the Talin explains. "If you were registered, the bio-identification monitor would have alerted when I carried you to this level of the private quarter section of the ship. The Talins who own humans don't live in this section. They live on the floor above, which has a communal area for the humans to gather and interact. The ship's monitoring system makes sure that humans don't accidentally wander into areas where they might get hurt. No alert means you're not registered."

That reminds Nalia of why Derani wanted to stop here. "That's right. I'm here to get registered."

"Then I'll register you," the Talin explains. "I have wealth. My family might not be the wealthiest, but we are hard-working and honorable. And one of the other families in my clan has a male human. I could introduce you two. I'm due to travel back to Talarian later this solar. My family will be very excited to meet you. We built a wonderful enclosure many solars ago but have yet to find a human. But we've kept it ready for inhabitation. It even has a small water feature because my sibling Dormean read that humans are very drawn to bodies of water." Her arms tighten on Nalia briefly. "You will be well taken care of."

Nalia can see that logic isn't going to work here. This Talin isn't concerned about the fact that she stole Nalia, so it's unlikely that a threat of reprimand or reprisal from other Talins is going to work. She needs to figure out some other way to convince this Talin to take her back to Derani. Her experiences with past negotiations tell her that playing nice and gaining information is key.

"That's a lot of effort to through when you don't even own a human yet," Nalia comments, choosing her words carefully. "I bet the enclosure is very nice. What should I call you?"

The purr intensifies for a moment but then quiets again. "You can call me Mistress Eoranan. I read somewhere that humans like to shorten names as a sign of affection, so if you wish to do that you can refer to me as Eora."

Nalia starts with the basics. "What do you do on the station, Eora?"

"I'm part of the maintenance crew that maintains the shell integrity," Eora says with a rumble Nalia hasn't heard before. Is that pride? Eora's next words cement that theory. "I'm a second-tier shell integrity controller. I expect to be first-tier within the next five solars. Very few positions on this station are more prestigious than that. Once everything is settled and you are registered to me, I'll move us to the level where you will have access to the communal areas. And I'll order you the best foods. You will always be well-fed."

Nalia keeps asking questions, hoping to find some crucial bit of information that she can use to get Eora to take her back to Derani. Or at least out of the private room where there's a chance she could call out or plead her case to another Talin to get the authorities on the station involved. She could even try to make a run for it.

No, that's a bad idea. Even if she gets away from Eora, who's to say someone else might not snatch her up and try to keep her? She has to admit the experience is novel. She's never been kidnapped and had the kidnapper promise to treat her well and feed her.

Over the course of Eora elaborating on her duties and status, her Ident beeps several times, but she ignores it. Nalia has a strong suspicion those beeps are announcements having to do with her. Do they know she was kidnapped or do they think she's running around loose on the station?

The image of her sneaking from hiding spot to hiding spot is so ridiculous it makes her chuckle despite the seriousness of her situation.

Eora must think that she caused the sound of mirth because she stops purring to exclaim, "You're happy! That's excellent. I'm confident you will adjust quickly to your new situation."

Before Nalia can protest, Eora leans over and rubs a cheek across the top of Nalia's head. The smell of warm bread fills her nose, and she immediately feels sick.

She doesn't even have to time to say anything before she's forced to lean over and vomit.

The station director doesn't rattle or rumble as she speaks, and her tone never changes. It's impossible to tell what she's feeling. But considering they've been engaged in this conversation for almost a full mark, she must be at least partially as frustrated as he is.

"I'm sorry, Captain Derani. As you well know, until a human is properly registered, proving ownership can be problematic. I only have your word that you own this Nalia-human. She's not in any database, and you have no paperwork to document the providence of your human, such as a bill of sale from a slave auction. With so little, how can I tell if one Talin has more rights over her than another?"

"This is intolerable!" Derani growls out. He can tell that his aggression isn't doing him any good, but he can't seem to calm.

He might be handling the director better if his body didn't hurt so much. He was still on his feet when station law-keepers showed up to break up the brawl, but he wasn't unscathed. Some of the Talins he fought fared much worse and were sent to medical, but he's sure several of his keratin plates are damaged to the extent that they will fall off so new plates can grow. The flesh under the keratin plates feels raw and tender and he might have mild damage to several of his internal organs.

Forcing himself to stand up straight despite the pain, he stares the director down. "My crew can verify Nalia's ownership."

"While I'm sure your crew would never lie, they might be encouraged to exaggerate on your behalf," she points out, her voice never wavering from a calm, reasonable tone. "I have no proof that this human was yours. She could belong to some other Talin who brought her here to be registered."

"Nalia can tell you!" Derani grounds out. "She's probably terrified right now. I came here to get her registered instead of waiting to get back to homeworld because she might be sick."

Those words cause an immediate reaction from the detached female. The station director rattles loudly with agitation and turns to face the sub-director behind her. "Make the station's law-keepers aware that we have a wild-caught lose human who might be ill. We need to find her and get her to the healers."

"Yes, Director," the sub-director responds and starts tapping and talking into her Ident.

Derani feels elated until the director speaks to him again. "Once we have the human safely in medical, we'll see about establishing who her owner is. Now if you will follow me, I'll take you to my office where we can better monitor the station."

"That owner is me," Derani insists as the director turns her back. He moves to follow, but Larimus's hand on his arm stops him.

"Captain Derani, we have the vid captures of her ship arriving and her getting off her ship with the Ollie," the engineer reminds him. "Normally I wouldn't bother turning them on, but I felt it was an auspicious occasion for my captain to gain a human, so I turned on the captures in that bay. Then the Ollie started shedding limbs, and I forgot about them until now."

That news makes Derani rumble with relief. "Excellent. Have them sent to the director's Ident as proof of ownership. We'll get Nalia back and punish whoever took her."

Suddenly the sub-director rattles with shock. Stopping in her tracks, the director looks over to her second in command. "What?" she demands with an impatient rattle.

Looking up from her Ident, the sub-director makes a mournful rumble. "She's at medical already. A second-tier shell integrity controller named Eoranan carried her in. According to Eoranan, the human is dying."

CHAPTER 19

The pain in Nalia's head is intense enough to keep her from opening her eyes, but at least she's not vomiting anymore. This is so much worse than when Yulian rubbed his bonding scent on her. So, so, so much worse.

"Oh, my dear, sweet, human! I'll get you to a healer. Please don't die!" Eora keeps repeating those words over and over again as she carries Nalia. The agony in her head is too intense for Nalia to respond. All she can do is focus on breathing. Hopefully, the healers will be able to alleviate this pain or at least knock her out.

"What are you doing?" an outraged voice asks, and Nalia slits one eye open far enough to see several Talins wearing long green tunics with matching green pants. Then the light is too much, and she moans and shuts her eye again.

"She's dying!" Eora announces with a panicked rattle to punctuate her declaration. It's all too much noise, and Nalia finds her stomach heaving. There's nothing left to vomit except bile, but her stomach doesn't care. She heaves, and the action makes her head hurt so badly her vision whites out.

"Set her down here. Hurry!"

Soon she's on a bed, and Talin hands are pulling and ripping at the soiled omnie to get it off of her. She doesn't fight them, but she mourns the loss of the beautiful garment as she hears it being torn apart so they can get it off her without making her move.

"Can you tell us where you're hurt?" one healer asks, her fingers gently feeling along Nalia's abdomen.

"Head," she croaks out.

She feels hands probe her head and hears puzzled rumbling sounds. "I don't feel any bumps or soft spots that would indicate trauma. Has she been having dizzy spells? I don't recognize her, so is she new to the station? Has she been registered somewhere else? I need her medical history." All those questions are thrown at Eora, who tries to give half answers.

"Derani." Nalia's not sure if any of them hear her at first. She tries again. "Derani." Then one of the green-clad healers leans in close.

"Derani?" she whispers, her voice gentle. "Is that your name? Can you say anything else, little one?"

"Captain Derani." She's proud to get those two words out, but it costs her. Pain slices through her skull.

"Captain Derani? Considering this human is unlikely to be a captain, I can only conclude that Captain Derani is a Talin important to her, perhaps even an owner?" The healer's voice is still soft, but her tone is aggressive. "I don't believe you're being honest with me, Eoranan."

"I have been deceptive," Eora admits. "But, do please save the human. She's a perfect example of her species."

"I will be discussing this with the sub-director," the healer warns. "For now, take her hand and speak comforting words. She's in distress and pain can cause further complications and issues above what's causing the pain in the first place. Do not let her thrash about or hurt herself. And above all, do not touch her head or raise your voice."

"I will follow instructions," Eora promises, and Nalia feels the Talin take her hand. The grip is gentle. The medical staff talk in the background as machines beep all around her while Eora talks to her.

"I didn't know you were ill," Eora whispers. "If you had only told me, I would've brought you straight here. But strange internal things go wrong with you humans all the time, so you might not have known you were ill. How odd it must be to have a body that can so easily malfunction. I promise to be much more diligent from now on. I won't let this happen again."

"Open your mouth, little human," the healer orders. "I'm going to put a wafer on your tongue. Let it dissolve. It will help with the pain."

The wafer doesn't taste like anything and not long after it dissolves, the pain in her head does lessen. It's not gone, but at least it's been brought down to a more manageable level. Eora is holding her hand and the scent of fresh-baked bread is still strong in her nose.

With the pain diminished a bit, her brain can function. She opens her eyes to inform the healers that they need to wash her hair and make sure Eora can't deposit any more scent on her. And they better damn well listen to her. She's not above yelling. Or crying. Whatever the hell it will take to motivate them.

No sooner has she opened her eyes than she sees Derani storm into the room.

"Where is she?" Derani shouts.

His loud voice makes her wince, but the medication is dulling the pain enough that she doesn't feel the need to curl up into a ball and wish for death. "I'm—"

"Lower your voice!" one healer hisses at him, and the censure in that one sentence is so pronounced, Nalia's surprised the healer isn't rattling. "How dare you invade one of my medical rooms like this while I have an ill human to attend to!"

Derani doesn't acknowledge the healer. He might not have even noticed her. His entire focus is on Nalia. If she could, she would sit up. Heck, she wants to get off the table and run to him. But the best she can do is keep her eyes open and trained on him as he strides across the room. She forgets that Eora is holding her hand until Derani tears the smaller Eora away and flings the Talin across the room. Eora hits a counter with a sharp cry of surprise. Vials and other items go flying from Eora's impact. The room falls silent, stunned by Derani's violent actions.

"I will deal with you later!" Derani threatens before he gathers Nalia into his arms and starts purring loudly. "Nalia, my little human, it will all be fine. I promise. I will get you the best treatment available."

Before she can explain why she feels like shit, she hears him take a sharp breath, and he reaches the correct conclusion all on his own. "Bonding scent? Who dared to rub their bonding oil on my human?" he keeps his voice level, but the quiet rage in those words is unmistakable.

"Has this human scent-bonded to you?" the healer asks, her tone all business. "That would explain all the symptoms." The healer turns away from the two of them and addresses Eora, who hasn't moved from her place against the counter. "Did you rub some of your bonding oil on this human?"

"I might have." Eora's petulant answer makes the healer rattle with irritation. "But she's mine now, so it shouldn't matter."

"Stupid, human-greedy Talin!" the healer admonishes. "You're the reason she's so ill."

"No, I didn't make her ill!" Eora protests, sounding a distressed rattle. "I'd never hurt a human! Never!"

One of the others in the room crouches down next to Eora. "You might not have meant to, but if a human scent-bonds to a Talin, another's bonding oil will make them sick. You're the cause of her misery."

Eora goes silent. Their eyes meet, and Eora sounds a disconsolate rumble. Despite her pain, Nalia almost feels bad for the Talin.

"I didn't mean to," Eora whispers. "I would never… you have to believe me. I've—" Suddenly she gets to her feet and bolts from the room.

"I want her punished," Derani insists as he holds Nalia in his arms, purring softly. The smell of him is helping to ease more of the pain, but not all of it.

"That's for the sub-director to deal with," the healer informs him. "Our concern at the moment is your human. I need to remove the foreign bonding oil from her hair and scalp. You will have to hold her still while I do this."

Unwilling to move her head, Nalia rolls her eyes to look up at the healer. "I'll remain still. Just get it off!"

Yulian barely rubbed any oil on her and she had to use the cleansing facilities three times to get it all off. Eora rubbed a huge amount on her with only one pass. Nalia can't imagine how many regular cleansing unit cycles she'd need to go through to get this much oil off, but it's daunting. If they have some kind of magical substance that can get rid of the oil more efficiently, she's all for it.

This time the healer speaks directly to her. "We have a compound that is very good at removing bonding oil, but it will feel odd. Don't be startled. It won't hurt you."

"Do it," Nalia grits out and shuts her eyes. Even if the compound makes her hair fall out, she doesn't care. Anything is better than this nausea and blinding headache.

"Sit her up," the healer orders. Derani keeps up the purring as he arranges her body into a sitting position. Her legs are dangling off the end of the exam table as Derani stands at her side, holding her tightly against his body. She doesn't think she could remain in this position if he wasn't do all the work holding her up.

She closes her eyes as an astringent odor hits her nose. The smell doesn't bother her, and when fingers start gently rubbing the cleaning solution into her head, it makes her scalp tingle.

"That her mane is so short is a benefit for the moment," the healer comments as she cleans. "But it's much better if you can have her grow it out. Humans are happier with longer manes."

What? That's such a random "fact" that Nalia wants to comment but doesn't have the focus. Then again, she shouldn't be surprised. She mentally adds this new tidbit in with the list of weird ideas the Talins have about humans.

The scent of fresh bread fades, and Nalia pulls in a deep breath of air with relief. The headache is now only annoying instead of debilitating, and her stomach is settling.

"There now, her face is relaxing. She's already feeling better," the healer coos as she works. For a species that doesn't have facial mobility, they've become quite adept at judging human facial expressions.

The healer's movements are slowing down, so she rolls her eyes up to see the healer intensely studying the top of her head. "I believe I've gotten it all off," she pronounces and straightens up. "If you would please scent mark her, we can see if any residual effects to Eora's inappropriate actions need to be addressed."

Nalia expects Derani to lean over and start rubbing his cheek against the top of her head, but he doesn't. He sounds a startled rattle and stares at the healer.

"You want me to scent mark her here? In public?" If his words weren't enough, his tone clearly implies that what the healer is asking him to do isn't the norm. The way his body goes stiff along with the other signs of distress means it might even be a major social taboo.

The healer sounds a soothing purr. "This is a medical facility, Captain Derani. No one will judge you here. We know you are rubbing bonding scent on your human in public for her own good not because you've scent-bonded her yourself and can't fight the marking urge. I'm sure someone of your rank would never be so weak as to scent-bond."

"I'm not sure this is wise," Derani mutters as he looks around the crowded room.

The healer sounds an impatient rattle. "This is about the health and well-being of your human. This is not about your fear of being thought of as weak-willed."

Her harsh tone makes Derani's spine snap straight, and he rattles out a threatening sound. Is he about to argue with the healer? Nalia's decided she's had enough of this. Reaching up with both hands, she cups Derani's face. He startles, looks down at her, and then purrs.

She was going to say something sarcastic about being shy, but his purring changes her mind. She can understand not wanting to look weak in front of others. It's not a far stretch to go from being thought of as weak to then being taken advantage of. As a human, she understands that at a fundamental level.

Empathy for his plight makes her touch gentle as she runs her thumbs over the engorged scent glands on either side of his face. Her thumbs are quickly covered in oil and the aromatic scent of orange and cloves fills the air around her.

His purr becomes more intense as their gazes lock. With deliberate slowness, she brings one of her thumbs to her face, rubbing his bonding oil onto the slip of skin between her upper lip and her nose. Then she goes back for more, this time rubbing the oil on her lips like a gloss. Never once does she break eye contact.

Her stomach calms completely and her headache vanishes. She takes a deep breath and smiles up at him, almost giddy to be free of the pain. She drops both hands to her lap. "This is good. You don't need to do anything that might bother you."

Her soft words spur him into action. He snatches her up, pulling her off the table and hugging her tightly to his chest. Then he takes several steps back so that he bumps up against a wall. He rattles out a warning to everyone, and at the same time, he purrs loudly for her.

He keeps up the purring and rattling as he rubs his cheeks against her head. She can feel her scalp saturate with his bonding oil, and the last of the tingling from the astringent cleaner dies out.

She gets the feeling that he stops only because his scent glands are empty of oil. So much boding oil is on her that it's dripping down her hair, but she doesn't mind. When he sets her down on her feet, she reaches up and runs her fingers through her hair, dispersing the oil and slicking her hair down against her scalp. She probably looks a bit like a drowned rat, but she can't imagine these Talins care much about that.

"Very good," the healer comments as she steps up. "How do you feel, Nalia?"

Nalia gives the healer a jubilant smile. "So much better."

Purring, the healer points to the exam table. "That's good to hear. Please go have a seat. Normally I'd ask owners to wait somewhere else while I examine their pets, but considering recent events, I can't imagine you want to be separated from your owner at the moment."

Nalia wraps her arms around one of Derani's arms possessively, and the healer sounds an amused rumble. "I see that I'm correct. Captain Derani will stay at your side for the exam."

"And she needs to be registered," he adds quickly.

"Can I assume you have proof of ownership or some kind of trade agreement?" the healer asks and

Derani sounds an irritated rattle. "My engineer is putting together proof of ownership."

"He can submit it to the sub-director," the healer states as she taps the table where she wants Nalia to sit. "After what's transpired, I don't require any further proof that Nalia is indeed your pet. But I need to make sure I follow protocol."

Belatedly, Nalia realizes she's naked and cold. While she was in pain, her body felt like it was overheating. Now that the pain is gone and the sweat is drying on her body, she feels chilled.

Letting go of Derani, she crosses her arms over her breasts. Shivering slightly, she awkwardly tries to get on the exam table. Derani makes quick work of it by simply picking her up and depositing her in the center.

No sooner is she sitting than fatigue sets in. Exhausted, she lies back and curls into a ball for warmth. Before she can ask for a blanket, Derani is ordering people around.

"My pet is chilled and without a warming garment. I require something that will warm her. It needs to be soft and comforting. And we need to hurry this exam. She should be in a familiar environment to rest and recuperate from her trauma."

Not only does no one protest at his high-handedness, but they all jump to do his bidding. Nalia grins and shuts her eyes, happy to let Derani take charge.

CHAPTER 20

By the time the exam and decontamination are complete, she's rested and ready to get out of medical. She's been poked, prodded, scanned, and asked a million questions. Some were standard: Is she reactive to some foods? Others were downright intrusive: Has she ever rutted with another human?

When the questions got too personal and she started refusing to answer, Derani stepped in and told the healer to move on to the next topic. He ended up having to do that three times. Now, finally, the healer has declared the exam finished.

"Nalia is a healthy female in her prime breeding years," the healer declares. Then she starts in on Derani, asking him all kinds of questions about what he feeds Nalia, what kind of sleeping spot she has, and what kinds of enrichment he provides.

It doesn't escape Nalia's notice that Derani doesn't mention their more intimate activities. He's assured her so many times that what he's doing is part of standard human care that she started believing him.

Now she's questioning the veracity of that. If it was part of standard care, the healer would ask about it or Derani would volunteer the information. But neither of them even comes close to the topic. At most, they talk about how she likes to "cling" to Derani while she sleeps and the healer assures him that's a common human need.

Not that she's going to bring up the subject. She doesn't want to risk losing her daily orgasm!

Eventually, the healer is satisfied and leaves to see to other patients. Wrapped in a warm blanket, Nalia isn't sad to see her go. The healer had been nice, but nothing about this situation was comfortable.

"Here is an omnie she can have." One of the assistant healer hands Derani a pale blue omnie. It's plain, with no gold or silver embroidery or fancy ribbon stitching along the seam lines. But as far as Nalia's concerned, it's perfect.

The moment Derani helps her put it on, not only does she feel warmer but less vulnerable as well. Snuggling down into the garment, she sighs with contentment as the soft, nano-infused, faux-fur lining warms her skin. This is so much better than the blanket.

Both Talins rumble with pleasure at the sound of her sigh. "I guess you like it," the assistant comments.

"It feels nice," Nalia agrees. "Thank you."

"Some humans run a little cold and wear their omnies all the time," the healer explains to Derani. "Especially as they become elders and their manes turn completely white.

"Thank you for providing comfort for my human," Derani says with a quick strike to his hard, badly grooved keratin pectoral plate with his palm. That's when Nalia notices that her Talin is a little worse for wear. He's standing stiffly and has deep gouge marks all over him from the fight.

"Maybe the healer should examine you," she murmurs.

He ignores her and keeps talking to the assistant healer who brought the omnie. "I can return it after we get back to the ship or I can pay for the garment before we leave."

"No need to do either," the assistant says without taking his eyes off Nalia. "We have a bunch of garments and other human items that have been donated by those who work on this station. Whenever a wild human is discovered on a planet or station, they are usually brought to us first."

The assistant sounds a sad rumble. "Often they're wearing a sorry excuse for a garment that is potentially infested with parasites. It's standard practice to dispose of the old clothing. Because no one wants the humans to suffer, many of those here on the station either bring clothes their humans no longer favor or have outgrown to us. A few bring brand new items they have bought."

Derani rubs a section of her sleeve between his fingers. "Was this one new?"

Nalia tries to grab his wrist so she can look at his hand, one finger looks swollen.

The assistant sounds an affirmative rumble to Derani's question. "Yes. This omnie was bought and donated by Senior Food Systems specialist Okianean. He doesn't have a human yet, but he's next on the list to receive a human when one comes in from the new bounty-system."

That gets Nalia's attention and distracts her from worrying about Derani. Whatever that is, it doesn't sound good. "Bounty-system?"

The assistant purrs as he answers. "The Apogee Assembly passed a law recently that puts money aside to pay bounties for humans brought to us by any other species. That extends our reach and allows us to rescue humans far beyond Talin-controlled space. We get wild-caught humans a few times a solar now, and our station boasts the largest human population of any other Talin station."

"You kidnap free humans?" Nalia really shouldn't be surprised by this news. After all, Derani felt it completely reasonable to ask her to accept slavery to save Hax, but her situation feels different. Derani gave her a choice. It wasn't much of a choice, but still, she could have taken her chances and left that ship with Hax. Humans hunted down by opportunistic bounty hunters feels different. More sinister.

"I can see by your expression you don't approve," Derani murmurs as she draws her into his arms. His hold is gentle as he hugs her smaller body to his bigger one. "If it makes you feel better, it took an entire solar of debates before the law was passed. Many didn't approve. It's still in the probationary phase."

"Almost all the humans brought here because of the bounty offered have been half-starved. And many of them suffer from some kind of debilitation from old injuries that we cured easily," the assistant adds. "Medical care can be expensive, and few medical personnel have experience with human anatomy, unlike Talin healers. Your kind is well-cared-for among us."

"I suppose," is all Nalia can think to say.

"If you were to talk to them, our pets would agree with me. They can speak for themselves," the assistant insists. "You need to remain on the station for at least another two marks so we can be sure the decontamination medication we gave you will have no ill effects. But that doesn't mean you need to stay here in medical."

Derani sounds a concerned rattle. "Ill effects?"

"Very rare," the assistant assures him. "But we want them to stay on the station to be safe. You could take her up to level three in the housing area. We have places designated specifically on that level for humans to meet and interact. Her bio-signature is in our security system so it's safe to take her anywhere in the Talin-only areas of the station."

Derani's arms tighten around her briefly. "Would she be safe among these other pets?"

"Most assuredly. At least one owner for each pet will be present. Often crowds of Talins ring the communal areas to watch the pets play. And a law-keeper is always posted there to make sure the pets are kept safe. Some of our crew are so eager to have a human that they can act irrationally on occasion."

"No joke," Nalia mutters under her breath, but both Derani and the assistant hear it.

"I would like to say what happened with Eoranan is uncommon, but I'm afraid it's happening more and more. Earlier this solar a pup was stolen before he could be bio-registered. He was only a few rotations old. It took the station law-keepers several marks to locate the poor little one. He was screaming with discontent by the time he was located but otherwise unharmed. The Talin who took him was dismissed and sent back to homeworld in disgrace. It was a deplorable state of affairs. I believe he died of the Fading not long after."

That's a story of woe if she's ever heard one. Nalia feels bad for everyone involved. The humans who had to suffer through their baby being kidnapped. The Talin who felt so desperate for affection that the only answer was to resort to abducting an infant. And that he died of the Fading points to how despairing that Talin truly was.

She glances up at Derani, who's asking the assistant questions about station security and law-keeper protocol. Dying from Fading could have happened to her Talin if they hadn't stumbled into each other. What a dismal thought.

"… I think taking Nalia up to level three isn't a good idea." That comment by Derani catches her attention.

"I want to see the other humans," Nalia says quickly.

"I'm reluctant," Derani answers.

"That's not a *no*," Nalia responds with a grin.

"I can assure you, she'll be perfectly safe," the assistant interjects. "And it's good for humans to interact with each other."

Nalia runs a hand over some deep grooves on one of his chest plates. "Or we could stay here so you can be examined by the healers too."

Derani sounds a rumble of distaste. "Very well. We'll go visit the other humans."

Ah, so it isn't just humans who don't like being poked and prodded! She grins up at him. "Thank you, Master."

"Why does it always sound like you're mocking me when you say Master?" he grumbles out.

Nalia's grin doesn't falter. "I don't know what you mean."

The human common area on level three is not what Nalia is expecting at all. She thought it would be like the thoroughfare outside of the docks—a large open area with a few benches and discreetly hidden elimination facilities. Perhaps a few kiosks dispensing drinking water, but probably nothing else. But the common area for the human pets is so much more.

She can't see much of it at first because it's solidly ringed with Talin bodies. Derani is carrying her, but even with the added height, all she can make out is the dome above the common area that pours in light from the star the station orbits. Unlike most stations, this one doesn't orbit a planet but is big enough to orbit a sun all on its own. The sunlight shining through the dome feels warm and inviting on her skin.

She expects the natural light to be the extent of the luxuries offered in this communal area, but she turns out to be wrong. Derani walks around the circle of bodies until he finds a gate in the waist-high decorative fence that demarcates the communal area from the rest of level three. With the break in the wall of bodies, Nalia gets her first glimpse of an environment she's never seen in space.

If she didn't know better, she'd think she stepped onto a planet. Underfoot is a green, spongy ground-covering plant, creating a soft floor for everyone to enjoy. Potted bushes and plants are all over the place, adding color and filling the air with a delicate perfume. Stone benches are scattered throughout the area, and she counts at least four different kiosks to get water.

At the center is a round area filled with sand. There looks to be a strange work of art in the middle of the sandy area. It's only when she watches a parent help their toddler climb and traverse the structure that she realizes it isn't an art installation but a structure for the children to play on.

On the edge of the sandy area, two parents help their child pile sand up into a mound. A Talin sits on the mossy ground on the outside of the sandy area, verbally encouraging the child and filling the air with proud rumblings. Occasionally one parent would look up at the Talin and smile before going back to playing with the child.

That's when she realizes none of the humans are alone. They all have a Talin or two by their side. Some of the Talins hover over their humans, watchful and even participating in games. Others are content to maintain a discreet distance and talk to other Talins, but Nalia can tell they're paying close attention to everything their pets are doing.

On the other side of the sandy area, a group of humans of all ages are playing some kind of game with a ball the size of her fist. She can't tell what the rules are, but when the ball hits the ground, half the humans cheer and the other half give each other rueful smiles. None of the Talin are playing the game with the humans, but they are keeping an eagle eye out. When one player trips and falls to the ground, a Talin hurries to pick her up and carry her to a bench, purring loudly the entire time.

So much is going on it takes Nalia a while to process her emotional reaction. She's a little surprised to realize that the thing she's feeling most is envy. These people have access to a more beautiful spot than any human she knows who lives on a station. And every single human she can see is round and healthy, with long, flowing hair and beautiful clothes. Like her, most of them are wearing collars that look like jewelry, and some of them are even wearing actual jewelry in their ears and on their wrists.

Everywhere she looks, people are smiling, laughing, and enjoying themselves. Her memories of humans having these kinds of carefree moments are few and far between. Could this be a special day? A specific event that brings them all together to play?

"Is today a holiday?" she asks as Derani walks them to an empty bench. Several humans and Talins in the common area have noticed their entrance and are watching her curiously.

"Not that I know of," Derani answers. "I believe it's an average day."

Nalia waves a hand around to show she's talking about the area and everyone around them. "This is an average day? All this is normal?"

Derani sounds a rumble of confusion. "Of course it is. Why wouldn't it be?"

Is Derani playing with her? "Because no one is working."

"I'm sure these Talins are off shift. I wouldn't worry, little Nalia. This station is adequately crewed. I'm confident that no one is shirking their duty."

She comments without thinking. "Do the humans and their owners all work the same shift?"

Derani is silent for a moment. Then he gently puts a finger to her cheek and turns her head so their eyes can meet. "No, Nalia. Our humans don't labor. You're too precious for that. I know other species use slave labor and will work those poor souls to death, but we don't keep slaves. We've never been a slave owner species. We have pets."

"But…" She wants to say, "But why?" Yet she stops herself.

She knows why Talins keep humans. It was obvious after she finished going through everything Mika sent with her. But reading about it and witnessing it are two different things.

Talins aren't allowed to love each other, but they can feel deep affection for their humans. They can't touch each other with affection, but of course, their human pets need comfort. They can't raise their own children, but humans are so fragile that there's no question a Talin should help the human parents with the child.

Humans allow the Talins to love, touch, and have children.

Only now does she truly get the difference between pet and a slave, seeing how effectively the Talins have created a concept of humans that fits their needs. Not only does Derani want to treat her like a beloved family member instead of an owned possession. It's the status quo among this species.

"How extraordinary," she comments.

He rumbles out a soft sound of amusement. "You will come to understand that your situation is very average among us. I'm treating you no better or worse than my fellow Talins would."

"Sure," she says with a shrug, not bothering to question him about their more intimate activities. He drops his hand away from her face and wraps her into a brief hug as he purrs.

"You will become accustomed to your life," he promises as he better arranges Nalia on his lap. She'd ask to go interact with the other humans, but she knows it would fall on deaf ears. Even if he won't admit it, he's rattled from losing her and then finding her in agony at medical. A little extra cuddling isn't going to hurt her and will go a long way in making Derani feel better.

A teenage girl walks over, a welcoming smile on her face. She stops a respectful distance away. "May I talk to your pet, sir?" she asks Derani.

"Of course, but be polite," Derani allows with a soft, encouraging rumble.

The teenager grins and gives Nalia a little wave. "Hi, I'm Lorn. Are you the one we heard about who was in the middle of the fight near the docks?"

Nalia gives Lorn an apologetic smile. "Probably. I'm Nalia."

Lorn nods gravely. "I'm glad to see you're fine. I heard that—"

She doesn't get a chance to finish that sentence. A large male Talin is suddenly there, pushing her behind him and glaring at Derani.

"Has your human been through decontamination? I heard she was wild-caught. That means she could be carrying all kinds of diseases and parasites that are deadly!"

Derani stiffens but doesn't raise his voice when he responds. "She's gone through medical. We are only here because they suggested Nalia might enjoy seeing other humans."

With that information, the male relaxes his posture and steps aside to allow Lorn access. "The healers are correct. Humans do like to interact with each other. Can I assume you haven't had her long if she's only now being registered?"

Derani sounds an affirmative rumble. "You're correct. But she's acclimating well."

The male eyes Nalia with a rumble of sympathy. "If she's recently wild-caught, that would explain the short mane and thin body. I'm sure she will do well under your care."

"Can I talk to Nalia now, Master Maneal?" Lorn asks.

"Certainly," Maneal agrees. "But don't touch, and speak gently. If she was in medical, she might not feel very well right now. Some of you become a little uncomfortable from the medication we have to give you."

"Sure," Lorn says dismissively and turns her attention back to Nalia. Maneal steps up behind her, wrapping his arms around her shoulders to hold her close.

"My parents own Lorn's sire and dam," Maneal explains to Derani. "Lorn's older sibling spent a solar here with me, and now it's Lorn's turn."

"I like the stations better than my brother," Lorn volunteers. "I think I'll make the rounds of the clan members who live on stations. Everyone's asking for me to visit. He went back to Talarian, but I'm not. I'm going to travel and see everything!"

Nalia is taken aback by Lorn's enthusiastic grin. "Sounds exciting?"

"It is!" Lorn confirms. "One family in our clan has a mining ship, and they visit all kinds of exotic places! I've already asked to spend a solar with them. They built a whole enclosure for me on their ship."

"I know they want you to visit, but don't get your hopes up," Maneal warns. "It's unlikely my parents will approve of you going someplace so dangerous as the clan mining vessel. Remember, you are family-owned, not clan-owned. My parents can say no to the other families."

Lorn pouts up at him. "But I want to!" she whines, making Maneal rumble out a chuckle.

"We'll see," is all he says. Then the group playing the game with the ball shouts across at them. "Lorn! We need you! Nanoc's owner said she can't play anymore. Come join us!"

Lorn's face lights up. "Okay!" Without even consulting Maneal, she ducks out of his hold and runs off to join the others.

Maneal sounds an amused rumble. "She's such a joyful human. Her sibling is more cautious and somber. He didn't like being in space and became despondent. He's doing well back with his sire and dam. But Lorn is the opposite of her brother. She's everything enthusiastic and happy. I regret that I can't keep her here. But I wouldn't want to deprive my sister of her visit."

"Do you worry that all the traveling might have an adverse effect on her health?" Derani asks.

"Not at all," Maneal responds, and the two of them discuss how to keep humans safe and healthy on ships and space stations.

While they talk, Nalia watches the humans and Talins interact and play. What a strange universe she lives in where one day she and Hax were struggling to make ends meet and the next day she's a pet and meeting more humans than she's seen since leaving her small colony so many years ago.

"Life sure can take some weird twists and turns," she murmurs to herself and snuggles closer to Derani.

CHAPTER 21

Derani glances down to find that Nalia is reading on the information square included in the purchases at the Kilkurn station. It's one of the smallest information squares he's ever seen and perfectly proportioned for her tiny hands. She carries it with her everywhere, tucking into her omnie when she isn't holding it.

At first, he worried about her obsessive reading behavior. But the literature claimed some humans find reading soothing and might do it for many marks at a time. It was interesting to him to find out that once he programmed the information square to give her access to the entire Talin UniBase, she now picks out random articles to read. When he examined the list of accessed articles, he couldn't find any rhyme or reason to her choices. His smart little human finds all kinds of topics interesting.

Perhaps he should assign her reading so they can discuss it at the end of the work shift. It might help to keep her clever mind occupied.

Curious, he leans over to see what she's currently reading. She's on her kneeling pad next to him with her back resting against his leg so he doesn't have to move far to view her screen.

Using Orina Treatments for Acute Catatonic Withdrawal Disease

He hisses out a breath and snatches the information square from her. She gasps and turns to face him, going on her knees as she moves. He waves the information square in the air. "You are not to read about these things."

Her mouth gapes open at his harsh tone. Then she sits back on her heels, crosses her arms, and lifts her chin defiantly. "I want to know what kinds of diseases affect Talins," she informs him coolly. "I need to be prepared if you ever get sick."

He rattles with distaste. "It is my job to care for you, not the other way around. You will cease reading these articles or I'll restrict your access to the UniBase."

Her brows furrow as if she's trying to puzzle something out. "Is this specific disease I was reading about bothering you? Or the idea of me reading about any diseases? If it makes you feel better, I'm not only focused on the Fading. Yesterday I was reading about plate rot."

Yulian makes a distressed rattle and both Melanem and Larimus turn in their chairs to regard her.

"What?" Melanem's voice sounds confused. "Why would you read about those topics?"

"Because it's important I learn about these things," she states with a stubborn expression.

Derani sets her information square on the control console next to his chair and then reaches down to lift her into his lap. Someone once warned him that some humans are abnormally industrious. If they aren't given some kind of task, they will "find" a job to do.

It's common to give the humans specially crafted squares of canvas for them to paint or draw on. Others carve figurines out of the softwood from the monhan tree. Some get obsessed with their useless projects and produce quite a lot.

But it looks like Nalia isn't interested in any type of craft. No, his human wants to obsess about learning. That wouldn't be so bad, but why did she need to focus on learning all about Talin weaknesses?

"These aren't suitable topics," Derani explains to her. "There is absolutely no reason for you to study Talin disease. Most especially Fading and Ending."

The stubborn expression doesn't change. "They are diseases, not state secrets. I don't see why I can't read about them."

Derani rattles out a strong, negative sound. "No."

Neither his rattle nor firm denial have any effect on Nalia's expression.

It's both good and bad that Nalia no longer startles at his rattles. He's glad she no longer fears him, but if she was still a little intimidated by his rattle, it would benefit him. Now she brushes off his attempt to intimidate her. He should know better. He's already learned his human doesn't respond well to demands, but perhaps her soft heart can be persuaded. With that in mind, he tries a different tactic.

"Please? It makes me uncomfortable to know you're reading about these things."

Her expression goes from obstinate to resigned. "Fine, I won't ask you any more questions."

He knows better than to leave it at that. "Or read about it."

Now she looks annoyed. "Or read about it," she repeats dutifully.

Melanem sounds a soft rumble of agreement. "Captain Derani is correct. These medical issues aren't something you should concern yourself with. Wouldn't you rather watch the vids on Talarian flora and fauna? We have some very interesting winged species that are fascinating to watch."

"And there are vids on our home solar system. We have several gas giants that are home to captivating micro-ecosystems," Larimus adds.

Yulian sounds an excited rumble. "I remember enjoying the vids and accompanying literature on the plavaxian migrations. I could send you an identification tag so you can watch them."

Derani hears Nalia say something about "kid stuff" under her breath; then she smiles at his crew. "That's very nice of all of you." He notices she doesn't tell them she's going to watch any of the suggested vids, only acknowledges their efforts.

Then she turns her attention back to him. "Can I still read about your governing structures and laws?"

That question surprises a quick rattle out of him. "If you like."

After he finished his required education, he focused his studies on ship technology, trade, and foreign cultures. He remembers the lessons on the assembly system and monarchy as dull and tedious.

When he had her memorizing the governing structures to tire her out, she didn't seem enthusiastic. Nalia will probably lose interest rapidly. Then he and the crew can urge her to more human-appropriate vids and readings.

"Great, thanks," she says with a smile and then snuggles her face against the small patch of exposed skin on his neck. Her warm breath fans across that vulnerable spot and his cursed mating shaft starts filling with blood. He knows that if a human wishes to cling to their Talin owner, it's wise to allow it to go on as long as the human needs. But he can't have the crew seeing him growing hard and ready for mating. He's the captain. His control should be beyond reproach.

His crew sound a few amused rumbles at Nalia's request to study their government, but they don't comment as they turn back to their individual consoles. As the others in the room go back to working in companionable silence, he focuses on getting his unruly body under control.

"Captain Derani, I'm getting a link-up request from a nearby repeater station," Larimus announces with a confused rumble.

"Who's requesting link-up?" he asks. Linking up to a repeater station is energy expensive, and he worries that his family might have suffered a tragedy if they're willing to use such an expensive resource when they know he's on his way back to Talarian.

Larimus's confused rumbling doesn't stop. "That's the strange thing. It's coming from Grander Citizen Ornianan and Grander Citizen Tuchianan."

Ornianan and Tuchianan aren't members of his clan, or even another trading clan. The families in their clan focus on colonization, and the couple in question even owns an entire colony. They spent a good portion of their careers building the colony up from scratch. What could they possibly want to speak to him about?

He debates briefly about leaving Nalia in the control room or taking her with him. But she feels too good in his arms to set down, so when he stands, he keeps her cradled to his chest. "I'll take this in the auxiliary control room."

He carries her across the hall and into the much smaller and cramped room that houses all the redundant systems. Regretfully, he sets Nalia on her feet and urges her to curl up in a nearby chair. He wishes he could sit and keep her on his lap, but he's going to need to stand for this meeting because Ornianan and Tuchianan outrank him. The added benefit is that they shouldn't be able to see Nalia unless he picks her back up or she moves to stand next to him.

He's not sure why they want to talk to him and he's worried that it might have something to do with their still un-married daughter, Captain Sherianan.

A marriage between their two families would be a benefit for both clans. He knows he should form a marriage contract eventually and that these types of meetings and offers will start pouring in soon. He's the correct age and highly successful, but he's been dreading it.

More so now that he has Nalia.

Once he's gotten Nalia situated, he checks that his belt is straight, his pouch is sitting on his right hip and his Ident is hanging just in front of his left hip. Then he squares his shoulders and looks up at the large display on the wall. "Accept link-up request," he orders, and the display on the wall in front of him comes to life.

He's greeted by the image of an elder couple sitting shoulder to shoulder, and when their eyes meet his, they both rumble in greeting. "Captain Derani, we're pleased we could get through to you. We have urgent need of your assistance."

Intrigued, Derani makes a welcoming rumble of his own. "Greetings, Grander Citizen Ornianan and Grander Citizen Tuchianan. What can I do for two such esteemed Talins?"

"I'm sure you're aware of the political divide that has recently become militarized," Ornianan begins.

"Of course." Derani can't imagine anyone who doesn't know about the attempt only last solar by an extremist part of the Traditionalist political faction to kidnap Commandant Holian.

No one knows why Holian's colony was invaded and he was targeted, but the rumors are that the Traditionalists believed he could provide them with all the information they'd need to attack the Prime Family. At the moment the monarch is a Reformist, but there is gossip that while her son follows her political leanings, her daughter is an ardent Traditionalist.

If that is their opening comment, this meeting can't be about arranging a marriage contract. Relief makes his shoulders relax, and he sounds a curious rumble. What would these political issues have to do with him? His family doesn't even work for the Prime Family, and none of his clan is involved in politics. They are a trading and merchant clan.

As if reading his thoughts, Tuchianan explains, "We have evidence that Prime Daughter Halieni is planning a coup against her mother, the monarch. We need to get this evidence to the monarch and her son, Searin. We could not trust many to do this. That's why we are contacting you directly. We need you to transport it here to Talarian."

Derani is so stunned by this request that he stands still and silent for several moments. Both Tuchianan and Ornianan rumble with worry when he doesn't respond right away.

"Captain Derani?" Ornianan asks gently. "Can you do this for us? For all Talins? We can't let this faction gain control. They would destroy us with stagnation. They would stop any social or political progress, causing us to weaken as a species. We can't let this happen."

"I should check with my family," Derani finally says. It's the best fallback answer he can give them.

Tuchianan sounds a disapproving rattle. "Absolutely not. This must be kept a secret. You are already on your way back to Talarian. The soldier with the information you need to pick up is at Tortuva station. It's barely out of your way. This will only be a minor inconvenience to you and a hugely important mission for your monarch and Prime Son."

Derani's mind fills with all the reasons not to get involved. If his clan finds out he's getting tangled in political intrigue, they could use that as an excuse to take away his ship. And he could be putting Nalia in danger. "I don't think—"

Ornianan cuts him off. "We are aware of all your deliveries to our Barvarian Colony. You hide behind a third-party intermediary, but we know it was you."

"I don't see how my making money by delivering supplies to your colony indicates I'd be willing to involve myself in this situation," Derani retorts.

"But those deliveries tell us a great deal about you," Ornianan responds. "We know very well that the margin for profit was low at the time. Even though you didn't make much and other more lucrative contracts were available, you did the run several times because few others would bother. You continued to make deliveries until we could secure reliable shipping from smaller haulers. That makes it clear to us that you are a citizen of integrity and honor. You wouldn't let those on Barvarian Colony endure deprivation, even if your bottom line suffered."

Tuchianan rumbles out an affectionate sound and wraps an arm around his wife, hugging her to his side. Derani is stunned into silence at the easy display of affection between the two Talins. When Tuchianan looks back to Derani, he stops rumbling to talk. "That is why we are asking you to do this and keep it a secret, even from your crew."

"I'm hardly going to be able to keep a guest coming on board the ship a secret," Derani points out wryly.

Tuchianan sounds an embarrassed rumble as Ornianan explains bluntly. "You'll need to leave them on Tortuva. Tell them it's a vacation. You will be generously compensated at two times the highest pay grade you've received so far. And we will pay for the crew to stay on Tortuva and take advantage of any of the diversions there."

Tortuva has a reputation as one of the most expensive and exclusive stations in Talin-controlled space. His crew would jump at the chance to spend time there, especially if someone else is taking care of the bills.

"Do you realize that you're asking me to fly my ship without a crew?" Derani clarifies.

Tuchianan rumbles in agreement. "We know you're more than capable of doing just that. Your trip three solars ago is well-documented."

"That was an extreme situation," Derani counters. "It's not something one plans."

He'd forgotten about it until Tuchianan reminded him. He and the entire crew succumbed to dielor poisoning, and he was forced to single-handedly pilot the ship for several rotations. It had been a horrible time, and the pain he endured was excruciating. Among other things, dielor affects the nervous system, causing the Talin body to send constant and severe pain signals.

He successfully flew the ship despite the agony, but there several times he'd almost passed out.

Derani rattles at the unhappy memory. "Piloting a vessel the size of Bountiful by myself is both unwise and ill-advised. My family and my clan will not approve."

"This time it will be much easier. You won't have to battle illness. And you won't be taking care of sick crew members. All you'll need to do is pick up a soldier named Palforma and deliver him to Talarian. We can even arrange for your crew to take passenger cabins on other ships so they can meet you back on the homeworld."

Derani keeps his gaze hard on them. "You haven't addressed my other concern."

"At the moment, your family and clan don't need to know about this trip," Ornianan states.

It takes effort to keep him from sounding a small rattle of agitation. "Of course not. I understand the mission requires stealth. But they will find out when my crew returns without me. I can't keep this a secret. Please don't be deliberately obtuse."

Ornianan sounds an apologetic rumble. "You're correct. That was unnecessary." She and her husband exchange a look and then she turns her attention back to him. "Once the mission is completed, the Prime Son will issue you a formal letter of gratitude. It won't be specific about what service you performed, but it will name you, the ship, and the time frame. Will that be sufficient to keep your family and clan from acting on any disapproval this trip might incur?"

A missive to him directly from the Prime Son is exactly the kind of accolade that will cement his reputation within the clan. And perhaps he won't be watched so closely any longer. The opportunity is too good to pass up. But no matter how strong the incentive, his gut churns. Plans like this never go as smoothly as these two would have him believe.

"Very well. Send me the information on Palforma. I'll send you our navigation data so you can best arrange our meeting to coincide with our arrival at Tortuva station."

The couple rumble with enthusiasm before the display blinks out. Derani turns to see Nalia looking up at him with wide, curious eyes.

"I guess it's a good thing I'm about to study Talin politics," she quips. "Looks like we're about to be neck-deep in them."

CHAPTER 22

After what happened at Hormin station, Nalia is a little nervous to go visit another Talin-owned station. That means she doesn't voice any objections when Derani picks her up to carry her onto Tortuva. She has no interest in getting kidnapped again and having anyone rub their bonding scent on her. She feels badly for the lonely Eora and advocated for the punishment to be light, but that doesn't mean she wants it to happen again. The bonding oil these Talins produce is powerful stuff.

The crew isn't with them as Derani strides down the docks and into the main station. After a brief conversation during which Derani explained he had "obligations" to see to, the crew left Bountiful with all kinds of plans to enjoy their unexpected vacation.

None of them asked a single question. Nalia isn't sure if that's because the crew is well-trained or if it's part of Talin culture. Or maybe their faith in Derani is just that strong.

Now she and Derani are off to meet the mysterious Palforma and deliver him to Talarian. Nalia has to admit that she's deeply intrigued by it all. It took them almost two rotations to get to Tortuva and Nalia spent all that time reading about Talin politics and the current struggles between Traditionalists and Reformists.

It's not a hard conflict to understand. When Talins first became a space-faring species, they suffered badly because couples would inevitably be parted for extended periods of time, especially during wartime. If the couple had scent-bonded—which used to be the common practice—they risked succumbing to Scent Collapse Disease, also known as Ending, if they were apart for too long. It almost always ended in a painful death.

No two couples reacted the same. Some succumbed to Ending after only a few rotations of separation while some could last almost an entire solar. But it all boiled down to the same thing. Scent-bonded Talins were dying, and the civilization was suffering as it tried to expand and fight wars over colonies and territories.

The monarch of the time declared that scent-bonding was killing the Talin species, and it needed to be stopped. The problem is that Talin females can't get pregnant unless they're scent-bonded. That's when the Talin practice of using artificial wombs was started.

Over the years, the monarch's original anti-attachment belief morphed into the conviction that most emotions should be avoided. No love between husband and wife. No overt affection between parents and children. Everyone is taught from a young age that foremost they must think of the good of Talin, then of their clan, then their family, and only lastly, should they consider their own needs and wants.

All of it comes together in Nalia's mind to form a picture of a species that has developed such rigid social protocols that scent-bonding with each other isn't just taboo. It's essentially illegal.

That's how human pets were added into the mix. It's considered perfectly acceptable to let a human pet scent-bond to the owner. And it's safe because they believed Talins aren't capable of scent-bonding to a human since humans don't have scent glands that produce bonding oil after all. But having a human scent-bonded to a Talin is perfectly fine, if not desirable.

It strikes Nalia as amusing to read all this advice on how to properly nurture a human. How to hold them. How to see to their emotional needs. It amazes her that this thinly veiled use of humans as a surrogate for love and affection is never questioned—at least not until now.

The current political conflict started when some Talins began questioning the status quo. After so many millennia, the scholars started asking the salient question: With all the modern advancements and the Talins' status as one of the most powerful species in the known universe, are all the taboos surrounding scent-bonding still necessary?

The backlash from these suggestions was severe, and the rise of opposing political parties emerged. Traditionalists see no reason to change Talin culture, and the more militant of them are talking about civil war. Reformists, ironically, want to bring back the original Talin culture from before they were forced to give up scenting-bonding for the good of the whole species.

Nalia can understand both sides but agrees with the Reformists. The writing is on the wall. The Talins are dying from Fading all over the place, and they can't ramp up the production of children fast enough to keep up. It's all being kept quiet, but if you look at the statistics, it's obvious.

Many of the humans back on the Wolder Colony would be horrified to find themselves embroiled in species-wide conflict. But Nalia finds it enthralling. How exciting is it to find herself in the midst of such intrigue?

She's always been fascinated by political maneuvering and plotting, and now she gets to be a part of it. A small part, but she'll take it. For the first time in her life, she feels like she belongs to something bigger and more important than only herself.

"Your heartbeat and respiration rate has increased," Derani comments as they wait in line to access a section of the station that's restricted to only Talins and their human pets. Everyone must pass through the bio-scanner one at a time to be registered on the station, so it has created a slight bottleneck.

"I'm excited," Nalia explains. "When we meet Palforma, can I ask him questions?"

Derani rumbles in amusement. "You can ask, but I doubt he will answer. I'm assuming discretion is a large part of his current mission."

"He might not talk to other Talins, but he'll probably talk to me," Nalia announces. "I'm only a human, after all. Who would I tell?"

"You make a good point," Derani comments as the line moves. "Being on this station isn't scary. Is it? I could have left you on the ship."

She glances around the crowd of Talins. "I'm not going to lie; it's a little intimidating. But honestly I'm not truly worried."

Especially since she's making herself pay more attention to the environment this time. If anything starts up again, she's ducking for cover. No more letting strangers snatch her up and run away.

"Would your human like a treat?"

The question makes both Nalia and Derani look up to see a female Talin holding out a sweet. Mika included a few bags of candy with all the purchases. After trying one of each, Nalia realized that several of the sweets were attempting to taste like the fruit-flavored candy she grew up with. This is one of those and her favorite.

Without even consulting with Derani, she grabs the sweet and pops it into her mouth. It's tastes like a cross between an orange and a peach. She forces herself not to chew so she can savor it longer.

Derani rattles in reprimand. "Nalia! You need to ask first."

The stranger rumbles in amusement. "Impulse control is not a human strong suit. Unless she has one of the blood-sugar diseases that some humans get, I'm sure one treat won't hurt her."

"She's perfectly healthy, but you're correct. She's rather impetuous."

The two of them chat about humans as the crowd moves forward. Nalia listens with only half an ear as she examines the Talins around her.

Many offer Derani a comment about her or good-naturedly express their envy. A few interact directly with her, but they speak to her as if she's a child. She doesn't take offense. It's always better to be underestimated.

Then she and Derani are at the bio-scanner and the conversation stops. He starts to set her down, but one of the Talins monitoring the pass-through makes a quick rattle to get their attention.

"You may carry your human through. I wouldn't want the scanner to spook her," she tells Derani. "I don't recognize her, so this must be her first visit. Welcome, both of you."

Nalia gives the guard a little wave, and the guard moves a few of her fingers back at Nalia. "You're a handsome human. Be good now and mind your owner."

"I will," Nalia promises, and the guard purrs.

"You're a lucky one, sir," the guard says when she looks up at Derani. "Enjoy visiting our station."

It's not as if Nalia hasn't experienced a walk-through bio-scanner before, so she isn't startled when she feels a slight pressure on her skin and then hears a few beeps. But she doesn't object to the guard's assumptions. It is nice to be carried by Derani. The crowd is friendly and hands-off, but she's still wary.

It takes only a moment, and then they're on the other side, striding fast to the meeting spot. This station isn't as populous as Hormin station, but because it's much smaller it feels far more crowded. The hallways aren't as wide, especially here in the Talin-only section of the station.

Derani confidently makes his way through the labyrinth of corridors until he finally gets to a door marked in Talin instead of Common so Nalia can't read it. Derani elbows the display on the door, and it beeps angrily at him. Displays with bio-locks don't like elbows; they like hands.

Before he can shuffle her weight around to free up a hand, the door opens, revealing a large and scary-looking Talin. Nalia gives a little gasp of surprise and shrinks back. Derani sounds a warning rattle and tries to step away from the open door.

With speed that leaves Nalia gaping, the stranger reaches out and grabs Derani by the back of the neck, his big hand covering the plates there before Derani can duck his head down to separate the plates and fend off the hand. Then he pulls Derani into the room. The force behind the pull is enough to send Derani stumbling.

Nalia pulls herself into a tight ball, expecting Derani to fall, which would cause her to hit hard when he lands on top of her. But that doesn't happen. Instead, she is plucked out of Derani's grip and then deposited gently on her feet. The stranger purrs at her briefly but then turns to face Derani, putting himself between the two of them.

"Who you?" It's the first thing this stranger utters, and his voice doesn't sound quite right to Nalia. It sounds like he's having to force the words out, as if his own throat is fighting with him as he tries to talk.

Derani's got his balance back, and he sinks into a fighting stance, claws out, quills up, and back plates rattling threateningly. "Get away from Nalia!"

The stranger glances behind his shoulder and purrs. "Nalia?"

She gives him a mute nod. "I'm scent-bonded to Derani, so don't try anything or I'll vomit all over you." As threats go, it's not an impressive one. She can only hope the threat of her ill-health will keep this Talin from doing anything to her or Derani.

Thinking his opponent is distracted, Derani tries to rush the stranger, only to find himself grabbed again and swung into a wall.

"No," the Talin says.

That moves makes Nalia go from concerned to scared. After the fight on the other station, she knows Derani has skills and strength. But this guy avoided the attack effortlessly and now is holding a struggling Derani as if he's a small child. She looks around wildly for any kind of weapon. A bag is sitting on a table close to her. She runs to it and rips it open, frantic to find something to use against this giant Talin.

To her surprise, she finds actual weapons. How did this guy get weapons aboard a space station where they aren't allowed? The monitors and scanners at the docks should have identified these items even before he made it into the main station area.

She grabs the weapon she is most familiar with, a short-range stunner, and turns to face Derani and the stranger. Any Talin could probably wield the weapons with one hand, but she needs two hands and has to balance the stock that would rest in the crook of a Talin's elbow on her shoulder. She hits the button that brings the weapon to life and steps a little closer. She doesn't want to risk hitting Derani even if the round would be painful but shouldn't cause any injuries.

"Derani?" the stranger asks at the same time she calls out.

"Let him go!"

The big Talin rattles with surprise when he sees her holding his weapon. Then he rumbles out a loud laugh. "No shoot."

He lets go and jumps back before Derani can claw or impale him with those wickedly sharp quills. Instead of continuing to attack, Derani cautiously steps backward until he's standing between the stranger and her. Then he reaches back and plucks the weapon from her grip.

"Hey, that was mine!" she protests, even as her fatigued arms drop to her sides. That thing had been too heavy for her to hold much longer.

"It's not a toy," Derani grumbles as he points it at the other Talin. "Now stay behind me. We're going to walk sideways until we get to the door display, and then we'll leave the room."

The other Talin rattles his displeasure. He opens his mouth a few times, trying to get words out, but only manages to vocalize hissing sounds. He rattles in agitation and bangs his chest several times with his open palm. She knows this is a greeting, but the way he's doing it almost looks like he's trying to force the words out by hitting himself.

"Me Palforma," he finally gets out. "Palforma. Palforma. You Derani. Nalia. Derani and Nalia. Me here and you here. Meeting to meet. Here to meet."

Derani doesn't relax at the Talin's words. "If you're Palforma, why did you attack me?"

"Not attack. Not hurt. Need you inside. No hall. Much exposed." Palforma points at Nalia. "Human? No record. No human. Derani humanless. Maybe not be Derani."

His halting speech is coming out a little better the more he talks, but it's painfully clear that Palforma is frustrated by his inability to articulate.

He taps his head, pointing to a misshapen part of it. She sees cracks in the armor plating there. When he turns his face to the side, she can see that he must have suffered a grievous injury to his head at some point. It's all long healed, but it has left him damaged. By the way he moves, his reflexes weren't impeded by the injury, so it must only affect the spoken language part of his brain.

"I'm new," Nalia explains. She stays behind Derani, only peeking her head around his bulk to talk. "I was registered a few rotations ago on Hormin station."

Palforma purrs as he regards her. "Where from?"

What does that have to do with anything? "Originally? I was raised on the Wolder Colony, on the Malmark planet of Mara."

Palforma makes a kind of grunting sound and lifts his eyes to meet Derani's gaze. "Wild-caught?"

Nalia harrumphs and crosses her arms. "That makes me sound like I was running around some jungle planet naked and eating grubs. I'll have you know I co-owned a ship." She holds up a hand at Derani before he can talk. "And yes, I know it wasn't much of a ship, but it was mine."

"It was yours, but maybe not entirely classifiable as a ship," Derani interjects. "Maybe an experiment gone wrong?"

Palforma roars out a rumble of laughter. "Like Lakin," he informs them. "Human Lakin. Wild-caught. Willful. Smart. Clever. So clever. All the clever." Then he sobers and starts rubbing at the scars on his head absently. "No plan now. Not safe. Nalia not safe with plan. Need new plan."

That makes Nalia step out from behind Derani. Not only doesn't he stop her, but he even lowers his weapon before he speaks. "I didn't think I needed to warn you I had a human. This mission is secret, but Nalia won't tell anyone. Besides, even if she speaks out, no one will pay attention."

"Not a go. Unsafe. Holian, Dalt, Searin will think and plan. Other ideas. Other messengers." He makes a sad rumble. "Delay! Every delay, more death. Every delay, more enemies."

"Wait, you're not going to deliver the evidence because you're afraid I'll be in danger?"

Palforma rumbles in agreement. "Danger."

"But all we need to do is get you to your homeworld. Right?" she looks up at Derani, feeling confused. "Isn't the homeworld only four or five rotations away?"

"Six," Derani answers.

Palforma rattles in disagreement. "Mali… Mali… Maligora station. Maligora first. Then Umeal Colony. Then Talarian. First, then second, then third."

"Neither of those stations are very far out of the way," Derani notes. She can tell by his tone he's thinking quickly. "If your visits are brief, each stop would only add half a rotation to our travels. I was assured this mission is critical, and I don't want to see the Traditionalists gain any more influence or power than they have already. This should have ended after Holian was kidnapped, but it seems that the head was not chopped off."

Derani glances down at her, and even though he doesn't make a sound, she knows he's thinking about her safety. She gives him her best confident expression. "I'm not afraid," she whispers.

That declaration makes him rattle out a decisive sound as he looks back to Palforma. "I wouldn't want it said that anyone from the Anize clan is cowardly. And my family, the Jorean, are well-known to lend aid and assistance when our people need us. We are and have always been loyal to Talarian and the monarch. Let me take you to Maligora and Umeal and then deliver you safely to Talarian. It would be my honor."

Palforma sounds an appreciative rumble. "Warrior heart," he comments. Then he looks down at Nalia. "You also, yes?"

"Sure," Nalia says with a smile. "I'm game."

"Not game," Palforma argues. "Serious."

"No, you're right, it isn't a game," she agrees, her expression sobering. "Even so, I'm in."

Palforma studies them, rumbling thoughtfully as he thinks. "Can't contact. Can't verify. On own," he explains, then points to Nalia. "You no… no… no help. Stay safe. No join in."

Those few words shock her. This is the first time any Talin has acknowledged her as a competent and independent being. He's telling her to stay safe and out of danger, not ordering Derani to monitor her. The sheer novelty of it has her gracing Palforma with a huge grin.

"Sure thing, big guy. I'll steer clear." Then she adds a word she rarely ever uses. "I promise."

CHAPTER 23

Although massive, Palforma moves with a stealthy grace that impresses Nalia. If she didn't have eyes on him, she'd never know he was striding behind Derani. He doesn't even make any sound as they walk across the platform onto the ship. That platform normally creaks and clatters with even her footsteps, but Palforma's footfalls are nearly silent.

"You're so quiet," she comments as Derani presses his palm to the ship's door display.

"Yes," Palforma agrees. "Need quiet. Not fast. So quiet important."

She gives him a quizzical look. In what world does Palforma think he's not fast? He sounds a rumble of amusement at the look on her face. "Dalt fast. Me not."

Nalia gives him a small smile. "Whoever this Dalt person is, he must be meteor fast because you're no slouch in the speed department."

A pleased rumble comes out of his chest. "Compliment. No deserve. But thank you."

"No, you're wrong, Palforma. And Nalia is correct," Derani comments as the hatch slides open. "Your speed is exemplary. It's obvious that whatever happened to your head hasn't affected your skills as a soldier."

A rumble that Nalia's never heard before comes out of Palforma, and he stands stock still as Derani steps onto the ship with her in his arms. When the other Talin doesn't move, Derani turns around and sounds a small worried rumble. "Are you well?"

Palforma remains still, but the strange rumble keeps going. "Not soldier. Only citizen now. Not worthy." He rubs his hand over the scars on his head. "Trying to be. Trying to prove. But failure is there. In my head. In my mouth."

The words sound even more forced than normal. The combination of emotion and the old head trauma are doing double duty to inhibit his language skills. Derani goes stiff, and she can tell he doesn't know what to say.

She knew guys growing up who always had to act tough. When they showed any kind of emotional vulnerability, the other guys would react badly. Not because they were cruel but because they didn't know what to do. This moment feels eerily similar.

That's when it hits her. Palforma's unfamiliar rumble is one of embarrassment. Like a human flushing from shame.

She decides to be bold. "I'm still learning about all of this stuff, but I can tell this mission is important. Even critical. Right?"

"Critical," he agrees.

"If it's that crucial, that means you must be superb. They probably had a ton of soldiers to pick from, and they chose you. So what if words don't come easily to you? You're communicating with us just fine."

Palforma stops his embarrassed rumbling for a moment; then he purrs. "Kind human."

"Eh, not always," Nalia quips. "Only to those who deserve it."

Then Derani does something she doesn't expect. "Palforma," he barks out. Palforma's gaze shoots up to meet Derani's eyes. Without breaking eye contact, Derani leans over and rubs his cheek over the top of Nalia's head. The scent of orange and cloves fills her nose, making her feel content and happy.

"Mine," Derani growls out.

Palforma rumbles out a laugh. "Understood. No worries. No take. The humans pick. Not us. Them. Sora picked. Lakin picked. This one picked. You, not me."

"As long as we are clear," Derani comments as he turns on his heels and strides into the ship.

It takes longer to get underway than normal because they don't have Yulian to man the navigation console, Larimus to monitor traffic, or Melanem to take over the communications.

Bountiful has all the latest technology, so Derani can reroute all functions to the console at the captain's chair. The consoles are designed to expand as more functions are accessed, so soon he's sitting behind a massive display of various programs. He might be highly skilled and have done this type of work before, but there is still a lot for one person to accomplish.

The first three marks are tense as he gets the ship out of the docks, into the queue to leave the station's orbit, and finally into the heavy traffic of the nearby warp corridor.

Nalia watches everything with interest, marveling at Derani's ability to multitask. Because her ship had been so old-fashioned by the standards of most species, she and Hax always had to pay the extra fee to be escorted by a tug-ship. That's why they rarely bothered with any of the bigger space stations. It was almost always cost-prohibitive. This might be the first time she's ever seen what goes into leaving a large station when you don't use a tug-ship.

By the time they hit the warp corridor, she's pretty sure she could take over monitoring the traffic. It's the least intense out of all the jobs because the ship's programming is so advanced and the sensors are extensive.

When they get closer to Maligora station, she'll suggest that Derani let her sit at one of the control stations. That gives her a few rotations to study.

Derani will probably say no at first, but she might be able to talk him into letting her help if she takes Yulian's console, the one closest to Derani. He could easily observe what she's doing and reroute the controls to his console if she does anything he doesn't like.

Excited, she pulls out her small information square and spends a few marks studying the Bountiful's systems, marveling at all the fancy bells and whistles. Derani glances down at her once but doesn't ask what she's doing. He's gotten used to the way she'll disappear into whatever she's studying.

She's memorizing one of the many program trigger key lists when Derani sounds a rumble of satisfaction and sits back in his chair. "We're in the line for the next full rotation," he explains. "Then we drop out of the warp corridor about half a rotation from Maligora station."

She looks up from her spot on the kneeling pillow. "Good job."

"Thank you, little Nalia. I should take you back to the cabin to make sure you get some rest before I'm needed to guide the ship again."

Her nipples bead and heat pools in her belly. Putting her to bed comes with at least one orgasm and sometimes up to three. Then she gets to fall asleep curled up in his arms.

Now when he mentions bedtime or even comments that she should take a nap, it causes a Pavlovian response in her. Hormones surge, and her clit aches with need.

"Sure, some bunk time sounds good," she agrees eagerly. Her prompt response makes him rumble out a chuckle. It gives her courage to voice her next suggestion.

"Maybe we could go all the way this time," she offers. He has yet to let her pleasure him. If she's sneaky, she gets to touch him, but otherwise, it's all about her pleasure and not his.

"Nalia." He puts a lot of warning into only one word. She sighs and gives up for the moment. Jumping to her feet, she stretches and watches as Derani carefully extricates himself from behind the expanded consol. "Do you need sustenance? Water?"

She shakes her head. The enormous meal he fed her before they left the docks to find Palforma will tide her over for many more marks. "Nope, I'm good."

He moves to pick her up, but she steps away. "Can I walk? I've been sitting so long that my muscles need to move."

The rumble Derani sounds is one of mild disappointment. "If you must."

She almost gives in, but she needs to start insisting that Derani let her walk more. All this being carried around isn't doing her leg muscles any favors.

The moment the hatch to the control room slides open, they hear some kind of commotion. Derani sounds a puzzled rumble and then goes quiet as he tilts his head to better gauge the sound. "It's coming from the activity room."

"Activity room?"

Derani looks down at her. "It's a multi-use room on the ship that can be utilized for large meetings, exercise, or storage. It's mostly used for training."

Because there's only one other person on the ship, all that commotion must be caused by Palforma. Her need to check on the big, damaged Talin overrides her eagerness to get back to the privacy of their cabin. "Then it's Palforma. We should make sure he has everything he needs."

A discontent rattle comes from Derani, but he doesn't stop her as she starts down the hall in the opposite direction of their cabin.

The door to the room is wide open, and they find Palforma training with what looks to Nalia like either a short sword or a long dagger. Whatever the weapon is, the Talin wielding it looks positively deadly.

Stopping at the open hatch, Nalia watches with wide eyes as Palforma moves with a degree of agility and athleticism she's never witnessed before.

When a training bot she didn't notice moves to strike the big Talin, Nalia only barely holds in a surprised shriek. She covers her mouth with both hands at the same time Derani sounds an amused rumble and pulls her tightly against him.

"There's no need to worry. Strict protocols are programmed into the combat training bots," Derani explains.

As if to prove his assurances false, the bot lashes out, and Palforma hisses in pain. The bot is wielding a weapon as fierce as Palforma's, and it looks like it grazed the big Talin's arm. It even broke one of Palforma's quills in half.

Derani makes an alarmed rattle behind her. "That shouldn't have happened. The bot must be defective. Let me get you to a safe place, and then I'll come back and deactivate it."

He starts to pull her away, but both of them end up freezing when Palforma sounds an enraged rattle so loud it echoes in the room. They watch transfixed as Palforma goes after the bot, cutting it into several pieces before it even has a chance to begin a defensive move. Bits of bot body twitch on the ground and Palforma cuts them into smaller bits, still rattling. But the rattles are only angry now instead of pure, unaltered rage.

"Damn," Nalia murmurs. "I'm glad he's on our side."

Derani rumbles in agreement. "He shouldn't have been able to do that. Practice bots are reinforced, and they are programmed to keep themselves from being destroyed. That's built-in programming, not something that can be manipulated like their aggression or skill levels. I don't think I've ever seen anyone able to dismember a bot while it was trying to retreat."

"Was is retreating?" Nalia asks. "Because I barely saw it move before it was in little bottie bits on the floor."

Derani rumbles in amusement at her language. "Because the bot caused a wound, it would need to retreat. Bot programming dictates that it must stop fighting at that point and allow the opponent to assess the training injury. Talin warriors are no good to us if they become grievously injured during practice. "

An embarrassed rumble brings both her and Derani's eyes up to Palforma. "Will replace. Sorry. Annoyance happened. Snick, snack, and bot done. Palforma done. Will replace."

"There's no need to replace it," Derani assures the other Talin. "But perhaps you shouldn't do any more bot training today."

"Done with bots," Palforma agrees and makes a pleased rumble. "Train with you now."

That makes Derani rattle in surprise. Nalia quickly puts herself between Derani and Palforma.

"No way," she announces. She points down to the still twitching bot arms on the floor. "Cut up all the bots you want, but you leave Derani alone."

A loud purr comes out of Derani, and he wraps his arms around her shoulders and nuzzles her hair. "Are you defending me, little Nalia?"

"I'm just making sure you don't make any bad choices," she explains.

"No hurt your Talin," Palforma promises. "He should train. Practice. Keep strong. You're trouble. I see it. Bold and fearless. Trouble, trouble, trouble on two little human feet." Palforma gestures at Derani. "Train. Teach. Learn. Not hurt." He seems to consider that last sentence and rumbles out a small laugh. "Not hurt much."

Derani stands stiffly against her and finally nods. "I can only train for a short while. Nalia needs to rest, and she doesn't sleep as peacefully if I'm not there."

"Sleep," Palforma echoes and sounds a rumble of approval. "Sleep with eyes open. Sleep with sound. Sleep with flesh on flesh. Always the best sleep."

Sounding an aggressive rattle, Derani steps around Nalia to confront Palforma. "Are you insinuating something?"

Palforma rumbles out another laugh. "No say. No reveal." He points to Derani and then to Nalia. "We are theirs. Our rumbles. Our rattles. Our flesh. All belong. You lie because she wants sleep. You obey. She order." His amused rumbling stops. "No human pick me. No human order me. Too damage. Too… too…" He can't get the last word out and slaps the side of his head with his palm as if that will force his brain to work. He sighs a sad rumble. "Want orders."

How did this guy go from deadly warrior to sad and childlike so quickly? Her heart breaks for him. She can't get him a human companion, but maybe she can comfort him in another way.

"Are you hungry or thirsty? We could go to the galley for something."

Palforma rumbles out an affectionate sound. "Nice Nalia. No. No. Good right now."

Derani rumbles out a thoughtful sound. "Palforma's correct. I need to train more. He's a warrior of superior skills. It would be a missed opportunity if I didn't learn from him."

Palforma perks up at his words, and Nalia realizes that Derani feels bad for Palforma also and wants to distract the big Talin from his sudden melancholy. She nods at his suggestion. "You're right. Practice is always a good idea. I'm not that tired anyway."

"Yes. Train. Practice."

Palforma practically runs to a far corner and fishes something out of the pile of items he must have shoved together to make room for him and the bot. He brings a large kneeling pad over and plops it on the floor near the door. Then he grabs up the bits of broken bot and tosses them into the same pile.

Nalia takes a seat while Derani removes his belt and hangs it on a nearby hook. He walks confidently to the center of the room and faces off with Palforma. For the next two marks, she watches Derani get tossed around by the exceptionally skilled Talin.

Each time the interaction is over, Palforma pauses and goes over what happened. He doesn't use many words, relying more on slow-motion recreations to explain to Derani what he did wrong and the appropriate countermoves.

When they start practicing with those long daggers, Nalia almost jumps up to protest. But it's obvious after the first go that Palforma will only touch Derani with the flat edge and is taking extra care not to cause any damage. She's not sure, but at one point she thinks Palforma winks conspiratorially at her.

By the time two marks have gone by, and they are approaching the first strike of the evening, Derani gets the upper hand on Palforma and wins a round. The big Talin rumbles with approval.

"Good! Much improve! Much good!" He lets Derani help him off the floor and slaps him on the arm. Derani is rattling with enthusiasm although she can tell by the way he's holding his body that he's physically depleted.

Slapping his palm to his chest, Derani sounds an appreciative rumble. "Thank you for your gift of time and skill."

Palforma slaps a hand to his chest. "More practice. More skill. Later. Yes?"

"I wouldn't miss it," Derani assures him. "You're an excellent instructor, Palforma. I've learned more during this one session than in all my training under professional combat teachers."

The compliment makes Palforma rumble out a pleased sound. "My yes. Nalia learn too. No hand-to-hand but with weapon. Little. Hidden. Can't take. Can't steal."

It takes her a moment to realize that he's offering to train her to use a weapon so no one can abscond with her. "That's a brilliant idea," Nalia says quickly before Derani can object.

Derani glances down at her, rattling out a negative sound. "No."

She smirks up at him. Doesn't he realize that "no" is only the beginning of the negotiation?

CHAPTER 24

As useful as he found the training with Palforma, Derani is very glad when the hatch to his cabin slides shut behind him. He sets Nalia on the bed, thankful that she didn't demand he let her walk. Every moment with Nalia feels precious, and he hates it when he misses out on holding her, even for a short time.

He doesn't know how he got so lucky as to not only run across a human to claim but one as clever and kind as Nalia. His human is one of the best the species has to offer.

"I need to cleanse myself," he explains. "I'll be back soon to massage you, and then we can spend a few marks resting before I need to be back on the bridge."

Nalia grins up at him. "Hurry. I'm eager for my, um, massage."

Rumbling out a joyful sound, Derani hurries to the cleansing unit. He's quick with the pumice stone, running it roughly over his body to clear away old keratin. He takes extra care with his hands, wanting to make them as smooth as he can for Nalia. She's never complained about his touch being too rough, but the last thing he wants to do is cause her any discomfort. Especially considering the skin of her sex is much more delicate than the rest of her.

Once he feels properly clean, he pulls on a fresh pair of pants and leaves the cleansing unit. Nalia's lying back on the bed with her eyes closed. Disappointed that his pet might already be asleep, he debates waking her up when she opens her eyes and ends his worry.

Sitting up, she scoots over and pats a section of the bunk. "About time you got done."

"Are you fatigued? Would you like to sleep?" he asks as he joins her on the bed.

"Massage first?" she requests hopefully and starts undoing the ties to her omnie. She shows no embarrassment as she pulls off the garment, telling Derani that she's not only content with their arrangement but eager.

So eager that he can smell her arousal already. He automatically begins purring for her.

Her next words stop him cold. "Why don't you ever take your pants off?"

Frozen in place, with one knee on the bed and one foot on the floor, Derani's rumble goes silent. "My pants?"

"Yes, your pants. You never let me touch you. You never let me please you. Don't get me wrong, I don't want you to stop touching me. But I want to use my hands and mouth on you too."

"We can't." Those words come out a lot less firm than he wanted them to.

Nalia sits up, folding her legs under her. She's much closer to him now, and her scent is having its usual effect. His pants are starting to feel too tight.

It only gets worse when she leans in until she can brush her lips against his. Then she swipes her tongue along the seam of his lips. Blood roars through his veins, and it takes all his control to remain where he is and not pounce on her.

"Nalia." Her name comes out like a whine.

"Derani," she responds, matching his tone. She reaches forward and runs her little fingers along the top of his pants, teasing the skin of his abdomen and making his muscles tense.

"You shouldn't do that, Nalia," he whispers but makes no move to stop her.

"My eyes work," she points out, and he feels thoroughly confused until she continues. "I can see this perfectly."

She brings one palm down to cup his hardening mating shaft. It's still mostly in the pouch, but the head is emerging and her palm is resting right on it. He hisses out a breath at the sensation. No one but him has ever touched him there. Even when he was apprenticing on another ship and would occasionally share pleasure with a crewmate, she never bothered stimulating him with her hand or mouth. It was his job to be hard and ready the moment she showed up. Then she would mount him, find her pleasure, and leave.

Nalia's soft touch is a thing of wonder. Somehow she's managed to short circuit his brain, and her palm isn't even resting on bare skin. The thick, durable pants keep her flesh from touching his.

"I want to touch this," she explains as she moves her hand up and down a little. "I want to hold it in my hands. I want to put it in my mouth. I want to run my tongue over it. I want to taste you, and I want to feel you inside of me. I've been patient with you, and I like the orgasms you give me, but something's missing. I need you with me when I come. I want all of you."

"Yes."

It's only when her hands slide into his pants that he realizes he spoke that one small word out loud. How inappropriate! What has he done? He should take it back. He should move away. He should—

Nalia's grip on his emerging shaft makes him gasp in a sharp breath and rumble with pleasure. He becomes fully engorged so quickly that it borders on painful, and when she squeezes him gently with her little hand, he shudders with pleasure.

"You're beautiful," Nalia murmurs as she uses her free hand to tug his pants down. Once past his hips, they fall to his knee but are trapped by where his knee is still resting on the bunk. It doesn't occur to him to move. Any movement might make Nalia stop, and if she stops touching him, he might die on the spot.

She wraps one hand around the top part of his shaft and then dips her fingers into the retreating pouch. Her actions make the pouch finish pulling back so the rest of his hard cock and seed sack spill out. She makes a small delighted sound and leans over.

"Beautiful and fascinating," she compliments him. "You're big and thick. I like it."

When she swipes her tongue across the head, Derani loses his breath. If he thought her hands felt good, that's nothing compared to her tongue and mouth. She works her mouth over the head of his shaft and sucks gently.

Derani isn't aware until that moment that a Talin can feel pleasure so intense as to put them on the verge of passing out.

"Nalia," he moans.

She pulls away, and he whimpers from the loss of her hot, wet mouth. Then her smell hits him. It's as intense as when she's ready to orgasm. That pushes him into action.

Kicking off his pants, he grabs her legs and tumbles her backward. With his grip on her calves, he pulls her legs apart. When he's pleasured her before, he would steal moments for himself. Admiring the sight, smell, and feel of her while his tongue and hands brought her to climax. The silken feel of dark curly hair at the apex of her legs. The sight of the soft folds of her sex opening to reveal the pink flesh. He would pull not only the scent of her arousal into his lungs but also the human scent of her skin. All of it would feed him later as he took care of his own pleasure in the privacy of the cleansing unit.

But today is different. He takes no extra time to admire before he dives between her legs. His engorged shaft rubs mercilessly against the bedcovers, taunting him after having felt Nalia's soft mouth. Focusing on his task, he parts the lips of her sex and puts his mouth on the little nub of nerve endings between her legs.

She cries out at the suddenness of it and struggles a little against him. Then she's pushing her pelvis at him, seeking more contact. Her taste floods his mouth, and his rumble of pleasure becomes more intense. He'll never get enough of this. Never be satiated, no matter how many times he gets to taste her essence.

"Derani!"

He's familiar now with the way her body moves and how her scent changes just before she finds her pleasure. She is very close now, and that only makes him increase the pressure and pace of his mouth and tongue.

But he goes a step further. Pushed by his own need, he moves one of his hands until it is below his mouth, teasing his fingers around her entrance.

He eases a single finger inside of her and is rewarded when she moans and moves against him. She is deliciously wet and hot, and without thinking, he adds a second finger. She cries out and starts convulsing as she reaches her climax. He doesn't stop stimulating her until she sobs and pushes at him.

Reluctantly, he eases his fingers out of her and sits back to take in his ravaged pet. Her eyes are closed, skin covered in a fine layer of sweat, chest heaving, and face flushed. She lies there with her legs spread, wanton and willing.

He starts to get off the bed, his own need rising in him. He'll go to the cleaning unit to finish himself off and then bring a small cloth to wipe down his beautiful human. His movement makes her eyes open, and a sensual smile forms on her lips.

Voice husky, she whispers, "Where are you going?"

"I'm not leaving the cabin," he promises. "I'll be quick in the cleaning unit and then come back to let you cling to me until you're asleep."

Her smile vanishes. She props herself up on her elbows, brows furrowing. "You don't want me?"

She glances down at his fully engorged mating shaft. It's throbbing in time with his heart, and when she sits up and reaches for it, he's helpless to move away. As before, her touch is gentle and inquisitive. His rumble turns desperate as her fingers glide over his taut flesh.

"I think you want me," she says in a coaxing voice. "We aren't done here yet." She wraps a dainty hand around his shaft and tugs. "Come back here. I want to know what this feels like inside of me." When he doesn't follow her urging, she frowns up at him. "Don't make me beg."

"I don't think—" he begins, but his refusal is cut off when she leans over and wraps her mouth around him again. What little willpower he could scrape together vanishes, and he moans and sways a little as sensation riots through him.

Somewhere in the back of his brain, he knows he'll regret this moment. Because he never let her touch him intimately and he never mounted her, he could keep the illusion that everything they did was still within the bounds of propriety. Still within acceptable actions.

But not anymore.

He can't fight his desire any longer. She must have sensed his acceptance because she pulls away from his shaft and looks up with a knowing grin.

Scooting back, she pats the bunk between her legs. "Come here."

He's all instinct and need now. When he moves on top of her, she wraps those beautiful human legs around him, pulling them tightly together and urging the tip of his throbbing mating shaft into her heat. He stutters at the feel of her—hot, wet, and tight. Fear hits him hard, and he sounds an anxious rumble.

What is he doing?

"Derani?" He opens eyes he doesn't remember closing to find her looking up at him with concern. "Are you okay? If this hurts, we can stop. I thought you would enjoy it too, but maybe I was wrong. I haven't read anything on Talin sexual practices yet, so this is my fault for interpreting your reactions in a human way."

Her care for him breaks the last barrier he has. "You're perfect," he whispers, and that makes her smile.

"You won't hurt me," she promises. "If you go a little slow at first, and let me get used to you, it'll be fine. I'm really turned on. And this is what I want." Her expression turns apprehensive. "If you want it too, I mean."

"Want," he assures her. "Want very much."

"You sound like Palforma," she giggles and then moans as he slowly starts pushing himself inside of her. "Derani! You feel so good."

He wants to argue that it's her that feels good. There is no way for him to describe the sensation of sinking into Nalia's warm heat. Pleasure unlike anything he's experienced before overwhelms him to the point that once he's fully inside of her, he's unable to move for a moment.

Even though he goes still, Nalia doesn't. She undulates under him, using her legs to move her body against him. It shouldn't amaze him that she's ready to reach another climax. He knows human females are capable of that. But what she's doing, by using his mating shaft, does all kinds of primal things to him.

Fighting his urge to pound into her, he moves his hips a little to see how she'll react. He's too tall for her to reach his face, so she peppers his chest with lip presses.

"Yes, please, more," she demands.

Bracing his body with his arms to keep from putting too much pressure on her, he moves with more intent. Her legs spasm around him and a breathy, inarticulate whine sighs out of her.

It's only by sheer force of will that he doesn't find his own release right away. He wants her to be pleasured again before he succumbs to his own climax.

"Harder," she demands. Arching his back so he can bury his nose in her mane, he moves faster, putting a little more force behind his thrusts. He's so close he's not sure he can last much longer.

Then she goes rigid under him, her legs tightening. Her eyes are tightly shut and her face tense. Breathy sounds of pleasure flow from her mouth. She's beautiful as she climaxes.

He lets himself follow her, emptying his seed sack into her velvety channel. The thought that he's filling her with himself makes his pleasure even more intense. He doesn't even realize he's rattling in triumph at the same time he's purring from pleasure until the roaring in his ears subsides.

Worried that he might be too heavy for her, he starts to move off, but she locks her legs around him. He could easily break her hold, but he wouldn't do that to his perfect little human.

"Stay," she orders, pressing her lips to a hard keratin plate on his chest. "Stay there just a little longer."

"As long as you wish," he promises. "Anything you wish."

He rubs a cheek into her hair, marveling at the smell of his bonding scent on her skin. He can detect the faint change in the smell of his bonding oil as it's soaking into her scalp, and he breathes it in greedily. Between his release and this perfect smell filling his nose, he feels more content now than he ever has in his entire life.

Then it hits him. He has scent-bonded to Nalia. He's done something with a human pet he's not supposed to do even with another Talin.

That thought should make him panic, but it doesn't. This moment feels too precious to ruin with doubt. Even if the consequences of his actions catch up with him, he's sure of one thing. He wouldn't trade Nalia or this bond for anything. Talin laws and taboos be damned. He's found something outside of culture and obligation to fight for. Even if half the battle was with his own inhibitions.

CHAPTER 25

Palforma slides his eyes over to glance at Derani as they wait in line to exit the docks at Maligora station. He's done that several times now, and this time Derani can't ignore it.

Turning to face Palforma, he sounds an impatient rattle. "What?"

He doesn't expect a burst of amused rumbles to come out of the Talin warrior. "Different. Different today. Body movement. Breathing. Rumbling. All different. Danced with Nalia. Danced with hands and tongues and other things. Dance left you better. More than you were. Being chosen is lucky for us. Good for us."

It takes Derani a moment to work out Palforma's meaning. He only barely keeps from rattling in surprise. "Don't speak of such things in public," he hisses.

Palforma sounds a dismissive rumble. "Everyone knows. Human and Talins. No eyes or earholes on us. We are fine."

"Everyone does not know," Derani argues. "Are you telling me that… that…" He can't bring himself to say it, even though he's leaning in close to Palforma and enough distance is between them and others in the line that no one can overhear.

Palforma sounds a curious rumble. "It's a secret that's not secret. A fact. A fact we pretend isn't there. The two species can pair. We can be the other half to each other. No shame. No blame. Only adoration. Love. Happiness." Palforma regards him silently for a few heartbeats and then sounds a sympathetic rumble. "Secret to you, though. New to you. All new to you. Congratulations."

Derani wants to ask questions, but then it's their turn through the archway into the rest of the station. They're not carrying anything illicit, so they have no issues. Soon they're striding into the shopping area.

While they were waiting in the queue to dock, Palforma showed him a map of the station and pointed out where they would meet his contact. He didn't board Bountiful with evidence against Prime Daughter Halieni, but at this station, he will take custody of it. Derani tried to ask why they had to stop at Umeal Colony also, but all Palforma would say was that the next stop was "part of the plan."

He should probably be more concerned about the fact that he's involved in this intrigue, but for the moment, all he can think about is Nalia.

She wasn't happy when he broke the news that she would be staying on the ship. After Palforma overpowered him so easily at their first meeting, he didn't want to expose Nalia to any further risk. The incident with the big ex-soldier turned out fine, but considering what they are here to collect, it's better she be kept out of harm's way.

She argued with him, claiming she wanted to see the station, but he knows better. She wants to be part of this scheme. When he proved intractable to her pleading, she threw up her hands and announced, "Try not to get yourself maimed or killed without me there to watch out for you."

That his adorable little human feels protective of him caused warmth to spread through Derani's body, chasing away the last of his doubts about their coupling. No other Talin, except perhaps his brother, cares this much about him. Not even his parents would bother warning him to be safe. They might issue proclamations about being a good Talin citizen and always bringing honor to his clan and family, but they'd never ask him to be safe.

And they certainly wouldn't press their lips to his earhole and whisper, "I love you."

Those three words made his scent glands fill so suddenly with oil that it trickled down his face. Far from embarrassed, he covered Nalia in his bonding scent, leaving her mane saturated. She giggled as he did this, and when he was done, she playfully wiped some of the excess away with a cleaning cloth.

That cloth is tucked in his belt pouch now. It smells of him but also of her. It's a comfort to know that at any moment he can pull it out, put it to his nose, and smell the unique combination of him and Nalia.

He should be upset over these recent developments. He should be in the midst of a moral quandary. But that kind of angst isn't in him anymore. One thing being with Nalia has made him understand is the fundamental perfection of scent-bonding.

He's sure that if other Talins only knew what kind of peace it brings to the mind and heart, they'd be demanding laws be repealed and taboos crushed.

But then again, there is the strong Reformist movement. He wouldn't be surprised to find many in that movement have scent-bonded with humans or even each other. All of it fills him with questions. Although he wants to ask Palforma more about humans and Talins pairing off, here and now isn't a good time.

It doesn't take them long to get to the meeting site. The small shop sells refurbished control units for comm arrays. When they walk in, two Talins are in the shop, one standing next to a display and tapping at it. The other one is at a shelving unit looking at several items for sale. The one tapping the display disappears through a back door as soon as Palforma and he enter, leaving only one Talin in the shop.

Derani's struck by this Talin's appearance. Palforma looks strange from his old head wound, but this Talin appears downright deformed. From what Derani can see, he's missing his quills, claws, and back plates. Was he tortured or in an accident? He couldn't have been born this way because their scientists make sure every embryo that matures in the artificial wombs are perfect.

The ragged nature of the scar tissue makes Derani suspicious that this Talin's body was damaged during war—either as a prisoner or while engaged in battle. Whichever the case, he must have survived something horrific.

Next to him is a human female who's holding an information square, reading something intently. She's standing with her shoulder resting on him, as if she can't bear the idea of not touching him in some way. She's probably average height for a human, which makes her small compared to her owner. Her mane is longer than Nalia's, but still on the short side for a human raised among Talins. That leads Derani to speculate that she's a recent acquisition.

Are they like him and Nalia? Do they share pleasure? Has this Talin scent-bonded with his human? His experience with Nalia and Palforma's assurance that it's widely done makes Derani question every human-owning Talin. How many of them are secretly bonded?

He and Palforma are halfway across the small shop when the human looks up and sees them. A smile blossoms on her face and she shouts, "Palforma!" before fearlessly launching herself at him.

The big Talin catches her easily and rumbles in greeting. "Hello, little Lakin. Trouble with fingers and toes. What do you break now?"

"I'll have you know, I haven't needed to break any ships lately," she declares with a giggle and graces him with a quick lip press on his cheek, well below his scent gland. Then he drops her gently back down to the floor. Her scarred owner strides up and tucks her possessively under his arm as he strikes a palm against his chest.

"It's good to see you well, Palforma," the Talin says and then turns to Derani. "You must be Captain Derani. I'm Dalt. This is Lakin. My parents are the ones who contacted you to help us."

Dalt? That's a very un-Talin like name. He doesn't know if he's ever met a Talin with a name so short. "Greetings, Dalt. It's my honor to serve the Prime Family."

"Has human now," Palforma announces to Dalt and Lakin with a gesture at Derani. "Smart, like Lakin. But doesn't break things."

"Hey, I only break stuff when I get kidnapped," Lakin protests with a grin.

Palforma sounds a teasing rumble. "Enclosure gate?"

"Those don't count," she argues, her grin still there. "But back to the topic at hand. Are you telling us that Captain Derani has a human? That's not in the records."

"I obtained her only a short time before you contacted me," Derani explains.

Lakin looks around. "Where is she?"

"Ship," Palforma answers. "Safer. New human. Wild-caught. Still figuring it out."

Lakin's expression turns worried. She takes half a step behind Dalt and wraps her arms around him, hugging him tightly. He rumbles out a soothing sound.

"Wild-caught? You mean like me?" she asks.

"Yes, but no," Palforma answers, making Lakin laugh.

"That clears everything up," she teases him.

He rumbles out an amused sound as he explains. "Co-owned ship. Ship in trouble and Derani save. No torture. No pain. Just choices. Scary because unknown but no pain."

Lakin's expression turns relieved. "That's good!"

The little human's questions and her reactions tell Derani that she suffered in her past. Poor thing, but it looks like she's in good hands now with Dalt.

To reassure this concerned human, he adds some details about Nalia. "She had an Ollie partner named Hax. He was incompetent and probably the reason their life was in danger. I sent him off to be with his people and kept her. That was the deal. I think she's acclimating well."

"Oh?" Lakin says, arching one delicate eyebrow before looking over to Palforma. "You'll tell me if she needs rescuing. Okay?"

Derani knows there's no way this pet could steal his Nalia, but her words fill him with irritation. "My human doesn't need rescuing, female," he informs her coldly. "She's happy and well-cared-for."

Lakin gives him a considering look, but before she can say anything, Palforma jumps in.

"Nalia happy." Then the big Talin points to the scent gland in one of his cheeks. "Scented and happy."

Expression softening, Lakin gives him a small smile. "I trust Palforma to know what's going on. A lot of Talins dismiss him because of the way he talks, but he sees everything. If he says Nalia's safe and happy with you, I believe him."

Derani doesn't bother pointing out that it's not her place to worry about someone else's pet.

Lakin must be one of those humans who is prone to devoting themselves to the welfare of others. It's an abstract concept that Talin literature notes can be a rare trait among humans. They can be devoted to known beings like family and their owners. But if they don't personally know someone, it's hard for most humans to form empathy. It's just the way they are.

Lakin is a rare human with enough empathy to be concerned with the well-being of another human that she's never met. He needs to treat her carefully or he might damage her emotional well-being. It's well-documented that humans with strong empathy can be easily upset. It makes him feel a little guilty about his earlier coldness.

"If you're worried about my Nalia, I can arrange for you to talk to her through a comm link-up," he offers and then looks at Dalt. "That is if it's something your master will agree to."

She moves her gaze to Dalt. "That would make me feel a lot better. I know you guys are good to us, but after what I went through with those Traditionalists, I feel like it's better to double-check. Especially if Nalia was free before she became a pet."

"And you could answer questions she might have," Dalt adds with an approving rumble. "But if there's a problem, you talk to me. You don't arrange anything without me. Understood?"

"Geeze, stop with all the dire warnings. It's not like I ran away," Lakin mutters.

"Yes, ran away. Not innocent." Palforma argues with an amused rumble. "Broke a gate, run away. Captured and caged. Broke gate again, run into the forest for Dalt. Broke a ship, wait for Dalt. Always breaking things. Always getting away. You're trouble with toes."

Palforma's teasing makes Lakin break out into laughter. "Those were all extreme circumstances," she protests. Turning her attention to Derani, she gives him a sheepish smile. "I might have a reputation. But don't worry. If Nalia's happy, I won't interfere."

"I think I'll be listening in on this conversation," he comments, eyeing Lakin with concern. "I'm beginning to believe Palforma's correct when he referred to you as trouble on two feet."

"Maybe," she answers impudently. "But everyone needs a hobby."

Dalt sounds an amused rumble. "Enough banter. We need to get moving. You and I need to get back to Kalor and Palforma needs to get this to Umeal Colony." He holds up a secure, nontypical information square.

These types of information squares can't be accessed by any computer unless it has the correct key-code, so it can't be hacked into through remote means. Even if it's stolen, it's keyed to specific bio-signatures so unauthorized persons can't access the information held inside. It's the most secure way to transport data but also slow because it has to be physically couriered from one place to another.

"This is keyed to your bio-signature," Dalt explains as he hands it to Palforma. "It's not keyed to interface with any other device. That's as secure as we could get. You know what to do."

Palforma takes the information square and rattles with tension. "I know plan. I know actions. I make sure this falls into correct claws."

Dalt rumbles out an encouraging sound and then turns to Derani.

"I thank you again, Captain Derani. If I'd known you had a human, I would have told my parents to secure another transport for Palforma, but it's too late now. I'd offer to take care of your human until this is all done, but…" He leaves the rest unsaid. What Talin in their right mind would give up a newly acquired human to another Talin?

"Nalia safe," Palforma insists. "No leave. No need. She's like Lakin. Bright. Blinding. Not intimidated. Quick, quick, quick."

"I trust your judgment, Palforma." Dalt's comment makes Palforma give a brief rumble of pleasure.

"Prove," Palforma says with eagerness. "Prove my worth again."

"You already have," Dalt argues. "You don't need to prove anything."

Derani realizes that both Dalt and Palforma were injured during the same incursion. These two are soldiers who came home broken from war. They might have survived, but neither man is whole. Yet Dalt is obviously happy while Palforma is coping.

Then he remembers Palforma's plaintive words about no human ever picking him as if that's the ultimate goal instead of honoring his clan or serving the Talin species.

Now that he has Nalia in his life, he can't fault Palforma for having that priority.

CHAPTER 26

Unlike the first time Derani left her behind on the ship, this time she's all alone and has the run of the entire place. She can't exit. He's locked down all the external hatches, but she's free to wander everywhere else.

It's nice to walk the ship at her leisure without Derani ready to pick her up and carry her off the moment she stumbles or takes a bad step. He also left her with access to all the information systems so she can pull up diagrams and manuals for the ship on any display.

Her bio-signature can't unlock any systems, but it's entertaining to read about the ship as she moves from room to room. The Amity was a single-engine standard O-frame hauler. The Bountiful has three engines, each one twice the size of the Amity's single engine, and is the much fancier A-frame hauler. It even has a comm array, so Derani only needs to use repeater arrays unless the distance he's trying to contact is extreme.

When the display she's reading pings to tell her someone's opening one of the outside hatches, her first reaction is surprise. The guys left only a little while ago. How did they get back so quickly?

She taps the display and anxiety hits her. The hatch that's being opened is a service hatch in the belly, not the main entry hatch on the side of the ship. That can only mean one thing. Someone is sneaking on board Bountiful.

She doesn't have many options and no way to contact Derani. Argh, why didn't she think to ask him to program his Ident's link-up address into her information square before he left?

Whoever is on board is either here to steal or sabotage. Unfortunately, if they're here to steal, the thing they might try to take could be her!

She's not a fighter and doesn't have access to any weapons, so her best option is hiding. If they are here to sabotage, it will be easy enough to help Derani track down whatever they might have touched once he gets back.

As long as she remains undiscovered.

Sprinting down the hall, she's thankful for the slippers that make her flight almost soundless. The best place to hide is in cargo bay one. It's the largest and has access panels in several places that she could slip into.

As the door down the hall opens, she hears voices calling out in the hall. "Nalia? We need to speak to you. We aren't here to hurt you! Please approach us. There is little time and we must speak with you urgently!"

Well, that answers the question of what the intruders' intentions are. They're here for her. She refuses to be stolen again.

Ducking into the cargo bay, she runs to a far access panel and pulls it loose. Nope, no way she's going to fit in there.

Looking around, she notices a battered box. Throwing open the door, she finds it's mostly empty. It's a tight fit, but she squeezes herself into the small space and closes the door over her.

It's a good thing she isn't claustrophobic because she's so wedged in she can't breathe in too deeply or her chest will pop the door open.

When she hears the bay hatch open again, fear spikes through her. This can't be good. Out of all the places they could search, they end up here?

"Are you sure this is correct?" one voice asks. "This area doesn't look comfortable."

The other voice makes a sound of agreement, but it isn't a rattle or rumble. It's almost like the sound Hax used to make when he was thinking about something. "I agree. This isn't a place a human would probably want to spend much time. She must think we are intent on hurting her and is hiding from us."

"How do we prove we mean no harm?" one of them asks. By the sound of the voices, at least three strangers are in the cargo bay now, and they're getting closer to her hiding spot. She hears a series of pings, and then the voices are right next to her.

"She's hidden in here," one announces, and she hears something tap on the box.

"She must be small to have fit in there," the other responds.

"Hax said she was tiny, a third of his size," the third voice adds.

Hax? They know Hax? She's about to ask a question when one voice starts talking to her.

"Nalia Gaborn, originally of the human colony of Wolder, we are here at our pod mate's request. It would please us greatly if you emerged. We would like to speak to you."

Feeling mildly foolish, Nalia opens the box door and wiggles free. In front of her are three Ollies, all watching her with curiosity. One of them has a bio-tracking unit strapped to his middle. Both she and Hax had their DNA on file in the Amity computer, so they must have used that to program the bio-tracker to look for her. No wonder they found her so quickly.

She asks the first thing that comes to mind, seeing these Ollies that claim to be Hax's siblings. "Is Hax well?"

"He is very well, thanks to you," one of them answers. "He suffered the loss of all his limbs on the journey back to one of our colonies after he was released from this ship. The governing services there were able to contact us so we could collect him. He is home and recovering now. We are all very joyful to have him back."

Relief fills her. "That's good."

She never told Derani, but she worried Hax might not be able to pilot all the way back to the Ollie colony by himself, even with the navigation already programmed for him. His anxiety couldn't just cripple him mentally, but it could quite literally cripple him physically as well.

It looks like her fears were justified because he shed all his tentacles on the trip. Poor Hax.

"He told the pod about your sacrifice," the one on the left explains. "He's alive because you willingly gave up your freedom."

"We're here to repay his debt," the one on the right adds. He points a tentacle to her jeweled collar. "We can't take you with us, so please don't ask. We can't risk that the Talin authorities might find out we were involved in your escape. But we can give you the means to free yourself."

The Ollie in the center holds out a waist sack. Because Ollie bodies don't have shoulders, they secure things to their person with bags tied around their body-stalks between their talking mouth and the top of the ring of tentacles around the base of their body-stalk. It would be too big for Nalia to wear around her middle, but she can sling it over her shoulder to carry.

"There are tools to open locked hatches, money, clothing, and a list of contacts that can help relocate or hide you once you're away from your owner. We suggest you wait until you're docked at a non-Talin-controlled colony or station before attempting to flee."

"We can't offer you sanctuary because Hax's pod is the first place they might look for you," the one on the right explains regretfully.

"We're sorry we can't do more," the one in the middle adds.

Nalia hugs the overflowing sack to her chest. "This is more than I ever expected. Thank you."

"Our Hax is special to the pod. We were all very fearful when he decided to work by himself. He's a delicate Ollie. Few would have put up with him, let alone cared for him as you did. Your kindness and selflessness have been noted in our pod histories."

Warmth fills Nalia. Not only is it good to find out that Hax made it home safely, but also to know that he's being looked after. Her last worry over her old life is gone.

"Tell Hax I regret nothing," she instructs the Ollie. "Tell him I still don't blame him and that I'm fine."

"We will report back that you appear healthy and undamaged," the Ollie in the middle agrees. "And that we were able to give you the tools to escape."

"We must go," the Ollie on the right announces as he holds up a small information square with one of his tentacles. We have a timer running, and it's rapidly approaching all zeros. "Our time margin is almost gone."

Impulsively, Nalia drops the sack and grabs the three Ollies up in a hug as best she can. "Thank you," she says. "It was brave of you to find me and I feel much better knowing Hax is safe."

The Ollies let her embrace them for a moment before shuffling away. She lets them go and picks the bag back up.

"We will leave as we came and re-secure everything," the one in the middle says. "There will be no evidence we were here. You will need to find a place to hide what we've given you until the appropriate time. Hax assured us that you are smart, so we are sure you'll gain your freedom as long as you plan carefully. Remember, if you are caught, you can't tell anyone we helped you. It could cause our pod great trouble."

"I won't," she assures them. She follows as they make their way to the belly of Bountiful and exit through the service hatch they came in. The drop they're forced to endure to get out through the hatch is too far for a human to handle, but they absorb the impact easily.

Once they're gone and the hatch is re-secured, she makes her way back to her quarters and upends the bag onto her bunk.

All the stuff they gave her makes her feel like a kid in a candy store. She finds an information square with a universal link-up number and an account loaded with funds so she can pay her way anywhere she needs to go. The amount they've given her is surprising and is more than enough to support her for almost an entire solar if she lives modestly.

She also finds tools. Some could break her collar off. Others can force doors open. The clothes could belong to any low-wage ship employee and would help her blend in on any dock or space station.

This bag full of items would allow her to escape Derani. It wouldn't even need to take much planning, just access to a large space station where Talins have little to no influence.

After creating a distraction, she could slip away. Once off the Bountiful, all it would take would be a change of clothes and removal of her collar. She'd be able to walk around and no one would look at her twice. Then she could purchase passage on a transport ship and could be gone before Derani even knows she's missing.

But she has no interest in getting away from Derani. She isn't going to tell him about the Ollies or their gift, but she isn't going to use it to escape either. She loves Derani and is starting to feel a lot of affection for Talins in general—at least the ones she's met so far.

But having these tools means she could leave if she wanted to. And that makes all the difference between feeling trapped and content.

Now to figure out where she's going to hide them.

CHAPTER 27

"Good," Palforma praises.

Nalia is red-faced and sweating, but she's feeling pleased with herself. They've been practicing for almost a full mark and Nalia's getting the hang of pulling the tiny practice dagger out and stabbing with it. Or pulling free of a Talin holding her and then pulling out the dagger and stabbing.

She's suspicious that Palforma is making it easy for her to get out of his grip, but she isn't going to argue. The guy is big, strong, and skilled. She'll take any break he wants to give her while she learns.

"I don't see why I can't learn to use a stunner," she complains as she stows the dagger up the sleeve of her omnie without looking. That was the first lesson Palforma taught her—to pull out her dagger and put it back without having to look as she did it.

"Need to grab weapons. Need to sight. Need to squeeze the trigger. Need to be steady. Very much to do in a hurry. Attackers no wait. Attackers no pause. This is quicker. Get distance. Get help." He taps the sleeve of her omnie hiding the tiny dagger. "Stunner big. Blaster big. Distance weapons big. Where hide?"

She glances down at herself. All the weapons he's talking about would be much too bulky to hide on her person, even with the omnie on. The tiny practice dagger is about the only thing she could reasonably conceal.

"You make a point," she grumps.

Palforma sounds a rumble of amusement. "Don't expect you to fight. Hide first. Pretend to cooperate second. Fight only if necessary."

"Yeah, don't worry. I know the drill," she assures him. "I'm not about to get into a tussle with anyone if I can help it."

Derani steps up behind her, sounding a soothing rumble. "Don't scare her, Palforma. It's unlikely she'll ever be in danger."

Palforma sounds a rattle of disagreement. "Right now, more likely. Right now, danger. Sides fighting and humans stuck between." He looks down at Nalia. "You rest, I work with Derani now."

"Good idea," she agrees, more than ready to sit down and take a breather. She pulls up her sleeve to take off the practice dagger and sheath attached to her forearm, but Palforma's rattle stops her.

"Keep on," he instructs. "Live with it. Learn it. Be used to it. Make part of you. Yes?"

"Sure thing," she agrees and tugs the sleeve back down. Honestly, the small sheath fits her forearm so perfectly that it could have been made for a human. That leads her to another question: Why would Palforma be carrying around a tiny dagger and sheath that are sized for a human limb? She wants to ask but is afraid that she might make Palforma sad. It's obvious he's desperate for a human of his own. He probably had this set made hoping to gift it to a human who "picks him."

"Good," Palforma says with an approving rumble. "You use if need to. No hesitation. No second thoughts. When in danger, you aim true. Yes?"

She understands that philosophy well. Any human out on their own lives by it or they don't last long. "If it comes down to it, I'll make sure my stab is just like you taught me. Right in one of the weak points."

Palforma rumbles with approval. "If it's them or you. Always needs to be you. They die; you live."

"Not that a Talin would want to cause you harm on purpose," Derani interrupts. "Most only want to steal you for themselves not cause you harm."

She gives Derani a sardonic look. "Like Eora? I'm pretty sure I ended up in medical because of her, sicker than I've ever been in my life."

Palforma rattles in rage. "Who Eora?"

"Easy, big guy. It wasn't like that. Well, not entirely like that," Nalia says quickly and then explains what happened.

Palforma's anger calms with the explanation, but now his focus switches to Derani. "This why train. Practice. Skills keep our humans safe."

"I did mention that my crew and I were greatly outnumbered. Didn't I?" Derani asks wryly.

Palforma doesn't answer. With a speed she's still not accustomed to, he picks her up and swings her onto his back. Instinct makes her wrap her arms around the big Talin's neck as he moves away from Derani. Weapons up, he takes up a defensive posture as if ready to engage Derani, even with her riding piggyback.

Sounding a warning rattle, Derani doesn't engage the ex-soldier. "What do you think you're doing?"

"Showing," Palforma explains simply. "Human cling well. She there, me here. Can protect, retreat, hands are free to fight."

Now that Nalia understands what Palforma is demonstrating, she makes herself a bit more secure on his back. She's not worried about cutting off his air because the armor plating around a Talin's neck isn't something her bare arms could crush. But she feels she needs to point something out. "I wouldn't be able to hang here that long. Even with my legs wrapped around."

Standing up straight, Palforma adjusts her a little and shows her where she can put her feet on the edges of the armor ridges on his hips. With that, she feels much more secure. "Okay, now I think I could hold on for a lot longer."

"Make clinging easier. Yes?" He moves a little, and she finds it isn't hard to stay balanced on his back.

"Much easier," she agrees, but even though she can hold on fine, Palforma's scent is bothering her.

As if reading the new tension in her, he reaches back and grabs her. Swinging her around, he hands her over to Derani with the easy strength of a Talin. "You now. Practice."

Nalia can't help but giggle as Derani maneuvers her onto his back. He's a little more awkward about it than Palforma, but that's when she realizes this is a technique the ex-soldier has practiced. He's deliberately figured out how to fight with a human on his back so he could defend them.

All kinds of warm feelings flood Nalia and more than ever, she hopes Palforma finds a human of his own.

"This feels unsafe," Derani comments once she's gotten herself situated on his back.

She tests her hold. "I'm pretty secure back here. Move around a little." Derani takes a few slow and careful steps, making Nalia laugh. "You can move more than that. I promise not to fall off. And I'll warn you if I'm going to lose my grip. Palforma's right. This a good thing for us to practice."

"Can help Derani defend," Palforma adds as he steps up close. He reaches a hand out to pretend to grab her. "Little dagger here," he explains as he points to a joint in his armor at his elbow. "Reach across, like this," he shows her how to pull her dagger and swipe across the vulnerable spot in one move. "Together greater. Better than separate."

"I see the wisdom in this," Derani agrees. They spend half a mark practicing different moves with her on Derani's back. It doesn't take long before she can figure out what Derani's going to do from feeling the shifts of his body under her.

That makes her think of sex and the next thing she knows, both Talin have stopped dead in their tracks and are sniffing the air.

Thoroughly embarrassed because she knows what they must smell, she drops down from Derani's back.

"I think that's enough for now," she declares, hoping her face isn't as red as it feels. "I need a break. You two go ahead and practice your stuff without me."

Derani hovers over her anxiously. "Your pores are exuding liquid even though you are no longer moving. This training was more vigorous than I expected, but you seemed to enjoy yourself. Should I have stopped everything sooner? Was hanging off of me too much?"

"Is that your way of saying I'm sweaty and gross?" she teases with a grin. "Honestly, I'm fine. Now it's your turn to be the center of Palforma's attention."

She gives him a little playful shove, which doesn't move him at all. Leaning over, he swipes a cheek across the top of her head. Orange and clove fills her nose and her smile widens. "And now I'm perfect."

Straightening up, he gives her a quick purr. "Hydrate yourself and rest. After Palforma and I are done, we'll all share a meal."

She's not hungry yet but knows she will be soon. "That sounds great."

As Derani turns back to Palforma, she saunters to the kneeling pad near the door. Several canisters of drinking water sit there, so she settles down and opens one up.

The water is cool and soothing to her throat. From the comfort of her seat, she observes Derani and Palforma practice. As with her, Palforma starts slowly. They go over the same move again and again until Derani can do it without thinking about it first. Then they add another move and then another one. Soon the two of them are moving back and forth across the open space, trading blows and blocks.

As she watches, her mind wanders. It's been an entire rotation since meeting the Ollies and getting the bag of goodies. Everything is tucked in one of the drawers Derani assigned her. It's the place she keeps all her slippers and a few other odds and ends. Derani lets her pick out her clothes each day, so he rarely has a reason to open any of those draws. Even if he finds everything, she's not worried about reprisal. He'll probably be amused more than anything else.

She's setting the half-empty canister on the floor when Derani goes flying by her, hits the wall near her and slides to the floor with a grunt. Surprised and worried, she scrambles over to him.

"Derani?" She pats around, looking for broken bones, but Derani opens his eyes and rumbles out a purr.

"I'm not injured," he assures her. Sitting up, he gathers her into his lap and starts petting her back as if she needs comforting.

Palforma hurries up to them, rumbling with distress. "No throw! No throw!"

Looking up at him, Nalia's eyebrows furrow. "Uh, pretty sure you threw him. Unless a ghost tossed him into the wall."

The big warrior drops to his knees and meets Nalia's eyes. His rumble has an appeasing tone to it now. "No mean. Not intent. No… no… not purpose."

"I was my fault," Derani explains. "I thought I could counter his last move, and he acted out of instinct. If I'd stuck to our practice, he wouldn't have thrown me."

Palforma rumbles out a sound of agreement. "Yes! Like that, yes."

"Ah, thought you could best the teacher. Did you?" she asks.

"I'm guilty," he admits.

He sounds fine, but the hit was hard enough to leave a slight dent in the wall plating. "Maybe we should call it a day and hit medical for a scan?"

Derani sounds an amused rumble. "Nothing is broken, and I'd like to finish practicing. Unless that would cause you undue stress."

She might be the one wearing a collar with the title of "pet," but she almost feels in charge. Or more accurately, she feels like an equal partner. Derani is willing to consult with her to avoid upsetting her. It's the definition of caring and not something she's used to at all.

Later, when they're alone, she's going to give him all the neck rubs he likes as a reward. He's still shy about asking for anything, so she'll have to insist. But a Talin this considerate deserves to be taken care of in turn.

At least she doesn't have to push for sex anymore. He is more than willing to comply when she asks now. That makes her grin.

"Go practice. Just don't get yourself hurt." That last sentence is half directed at Palforma.

"Check instinct. Careful. Won't damage." Palforma pauses a moment and then sounds a rumble of amusement before adding, "Much."

Almost a full mark later, Palforma is finally satisfied with Derani's progress and calls a halt to their session. After banging their palms against their chests, Derani is striding toward her when an alarm sounds. It's not one she's heard before, but it must be serious because Derani hurries to a nearby display and taps it.

"Something's wrong," he declares with a rattle. He turns to Palforma. "Do you have the secure information square?"

Palforma rumbles out an affirmation as he points to his weapons bag. "Always in sight."

"Good. Grab it and follow me to the control room. I'm going to need your help." Both his tone and body are tense.

Nalia scrambles to her feet. "Derani, what's going on?"

"I think we might be under attack. I need you to secure yourself in my cabin."

She shakes her head. "Hell, no. You'll need all the help you can get."

Derani sounds a loud irritable rattle. "I need you safe."

Palforma sounds a calming rumble at the same time an alarm echoes through the ship again. He talks once the alarm quiets. "Better together. In sight. In reach. No waited time if have to run. Grab and go."

Derani makes a frustrated rattle. "Fine! But hurry!"

He turns on his heels and races out of the room. Nalia is about to follow when Palforma grabs her arm to stop her. Puzzled, she looks back only to have him drag her to his bag.

"What—" she starts but is interrupted when he pulls something out of his bag and shoves it at her. She takes it automatically and then realizes he's given her a real dagger the same size and shape as the practice one.

"Take," he orders her. "Hide. Use. No be brave, but no hesitated either. Yes?"

Quickly, she pulls up her sleeve and tugs off the practice dagger and sheath before putting on the stiffer sheath holding a small but wicked blade. The extra weight feels comforting on her arm.

"Thanks, Palforma," she says and grabs him in a quick hug around the waist.

He gives her one quick pat on the back and then pulls away. Picking up his bag, he points to the open door. "Join Derani. Trouble followed me."

They hurry out of the room and head down the hall toward the control room. She tries for optimism. "It could be nothing."

Palforma sounds an aggressive rattle. "It is something. Something disloyal. Dishonest. Unworthy."

She wants to ask a question but all kinds of alarms sound as they step into the control room.

Derani is rattling with anger. "We're under attack."

It looks like Palforma is correct. Trouble found them.

CHAPTER 28

This is not the first time Derani has dealt with an attack, but it is the first time he's had to enter into combat without a crew. His ship might be designed for trading, but no Talin worth anything would have a completely defenseless ship. At least this time he's on a ship that has automatic gun targeting and better maneuvering capabilities. Hopefully, that will be enough to make up for his lack of skilled crew.

"Nalia, take Yulian's station," he barks out once he's silenced the alarms. "Palforma, take the station to the far right. I'm going to give you control of the aft gun. They're targeting our engines. All hits have been deflected so far, but it would only take one shot to disable us."

Both Nalia and Palforma take their designated seats without comment. Nalia sends out distress signals and requests for Talin support even before he needs to order her to.

"This is the Talin merchant ship Bountiful," she broadcasts. "We are under attack by unknown assailants. Requesting aid."

As she puts that distress call on repeat along with their current coordinates, Derani feels one of the rear guns fire. The ship shudders slightly, and the navigation system is thrown into a frenzy trying to compensate.

He ignores that for now. The moment he got to his console, he set the system to use maximum engine capacity so they could try to gain distance on the less powerful ship chasing them, but keeping the original destination is too far away to be helpful. They need to find help closer. His focus is on looking at a list of the closest stations, colonies, or planets that can lend aid to a ship under attack.

Again, it's almost like Nalia is reading his mind. "Brinmare is closest but Declow's perimeter satellites are an equal distance and would probably give us a better protection than trying to get into Brinmare's orbit."

When he looks over at her, he notices her eyes are closed. It's curious, but he doesn't have time to ask her why or worry about her. First, he needs to get them all to safety. Then he can figure out why his pet is sitting there with her eyes shut as she talks.

"Neither of those two are Talin," Derani notes as he brings up those two options.

Eyes still closed, Nalia nods. "There are no Talin-controlled or owned colonies or stations within range. But Declow is Delorta, and I know the Talins have a bunch of exclusive trade agreements with them. They should protect us."

"But at what cost?" Derani mutters and starts setting a course for Declow.

"Anything's cheaper than all of us dying," Nalia points out as she opens her eyes to regard him with a furrowed brow.

"Delortas are strange about our pets," he tells her while he stares at his display and waits for the data to come back.

"Huh, I didn't know that," she murmurs as the calculations begin appearing on his display. The numbers make him realize that Nalia made the right call. Declow station's defensive satellites are slightly closer than Brinmare. If the ship chasing them fires at them once they're within range of the satellites, the guns on those satellites will vaporize it. To put it mildly, the Delortas take station safety and aggressive behavior seriously.

Now they need to survive long enough to get in range of Declow's satellites.

Derani had the Bountiful outfitted with two large guns—one fore and one aft. The enemy ship is behind them, so Palforma doesn't have to divide his attention between the two guns. He's rattling aggressively as he sets up to fire the aft gun again.

The ship shakes and shifts.

The sound of Palforma's frustrated rattle tells Derani he missed.

"Deflectors," Palforma hisses as he sets up another shot.

"Try targeting the area right behind the maneuvering thrusters on the belly," Nalia suggests. Derani hears Palforma's rattle of surprise at the same time he looks over at his pet.

"Why?" he asks for both of them.

Her eyes are open now, and she's looking at the display on her console. She glances up long enough to answer. "I worked on a ship like that once, and the deflectors have a seam line right there. You'll have to do some fancy targeting with an autopiloting round, but if you can hit there, it will do damage even with the deflectors on. If the hit is good enough, it could cripple the ship."

Derani swings his gaze to Palforma. "Try it."

Palforma bends over his console and starts tapping, muttering indecipherable words to himself as he works. Soon the aft gun fires, and he checks the rear sensor data. The ship chasing them falters. Momentum keeps it coming, but now the Bountiful is quickly gaining distance.

"They shut down their engines," he reports as he switches from one sensor to another.

"Oh shit! Brace yourselves!" Nalia shouts as she throws herself against the back of her chair and grabs the sides. Derani only has enough time to look down at his display when the ship bucks violently around him.

His expanded console keeps him in his seat, but the intense movement confuses all his senses for several precious submarks.

"Hit," Palforma calls out as he scrambles to get back into his chair. Nalia is leaning forward over her console and tapping a display.

"I can't shut down engine two," she calls out. "I don't have the authority. Derani, you need to do it."

Shaking his head to clear it, he straightens up and sees that half his console displays are cracked and broken. He moves to one still working on the far left and brings up the command sequence to shut down the engine while keeping the other two engaged.

"What happened?" he asks as he works.

"Got hit," Palforma answers tersely.

Derani sounds an annoyed rattle. "I know, but I thought you disabled them."

"I heard the shot. It was from their port gun, not the belly. I think it was a desperation move because they're fucked now. Firing that gun sent them spinning and they can't stop it without the maneuvering thrusters that Palforma shot off."

Looking up, she points down at something on her display. "They're headed straight into that gas giant. It'll crush them."

"Forget about them. We need to make sure we don't end up in a gas giant also," Derani comments grimly as he checks the displays that are still working. Both engine one and three are fine, but engine two will need to be replaced. The problem is that the engines have linked fuel systems, so shutting off engine two means engine three will run out of fuel within a quarter of a mark.

Running on one engine isn't an option. Going forward isn't the issue, but slowing down is. With only one engine, it will be almost impossible to flip the ship over and slow themselves down by firing the engines in the direction they're going. He normally uses that braking maneuver when going to places without warp corridors.

He does some quick calculations. They have enough momentum now that if he reduces the burn rate, they should have enough fuel to perform a braking maneuver once they reach Declow station.

"Declow is responding," Nalia calls out. "They're willing to meet us with a tug-ship if we need it."

"Redirect the comm-link to my station," Derani orders her.

"Sure thing," she answers and taps away. Soon he sees it on his console. He's quick to work out the logistics with Declow, as well as payment for the tow and the use of a bay instead of a docking slip. Further negotiations will need to wait until they can assess the damage to Bountiful.

Once he's finished, he checks the stats on the engines. Number three is already sputtering, despite his earlier calculation that it would last long enough to get to Declow. Good thing the tug-ships can grab and slow a ship as well as guide it to the station.

"In less than a mark, we will be on Declow," Derani announces to his impromptu crew.

Nalia makes a sound by pursing her lips. It takes a moment for Derani to remember that humans call it a whistle. "It's going to be expensive to have the repairs done there. But they have some of the best repair shops in this sector, so I guess if you can afford it, we'll be okay."

"I can afford it," Derani assures her and then pushes his almost useless console out of his way. Bounding to his feet, he covers the distance between them in a single stride and plucks her up from her chair.

"You're brilliant," he announces, hugging her to his chest.

She snuggles against him. "I didn't do much. But if you want to reward me, there's that cocoa powder in the galley you still haven't let me touch."

"Forget that powder. I will mine you whole chunks of the mineral myself!"

Lifting her gaze, she wrinkles her nose at him. "It comes from a tree. I think it's a nut. But I'd be happy with the powder. I don't need an entire tree."

"I'll find you whatever you desire," Derani promises. "I'm astonished at your skills and calm demeanor under dire circumstances. Now I understand better how you were able to survive with that Ollie for so long. You're truly a unique and capable human."

"Agreed," Palforma says with an appreciative rumble.

Derani looks over at him, checking for injuries, but the big Talin looks fine. "This attack doesn't make any sense."

"They were trying to stop us, not destroy," Nalia points out. "Maybe they thought we were hauling valuable cargo."

That's when it hits Derani. He slides his gaze to Palforma. As usual, the big Talin's bag is slung across his shoulder. Suspicion fills him. "It's you. Isn't it?"

Palforma jerks as if Derani hit him with an electrical current. "Not this way. Not the plan. Follow me, but wait. Get me alone. Too soon. Too soon for this."

Nalia taps Derani on the shoulder. "Put me down, please."

A rattle of reluctance comes out of him, but he lets her slide down to stand on her own feet. After she's turned to face Palforma, he drapes his arms around her. He's not ready to let her out of his reach yet.

His little human's eyes narrow as she regards Palforma suspiciously. "Did you know we were going to be attacked?"

Palforma sounds an uncomfortable rumble, halfway between embarrassed and ashamed. "Not here. Not now."

Nalia's voice is impatient when she speaks. "I don't understand. You expected to be attacked but not on the Bountiful?"

Palforma slaps a hand on his bag. "Have information square. Nothing real. Nothing helpful. Most fake with little truths sewn in. They want. Make them steal so they think it's real. But not here. Not now. Later. Attack me on Umeal Colony. Take it there. Only me in danger. No one else."

"That's a solid plan," Nalia says, and Derani can hear the admiration in her voice. "Trick them into stealing fake data." She pauses for a moment, thinking. "And if my guess is right, the info they are trying to steal would end up outing them. Right? I read that one of the issues you guys are having is that you don't know who is a militant Traditionalist and who isn't. Who wants to overthrow the entire government and who is still a loyal Talin first and Traditionalist second? If you can make them reveal themselves, it would be a lot easier."

Palforma rattles out a shocked sound. "How?"

The big warrior isn't the only one who's shocked. Derani can't believe his little human is so perceptive. He knows she's smart, but this type of deductive reasoning is beyond the pale.

Nalia makes a derisive sound. "I can read. It's all on the UniBase."

"What do you mean it's all on the UniBase?" Derani questions.

Her eyes unfocus as she speaks. "In his article titled 'The Power of Traditionalist Mindset,' Javron of the Purlian Clan posted the idea that Talins have outgrown the Traditionalist ideals. But because Talins are fearful of being perceived as weak by other species, they are reluctant to change any of the laws or ideologies." She opens her eyes and smiles at him. "That article led me to read all about Traditionalism and Reformism."

"Much to read," Palforma grunts.

"There sure is, on both sides," she agrees. "By the way, I'm really glad you're a Reformist. Some of the Traditionalists have scary views regarding humans."

Derani sounds a rumble of curiosity. "You sounded like you were quoting Javron. Did you memorize this article?"

"Not really," she says with one of those adorable human shrugs. "I mean, I don't mean to memorize stuff. I don't know how it works, but I can always remember what I read. My mom said her grandmother had a similar talent for remembering."

"Amazing. What else have you learned?"

"Well, Javron referenced a report by Himorl, so I read that one next. Himorl was a little dry because she's a numbers person, but she does a good job of explaining the numbers at the end of her report." She closes her eyes again. This must help her recall what she's read. "The trend toward Reformism is clear. If current inclinations continue, within three generations we will probably see a reversal of laws regarding marriage, scent-bonding, childbirth, and child care. Semocheli's work on birth and death rates per providence provides further evidence to support the conclusions of this report."

A rumble of amusement comes out of Derani. "Can I suppose you read Semocheli's research next?"

Blinking her eyes open, she gives him a big grin. "Yup, want me to quote it?"

"I don't believe that will be necessary," he replies. "You have a singular skill, Nalia."

"I'm not sure you could call it a skill," she demurs. "I was born this way."

"But you've taken the time to read all those articles, reports, and research on the UniBase. That's dedication," he argues. "It's one thing to read all those things and remember facts. But you put all those facts into a cohesive understanding of Talin culture and politics. That's an example of both talent and dedication to learning." Then something occurs to Derani. "That's how you knew what was close to our location? Have you been memorizing trade routes and species in this sector?"

"And what kind of political agreements they have with Talins." Her expression suddenly turns anxious. "It seemed like a good idea. Are you upset?"

"Absolutely not. You're an incredible human, Nalia," Derani declares and watches the skin of her face flush from pleasure at his praise.

Unfortunately, Palforma's next words extinguish his joyful mood.

"Probably more. Out there. Waiting. Back up to the first ship. Need to plan. Prepare. Don't want Nalia hurt. Don't want Derani hurt. Buy you ship. Buy you transport. Get you away from me."

He might not like Palforma's words, but Nalia's response fills him with dread.

"We aren't abandoning you, big guy," she insists, her expression turning stubborn. "There's no way we're leaving you to deal with this on your own. That's a good way to end up dead. No one's dying on my watch, not if I can help it."

CHAPTER 29

They have to leave the ship while it's being repaired, so now she needs to pack enough for a few days on Declow station. Normally that wouldn't an issue. She's a quick and efficient packer. The problem is that Derani decided to help her pack.

"The Delorta homeworld is an ice planet so they keep their stations cold compared to what other species are accustomed to," Derani explains as he rolls up an omnie. "We'll be able to raise the ambient temperature in the room we rent, but the rest of the station will be almost inhospitable to you."

"Right, but I don't think I need all three omnies," she protests. "I can see wearing two at one time, but not all three. And packing all six sets of slippers seems excessive too. You said repairs should be done in a few rotations."

"It could be longer, and once they start work, we won't be allowed back on board," he warns her as he shoves more items into her bag. With a small smile, she gives up and lets Derani pack almost everything.

Once he's done, the pack is just about as big and as heavy as she is. In contrast, the bag he packed for himself is only a little bigger than his belt pouch.

She tries to pick up his bag because he has to carry hers, but his rattle stops her in her tracks. Rolling her eyes, she steps back and lets him carry everything.

They meet up with Palforma at the ramp leading off the ship. A strong breeze moves her hair as the outside hatch opens and the pressure between the bay and ship equalize. Then cold hits her. She's only been on one ice planet before and this station feels only a modicum warmer than there.

Experimentally, she opens her mouth and breathes out, noting the way her breath fogs from the cold. Now she understands why Derani was so insistent on packing as many warm articles of clothing as he could. He warned her it would be cold, but she didn't expect this place to be kept at such a shockingly low temperature.

She glances first at Derani and then at Palforma. Both are wearing their pants and belts but no other clothing. Not even boots on their feet. Neither seems bothered by the cold.

She tucks her hands inside the sleeves of her omnie and wishes she had a scarf as she follows Derani down the ramp.

As they get to the bottom of the ramp, she can see a vast bay stretching out all around them. It's busy with crews of Delortas working on ships, shuttles, and comm arrays. A small group of Delortas are headed toward them, probably the crew to do the repairs on the Bountiful.

When her mom saw a picture of a Delorta, she claimed they looked a lot like a mythical creature on old Earth called a centaur. They have four stocky legs to ambulate with and a tall torso at the front of their bodies, equipped with four arms. The lower two arms, called strength arms, are short and densely muscled. The upper two are referred to as reaching arms, long and lean with four fingers, two on either side of their palm. Their bodies are covered in thick fur in various shades of brown and deep green. Their faces are mostly humanoid, with two eyes, a noise, and mouth. But their mouth is large, and their eyes are small and hard to see behind all the fur on their face.

Although she's read about them and seen vids, this is the first time she's ever seen one in person. She desperately wants to feel the texture of the fur but knows better than to touch another species. It can be dangerous to even ask. In some cultures, verbalizing a request to make physical contact can be considered an insult. She hasn't read up on the Delortas yet, so she isn't sure. And the last thing she wants to do is to cause an international incident between the Delortas and Talins.

But they all look so soft and fluffy! Some have fur so thick and long that it dangles down to obscure their legs almost to their squarish feet.

"Captain Derani," the Delorta in front of the group greets him. "It's an honor that you've chosen our station for your repairs. We're happy to assist such a distinguished Talin. My name is Tal-tok, and I'm the bay chief." As he introduces himself, Tal-tok bends both front legs and does a kind of bow. Derani bends his knees to mimic the movement.

"The honor is mine," Derani answers. "This station and those who run it are well-known for their quality work."

Tal-tok nods solemnly. "We have also secured accommodations for you. I'm afraid we are very busy at the moment, so there is only one room available. But it has several sleeping platforms and plenty of cushions to make beds on the floor, so you and your crew should fit."

"It's only me, Palforma, and my pet," Derani explains, gesturing behind him at Palforma and then down at Nalia. When Tal-tok's eyes drop to her, she waves and remembers not to smile. Most species see the showing of teeth as a threat display, so humans learn quickly to curb that impulse.

Not only does Tal-tok not wave back, but he also hisses out a breath and stamps a front foot. "What is the meaning of this?"

Confused, Nalia takes a step back and half hides behind Derani. "I'm sorry. It was a wave. It didn't mean anything bad. I promise. Humans do it to greet each other. Or to say goodbye."

Derani drops their bags and sweeps an arm around so he's half holding her to his back. He sounds a warning rattle. "My pet is no threat to you."

Stomping a big foot again, Tal-tok glares at Derani. "I know what a wave is. Don't be daft. That's not why I'm outraged, you thieving Talin!"

The dozen Delortas behind Tal-tok mumble angrily among themselves and also stomp their feet. Nalia is in shock. What's going on here? Tal-tok was so gracious a moment ago, but now he's calling them thieves. Does he think one of their packs belongs to someone here on the station?

"We haven't stolen anything, and we aren't here to steal. We're here because the ship needs repairs," she announces quickly. "You can look in our bags if you want to, but they're full of our stuff. No one else's, I swear."

When the Delorta shifts his gaze to Nalia, his expression softens and his voice is kind. "He stole you, little human. I know a collar when I see one. He can cover it in all the jewels he likes, but it's still a collar. No sentient being should be owned. The practice is an abomination."

Now she remembers a line in one of the treaties between the Talin and Delorta that struck her as odd when she read it: *All possessions will be honored, independent of moral or political beliefs.*

That strange line makes more sense now. The Delortas don't approve of slavery to the point that the Talin government had to have it stipulated in the treaty that the Delortas couldn't set a "possession" free. As a pet, she falls under that heading as an owned being. Her status as a pet is upsetting everyone.

She knows from that treaty that the Delortas can't legally take her away from Derani, but it looks like they might want to anyway, despite the political repercussions.

Palforma moves up to stand next to Derani, rattling threateningly. Several of the Delortas behind Tal-tok step forward, stamping feet and pulling back lips to show off rows of uneven, sharp teeth.

A Delorta gallops across the bay, his hard soled feet loud against the steel plating of the floor. He skids to a halt between the two groups and stomps a back foot with enough force to leave a dent in the deck plating. "What is going on here?"

"This Talin owns a human," Tal-tok spits out.

The new arrival grimaces and takes in their small group, spending a few extra moments staring at Nalia's collar. Self-consciously, she runs her fingers over it. If she's honest with herself, she's forgotten she's wearing it. The thing has become a comfortable and familiar weight around her neck.

"This is an unfortunate turn of events," the Delorta says as he looks at Tal-tok. "All of you go to work. I'll deal with this." Then he addresses Derani. "If you would come with me, we can settle this in my office. I'll even turn the temperature up to make all of you more comfortable."

Although he's not even looking at her, Nalia can tell his remark is aimed at her. The other Delortas visibly relax with his words. They pick up the tools and parts they dropped and begin moving away. They're still grumbling about "archaic practices" and "making souls light with dishonorable deeds," but their body language is much calmer.

Derani focuses on the new Delorta and sounds a low warning rattle. "You will not take Nalia away from me."

"Of course I won't. I'm bound by our treaty," he replies, his tone chilly and formal. "And as much as I regret the weight it will take from my soul, I'm forced to ignore this atrocity."

"Nalia is not an atrocity. She's a clever, sweet, and wonderful human," Derani growls out.

That startles the Delorta. His eyes widen, and he takes half a step back before seeming to catch himself. "Why don't you follow me, and we can finish this discussion in my office, away from the others. I'm afraid most Talins know better than to bring a pet here. It doesn't go over well. The sooner we get both of you out of sight, the better."

Looking down at Nalia, the Delorta points to himself. "I'm the station coordinator, Mye-nac. If you come with me, I have refreshments you'll find palatable and warm blankets to bundle in."

Nalia isn't sure about this turn of events. She's gotten used to being treated like a pet, communicated with as if she is a lower intelligence than everyone else. Heck, even before she met Derani, a lot of species treated her like she was mentally deficient. But Mye-nac went from being upset at her very presence to inviting. It's confusing.

"I... uh... thanks?"

Mye-nac nods in approval. "You don't need to fear me or any Delorta. We would set all sentient creatures free if we could. It's only because the Talins are so numerous and strong in the neighboring sector that we allowed the language in the treaty. However, you're the first one that's ever been brought on board. We weren't prepared to see a collared being."

Understanding dawns. It's not her. It's that she is owned by Derani. That's a relief. She'd hate to think the Delortas didn't like humans in general.

She rubs her fingers on her collar. "I can see how that would be upsetting."

He pauses for a second, his eyes flicking to Derani and then back to her. "Are you in pain?" he asks softly. "We have an excellent medical suite here."

For a moment Nalia doesn't understand why he'd ask her that, but then she remembers that part of the treaty mentions that in a state of emergency the Delorta can act as they deem necessary to preserve life. Mye-nac is trying to find any excuse to separate her from Derani, even if he has to call something trivial a "medical emergency."

It's all very sweet but unnecessary.

"I'm not in pain or hungry or cold," she assures him. That last one is only a little bit of a fib. The slippers and omnie are doing a good job of keeping her warm despite the freezing temperature of the station, but the cold is making her eyes sting and her nose run. And her fingers are losing feeling. She puts the opening of her sleeves together so she can join her hands to keep her fingers warm.

Derani is sounding a threatening rattling as he growls at Mye-nac. "I take good care of Nalia. She doesn't need your intervention."

She moves closer to Derani and bumps him with her shoulder. "It's okay," she assures him. "No one is going to take me from you." Then she leans a little closer as she whispers, "At least not without a fight."

Her words have the desired effect. Derani stops rattling threateningly at the Delorta. He turns to pick her up and cuddle her against his chest. Even though he doesn't rub his cheek against her hair, she can smell oranges and cloves. His scent glands must be full to bursting if the scent is that strong without it being in her hair.

Mye-nac shifts in place anxiously. "Is she injured?"

"No, but you scared her," Derani barks at him. Nalia keeps from making an annoyed sound at Derani's lie. She's not scared. He is.

Mye-nac jerks at Derani's loud words and then sighs. "That wasn't my intent. It seems I've mucked this all up. Do please follow me so we can finish this discussion elsewhere."

"Or I could take my pet to our room," Derani challenges him.

Inclining his shaggy head, Mye-nac moves one of his long arms to indicate the surrounding bay. "And we could end up having to work very slowly on your ship, Captain Derani. You came at a busy time for us. It would be a shame if we had to put your repairs at the end of the queue."

To Nalia's surprise, Palforma speaks up to address Derani. "Mye-nac, good intentions. Isn't planning to steal or harm. Safe to follow."

Derani looks over at the ex-soldier. "It's clear he wants to find any excuse to take Nalia away from me."

Palforma sounds a rumble of amusement. "So too would many Talins." Then Palforma points to Nalia. "She not dumb. She decided. Picked her Talin. Won't be parted or manipulated. Trust your human."

Nalia reaches out and affectionally bumps Palforma's arm with her fist. "Thanks for the vote of confidence, big guy."

Derani rumbles out a sigh, clearly telling the world he feels maligned. "I've never once thought or said that you had less than optimal intelligence."

"For a human," she adds and can't help the laugh that bubbles out of her when Derani rumbles out a long-suffering sound.

"If you would follow me," Mye-nac says as he turns to lead them through the bay. Palforma picks up all their bags as Derani falls in step behind Mye-nac with her in his arms. Despite her confident words, she's feeling a little intimidated as every Delorta they pass stares at the two Talins. Some even hiss at them in distaste. The animosity is palpable.

She can't wait until they're off this station.

CHAPTER 30

Once they are seated in Mye-nac's office, he hands Derani several blankets and then leaves the room, promising he will return shortly. Despite the self-warming omnie, Derani can tell his little human is struggling with the frigid temperature of the station. He wraps the heaviest of the blankets around her, even pulling it up so it covers her head until only the top of her face is visible. Then he tucks her tightly against his body.

It would need to be far colder to ever bother him or Palforma, but his body will at least produce some heat to help combat the chill for his frail human. He wishes the blanket was made of the same self-warming microbes as the omnie. Perhaps he should look into acquiring something like that.

"I'm worried about that second ship," Nalia comments in the silence, making both him and Palforma stare at her in surprise.

Palforma leans a little closer to her. "What?"

"They were supposed to wait. Right Palforma? Wait until you were alone and vulnerable planetside on Umeal Colony? That's what you alluded to, back on the Bountiful."

When Derani sounds a questioning rumble, she continues.

"It makes sense. I read about that colony. Bad security, no surveillance outside the port, and a lot of places it would be easy to land with no one on the planet knowing about it. They could have landed in one of the remote places, found you in the only city there, gotten the information square, and left. Instead, they did it the hard way by attacking the Bountiful."

Palforma rumbles out a sound of admiration. "Quick mind. Yes, Umeal Colony was the plan. No longer plan."

Derani rumbles out an inquisitive sound. "What point are you trying to make, Nalia?"

"The more difficult attack on the ship tells me that their information isn't great; otherwise, they'd have waited. They might not have even known he was going to stop at Umeal. Or they weren't confident in that intel. That pushed them to attack an entire ship and potentially lose the info they want from Palforma instead of waiting and risking having him make it back to Talarian."

"But what makes you think there were two ships?" Derani pushes, fascinated by his human's quick mind. "That was only a guess on Palforma's part. We never saw a second ship."

"That's obvious. There must be a second ship. The ship that attacked us couldn't have boarded us. They were a Star Fairer class ship. They have a hard time docking at irregular stations, let alone trying to dock on an unwilling ship. There must have been a second ship hanging back, ready to latch on once we stopped fighting or thought the fight was over. They probably didn't expect us to have any working engines after dueling with the Star Fairer."

Now that she lays it out, Derani feels like a fool for not thinking of it sooner. "Your assessment is no doubt correct. There must have been at least one more ship."

"Follow here?" Palforma asks.

"I'm sure they must have," Derani confirms. "The question is if they'll dare to come onto the station to get us. We need to figure out how to get the information square to them while making it look like we're trying to protect it. And we need to do it here before the repairs are done."

Palforma rumbles in agreement. "Safer here. For all three of us."

Any further plotting and planning are put on hold when Mye-nac comes back into the room carrying decorative baskets full of items. "These are all human safe," he declares and sets them on the floor next to the low, backless, platform-like chair Derani's sitting in. Mye-nac makes himself comfortable on a chair across from him and Derani realizes that the part he's sitting on are what the Delorta use to support their bellies. Mye-nac lowers his weight onto the low, cushioned platform and folds his legs under him.

One basket has several drinking canisters, and Nalia works an arm free of the blankets to reach for one. Derani tightens his hold on her and rattles a warning. "How can you be so sure they're safe for human consumption?"

Mye-nac doesn't even look fazed by the question. "Why would I wish to hurt another being? That would only take weight from my soul."

"Weight?" Nalia asks, clearly fascinated.

"Every time we act badly, we lose weight to our soul. When we act well, we add back weight. If our soul is heavy enough when we die, it will fling off into a far galaxy and form a star. If there is some weight but not enough, we will become a planet, forced to circle someone else's soul-star."

Wiggling a bit until she can sit up and lean forward, she pushes for more. "What about if there is very little weight?"

By the way his face lights up, it's obvious that Mye-nac is delighted to share his culture and religious philosophy with Nalia. "Then we become meteors and spend our afterlife insubstantial. Souls who exist like that are doomed to the dark, blackness of space. We think they probably kill off the ethereal part of themselves by flinging themselves into a planet or sun, giving their minute weight to a stronger soul. That means they have no chance to be reborn when the universe starts over again."

Nalia nods. "That's an interesting way to look at the afterlife. So everything is about trying to make the soul denser?"

"Exactly, dense. Like stars and planets. That's why we feel so strongly about sentient beings and freedom. If you don't have the freedom to make choices, your soul doesn't have a chance to become heavy or light. You could end up nothing but dust, unable to even fly through space. It's a horrible fate we don't wish anyone."

"That's so beautiful," Nalia comments and, to Derani's surprise, her eyes get misty.

"Are you about to cry?" he asks, feeling mildly concerned.

She sniffs and looks up at him. "It's all so touching, the idea of soul-stars. But no, I'm not going to cry. The cold is making my nose run and causing me to sniff, so you can loosen up."

Derani can tell from her tone that she's teasing him, and that makes him relax back on the low-slung chair.

"The canisters are full of basic nutrient-rich liquid," Mye-nac explains. "It's warm and sweet to the taste so it will be a lovely treat for Nalia." He plucks one out and tosses it to Palforma before pulling something out of the pocket of the utility vest he's wearing and throwing that as well. Palforma easily catches both and rumbles with interest when he looks at the item from Mye-nac's vest.

"Basic bio-tester," Palforma comments. Without instruction from Derani, he pops open the top of the canister and holds the bio-tester over the steam rising from inside. The bio-tester beeps, and Palforma reads the tiny display.

"It's safe. Drinkable. Her and us," he declares and tucks the bio-tester in his belt pouch at the same time he hands her the canister. Derani trusts Palforma, so he lets Nalia take the canister. She sniffs it first and then tentatively takes a sip of the contents.

"Oh, this is good," she comments. "Thank you, Mye-nac."

"My pleasure," Mye-nac replies and then focuses his gaze on Derani. "I have a proposal for you, Captain. I have funds at my disposal to spend as I see fit. I'd like to use those funds to buy Nalia from you."

Derani doesn't even have to think about it. "No."

"Don't answer now," Mye-nac insists. "I'm going to send you a formal letter of inquiry with the amount we can pay. I promise. It's quite substantial."

Before Derani can refuse again, Nalia speaks. "Why do you want to buy me? Most species don't think much of humans."

"We would want to free you," Mye-nac explains. "We could provide you with some funds so you can book passage, or we could find you a job here if you're afraid to go out in the universe and risk re-capture."

"But why?" she repeats. "Why waste all that money on me? I'm nothing special."

Derani wants to argue that fact, but Mye-nac is quick to answer her. "Every living creature is special," he argues. "All sentient beings deserve to live a life of their choosing—a life that will add weight to their souls."

Nalia takes another sip before asking her next question. "Won't you get in trouble for spending this money to purchase me?"

"The fund is specifically created for such occasions as this. All contributions are voluntary, and if we use the fund to free an enslaved being, everyone who contributed will have weight added to their souls."

"You could buy dozens of beings at an auction house," she points out.

Mye-nac shudders with revulsion. "We can't go near those places. Even being close to one takes weight away from the soul. Those who work there are doomed souls."

"Doomed isn't the word I'd use," she mutters. "Assholes come to mind."

"But our focus is on you, Nalia. The here and now. The weight we can add to souls by helping you."

"I don't think—"

Derani didn't mean to cut off her words, but he's so irritated at Mye-nac that he can't stop the loud, angry rattle that makes all eyes focus on him.

"You will stop speaking to my pet about this," he orders. "Our treaty is clear. You can't steal her from me. And I won't be selling her, no matter what offer you make."

"I'm sad to see you so stubborn," Mye-nac states softly. "I hoped to add weight to your soul as well. Nevertheless, I'll be sending you an offer. You are welcome to enjoy the communal areas on the station, but I would suggest you stay in your room as much as possible. You won't be received with joy in any of the establishments here."

"Before we leave this meeting, I need you to do something for me. If any other Talins come on board the station, it's important that I be informed." Derani expects that Mye-nac will refuse his request, but the Delorta blinks slowly in confusion and asks a question instead.

"Don't you have access to your homeworld's UniBase? That should have all Talin ship movements. You don't need me to tell you when a Talin ship docks here."

How to explain without giving away the fact that a Talin conspiracy is at play? That last thing he wants is for other species to find out that the Talins might be on the brink of a civil war.

"It's really Talin ships we're interested in. We think a Talin ship might have been stolen," Nalia answers Mye-nac. "It could try to land here for repairs. We didn't get the ident codes on the ship, so it would be helpful if you could keep us apprised of any Talin ship that requests docking."

Mye-nac looks surprised but nods in understanding. "Some in this sector do such things. I'll need to verify that it's acceptable to share that information with you according to our treaty. I'll contact you as soon as I know it's allowed. Do you need access to our interstellar comms so you can report this to the appropriate authorities?"

"That would be helpful," Derani agrees as he hugs Nalia tightly. His quick-thinking human is a treasure beyond his wildest dreams.

"I will arrange it for you," Mye-nac says as he stands up. "I think we might even have an open slot coming up. Allow me to escort all of you to your room, and we'll contact you about the interstellar comm as soon as I have a time slot available for you."

Derani stands, keeping Nalia held high against his chest. He's not ready to let go of her, and she'll probably stay warmer if she stays wrapped in the blanket Mye-nac provided.

She drinks the rest of the warm liquid in the canister and holds it out for Mye-nac to take. "That was delicious. Is there any way I could have more of it?"

Mye-nac looks pleased with her request as he sets the empty container on a nearby table. "Of course. I'll have a basket of canisters sent up." Turning, he leads them out of the office. "Come along. I'm behind on my work today, so I'm afraid I must be quick now."

It doesn't take long for him to escort them to the rented room. It's about the size of Derani's cabin, with only two sleeping platforms similarly styled to the low furniture in Mye-nac's office. At least the beds are big and should be able to accommodate a Talin body. And

Nalia is so tiny she will easily fit into one bed next to him without any effort.

"I suggest you stay in the room for now," Mye-nac reminds them. "I'll keep you updated on comms access as well as your other request. Order anything you need from the galley. It can be delivered here."

Mye-nac looks down at Nalia, still held securely in Derani's arms, and addresses her directly. "You can leave the room without fear. In fact, many here would like a chance to meet you. You're the first human I've ever met, and your tiny stature is intriguing. I know other Delortas will feel similarly."

"She will not be leaving this room without me," Derani growls out.

Nalia's answer is more diplomatic. "Thanks for telling me, but I think I'll stick close to Derani for now."

Mye-nac ignores Derani and maintains eye contact with Nalia as he bows with his front legs before turning and leaving without another word.

Palforma drops their bags onto one of the beds and rattles with irritation. "Meddling herbivores," he grumbles.

"Put the Delortas out of your mind," Derani orders. "We need to focus on how to convince the Traditionalists to go for the information square here instead of waiting to attack our ship once we leave Declow."

Palforma rumbles out an agreement. "I have idea. Need to use comms."

Derani sits on one bed, settling Nalia on his lap. The room is substantially warmer than the rest of the station and she's already looking more comfortable.

"Tell us," Derani orders.

By the time Palforma is finished with the simple but effective plan, Nalia is nodding enthusiastically. "That sounds like it should work. Not too many moving parts to go wrong. I like it."

Her praise makes Palforma rumble with pleasure. "Still need comm access."

No sooner does he say that than a display on the wall lights up with a soft chime and calls out. "Interstellar comm access granted to Captain Derani in communal room 2251. Please note the time and arrive early for best access. Tap room number for a map."

"Looks like that's not going to be an issue," Derani comments wryly. Setting Nalia down on the bed, he stands up. "You need to stay here for now. We won't be long."

Nalia smiles up at him and makes a shooing motion with her tiny human hands. "I'm good. I've got some more of that warm, tasty drink coming and an information square to keep me entertained. Go lay the groundwork for our plan."

CHAPTER 31

Dalt's roar of anger is so loud that his little human has to pet his quill-less arm and whisper soothing words to calm him down. Palforma glances over at Derani while they wait, giving the distinct impression that he didn't expect this reaction.

"Have alternate plan," Palforma assures Dalt when he finally quiets down. "Won't fail again."

Rumbles of worry sound from Dalt. "I'm not angry that you failed. I'm angry that they attacked the ship. You could have all been killed. I told Holian there was little risk to you or Captain Derani. This is my fault."

Suddenly Lakin is there, jumping into Dalt's arms and wrapping her arms around his neck. Automatically, he brings his arms up to hold her against his body and starts rumbling out a soothing sound. More now than ever, Derani notices that this Talin's rumble doesn't sound quite right. His soundbox must have been damaged because his rumbles are broken up and not as melodious as rumbles should be.

It doesn't seem to bother Lakin. She clings to her Talin with no hint of dislike or disgust.

"Don't be dumb," she whispers fiercely and then leans in close to put her mouth to his earhole. The back of her plain collar is hidden by her hair as she whispers to Dalt. Derani can't hear what she's saying, but by the way Dalt's body relaxes fractionally, her words are having the desired effect.

As much as he wants to leave these two to interact uninterrupted, the counter on the corner of the display shows how little time they have left in this link. Derani sounds a polite rumble to get their attention.

"No one was hurt," Derani tells them the moment he has Dalt's and Lakin's eyes on him once more. "My ship is being repaired, and as Palforma mentioned, we have a plan."

Lakin nods eagerly. "I'm all ears."

What a strange thing to say, but Derani lets it go and quickly lays out Palforma's plan before explaining to them what is needed.

"It should be easy enough to leak your location," Dalt agrees. "I'll also make sure it's clear that Palforma is using you as a means to an end. That you aren't caught up in this." He pauses for a few submarks, and Derani gets the impression he doesn't want to say something. When he does talk, his hold on his human seems to have tightened slightly. "How is your human? Was she very upset from the attack?"

Lakin gives Dalt a sharp look that Derani thinks might be irritation. Is she jealous of Dalt's concern over another human? She didn't strike Derani as anything but confident and secure with Dalt as her owner.

Unsure about the dynamic going on, he gives Dalt a vague answer. "Nalia is very well."

"Then she wasn't traumatized?" Dalt persists.

"Really?" Lakin asks with mild outrage in her voice. "You have to push about this? He already said no one got hurt."

"But she might be mentally damaged," Dalt argues. "He never mentioned her emotional state. If she is having issues, it would be good for him to bring her to Kalor. It's peaceful and safe here."

"Not always," Lakin grumbles and then focuses her gaze on Derani. "Well? Is Nalia showing signs of emotional trauma?" He can't be sure, but he thinks her tone might be sarcastic. Her expression could certainly be classified as irked.

"She hasn't expressed any ill health to me," Derani answers, choosing his words carefully. "In fact…" Should he tell them the role Nalia played in their escape? He's reluctant to let Dalt know he needed her to act as crew, but he's also so very proud of his capable human.

He gives in and rumbles out a prideful sound as he talks. He can't keep her talents a secret.

"She is the cleverest human. She's the one who knew where to target the ship for a successful strike, and she also worked out where we could go for repairs. Even as the ship bucked and almost threw her from her seat, she remained calm and quick thinking." He knows his prideful rumble is getting loud, but he can't seem to stop it. "She's the most wonderful of humans."

Lakin shoots Dalt a triumph look. "See! Not only isn't she 'emotionally damaged,' but she managed to kick ass. I keep telling you to stop underestimating us. We're a hell of a lot tougher than any of you think." Lakin's expression softens as she focuses her gaze on Derani. "Nalia sounds wonderful. I can't wait to meet her someday."

Relieved that Lakin isn't jealous, Derani sounds an affirmative rumble. "She is a sociable human like you. She's made friends with the Delortas here."

Lakin laughs. "It's easy to make friends with Delortas. Those guys are really sweet. They have an entire colony of freed slaves and refugees. I've made deliveries to the colony a couple of times."

"Were those deliveries legal?" Dalt asks, and Derani gets the feeling he's teasing his pet.

"They might not have been entirely legal, but they were definitely morally lawful," she responds promptly, gazing up at her owner with loving eyes.

Dalt rubs a cheek across the top of Lakin's head. Despite the grossly inappropriate display of affection, Derani doesn't find himself repulsed. Instead, he longs to get back to their room so he can do the same to Nalia.

"When can we expect our location to reach the Traditionalists?" Derani asks, breaking up the intimate moment between Dalt and Lakin.

Dalt rumbles out a sharp note, a combination of embarrassment and surprise at realizing Lakin completely distracted him. Lakin absently runs her fingers through her mane to distribute Dalt's bonding oil as she answers Derani's question.

"We'll set up a transmission to be overheard today," she promises. "It won't be hard. We're back on Kalor, and I know which one of our satellites is being monitored. We'll send it with only a low-end encryption, so it shouldn't take long for them to decode it. If we make it too easy, they'll get suspicious."

"If the second ship stayed close, it shouldn't take them long to get to you. I'll contact you if we get any further information, but otherwise, we should try to keep the channels quiet."

Derani sounds a rumble of agreement. "We'll contact you the moment the information square is taken."

Lakin's expression is one of approval. "That would make sense. If our agent lost the data on that square, and it was real, he'd panic and contact us right away." Then she gives him a big, toothy grin. "After this is all over, if you feel like having a vacation. Come to Kalor. It's great here."

"Perhaps," Derani hedges and wonders about Lakin's insistence. Part of him thinks it's genuine interest in meeting another human, but he's also sure that Lakin would intercede on Nalia's behalf if she decided the other human wasn't happy. "But first we need the Traditionalists to think they won a victory."

They talk for a little longer before the time is up and the display goes blank. The moment the link is broken, the door opens and Mye-nac appears. "I'm afraid I need to speak with you about your ship, Captain Derani."

After setting the temperature as high as it would allow, Nalia stood right next to one of the room's heating elements, soaking in the heat with a contented sigh. Between her omnie and the borrowed blanket, she wasn't going to get frostbite, but she was still uncomfortable. Now she's starting to feel normal, but warm and toasty is probably going to have to wait until she's back on the Bountiful.

The door display's chime sounds, but before she can even move a face appears on the display. She doesn't recognize this Delorta, so she hesitates.

"Human Nalia?" a voice calls out. "I'm here with more tea. Mye-nac said you requested another serving."

Happy to have more the delicious drink, Nalia abandons her spot next to the heating element and hurries over to tap the display and open the door. To her surprise, three Delortas are waiting in the hall, all of them massive. At least half a size again bigger than Mye-nac.

"Oh, uh, hi," she greets them and holds out her hand for the canister the one in the front is holding. The Delorta doesn't hand it to her.

"Mye-nac told us that your owner and the other Talin are in one of the comm rooms. Those rooms are on the other side of the station. It will be awhile before they get back. We've come to sit with you, talk, and share sustenance."

"Okay, sure. Thanks," Nalia says and moves back to let them in.

Full of confidence and friendly energy, the three walk in. Bemused, Nalia watches as they make themselves comfortable on the few pieces of low-slung furniture in the room. They make quick work of setting out massive cups that look like they were carved out of stone, bowls of food, and half a dozen canisters of hot, steaming tea.

"Come join us, Nalia," one of them invites, patting a pillow on the floor.

Sinking onto the pillow, Nalia reminds herself not to smile widely enough to show teeth. "I'm pleased you decided to visit," she says after a brief hesitation. She's racking her brain for anything she's read about Delorta culture, but honestly, there isn't much. This is her first visit to this sector, so she never had a reason to research them before.

One of them hands her a stone cup that's so heavy she's forced to hold it with both hands. She takes a sip and finds it's the same stuff Mye-nac served. She's really going to need to see if they'll let her take some with her.

The Delorta next to her introduces the group. "My name is Ome-cal. Mye-nac is in my unit. These are my sisters, Ome-rea and Ome-lye."

"Is it okay to ask questions?" Nalia hopes it is because she's bursting to ask about so many things.

"Certainly, questions are one of the most efficient and pleasant ways to gain knowledge," Ome-lye answers.

"What's a unit?"

"Unlike many others, our species isn't binary. We have three genders. Lifebearers, nurturers, and providers. As the name indicates, lifebearers, like me and my sisters, grow and birth the young. You might have noticed we are substantially bigger than the nurturers or providers. Our young are very large when they're born. That means that the bigger the lifebearer, the better chance both mother and child have to survive. Our nurturers and providers are both needed to fertilize, so our units need to include at least one of each."

"I can see how much bigger lifebearers are, but I'm not sure if I've met nurturers or providers," Nalia admits. "I don't know much of anything about Delortas except for the excellent reputation of this station."

That makes all three of them laugh. They do it without opening their mouths. Instead their nostrils flare with their sounds of humor.

"Then it's our pleasure to educate you," Ome-lye states.

Ome-cal continues the explanation. "Nurturers are the smallest of us, and their fur is the longest. Some say that the longer the fur on a nurturer the more fertile they are, but I doubt the veracity of that."

Ome-rea speaks over her sister to tell Nalia in a humorous tone. "If you met my Lar-may, you won't doubt it."

"Lar-may is a lovely nurturer," Ome-cal agrees with a chuckle.

Then she addresses Nalia. "I know you've met my Mye-nac. He's a provider, and a typical size. Almost everyone on the station is a provider. They outnumber the lifebearers about three-to-one, so normally we will enter into a unit with two or three providers to one lifebearer. The nurturers outnumber us two-to-one, so our units often have two nurturers as well. It's important to us that everyone be able to participate in unit life."

Ome-rea speaks up. "Without a unit, a soul can become light and forget that the purpose of life is to help others. Generosity of the soul starts within the unit."

"Yes, exactly," Ome-Cal agrees.

"Only six lifebearers are on the station at the moment," Ome-rea continues. "We cannot gestate in space or on a colony. Our homeworld is the only place we can maintain a pregnancy and give birth. We aren't sure why, but most think it's because of the minerals in our ice. Most of the Delortas who work here or on the colonies are young providers who aren't part of a unit yet but are eager to earn wealth so a unit will notice and ask them to join."

"Not every provider is so eager. Some are more interested in adventure," Ome-cal adds with a little closed-mouth chuckle. "Look at our sibling, Ome-ark. He's several sectors away with no intention of coming home anytime soon."

Ome-rea makes a fretting sound. "I hope his soul doesn't lose weight while he's away."

"That's not for us to worry about," Ome-lye states gently. "Those are his choices to make."

"How many siblings do you guys have?"

"Only ten," Ome-rea answers. "But with three of us being lifebearers, our birth unit was considered very blessed."

Nalia's eyes go wide. "Ten isn't many kids?"

That question makes them all do a closed-mouth chuckle. "It used to be that most units strived to have at least fifteen offspring, but ten or less is becoming more common."

"That's a lot of kids," Nalia thinks out loud. "But then I guess it's easier to raise that many if there's more than only two parents taking care of them."

"Our units organize well around the raising of offspring," Ome-rea agrees.

They answer all her questions about the way they organize the unit as well as getting more details about their society and culture. The time passes quickly, and Nalia's not surprised when Ome-cal brings up the collar around her neck.

"We could remove that for you, if you like," she offers and digs around in one of the pockets of the vest she's wearing. It seems that the vests are standard clothing for Delortas, independent of gender or job. Finally, she holds up what she was looking for. Nalia doesn't recognize the tool but assumes it's some kind of disrupter that would fool the collar's locking mechanism.

She doesn't say no right away. Absently she strokes the collar as she stares at the tool in Ome-cal's long fingers. "I don't want to get anyone in trouble."

"We are attempting to buy you," Ome-rea points out. "But if we are unable, you should have the means to make choices."

Ome-cal holds out the tool. "Take it in case you need it later."

Unlike the heavy tool the Ollies gave her to get the collar off, this one couldn't accidentally hurt her. She accepts the disrupter and tucks it into a fold of the omnie. She'll need to find a more secure place later, but this will work for now.

"And you should take this," Ome-lye holds out an item on a string. Taking it, Nalia finds that it's an average-looking stone with a hole drilled in the end and a bit of twine threaded through.

"That's from one of the rings that surround our homeworld," Ome-lye explains. "It's considered good luck to wear one. If you are suffering from anxiety or bad thoughts, you should grip the stone in one hand and pull the cord through it with the other. Try it."

Although it's only a bit of off-white stone, Nalia is touched by the gift. She puts it around her neck and then does as Ome-lye explained and pulls the cord. As the cord rubs against the stone, a pleasant smell hits her nose.

"These stones are soft and easily cut into. The cord is made of a very strong polymer so as you move it through the stone, it loosens and aerates a tiny bit of the rock. That's what causes the smell."

"It's a soothing scent," Nalia agrees. "And the motion is relaxing as well."

All three look pleased with her, and Ome-rea says, "Exactly."

"Keep moving your rock so our conversation doesn't cause you undue stress," Ome-lye instructs. Nalia does as asked but more to appease them than any belief that this agreeable smell is going to keep her mood elevated.

"Is there more you need to tell me?" she asks.

"It's common for slaves to fear freedom," Ome-lye begins. "If they've been slaves for a long time, freedom can be intimating. Choices are never easy. Wants have to be measured against the lightness they will cause."

"I'm not afraid of freedom," Nalia assures them. "I was free before Derani, but I'm not sure I want to be free. I don't think I want to be parted from Derani."

Instead of being upset, all three Delortas beam at her. Ome-lye speaks first. "You are contemplating your choices. This is good."

"And now you can act if you wish to gain your freedom," Ome-rea adds. "Should you choose to no longer be a slave, all you need to do is run away and contact us. We will secure you transport back here."

She's not sure how she got to be so lucky as to have not only the Ollies try to help her but now these Delortas, who are virtual strangers. It's heartwarming to think there is compassion in the universe.

"I will remember your offer," she promises. "And your kindness."

CHAPTER 32

Derani notices that the room smells strongly of Delorta the moment he enters. The scent of the quadrupeds is far stronger than when he left several marks ago. At least one has been in here while he and Palforma were gone.

He should have been suspicious when Mye-nac found all kinds of reasons to detain the two of them in the bay with questions that didn't need his input. The Delortas know their jobs well, and dragging him into the discussion of parts and repair techniques was unnecessary. Now he realizes that he and Palforma were being deliberately waylaid so other Delortas could visit Nalia and possibly steal her.

Only the sight of Nalia curled up in a nest of pillows and blankets next to a heating element keeps him calm. When she looks up from the information square she's holding and smiles at him, pleasure blossoms deep in his chest. They might have tried to talk her into running away, but it's obvious she refused.

That makes him realize an uncomfortable truth that he's worked hard to ignore but can't any longer. If Nalia decides she wants to get away from him, she will probably be successful. It might take her time, but unless he wants to keep her bound hand and foot, there's no way he could hold on to her if she becomes determined to leave.

The thought of losing her makes him feel a cold that has nothing to do with the low temperature of Declow.

Needing the comfort of her touch, he strides across the room and scoops her up. He sits down in the nest she created and cuddles her, rubbing his scent glands into her hair.

"Why were Delortas here?" he asks.

He expects her to become stiff and prevaricate, but she does neither. She makes a soft humming sound and snuggles against him as she explains.

"They wanted to make sure I knew I could be free if I wanted to be. They're really big on individuals being able to make choices. You know, because of the souls needing weight thing. Did you know that if you call someone heavy among the Delortas, it's not an insult? You're basically telling someone they are kind and generous, not fat."

"What's fat?" Derani asks, nuzzling her hair. His question makes her huff out a laugh.

"What I'll be if you always carry me around," she quips.

"So fat means pampered?"

"Ha!" she barks out. "No, not really. Anyway, among humans being called fat is usually an insult like being called ugly."

"So some Delortas came here to take you away from me?" he clarifies. He can hear Palforma rattling with agitation at his question.

"I talk to them!" he declares aggressively in his familiar stilted speech.

"No need," Nalia assures him. "They were very polite. All they did was talk. I promise. Besides, wouldn't you want them to be ready to intervene if they saw a human being treated poorly?"

"But you not… not… not bad. Not treated bad. Good here—" Palforma is upset enough to tap at his head as he struggles to get his words out.

Derani lets Nalia move out of his arms. She goes to the struggling Talin and grabs one of his hands, holding it in her two smaller ones.

"Hey there, big guy. It's okay. I'm not leaving. I'm happy here. I made sure they understood that. They don't think I'm being mistreated, but it's hard for them to get past this." She lets go with one of her hands to tap her collar.

Palforma's rattling stops, giving way to a soothing rumble that's probably more for him than Nalia. "Not go. Not leave Derani. Humans die out there. Die young. Killed. Lost. Can't… no more death."

"I'm not planning on dying. At least not soon," she teases him. Then she shivers a little, and he pulls his hand away from her and gives her a gentle push back to Derani.

"Warm self," he orders. "I'll scout station. Look at angles. Check places. Will be back, three marks." With that, he turns on his heels and leaves. Derani sounds a rumble of amusement. Palforma might be a skilled warrior, but subtlety and tact are not his strong suit.

"Did he leave to give us time alone?" Nalia asks with a chuckle as she settles back down in his lap.

"I believe he did," Derani agrees.

"Might as well take advantage," she murmurs and presses her lips to his chin. Eager for more of her lip presses, he angles his head down so she can have better access to his mouth.

He adores the way she eagerly puts her lips to his and sweeps her tongue into his mouth, completely unfearful of his sharp teeth.

She twists around so she's facing him, and then he feels her fingers probe until they find his belt. She efficiently unbuckles it and slides it out from around his body. He hears it clunk as it hits the floor; then her little fingers are tugging his pants out of the way.

His mating shaft started swelling the moment Palforma left the room, so the tip is already emerging when Nalia runs her fingers around the end of the flesh still covering most of it.

He doesn't stop her searching hand, but he voices his concern. "I'm worried you might get cold."

"Then I guess we better figure out how to do this mostly clothed," she responds with a light laugh. He goes stiff as she forces her fingers into his tight flesh pouch. The feeling is indescribable and turns off his thinking brain momentarily. She works most of her hand inside, and by the time she stretches the pouch to where her fingers and palm can close around his mating shaft, the smell of her arousal has reached his nose despite the layers of cloth covering her.

The scent of her need hits him hard, and he rears up, forcing her onto her back. Her hand is trapped in his pouch, but he's careful to keep from hurting her as he brings his face down and gently bites at her neck. He found out by accident that she likes these soft bites and now includes them during their coupling. He's cautious not to pierce her skin with his sharp teeth, even when she moans and pushes harder against him.

Moments later, his shaft is fully engorged. The pouch pulls back, letting his erection and seed sack loose. Nalia makes a happy sound as she wraps her little hand around his mating shaft and squeezes. The pressure feels good, but not as good as when he's buried deep inside of her.

But no, he refuses to do that until she's climaxed once. She's so tiny that he's worried if he tries to mount her before she's ready, he might hurt her. Better to soften and warm her passage by thorough arousal before trying to sink deep inside her.

"Derani," she moans out when he pulls her hand away from his shaft and forces it onto the bed over her head. At first, when she said his name during rutting, he thought it was because she needed to tell him something. He soon learned that when she's pleased or needy, she will say his name in that breathy way. All it means is that she's aroused.

"I've been watching more vids," he tells her as he gently nips at her flesh.

"Yeah?" her voice is unsteady.

He pulls the length of the omnie and the wrap under it out of his way so he can part her legs. He deliberately doesn't take them off. The room might be warmer than the rest of the station, but it's still far too cold for a human to be comfortable. He needs to keep a close eye on her. If she becomes chilled, he'll need to figure out a way to please her while still keeping her swaddled in coverings.

Moving between her legs, he leans in close. He adores the feel of the curly hair that frames her beautiful sex. He especially likes how it soaks up his bonding oil as well as the straight black hair on her head. The combination of his bonding sent and her scent is such a heady smell that he's sure it's addicting. On the rare occasions she wears undergarments, he's taken them away to store in his belt pouch so he can smell them when she isn't around.

"What have you been watching?" she asks when he rubs his cheek against the inside of her leg and then on the soft fur above her sex.

"These vids are a studying of all the ways humans can copulate," he answers. "There are dozens. In this last one, the male teased the female's back hole."

She stiffens slightly at his words, but he's not worried. She stiffens all the time during coupling. However, her words make him pause. "You're not going to try to rut me there. Are you?"

"No," he assures her as he rubs his fingers through the curls to gather oil and then trails them down until he can circle his fingers around that tight hole. "But the male in the vid teased the female with his finger and she liked it a lot. I thought I would do that to you." As he talks, he massages her there, his oil making his fingers slippery. He knows she likes it when he uses bonding oil on her breeding hole, so he thinks she should probably like this as well.

The Talin scholar recording the vids pointed out that there are more nerve endings in the human's back hole, and if properly stimulated, both males and females could find it more than a pleasant experience. It's an erogenous zone that Derani hasn't explored yet.

"Be gentle," Nalia murmurs and then wiggles a little as he presses a finger against her. He can feel her body fighting him, so he stops pushing and goes back to rubbing his finger back and forth. As he does, he bends his head forward to lap at the little nub that gives Nalia so much pleasure.

He knows now that if he draws it out, her climax will be more intense. Instead of sucking her into his mouth, he teases that little bundle of nerves with his tongue and lips until she's squirming under him. He can also feel her tight hole loosening. He pushes gently, and this time she doesn't tense, so the tip of his finger slides in.

"Ugh!" Her startled sound makes him freeze, worried he might have caused her pain. But then she makes a frustrated sound and cries out, "Derani!"

The need in her voice is clear. She wants him to continue. He doesn't let up tormenting her clit as he works a second finger into her. With his other hand, he tugs at her wrap enough to reach one of her breasts. The nipple is beaded, and she's making all kinds of needy sounds when he cups the heated flesh in his broad hand.

Now she's undulating her hips against his mouth and hand. She's alternately begging and demanding with breathless, one-word pleas. "More. Please. More. Harder. There. Oh! Harder!"

Then he rumbles, knowing she'll feel the vibration. It has the desired effect as she moans again and strains to press herself more firmly against his mouth.

When he sucks determinedly on that little nub, it's more because he's ready. He's too aroused to wait any longer to sink his mating shaft into her.

It only takes a few moments before her body clenches and he can feel the muscles around his finger flutter as she climaxes. Her legs close hard around his head as she cries out. Her essence floods his mouth as her body succumbs to pleasure. He adores this part.

She's still gasping for air when he pulls away and rears up to place his shaft at her entrance. He knows he should take more time. He should stretch out her climax with his fingers and his mouth, but he is greedy and can't wait any longer. Her little mewling, "Yes," only encourages his eagerness.

As usual, he has to ease the throbbing head of his mating shaft into her. She is so small and tight that he marvels she is able to stretch to accommodate him. Far from hurting her, she admits she loves how big he is. Still, he's cautious. Even driving need doesn't push him to move faster than the normal, slow, easy slide inside of her.

She moans and wraps her legs around his hips, urging him to sink deeper. Her expression is nothing but pleasure, and when she opens her eyes and looks at him, he sees lust and love mingled together.

The look is his undoing. His chest swells with adoration for her, and he can't hold back his need to move in her liquid heat. He tries to keep the pace metered and slow, but his instincts take over and soon he's thrusting at a brutal pace.

Far from objecting, Nalia tightens her legs, closes her eyes, and braces her body with her arms over her head and her hands flattened against the nearby bulkhead.

A rumble of pleasure sounds from his chest, continuous and strong. That tips Nalia over the edge, and he feels the feminine walls surrounding his mating shaft tighten around him. The moment he realizes she's climaxing again, he can't help his body's reaction, and he floods her with his seed.

Still inside of her, he hunches his body over so he can rub his scent glands over every bit of exposed flesh he can reach. Her chest, shoulders, face, and hair all end up glistening from his bonding oil. Pulling back, he gazes down at Nalia. His human looks flushed and sated. When she opens her eyes and smiles up at him, his heart blossoms with feelings of affection and happiness.

"I love you," she whispers.

Even though those words aren't in the Talin lexicon, they still affect him. His spent mating shaft wants to engorge again even as it is already half shrunken and close to pulling out of Nalia's heat. Warmth builds inside of him like he's never felt before. When the words fall from his mouth, there's no hesitation or shock. They only reflect what he's come to understand as an undeniable truth.

"I love you, my sweet, perfect Nalia."

CHAPTER 33

Derani didn't like the idea of leaving Nalia alone in the room, but it's the safest place for her. At least for the moment, especially with Palforma in there with her, waiting for his signal.

The plan is simple. Once he's is in place, Derani will contact the warrior. Palforma will leave the room with the information square and parade in front of the Traditionalist, pretending he doesn't notice them. Then he'll wander into a section of the station that's not monitored. At that point, they should be bold and attack Palforma. He'll let them steal his bag, and it will be all over. Derani will wait at a discreet distance, ready to jump in and help Palforma if any of the Traditionalists look like they want to take the attack too far.

The problem is that he can't find them. Palforma saw the ship land. He was walking by a large windowed area and saw an ancient and poorly maintained Maro class ship docking. Not only did it have Talin markings on it, but he also saw fresh scars on the hull that looked like this ship had taken a hard impact like the kind that will happen when one ship tries to stop another ship from being sucked into the gravity of a gas giant.

As if to cement the evidence, the ship also had a brand new and badly installed parasitic hatch attached to its belly. Pirate or rescue ships use the same hatch to latch on to another ship and either board it or rescue the souls on board. Maro class ships don't normally have parasitic hatches.

Jumping to the correct conclusion, Palforma hurried back to the room before they could finish docking to inform Derani.

That was long enough ago that they should have made it onto the station, but Derani can't find them. He's tried to contact Mye-nac for information, but the Delorta isn't answering his request.

Now, after searching all over the common areas of the station and not finding a single other Talin, he's getting a bad feeling that something has gone wrong.

Giving in, he unsnaps his Ident from his belt and taps at it, trying to hail Palforma—nothing.

Concern turns to worry as he finds a wall display and hails the room. Still no answer. Panicked, he sprints back to the room only to find the door open and the room in shambles. Both Palforma and Nalia are missing.

An empty and dented canister is still rocking on the floor. They must have been attacked and abducted only submarks ago. The Traditionalists could only get back to the dock in two ways, and he came by one of them. Knowing they must be taking the slightly longer but more secluded path back to their ship, Derani sprints off after them, desperate to save his pet and his new friend.

When he hears the stomps of angry Delortas, he knows he's close. Rounding a corner, he finds himself almost at the docks. He can see about two dozen Talins followed by several angry Delortas. Two of the Talins are dragging an unconscious Palforma and another has a bag large enough to hold Nalia slung over his shoulder.

Many of them are staggering, and several are forced to lean on others as they limp to the ramp. Palforma must have hurt many of them in the fight, but no Talin could stand against two dozen opponents.

They ignore the stamps and shouts from the Delortas as they stumble up the ramp to their ship. Because the ship isn't in a bay, it will be easy for them to disengage and leave once they've boarded. Declow isn't a trading hub. It specializes in refueling and repair.

Without enough traffic to require a strict exit and entry queue, their departure won't be delayed.

Desperate, he sprints down the hall toward the ramp, determined to stop them from leaving. One traditionalist sees him coming and violently pushes at the men in front of him until they all fall into the ship. The hatch is closing when Derani gets to the bottom of the ramp, but he doesn't stop. Keeping his momentum, he crashes into the closed hatch.

"Cowards!" he screams. Of course, they don't open the door, and he's forced to move back as the secondary hatch slides shut to secure the docks. The plates under his feet vibrate slightly as their ship rumbles to life. Has he failed both Palforma and Nalia?

No! He's not done yet.

"Mye-nac!" he shouts as he turns and takes in all the startled faces around him. "I need Mye-nac! *Now!*"

Nalia is angry. No, angry is too mild a term. She's furious. Incandescent with rage. Yes, that's it! If her anger could physically manifest, she'd be as bright as a star at the moment.

Because she's infuriated, she hyperventilates inside the damn sack they packed her in. She can feel tears running down her face, and her chest is getting tight. She can't scream because of the gag they stuck in her mouth, and struggling isn't much of an option after they bound both her hands and feet.

At least they didn't search her. She can't move enough yet, but the moment she gets out of this sack and no one's looking, she's digging out the little disrupter that lifebearers gave her. Then she's going to get free of her restraints and rain down hell on these assholes.

Well, she probably won't be able to rain down hell, but she will make their lives hard! Put in the right place, disrupters can cause absolute chaos.

"Put them both there," the leader says. To her surprise, she's set down gently. Then she hears a hard thump as something big lands next to her. Poor Palforma.

The man put up an amazing fight, but there were so many of them. They opened the door to their room and attacked with no warning. One moment she was telling Palforma about her time with Hax. The next thing she knew, the room was filling with rattling Talins.

Even with so many attackers, she thought Palforma might still win, but then someone pulled out a stunner. How they got a stunner onto the station is a mystery, but it probably has something to do with the fact that they could open a locked room door without the display even making a chime of warning. Someone on the station assisted them.

That Delorta's soul is going to be so light it will be particles when they die, Nalia fumes. *No, they'll be sub-particles!*

"Should I pull the human out of the sack?" a voice asks. She hears the same Talin who's been carrying her. "She could have trouble breathing."

"I agree," another voice adds. "She could be already suffering from insufficient respiration. "

She hears a burst of irritated rattling. "Fine, but it's on you to complete your tasks and keep the human out of trouble."

A loud rumble of pleasure sounds at the same time a voice asks from a different location. "What will we ultimately do with the human?"

"If she's well-behaved, Detrion will probably add her to his collection. Otherwise, he might have her put down or sold to a market."

"Shouldn't we get a say about who gets her?" the first Talin asks. "We are risking our lives and freedom for this information."

"I agree with Aroginean. We should hold a nonbiased lottery among everyone on board who has a wish to own her. No human should be wasted just because another might consider them badly behaved. We have ways to train a human to be a good pet."

A rumble of exasperation comes out of the Talin in charge. "Aroginean, Julimian, we can discuss this after we are safely away. Captain Derani might not have a ship to chase us, but we don't know if Palforma requested a second ship to fetch him. We need to get away from this station as quickly as we're able."

Aroginean and Julimian grumble out agreements. She hears footsteps walk away as the sack is ripped open. Harsh light makes her eyes water, and she hears twin purring as gentle hands lift her off the floor.

"Don't weep, human," one of them says as he cradles her against his chest. "You're safe. Aroginean and I won't let anything happen to you."

"Is she in pain? Is that why liquid pours from her eyes?" Aroginean asks.

"It's probably from fear and discomfort. I saw a human pup wail only because he tripped himself to the floor. He was soothed quickly with some holding and rumbling."

"Should I come close and rumble with you?"

Accustomed to the light now, Nalia looks up at the Talin holding her and then startles as the second Talin snuggles in close so she's wedged between them. Both of them are purring, and she might have found it nice if she wasn't still bound hand and foot.

Not to mention kidnapped!

Making inarticulate sounds behind the gag, she struggles against her bonds. Both Talin's stop purring. "What's she doing?"

"I think she's upset at the gag," Aroginean says as he reaches up to untie the cursed thing. "Humans have all kinds of odd and problematic ducts in their face and her nose might be partially blocked from her weeping." He pulls the gag free and coos. "There now, isn't that better."

Finally free of the gag and able to talk, Nalia says the first thing that pops into her head. "I'm scent-bonded to Captain Derani!"

Neither Talin stops purring as Julimian speaks. "It's good that you told us. We can get you medication that will keep you from getting separation sickness and allow you to bond to a different Talin."

"We don't want you to be fearful, little human," Aroginean assures her. "We won't let Nearlon give you to Detrion. His family owns three humans already. He doesn't need you."

"And I've heard that he doesn't treat his pets well," Julimian adds. "We will make sure you belong to us."

Aroginean leans in and looks like he's about to rub his scent glands on her, but then he remembers that she's scent-bonded and rears his head back. "You should know we can take good care of you. We're both of the Hakian Clan. Our clan is famous for their engineers and technicians."

"My family even has a large empty enclosure all ready for you," Julimian explains. "And Aroginean's family compound borders ours, so his family can visit often."

"That sounds wonderful and all," Nalia says to keep her tone reasonable. "But I belong to Captain Derani."

To her surprise, neither Talin gets upset. Both of them pause their soothing rumbles to make sounds of amusement.

"Not any longer," Aroginean explains. "No one will find you when we get back to our clan homes on the Omeanin Colony."

As she tries to figure out what to say next, she notices Palforma lying on the floor, motionless. So much blood is on his face that some of his features are obscured. She cries out in distress and struggles in Julimian's hold.

"Palforma!"

Aroginean sounds a dismissive rattle. "Calm yourself. He's alive. He's being taken to Detrion so he can be interviewed."

"Please, can I see to him?" Nalia asks and doesn't try to stop the tears that pour down her face. The sight of fresh tears makes both Talins increase the volume of their purring.

Julimian turns his body so she can't see Palforma any longer, and Aroginean steps away to open the door.

"We can't let you near him. He's an odd one, damaged and unstable. Nearlon told us he can barely talk. Poor soul, it might be a mercy to end his life."

"No!" Nalia's shout makes both Talin's rumble in laughter.

"Tender-hearted human," Julimian murmurs as he carries her out of the room. "Your kind aren't concerned enough about worthiness, only affection. If you understood better, you would know that he isn't worth your fondness."

She catches a glance at Palforma's still form before Aroginean closes the hatch behind them and then pats her on the head. "Don't fret. We'll take good care of you."

CHAPTER 34

"This ship is worth only half of the Bountiful's value," Mye-nac argues, even as he taps on an information square to close the deal. "I don't want to cheat you and risk losing weight."

Rattling with impatience, Derani steps closer to the Delorta so he can see the information square. "That doesn't matter. I need it."

"This craft can't be used for trade," Mye-nac points out unnecessarily. "It's only good for speed and stealth. We only have it because it was—"

Derani's rattle gets loud enough to cut off Mye-nac's words. "I don't care. Get this done! They have Nalia and Palforma!"

"But they are also Talins. It should be fine," Mye-nac says blithely as he hands the information square to Derani. With barely controlled violence, Derani snatches it out of his hands and taps his activated Ident to the display. The information square's display flashes and then shows the completed transaction details.

Without looking, he tosses the information square back at Mye-nac and bolts for the ship he traded the for the Bountiful. The thing is small, sleek, and fast. It's nothing a merchant trader would want and everything Derani needs if he's going to catch up to the Traditionalists.

When this is all over and he has Nalia and Palforma back, he'll deal with the consequences of trading the Bountiful for an impractical ship worth half its value. His clan will be furious with him. His family might even disown him. As an outcast, jobs will be hard to find, and it will be unlikely he'll ever captain a ship again.

But what does any of that matter if he doesn't have Nalia?

Relieved to find that the sleek ship is already fueled and prepped, he takes the only chair in the cockpit. He runs through the engine start and warm-up far faster than is safe. He was able to get the Delortas to tell him which heading the other ship took before it was beyond their satellites, so he's got an idea where the Traditionalists are going.

It helps that Dalt and Lakin explained that the Traditionalists like to do ship-to-ship meetings instead of going to a station or planet. The best place for ships to hook to each other is in a stable orbit around a small planet or planetoid with enough gravity to assist with docking, but not so much that they are forced to constantly burn to keep their orbit from deteriorating.

Derani uses that information along with their last known heading to figure out the closest planets that will work. It becomes easier to narrow down the search knowing they wouldn't want to be near any settlements or stations.

After all the criteria are taken into consideration, they could only be going three places. He will check the closest one. The speed of this ship should mean that even if that guess is wrong, he'll be able to overtake them by the second or hopefully still be able to catch them if it turns out to be the planet farthest away.

No, no "hopefully" about it. He must be certain and catch up. He must get Nalia and Palforma back. To contemplate otherwise is to invite failure.

He has never failed.

His Ident is already linked with the ship's systems, so he shouldn't have been surprised when the display in front of him flashes with a comm link request. Impatient, he slaps at the console, and an unfamiliar Talin comes into focus.

"Captain Derani?"

"I don't have time to speak with anyone right now," he barks out.

"Make time," the Talin commands. "I'm Commandant Holian, and I'm the one who's in charge of this mission. Where is Palforma? He should have checked in by now."

"Then you're the one I'll blame if anything happens to Nalia or Palforma!" Derani growls.

He's not sure how he expected Holian to act to that vague, threatening statement, but the commandant remains detached and unperturbed.

"Tell me what happened," he demands, his voice full of authority but no emotion.

In clipped words and halting sentences because he's distracted with piloting an unfamiliar ship, Derani explains. When he finishes his quick account, Holian reacts decisively, his words unexpected.

"You're taking the correct actions," Holian assures him as he looks away and starts tapping at something off screen. "I'm going to send you a secure link that will allow us to track you. I'll coordinate ships, but you will still be the first one there. Stealth will be your best asset. If you see an opportunity to board one of the other ships without detection, take it. Otherwise, monitor but don't engage until help arrives."

"No, I—" Derani's argument is cut short when Holian holds up a hand. The man doesn't even rattle, but his presence is powerful enough to make a raised hand cause Derani to fall silent.

"I understand," is all he says, and then the display goes blank. Submarks later a secure link request comes through, and he accepts it without thought.

Now he focuses his complete attention back on pushing the ship faster than it was ever designed to go.

These guys aren't too bad—for kidnapping, traitorous scum, that is.

Julimian and Aroginean carried her to a galley to get her something to drink and check her over for injuries. They fuss over a few bruises, and Julimian ends up running to fetch some salve from his bunk. The stuff doesn't smell great, but it doesn't hurt when they liberally slather it on her, so she keeps her mouth shut.

The longer these two fawn over her, the more information she can gather. Already she has the basic layout of the ship and knows where they're heading to rendezvous with another ship.

They took the restraints off her wrists. But they refused to take the ones off her ankles. "We don't want you able to wander around and get hurt," Julimian explained as he tossed the wrist restraints into a corner. "This ship isn't human safe and touching the wrong thing could do serious damage."

"Or kill you," Aroginean adds.

They aren't kidding about the injury and death warning. This ship is in such poor condition that she constantly notices disrepair death traps. It isn't even that old, but she's pretty sure the Amity was in better working order than this thing.

Every corridor she sees has panels pulled off, exposing electronics, biosystem piping, and other delicate ship systems. One power conduit even looks like it has been hastily repaired using parts off a different ship. It's so badly put together that the floor plates in that section can't be put back on and only half the corridor is usable.

She can also feel the telltale, light-foot sensation that happens when grav drives aren't working right. She wouldn't be surprised if the inside of the ship suddenly went weightless. That would explain why random items are scattered all around the place. When grav drives go wonky, everything can end up floating all over. By the looks of the ship, that's happened several times, and no one bothered cleaning up afterward.

The Amity's grav drive was so faulty that she and Hax got good at moving around without it. That skill might be an advantage for her here.

Aroginean taps the drinking canister in her hand. "You should drink more."

Rumbling in agreement, Julimian leans close to her. "Are you sure nothing hurts? We don't want you to be stoic." Julimian looks at his cousin, Aroginean. "If we need a healer for her, we could go to Molpa Colony after all this is over. They're the closest."

"But she's registered," Aroginean reminds him. "If they run her through the UniBase, they'll see who she belongs to and she'll be taken away."

Julimian sounds a frustrated rattle. "But what if she's hurt? Or gets sick? What will we do?"

"We need to find a healer who will be sympathetic to us," Aroginean states with confidence. "I'm sure we will find one with our ties to the Traditionalists."

It doesn't escape Nalia's notice that while they both seem concerned about her health, neither has bothered to listen to any of her responses so far, at least when they give her a chance to respond. If they did, then they would give her something for the nasty headache brewing behind her eyes. She's pretty sure it's from being close to their scents, but at least they aren't trying to rub their bonding oil on her.

Julimian smells like grass, and Aroginean reminds her of almonds. They both rubbed something over the scent glands on their faces, probably to keep their glands from overproducing. She can only be thankful for that.

"How many Talins are on the ship?" This is the third time she's asked this question, and by some miracle, Julimian responds!

"Are you scared? You don't need to worry, Aroginean and I will keep you safe." Julimian purrs as he talks. "We were the ones who were first in the room and grabbed you, so we've decided you belong to us. Don't worry. We're the most skilled here. Nearlon won't take you away. He doesn't dare."

"Soon it will be only the three of us," Julimian adds to comfort her. "We have a ship of our own, tethered to a nearby moon. Once everything is over, we'll get on that ship and leave. Even if they try to have a lottery to decide who owns you, we'll make sure we win. We're good at manipulating those things."

She could try asking about the ship they're meeting, but it's probably pointless. Even though she knows these two aren't deliberately keeping information from her, their inability to answer even the simplest question is driving her nuts. Time to try another tactic.

Making her eyes wide and fearful, she clutches the drinking canister to her chest and hunches her shoulders. "Am I going to die?"

Both Talins are purring loudly now. "No, of course not. Why would you think such a thing?"

"Because of the ship," she answers, pointing to a nearby wall where all the panels have been pulled off to expose the delicate tritronics.

Neither of them bothers to look where she's pointing, but Aroginean rumbles out a laugh as his gaze slides over to Julimian. "I can't blame the little human for being worried. This ship is a worthless heap."

Also sounding a rumble of laughter, Julimian kicks a broken bit of hardware near his foot. "It was the only other untraceable ship we could get. At least we won't be using it after we meet up with our compatriots. I'll be glad to never step foot on this thing again."

Rumbling out an affirmative sound, Aroginean tugs the empty drinking canister out of her hand. "We'll be off this ship within the rotation. If your fear is causing you too much distress, we can give you a medication. It will make you sleep and then you can wake up on a whole different ship."

Now that she's no longer holding anything, Julimian wraps his arms around her and pulls her backward across the small table. Aroginean straightens up to watch as Julimian hugs her to his chest, her legs extended across the table in front of them.

"That's not a bad idea," he comments. "You would sleep peacefully, and the two of us could hold you and keep you safe until the medication wore off. Our personal ship is well accommodated, with a full-sized cleansing unit. We could bathe and groom you. You would wake up clean, dressed in a new wrap, and safe from stress."

Tensing up at the idea of being knocked out with drugs, she hurries to put that idea out of their minds. "I'm allergic!"

"That's unfortunate," Aroginean states as he looks at Julimian. "Human systems don't process most of our medications well. We would need human-specific drugs to give her. I'd forgotten." He sounds disappointed that they won't be drugging her unconscious.

Julimian doesn't answer him. "Do you know what you're allergic to?"

"Uh, no," Nalia answers. She's at a loss to name a single drug at the moment. It doesn't matter because neither Aroginean nor Julimian makes surprised rattles at her statement.

"They probably didn't bother to tell her," Julimian says with confidence. "She's human. It's not as if she would remember the proper names of medications."

The ship shudders around them, and the grav drive goes offline. Julimian holds her tightly as they both start floating. Neither Talin makes any noises of alarm. It only takes a few submarks before the grav comes back on.

Unfazed by the fluctuations of gravity, the Talins' feet hit the floor hard, but neither appear bothered by the whole interlude.

Before either can speak, the display in the room crackles and the disembodied voice of Nearlon shouts out. "Julimian, Aroginean, you're needed in the engine room."

Both Talins stiffen. "Going," they shout out, almost in perfect unison.

Julimian carries her cradled to his chest, and they all make their way aft. The noise hits her hard when the hatch to the engine room slides open. It's utter chaos inside. Several other Talins are already in the room, rushing around as alarms blare.

Setting her down in a corner near the door, Julimian rumbles out a last purr. "You stay here. If you try to move, I'll be forced to restrain more than your feet," he warns her. She nods once, and he hurries to assist Aroginean, who's already jumped in to help.

With everyone distracted, she pats at her omnie. If she's lucky, the disrupter the lifebearers gave her is still tucked in the waistband where she put it. She'd forgotten about it falling to the floor when Derani undressed her. When the room was invaded, she ended up landing on the floor right next to where it had fallen. She had barely enough time to snatch it up and tuck it away before Palforma was pushing her to a corner and trying to defend her.

With Palforma incapacitated, they searched the room and found his bag with the coded information square, but then they decided that wasn't enough. Abducting Palforma meant they had someone to torture for more information.

Then they argued about her. Not about taking her. Every single Talin agreed she shouldn't be left behind. They argued about who was going to get to put her in a sack and who got to carry the sack.

Julimian and Aroginean won the argument. Nearlon might be officially in charge, but it turns out these two are the only reason the ship is working. Now she wonders if even those two can keep something this broken in operation.

Something in the room makes a horrific grating noise, and she looks up in time to see a Talin sucked into a compartment. He disappears screaming as several others fruitlessly lunge to grab him. The tube he disappeared into is tossing up violet light and some kind of substance that quickly eats pin-sized holes in anything it touches.

Now would be a good time to get out of here!

Everyone is so distracted that she forgets caution and pulls herself to her feet. That helps her search the thick omnie. She finds the disrupter tucked away and only moments after she digs it out, she's free of the leg restraints.

She hears another scream as she runs out into the hall. The sound of her footfalls are masked by the earsplitting pandemonium of the engine room.

No matter what Julimian and Aroginean told her, this ship isn't going to last much longer, let alone make it to rendezvous with another ship. She needs to get back to Palforma and then find some way to get the two of them to a lifepod.

It doesn't take her long to retrace her steps to the room they dumped Palforma in. Peeking through the open hatch, she sees him in the same spot. He's restrained now, but she's sure that's only a precaution. He doesn't look like he's regained consciousness yet.

Two other Talins are in the room, both leaning over the same console and tapping at it as they talk in tense tones. She doesn't know how to get them out of the room, but they're both facing away from the hatch. With time in short supply and feeling a little desperate, she tip-toes in the room and to Palforma.

He doesn't move when she touches his arm. He's out. Damn, how the hell is she going to get him to a lifepod? But first things first. The disrupter makes quick work of the shackles on his wrists and ankles. She leaves them in place, but unlocked. If anyone looks over, it'll appear that he's still bound.

Now she needs to get out of the room. First, she needs to distract the guys and draw them out of the room. Then she needs to perform some kind of magic that will carry Palforma for her!

"What is this?" The exclamation is followed by a rattle of surprise. Nalia looks up to find both Talins have noticed her. They both rush her, but the one who gets to her first swings her up in his arms and turns so the second Talin can't touch her.

"She belongs to me now," he crows out and carries her to a corner of the room and sets her on a tall table.

"I have equal rights to her!" the other Talin argues.

This is not good. "I need to find Julimian and Aroginean. I got scared and ran away, but now I can't find them."

"They lost you, so you're mine now," the Talin holding her argues. Then he looks over to the other Talin. "Did you know these humans are breeding compatible with us?"

"I've heard that, but I thought it was a rumor," he responds as he steps up behind the Talin holding her, peering at her over his shoulder.

"It's not a rumor. It's true. And some Talins even treat their humans as if they're equals," the Talin holding her declares with derision. His rattle of disgust is loud, and his hands tighten on her painfully, forcing a gasp out of her lips.

His buddy's rattle of disgust is as loud as his exclamation. "Equals? That's repugnant!"

The Talin holding her tugs at her omnie. "I've seen the humans rut with each other, and I've wondered what it's like. Then I found out that they're compatible with us. I even heard the Talin owners enjoy it specifically. They aren't merely using their humans as a substitute."

"I'm surprised that they don't end up all torn apart after rutting with their owner."

That makes him pause with the front of her omnie in his hands. "They are soft, but I've been told they can be resilient."

Nalia tries to hold the edges of her omnie together, but the fabric rips. "He's right! You'll kill me," she states quickly and tries to keep the panic at bay. "If you try to have sex with me, you'll kill me. You're too big!"

That makes him pause again and sound a rumble she associates with Talins thinking something through. "I will examine you to see for myself," he declares and then looks to his buddy. "Help hold her. If I determine we can fit, you can take a turn as well."

Sounding an aggressive rattle, the other Talin quickly rounds the table and grabs her flailing arms. Even though she knows it is useless, she keeps fighting. She kicks out at the Talin trying to part her legs and screams curses at them.

"I wish we had a gag," the male holding her arms down comments. "Her voice is grating on my earholes."

The Talin gripping her thighs stops long enough to lean over her. "Quiet or I will do something unpleasant."

"Unpleasant?" she screeches at him. "What do you call raping me?"

"This isn't rape," the Talin insists. "I've read all about human anatomy. Your breeding hole is always open and ready to be used. That means you can't be raped. We would never force a female."

Is he even listening to himself? "*I don't want it!*" she screams at the top of her lungs, making both Talins flinch. "Don't touch me! Don't touch me! Don't touch me!"

Now she's realizing how wrong she was about the concept that Talins don't rape. It appears they do, but they don't call it that. Damn Talins and their semantics!

"She's poorly behaved," the Talin standing near her head comments. He sounds disappointed. Good! "She didn't make this much noise with Julimian and Aroginean. Don't humans normally want to please us?"

"Maybe she's defective," the male holding her legs comments. He lets go of one of her legs and grabs her jaw, putting enough pressure into his hold that she's worried he's going to do damage. Tears start pouring out of her eyes from the pain. She's never felt so helpless in her life.

"You are an animal," he explains, his tone bordering on exasperated as if he's had to explain this multiple times before. "You should want to do anything to make me happy. To please me. If I want to rut you, as your kind does to each other all the time, you should let me."

Whimpering, she blinks up at him and tries to talk through his hold. "Yes."

He lets go of her. "What did you say?"

"Yes, I'll be a good pet." Saying that makes bile rise up her throat, but she forces more subservient words out of her mouth. "Let me show you how we please each other. You'll like it. All the males I've been with have liked it."

Both Talins rumble with interest. "What do you want to show us?" The one holding her wrists lets go and steps back. The one at her legs releases her thighs but doesn't step away. Trying to control the shaking in her hands, she sits up and tugs at the waistband of the Talin in front of her.

"You need to take this off," she explains. With an eager rumble, he steps back and unbuckles his belt. He drops it to the floor next to him and then pulls off his pants. She can see the head of his cock emerging from the protective pouch.

"I knew all you needed was some discipline. Those Reformists all spoil their pets and that makes you think you're better than you are. You forget that your entire purpose is to please us. To make us happy. To serve us. Not the other way around."

She doesn't respond as she slides off the table. Her shaky legs barely support her, and she's forced to grip the table to keep from stumbling.

As she gets her balance, the other Talin steps around and stands next to the first one, also dropping his belt and pulling off his pants. If this wasn't such a dire situation, it would almost be funny. It reminds her of one of the old Earth pornos the young men of her settlement used to pass around clips of.

"Hurry. Show us how you please the males," the second Talin demands. "Show both of us."

"I can only please one male at a time," she murmurs, keeping her head bowed in submission.

"Fine," he says. "But be quick about it. We still need to work on decoding the information square."

She can feel their eyes on her as she sinks to her knees. Rattles of excitement and rumbles of anticipation emit from them. As she draws up close to the first Talin, she acknowledges to herself that this plan is idiotic and will probably end in her death. But she's going to take at least one of these guys out with her.

"You're very large," she tells him, even though she can tell even before he's fully emerged that neither of them are as big as Derani. "Please don't push into my mouth as I do this. It could damage me. My other master had great restraint and didn't accidentally hurt me."

Rattling in indignation, he shoves his hips at her. "My willpower is beyond reproach. I will remain still as you please me."

"Of course," she agrees and makes a show of licking her right hand from the bottom of her palm to the tips of her fingers. Then she reaches those fingers up to play around the edges of the flesh pouch. It's starting to pull taut, and it won't be long before it completely retracts as he becomes fully engorged. It's now or never.

She wiggles her fingers into the pouch, trying hard not to let the revulsion show on her face. With the other hand, she performs the difficult maneuver Palforma had her practice. When both hands are where she needs them to be, she sends a silent prayer to the universe.

With her right hand, she grips his delicate seed sack, squeezes with all her strength, and pulls. At the same time, she brings up her left hand and cuts straight across her with her dagger, slicing the sack from the Talin's body in one smooth motion. The Talin screams in pain and crumbles. She drops the severed seed sack and dives for the blaster holstered on the Talin's dropped belt. Because her hand is slick with blood, it's hard to pull the thing loose.

But it's too late. The precious moments she lost getting the blaster loose allowed the second Talin time to react. He knocks the blaster out of her hand and then kicks out at her. It's only a glancing blow, but it's enough to knock the wind out of her and send her tumbling.

At least she still has the knife clutched in her left hand. She quickly switches the blood-covered dagger to her dominant right hand.

With an enraged rattle, the second Talin looms over her, drawing up his foot to stomp on her head. There's nothing she can do. Even if she had enough breath in her lungs to move, she's up against a wall with no place to go.

She's going to need to stab his foot as it comes down on her. She'll only have one chance, and if she doesn't do it right, she's dead.

Before the foot can descend, the Talin suddenly disappears. He goes flying into a far wall and then Palforma's scarred face is there. He's rumbling with concern, and his hands are gently patting her body.

"Holes? Blood? Pain?" It takes her precious moments to realize he's asking her if she's wounded or injured.

"Fine," she gasps out. "I'm fine."

She sees movement behind him, but before she can do anything to warn him, Palforma moves with a speed that is almost too fast to track. With the grace of a dancer, he ducks sideways. With a move that looks deceptively casual, he reaches out and grabs the Talin by the foot he was going to use to kick Palforma in the head.

As he stands, Palforma twists the foot and Nalia hears it snap as the Talin howls in pain. He drops the foot, and the guy falls to the floor, clutching at his leg.

"Disfigured trash!" The guy whose seed sack she ripped off is on his knees and pointing the blaster she tried to steal from him right at Palforma. "We should have killed you in the room back on Declow."

Palforma doesn't waste time on glib replies. With no hesitation, the ex-soldier is on the guy before he can fire a shot. The blaster goes flying and Palforma lifts him off his feet with one hand around his neck.

"Bad!" he pronounces. "Rotten."

He probably has better curse words in his head, but she's sure he's too worked up to get them out. Then the ship shudders violently around them, and the grav cuts off.

She hears Palforma's surprised rattle as they all start floating. Quickly she tucks the knife back in the sheath strapped to her left forearm and then reaches for the edge of the table that's bolted down, but she's nowhere near close enough to grab it. This is going to hurt when the grav drive comes back on and she falls to the floor.

"Critical structural failure. Make your way to an available lifepod. The paths are lit and indicating available pods."

The computer's voice sounds out through the ship, urgent but calm. Before the voice can repeat the sentence, the ship shakes violently, and she hits the bulkhead. Scrambling for a handhold, she gets her feet pointed down before the grav drive comes back on.

"Critical structural failure. Make your way to an available lifepod. The paths are lit and indicating available pods."

She lands on her feet and looks up in time to see the Talin who Palforma was holding by the neck, sprinting from the room.

"Davianan, come back! Don't leave me behind!" His friend with the broken foot screams as he rumbles with distress and starts crawling after him.

Then Palforma is there, snatching her up and sprinting down the hall, following the bank of lights that point them to the closest lifepod. They're almost there when the bank flickers and then changes direction. The lifepod they were going toward has been launched.

"Critical structural failure. Make your way to an available lifepod. The paths are lit and indicating available pods."

With the speed and fluidity that she's coming to associate with Palforma, he changes direction to follow the new bank of lights. By the second turn down a long corridor, it blinks and changes directions again. The lifepods are being loaded and launched by the Talins onboard. There's a good chance they might not make it to one.

Palforma doesn't sound a rumble or rattle as he sprints, hurdling over bodies or broken bits of the ship as he runs. Nalia glimpses several bodies, one of which is almost cut in half from where the level above collapsed in on the corridor. Even from the brief look she gets as Palforma runs by, she can tell the lifeless body is Julimian. He's still gripping a hand. Even though she can't see his face, she's sure the hand he's holding belongs to Aroginean.

She'll figure out how she feels about that later. If she survives.

The light bank flickers and changes direction again. She's got a sinking feeling this might be one of the last pods. She already knows there weren't enough working pods to begin with. She heard the guys grumbling about that as they carried her on board.

They hit a corridor and find two Talins fighting over a pod. Palforma takes to bounding leap past the battling Traditionalists and shoves her into the pod. He doesn't have time to close the door before both fighters are on him.

She doesn't know how he does it, but he fends them both off. He's moving slower and showing his fatigue. The man's been beaten up, stunned into unconsciousness, fought multiple Talin, and then sprinted through a ship carrying her. That he's still moving at all is amazing. That he is fighting and winning makes him astounding.

"Go!" Palforma roars to her.

"Not without you!" she cries. She can't imagine leaving this brave Talin behind.

"Go!" he repeats and backs up as he fights. He slams a hand down on the controls. "Derani find you."

She realizes what he's doing a moment too late, and the door to the pods shuts. She puts her face to the small port and screams. "No! Palforma, no!"

The pod shifts as it prepares to launch her. She sees all the lights in the corridor blink off, and they don't start up again. That can only mean one thing; she's in the last pod.

Palforma battles the two Talins and manages to either kill or knock them both out. Her last glimpse is of him turning to face the launching pod. He brings up one of his big hands and slaps it to his chest. She can't hear it, but she knows he's rumbling a goodbye.

Sobs bubble up her chest. "Palforma!"

And then the pod launches, and she's hurling through space.

No! Palforma can't die! He's too brave and fast to die this way.

Maybe the lights came back on? Maybe there's another pod. Frantically, she searches the small area out of the window she can see. The ship looks even worse from the outside, if that's possible. She can see the engine section, and the healthy blue glow isn't there. Instead, there's the orange/red light of a failing fuel system. She knows that light. Anyone who works on a ship knows what that light means. The engine is about to go critical.

There has to be another pod. There just has to be. She watches the ship, waiting to see another pod launch. She wills with all her might to see the minor explosion that signals the launch of another pod.

As she watches, the ship deteriorates. The cargo bay explodes out, ejecting all kinds of flotsam along with the last of the atmosphere on the ship. No sooner does that happen than the entire structure fails and explodes.

Sobs rack her body as she floats in the small space of the lifepod, her tears forming globules that drift around her head.

She doesn't know how long she floats in silence. It couldn't have been long because she's still crying when Derani finds her.

When he pulls her lifepod onto a ship she doesn't recognize, she doesn't have the energy to ask a single question. All she can do is fall into his arms and hold on to him with both hands as she sobs her heart out.

CHAPTER 35

Derani holds Nalia tightly to his chest as he walks them down the well-groomed trail. In front of them, Dalt is carrying his weeping human, Lakin. Holding a single glowing ormit gem cupped in both hands and wearing his full military regalia, Holian walks with a measured pace at the front of the procession.

A glance behind him reveals a long line of Talins and humans following. Some Talins are rumbling out soft, sad sounds while many of the humans are openly crying. He didn't know Palforma long, but considering the Talin sacrificed his life to save Nalia, he can understand why so many are taking the long trek into the jungle to participate in his mourning ceremony.

By the time he arrived and recovered Nalia, there wasn't much he could do. His ship wasn't set up to sift through the wreckage, so he couldn't look for Palforma's body. He was also worried that whatever ship the Traditionalists originally planned to meet might come searching. Once he recovered the lifepod with a human life signature inside and found out Palforma didn't make it, he burned hard to get them away.

Holian coordinated ships to converge on the spot later only to find a junk trawler had sifted through and picked up a lot of the wreckage. They picked up the lifepods but found dead Talins inside. Nalia got lucky to be shoved in the only working pod on the entire ship.

In the end, Derani lost his ship, Nalia was traumatized, Palforma sacrificed his life, and the fake information didn't even get into the correct hands.

The plan wasn't an utter failure, though. Thanks to Nalia's memory, they now have a name to focus on—Detrion.

As an outspoken proponent of Traditionalist values on the Apogee Assembly, Servant Citizen Detrion must be one of, if not the major organizer of, the armed Traditionalist insurrection. Now that they know who to focus on, both Holian and Lakin are confident they can figure out a new way to make the man expose himself and his followers.

Derani understands that the mission was for the good of Talin civilization, but he's still not sure it was worth Palforma's life. The man already sacrificed his ability to articulate. He shouldn't need to give up his life as well.

As he's supposed to do during the mourning ceremony march, Derani remembers every aspect of Palforma that he admired. It's not hard. The male might have been damaged, but he was kind and honorable. And in the end, he saved Nalia's life. For that, Derani will always remember Palforma as the worthiest of Talins.

The walk into the jungle takes several marks and finally ends at a cleared area at the edge of a cliff. Holian made sure the area was ready for everyone who would want to attend. The jungle has been carefully cut back to make room and pillows and blankets have been spread out over the bare dirt. Derani follows Dalt and takes the blanket next to the one he settles on.

Neither Lakin nor Nalia try to leave the laps of their Talins as everyone files into the clearing and takes a seat. Holian stands at the cliff edge, silently holding the gem, and waits. Once everyone is seated, he speaks.

"We are here to bid Farwell to one of our own. Say his name so he may be remembered."

Everyone responds to the cue. "Palforma."

"We will stay here until everyone has had a chance to step forward and voice their remembrance. I'll go first. When I met Palforma, he was already showing promise as a raw recruit."

Holian goes on to describe a male of worth who never stopped striving to do the best he could—first for his fellow soldiers and then for Holian and everyone who lived on Kalor. By the end, the stoic commandant finally lets out a miserable rumble as he utters, "Say his name so he may be remembered."

"Palforma."

Dalt stands and steps forward, taking the glowing gem from Holian. He tells everyone about Palforma's fierce loyalty and kindness. How even he didn't realize how strong Palforma was until after the man was injured and fought to form words, even when the healers said he would never speak again.

As Dalt apologizes to his friend and colleague, Lakin stands up to join him, wrapping her arms around his waist and openly weeping. Dalt can't hug her back because he has to use both hands to hold the gem up, but he rumbles out a soothing sound as he finishes, "Say his name so he may be remembered."

"Palforma."

One by one, almost everyone takes a turn to talk about Palforma. None of the stories surprise Derani. They all reflect the male he came to know and learned to respect during their brief time together. It takes many marks, but eventually, everyone shares their thoughts on Palforma.

The last one to talk, a tiny human female, looks up to Holian after she's finished and holds the gem out. Before he can move to take it, Nalia stands up.

Derani makes a worried rattle, but she smiles down at him through her tears. "I'll be quick," she promises. "They need to know how brave he is."

He lets her go, proud of his beautiful human, as she walks with a straight back and her chin up. She takes the heavy gem from the little female and turns to face the crowd.

"It's my fault Palforma's dead," she announces loudly. She isn't crying any longer, but her eyes are red and swollen from the tears she's been shedding for the last few days. "He died saving my life. He died because he pushed me into the lifepod and then fought everyone else off so they couldn't steal the pod from me. He died as he lived, protecting others. I didn't know him for long, but he gave me this and showed me how to use it."

Carefully, she sets down the gem and pulls the small dagger from inside her long-sleeved wrap. When she holds the weapon up, it gleams in the setting sun. "My mom told me about a custom among our people from our days on old Earth. Back when we grew our hair long. Before we worked in space and had to keep it short for safety reasons."

With one hand, she gathers her hair and then takes the dagger and starts cutting it off in jagged hunks. "We would cut our hair when a loved one died. As it grew out, our pain was said to lessen. As our hair got longer, our memories were only of joy and not sorrow."

She hears a few gasps as she cuts, but Derani can't bring himself to stop her. Nalia's been inconsolable since he found her floating in space in the lifepod. That makes him willing to let her do almost anything if it will make her feel better. Letting her cut off her beautiful mane is nothing if it will help her heal.

When she's done, the ground at her feet is scattered with her mane and what remains on her head is rough and lays in untidy, irregular locks. But at that moment, she is more beautiful to him than ever.

"I invite anyone to come up and I'll cut their hair for them," she invites and there is dead silence for a moment. Then Lakin is standing and rushing to her.

"Mine too," she requests as she rubs at her eyes. "Do mine too."

Dalt rattles out a protest, but Lakin regards him through narrowed eyes. "I know you're not about to tell me what to do. Are you?"

That makes the humans chuckle and the Talins rumble out in laughter. Derani found out quickly that Lakin is a force to be reckoned with, and to go against her express wishes is to risk having your technology broken at very inconvenient times. According to the stories he's been told, Lakin cannot be contained if she doesn't want to be.

"Please be careful with your weapon," Dalt requests, and Nalia gives him a small nod.

"Don't worry. Palforma taught me well."

Nalia makes quick work of cutting off Lakin's mane and no sooner is she done than a line of humans are waiting to have their manes cut. Derani notes that a few of the Talins protest, but only slightly, and Holian remains silent in tacit approval.

When every human who's willing has let Nalia cut off their mane, she puts the dagger back, bends to gather up the hair, and steps to the cliff edge.

"Palforma!" she yells at the top of her lungs as she flings the hair off the cliff. The other humans hurry to follow.

"Palforma!" they cry out as they fling the remnants of their manes and then all clutch at each other. A few start crying again. Derani is relieved to notice Nalia seems to be finished with her tears. At least for the moment.

Holian steps up and picks up the gem. "You will be missed, my friend. May you sit with the ancestors now and be part of their wisdom that guides us all."

With those words, he violently smashes the gem against a rock. The thing cracks open and the glow dies.

"Palforma."

CHAPTER 36

Idly, Derani watches as Nalia finishes her morning drink while reading the stats on the ship he traded for the Bountiful. They've been on Kalor for several rotations now, taking a break and enjoying Holian's hospitality.

It's been an eye-opening experience for Nalia. First, it was seeing so many happy pet humans. Then the grandeur of Holian's compound. And finally, when Lakin demonstrated how she could take off her collar whenever she likes.

He's not sure what Nalia was more impressed with, the fact that Lakin's collar is keyed to the bio-signature of the human wearing it, or that the collar had hidden tools on the inside.

She hasn't asked him for a collar like it yet, but he's sure she will.

But that's in the future, along with everything else. They'll need to figure out what they're going to do once the two of them are ready to leave Kalor. The new ship might be fast, but it has almost no cargo hold and uses an expensive fuel.

Derani let her look at his finances, and even if they sell the new ship, there isn't enough to buy back the Bountiful, even with his savings. The moment they could, Nalia contacted the Delortas to inquire about the Bountiful only to find they had already sold it.

The Delortas promised to forward the contact information so Nalia could inquire if the new owners might sell, but that's probably fruitless. The cost would be prohibitive. And as a soon-to-be outcast, he has no clan or family to ask for a loan.

"We can't buy back the Bountiful, but we could get other cargo haulers," Nalia points out. Derani focuses his gaze on her and rumbles out a soothing sound.

"Are you worried about our future, little Nalia?" he asks. He takes her drink and sets it down on the small table before pulling her onto his lap.

They've been staying in a small guest house on the outskirts of Commandant Holian's compound. They can see the main house from the front door, but the cabin is far enough away to feel cozy and isolated. It was even stocked with food and all the items a human might need, including clothing. It's a good thing too because Nalia arrived with only the clothes on her back, and those were fairly dirty and ripped. All her things were either left on Declow or got sold with the Bountiful. At the moment, neither of them owns much more than what they have with them.

"I'm not worried," she assures him. "But I want to help you figure out our next move. We're in this together now. You and me."

"So you don't wish to leave me?" he asks. He nuzzles her short mane and rubs his scent glands over her. She snuggles against him and pulls in a deep breath through her nose.

"Nope. Your paperwork might say you own me, but that's only half the story," Nalia tells him confidently.

"What's the other half?" Derani asks.

"That you love me. That you see me as an equal. That, in a way, we own each other."

He pulls back so he can see her face. She's smiling, but it doesn't reach her eyes, and her body tensed up with that last sentence. His sweet human isn't entirely sure of his reaction, so he keeps purring and casually reaches up with one hand to unlatch her collar. It beeps once and then falls into her lap, forming a small pile of linked jewels.

"Derani?"

"Yes, my wonderful, beautiful, talented human. You are correct. You own me as much as I own you because if you're not happy, I won't be happy. You tell me what you want our future to be and I'll do my best to make it happen. Do you want to live here on Kalor? I'm sure Commandant Holian can find employment for me. Do you want to go to Talarian? I'm sure I can find work there. Do you want to leave Talin-controlled space? Any number of shipping fleets would hire me. We could travel anywhere you want to go. Tell me what you want, and I'll make it happen."

She sits silently for a moment and then throws her arms around his neck and clutches him tightly. "I love you so damn much," she whispers.

"I hope that's a good thing," he teases her. "I hope that whatever a damn is, it's very large."

"Very big. Damn big," she replies with a giggle.

A knock at the cabin door makes Derani rattle out a sharp, annoyed sound. "We aren't receiving guests at the moment," he calls out.

"Are you naked?" Lakin shouts through the door. "Dalt tells me you're not having sex because he says he'd be able to smell it. Which is super creepy, but these guys aren't embarrassed about stuff like that, so I'm learning to let it go."

By the time Lakin's finished her little monologue, Nalia is laughing and climbing off his lap to answer the door. He stands also, hopeful that he'll be able to hear what Lakin and Dalt need to say and then get them to leave. He wasn't done holding his human yet.

"What's up?" Nalia asks as she swings open the cabin door to reveal Lakin, Dalt, and Holian. "Oh wow, the whole gang's here. Come on in." All three step inside and make themselves comfortable, including Derani who resumes sitting and pulls Nalia back onto his lap.

Holian speaks first. "It's been brought to our attention that you were forced into an extremely disadvantageous trade after Nalia and Palforma were kidnapped on Declow."

"True," Nalia answers for him. "It's funny you should mention that because we were about to discuss what we were going to do next."

Eyes sparkling with excitement, Lakin leans forward on Dalt's lap. "That's why we're here. We spent most of yesterday on the comms talking to some important Talins, and we think we've got an offer you're going to like. Really like."

Derani's intrigued. "What offer would this be?"

"Prime Son Searin wants you to go to work for him," Lakin bursts out as if she can't hold in the news any longer. "His people were able to buy the Bountiful from the Delortas on Declow. It's all finished with repairs and heading this way."

He knows he should be overwhelmed with joy at his good fortune. What Talin wouldn't want to work for the monarch's son? But he feels cautious. "Why? Why me? Why now?"

"Two colonies are very important to Prime Son Searin. One belongs to Dalt's parents," Holian explains.

"That's the Barvarian Colony," Lakin interrupts, making Dalt rumble out a sound of amusement. "The other one is a colony he is starting himself called the Calandal Colony. Not much is there yet, but they're improving and growing quickly."

"But why would you need me? Anyone could make deliveries to those colonies," Derani protests. After a quick look at Nalia's face, he can tell she is as suspicious of their motives as he is. "Is this out of guilt?"

"Of course not," Holian says.

At the same time Lakin announces cheerfully, "Only a little bit."

That makes the normally silent Holian rattle out a sound of mild frustration. "Lakin."

She throws him an unrepentant grin. "Sorry!" Then she looks at Derani and Nalia. "But to be honest, it's slightly guilt motivated, but not much. Mostly we need you guys. We need loyal people who won't use the information about those colonies in the wrong way."

"What information?" Nalia asks before Derani can.

"Those colonies are going to be like here," Lakin explains. "They're going to be safe places for both Talins and humans. Places where love and affection aren't taboo. Where children don't need to worry who their parents are."

Nalia's eyes go wide as she exclaims, "Oh!"

Yesterday they were given a full tour of Holian's compound, which included the very well-protected center of the house. There, for the first time, Derani met Talin-human hybrid children.

The moment he saw them, he suddenly wanted one so badly with Nalia that it felt like a physical pain. That's one reason he isn't concerned about his future career. Something far more important has taken residence in his head—the image of Nalia as a mother. Nalia as his scent-bonded partner and mother of his children.

"Yes," he says without thinking. "Yes, we will help build more colonies like Kalor. But I want land. I want a holding on one of the colonies. I want a safe place for our children to grow."

"Hold up there, buster." Nalia looks up at him with amused eyes. "Our children?"

"Yes, my heart," he replies. "As many as you wish to grace me with. And we will raise them and show them what it is to be a family."

"Awww," Lakin whispers loudly.

"Perhaps we should leave," Dalt comments as he stands.

"I will inform Prime Son Searin that you've accepted his offer," Holian comments as he also stands to leave.

Derani sounds a rumble of agreement as the others depart, but he never takes his eyes off Nalia. He's finally figured out what is important, and there's no way he's ever going to be distracted again.

Nalia stands next to Derani as the crew boards. They look happy to see Derani, and then they all stop and take her in, rumbling with amusement.

She stands still so they can look their fill. She's wearing a wrap and omnie in the same color as Derani's pants. She's also wearing a belt complete with a pouch full of tools on one hip and an Ident square dangling at her other hip. Although the Ident is half the size of Derani's, it's keyed the same as his, so for all intents and purposes she can pretend to be him to any computer out there.

She and Derani talked at length on the trip back to the homeworld about how they would present her to the crew.

Eventually, she wants to be part of the crew with a job and responsibilities, but that's not something they can spring on the them suddenly. They're going to have to ease the other Talins into it.

The belt and Ident were Derani's idea, so they get used to seeing her with tools. For now, she's going to stay at his side and use the information square to learn all about the ship, the colonies, and anything else she feels like reading. Over the next few trips to bring supplies to the colonies from various planets and stations, Derani will give her minor tasks and tell the crew to indulge her.

It won't take long before they get used to little Nalia running around the ship with assignments of her own. At some point, Nalia knows they're going to need to figure out who they're going to trust because even though she's on suppressants now, they will have children. But by the time that happens, they should know who on the crew can be trusted with their secrets and who will need to find work elsewhere.

For now, she's excited. Working with Derani is a far cry from her and Hax struggling to get by. Derani's status as a well-respected Talin merchant and cargo hauler opens all kinds of doors that she and Hax couldn't even knock on.

Self-consciously, she rubs the new collar Derani got her. It's jeweled, like the original one, but this one has a special release so she can tug it off any time she needs to. Holian also suggested putting a tracker in the collar, which she agreed with. She's not planning to get kidnapped again, but if it happens, she wants to be damn sure Derani finds her.

"Don't you look adorable," Melanem coos as she takes in Nalia's outfit.

Larimus takes a small step closer and sounds an admiring rumble. "That Ident even looks real."

"You look very important," Yulian assures her with an indulgent rumble.

They all ask her what kind of important things she keeps in her pouch as they board and make their way to the control room. Settling on the kneeling pad next to Derani's captain's chair, she watches everyone get to work.

It's time to set off on the first of many new adventures.

EPILOGUE

Every alarm is blaring throughout the ship. Every single one. They're filling Palforma's throbbing head with noise and making it hard to think. It doesn't help that it feels like every part of his body hurts.

As he watches the lifepod shoot off into space toward safety, he leans heavily against the bulkhead and then sinks to the floor. The Talins he fought lay limp and lifeless around him. Serves them right—gutless, dishonorable fools.

He sighs out a sad little rumble. He didn't expect to die on this mission, but he's not exactly surprised it's going to happen.

"Please proceed to the nearest escape pod or shuttle."

The ship's voice calls out in Talin, then Norik, and finally in universal Common language. The ship's system knows he's here and alive, so it's been saying this same sentence over and over again.

As much as he wants to take the computer's advice, Nalia just launched in the last lifepod. The computer knows that too or it would be flashing light banks down the halls to direct him to an available lifepod.

"Please proceed to the nearest escape pod or shuttle."

Now he feels like the voice is taunting him.

Show me to a lifepod or ship and I will, you stupid computer, he thinks as he sounds an annoyed rattle.

Should he kill himself before the ship explodes? Would that be a more or less painful death? He's not sure. It probably depends on how spectacular the explosion will be. His clan and family are famous for producing soldiers, not scientists or engineers. He trained all his life to be an effective member of the Talin elite military. That means questions about physics and engines are beyond him.

"Please proceed to the nearest escape pod or shuttle."

Is he going to die with this voice being the last thing he gets to hear? That seems unfair somehow.

"Please proceed to the nearest escape pod or shuttle."

"...nearest escape pod or shuttle."

"...pod or shuttle."

Shuttle!

He was barely conscious enough to notice it, but now the image of the shuttle comes to the front of his thoughts. A broken-down short-range shuttle sits in the bay he was carried in through. It was barely more than a high-orbit planet jumper, but it's a ship.

Endorphins hit him hard as he scrambles to his feet and sprints to the bay. He ignores the pain and damage to his body as he moves. He has to shove a stuck hatch open, basically ripping it out to get into the bay. Then he rattles with triumph—a shuttle.

Getting inside the tiny craft isn't easy, and then he's forced to squeeze himself into the only seat. He hits the control console to bring it to life, his limited training in basic piloting skills helping him activate everything.

The display comes on, but one message flashes at him—engine inoperable.

He's unfazed. He doesn't need working engines, only life support. As long as the shuttle will hold atmosphere long enough for Derani to get him, the state of the engine doesn't matter.

And he knows without a shred of doubt that Derani is coming.

It feels like he bangs every injury as he gets back out of the shuttle so he can quickly program the bay door. The countdown sounds as he rushes back to the shuttle and squeezes himself in. He's forced to manually shut the hatch behind him because the automatic machinery is damaged. The visual read-outs are all working, so he knows the door seals after he closes it and the limited life support systems come on. Strapping himself in, he watches the countdown on the bay door through the ship's tiny porthole.

The counter flashes at zero and then the bay door starts to open. It isn't meant to open with atmosphere still in the bay or the hatch to the rest of the ship ajar. The moment the bay door cracks the seal, the entire door fails. It normally wouldn't do that, but it must have sustained some damage.

As he had hoped, explosive decompression pushes the shuttle out into space. Momentum keeps him moving away from the doomed ship, but will it be enough to get him out of blast range?

At least he can't hear the infernal computer telling him to leave any longer.

Then the ship explodes. He doesn't hear anything at first. His shuttle is tumbling so he can only see the bigger ship for a few submarks through the porthole each time the shuttle revolves. He has no idea how long he spends tumbling before he sees a ring of bright light emanating from where the ship had been on one of the tumbling revolutions.

Before the shuttle can complete another full roll, the shockwave from the explosion hits. The noise deafens Palforma and causes enough pain to his already brutalized brain that his body shuts down in self-defense.

He's not conscious, so he can't see Derani's ship arrive and pick up the lifepod holding Nalia or watch it travel away. It is probably a blessing that he can't watch it leave him behind to float in space alone with the rest of the detritus from the destroyed ship.

He doesn't wake when a massive junk trawler picks through the debris and pulls his shuttle on board. His abused brain only comes back online as hands drag him from the severely damaged craft.

When he opens his eyes, he sees alien faces looking down at him, all chattering in a language his translator doesn't know.

His brain still feels mushy, and his body is uncooperative, but he stumbles to his feet and clumsily strikes out at the air to keep these strangers away from him. He can't manage a single word at the moment, but his movements speak for themselves. They all step back and give him room, still speaking in indecipherable, excited voices.

And then, in the sea of unfamiliar, he sees a small, delicate human face. She's looking at him with curiosity, her beautiful dark eyes full of sympathy. She holds something out to him, but he ignores her offering.

His wounded mind is finally able to produce one word, and he roars it out as he rushes to her.

"Mine!"

Dear Readers,

Thank you for reading *Negotiating Captivity*. If you want more Human Pets of Talin the next book is ready for you to read: *Fighting Captivity*.

I hope you enjoyed *Negotiating Captivity* enough to leave a review! As an indie writer without the support of a publishing company, I need all the help I can get. Your good reviews keep me writing.

If you have any questions, comments, or suggestions feel free to contact me via email: author@rk-munin.com

Want some free novellas or buy signed paperbacks? You can find everything on my website:

www.rk-munin.com

Have a fruitful rotation,
Rye

OTHER BOOKS BY RK MUNIN

-Science Fiction-

Hissa Warrior Series
Rescuing Halin (Mian and Halin)
Buying Tiran (Mara and Tiran)
Tempting Selon (Lara and Selon)
Defying Kilan (Deena and Kilan)
Healing Mavito (Raleen and Mavito)
Claiming Yopin (Mouse and Yopin)
Teasing Woken (Safena and Woken)
Defending Revin (Kamaril and Revin)
Trusting Warik – Coming soon

Human Pets of Talin Series
Loving Captivity (Sora and Searin)
Escaping Captivity (Lakin and Dalt)
Negotiating Captivity (Nalia and Derani)
Fighting Captivity (Zia and Palforma)
Tender Captivity (Jinna and Holian - This is a novella you can get for free by signing up for my newsletter)
Craving Captivity (Lasha and Tamerin)
The Twelve Nights of Halloheen: A holiday mashup novella (Isla and Tisuran)
Stealing Captivity (Kasi and Ignatias)
Redeeming Captivity – Coming soon

Origins (A Human Pets of Talin Series)
Creating Captivity (Ari and Bazium)
Gossamer Chains (Rain and Hesarium)
Golden Cages – Coming soon

-Paranormal /Urban Fantasy-

Ours Evermore Series
Two Wolves for Soren (Soren, Kalli, and Quinn)

A Hacker, Vampire, and Chimera Walk into a Bar….(Tobias, Briar, and Memphis)
When Darkness Meets Dawn (Imani, Lex, and Mac)
Tag, You're It (Novella)
Kidnapping Their Third (Cora, Pike, and Kimble) – Coming soon

Alpha Series
Alpha Mage (Emma and Kade)
His Alpha Mage (Avery and Jason – Novella)
Alpha King (Cathleen and Lazlo)

New Clan Series
Stray Wolf (Steph and Eli)
Lost Lion (Maeve and Cyrus)
Reluctant Cervid (Tavi and Donovan)
Broken Thorn (Sabina and Theodosius)

9 781962 699167